Gnaritus: Every Life Matters

Nina Wirk

I dedicate this book to all the people whose lives have been marginalized; always remember you are children of the universe.

Contents

1

Tilting at Windmills

IT WAS THE day everything changed. Surina woke up on her fortieth birthday with her head spinning from a dream. Since she had stopped dreaming a long time ago, it was unusual for her to dream in the first place, let alone about a comet. What's more, in this unsettling dream, she was riding on a glowing blue comet as it swept past the sun and Earth at a dizzying speed. She remembered feeling like a giddy surfer catching a once-in-a-lifetime wave of awesome majesty. Then, just as it had materialized out of nowhere, the comet vanished into a thick cloud of dust beyond the edge of the solar system, blazing an iridescent-blue trail in its wake.

Since today was also her birthday, she felt a heightened sense of urgency in deciphering the meaning of her dream. Was it a prescient dream or just another nonevent? As she pored over the online encyclopedia during breakfast, she became even more crestfallen when she read about comets as omens of troubled times, perils, and calamities ahead. What an inauspicious start to her birthday, she thought. However, the idea of any celestial body foreshadowing doom seemed hard to grapple with, for she could remember only the sheer exhilaration of exploring the entire universe by hitching a ride on a comet. As she scrolled down the computer screen, her face lit up when she came to the far more reassuring interpretation of a long journey, transformative change, or personal expansion. In any event, she much preferred comets as harbingers of transformative change and would just try with all her might to forget that they could also spell catastrophe. Hence, *transformative change* became her new mantra at work, although it was unlikely in a job like hers.

After she had settled into the complacency of her comfortable, quotidian routine at work, she forgot all about far-fetched things like comets. As the lackluster day dragged to its predictable conclusion, her wristwatch flashed with a message summoning her to the medical director's office at once. With her heart sinking to the floor, Dr. Surina Mathew wondered why this long-dreaded and feared meeting had arrived on her birthday like an unwelcome guest.

Before going to the medical director's office, she smoothed her unruly curls, not that anyone would notice, but it was important to her. Try as she might to tame her thick, curly black hair by tying it in a ponytail, somehow loose tendrils always managed to escape, giving her a somewhat unkempt, windswept look. Apprehension overshadowed her bronze face and chiseled features. She felt harried and worn out by incessant overwork. Her thin frame appeared even frailer in her oversized white lab coat. The weight of the hodgepodge of medical paraphernalia filling the pockets of her lab coat made her walk with a stoop. As she trudged toward the android security guard station at the end of the gleaming white hospital ward, the nurses and doctors gave her momentary knowing glances. Then, with an air of resignation, they returned to their work rounds. The stodgy android security guard greeted her with his usual vacuous smile. His lifeless eyes scanned her badge for the twelve-digit identification number and scrutinized her face.

"Hope you had a good day, Dr. Mathew," he said in an unctuous voice.

Surina nodded in the affirmative, out of force of habit only, for her day at that moment had taken a sour turn. Each standard-issue android resembled a bland Ken doll with a height of six feet and a muscular physique. From a distance android security guards proved difficult to distinguish from humans; however, close up their dimpled smiles, cadaverous complexions, and eyes with fixed pupils gave them away. The unrelenting cheeriness of their voices, in spite of the gravity of the situation, also distinguished them from humans.

Seconds later, when the door swung open, she gave a last wistful look at the spotless ward that had almost been her second home for the past ten years. Unable to linger any longer in the doorway as the door slammed shut, she passed into the clamor of the foyer. Anxious families paced the hallway and waited for updates on their relatives. She dragged herself into an elevator, and the claustrophobic silence engulfed her as it sped up the seventy-eight floors to the top story of the hospital.

As Surina stepped out of the elevator, an android secretary at the reception desk ushered her into the office. The medical director, Dr. Robert Hurpan, sat enthroned at the center of a steel table, which stretched the length of the room. A staid, stout woman and an android flanked him. Their faces, like their suits, were drab and expressionless. The monolithic Spartan room, occupying the majority of the seventy-eighth floor, appeared as grim and unwelcoming as its occupants. As she sat down facing the glum trio, the lack of any cushions on the steel chairs doubled her sense of uneasiness. The medical director extended her the courtesy of a perfunctory nod. He cast a sinister chill in the room as he peered at her through the circular, gold-rimmed spectacles resting on the bridge of his curved nose. Surina thought his nose resembled the beak of a vulture. While tapping his pen on the table with impatience, he spoke in an indifferent tone as if reading from an oft-repeated script.

"The head of Human Resources, Mrs. Jane Woodford, and our android security chief, Rex, are also present at this meeting," he said with a voice like a booming foghorn. "Dr. Mathew, you have served the Greysville Quadrant Hospital for ten years and are forty years old today. Pursuant to the Relocation Policy to the planet Gnaritus, in one week on July twenty-eighth, 2200, you will leave Earth to join the hospital staff on Gnaritus. I'm aware you are a physician-scientist with both an active research laboratory and clinical responsibilities. Nevertheless, on Gnaritus you will perform only clinical patient care duties. The Relocation Council of the World Governing Body has approved your departure."

Jane Woodford's well-practiced, slick veneer of concern always came in handy during meetings such as these. Without any hesitation, she dived into her role of trying to hearten Surina in coming to terms with her expendability.

"You know the reality of the situation, Dr. Mathew," she said in a honeyed tone that feigned succor. "Despite over two hundred years of space exploration, we have found only a single planet, Gnaritus, capable of hosting a space colony. Gnaritus means knowledge in Latin, which is a lofty ideal by all accounts, but it's far from being a perfect planet. Since Earth is our most habitable planet, we must preserve its limited resources. As you have no family or children on Earth, there are no reasons to postpone your relocation."

Jane was a seasoned Job's comforter and only aggravated Surina's distress. She paused for dramatic effect and glowered at Surina with bulging eyes in an accusatory way. A menacing tone replaced her usual oleaginous manner as she spoke. "Your supervisor, Dr. Rod Stinguard, the chief scientific officer of the Cancer Unit, has indicated the direction of your research is not promising. In fact, the scientific community doesn't put much credence in your data. Your marginal publication record in reputable scientific journals is also not of the caliber expected of someone your age. Thus, Dr. Stinguard has not recommended any delay in your departure to Gnaritus.

"We know of your objections to the release of the viral vector, but Dr. Stinguard believes it to be ready. We have sifted through reams of data ourselves and reached the same conclusions as Dr. Stinguard. Without a doubt, the viral vector is sound and will save humanity from the scourge of cancer. Overall, Dr. Stinguard and many others feel you don't fit into the mission here. There's no place for you on Earth and no reason for you to stay here anymore. As a consequence, you must step aside for the next generation. The climate on Gnaritus is harsh, but it hosts a self-sustaining space colony with all the necessities. Remember, you'll be in good company with millions of others."

Surina wanted to clarify her views one final time, but she could only stammer in a diffident manner. "Um, I'm only saying that Dr. Stinguard needs to do more testing before the global launch of his viral vector. Even though I believe in gene therapy, as it has helped to treat and prevent many conditions, the distribution of this particular viral vector is fraught with danger."

Out of the blue, the medical director's face turned crimson as he adopted a pugilistic mien. The veins in his bull neck became engorged with blood, and his nostrils flared. The gainsayer had no qualms about interrupting her to deride her in his strident voice. "Such piffle! Of course, we're well aware of your opinions but disagree with you. You should stop tilting at windmills. You're in the habit of kvetching with incendiary comments not only on this occasion but also many times before. Your recusant tendencies will get you nowhere. Your account of the viral vector doesn't dovetail with the opinion of the most august scientific committees in the world. Since the Stinguard viral vector has enormous potential to save countless lives, there is no need to delay the launch. Rex will accompany you to your lab."

After finishing his peppery diatribe, the medical director turned his attention to a stack of papers and began jabbering away with

Jane Woodford. Surina almost gagged on the nauseating odor of Jane's sickly sweet perfume and the medical director's pungent aftershave. To put it another way, it resembled the smell remaining when incense cannot entirely mask the stench of death. Since Rex was immune to any odor, he maintained a fixed thin smile throughout the unpleasant proceedings. While Surina reeled from the acrid smell, the comet once again orbited her head.

Questions raced through Surina's mind. Despite her ten years of toil and moil at the hospital, it had taken the medical director less than two minutes to dismiss her on her birthday with a shrug. Was that the extent of her relevance to the hospital? Why had she even expected bouquets and plaudits for all her travails when brickbats were the norm? Even though governments worldwide accepted the Relocation Policy as necessary for the Earth's survival, why were members of the powerful ruling elite exempt from it?

All of a sudden, the shocking realization of her premature departure—as the usual age of resettlement was sixty years—overwhelmed her. Even worse, her vain hopes of her accomplishments in medical research being enough to maintain her place on Earth seemed altogether foolish to her now. She had wondered about her place in the world all her life. Well, today she had an answer. There was no place for her. Was she being cast out by virtue of not fitting into Earth's society? Perhaps she should not have raised any questions about the Stinguard viral vector, a sacrilegious act by all accounts in such a stultifying, myopic world. In any case, having a cockalorum like Dr. Stinguard for a supervisor had stacked all the cards against her, making her chances of staying on Earth nonexistent from the beginning.

Then Rex chimed in with his singsong voice. "Dr. Mathew, there is time now to clear your lab for the next occupant."

The medical director continued to gabble with Jane Woodford at the table as Rex marshaled Surina out of the stuffy office in a brusque manner and into the elevator in the hallway. As the external building elevator whished down to the lobby, she saw the fading rays of the setting sun that drifted as shimmering ripples on the lake in front of the hospital. In the distance, the sparkling emerald green shrubs and trees on the rolling hills made a picture-perfect backdrop to the hospital. Although the Earth had never seemed so beautiful to her as today, in one week she would never see it again. Nevertheless, she understood how certain unexpected events could transpire in the lives of hapless, ill-starred individuals such that nothing would be the same again. She had already reached her point of no return! What else could she have expected? After all, she had dreamt about a comet last night.

2
Packing Boxes

SINCE SURINA MOVED like a noctambulist with legs of lead, Rex shepherded her through the main entrance hall of the hospital to the only passageway leading to the medical research facility. On the left side of the imposing lobby, with its cathedral ceilings, a gaggle of visitors to the hospital kept their eyes glued to a giant screen. Here and there, a handful of patients in white hospital robes sat beside their intravenous poles. The masterful film riveted the audience to their seats, with images of a devastated Earth, followed by idyllic green forests, babbling brooks, and the ocean teeming with fish.

"For a hundred years, the Earth has been healing itself," began the orotund narration accompanying the footage. "We once believed the environmental harm from the pollution of the twenty-first century to be irreversible. However, when the greenhouse gases fell to preindustrial levels toward the end of the twenty-second century, the seas became crystal clear, and the Earth began to heal. The flora and fauna have flourished in the new temperate climate.

"At the peak of the noxious greenhouse gases in the twenty-first century, the solar radiation ravaged the Earth and mutated the human DNA. Some other words for DNA are deoxyribonucleic acid, the genome, or the building blocks of life. DNA contains the genes that provide the code for each cell of the body, much like an instruction manual. So far we have been unable to repair the cancer-causing gene mutations that successive generations can also inherit. As a result, the cancer rate is skyrocketing. Cancer is sweeping Earth like a plague. No one is immune. Even children are developing cancer at earlier ages. Over the span of just a century, the human population has plummeted from nine billion to one billion due to the astronomical cancer rates. There is a threat that the Anthropocene epoch, or the Age of Humans, which began in the eighteenth century, will end.

"Over the past decade, gene therapy has saved countless lives by preventing conditions such as Alzheimer's disease and multiple sclerosis. At long last, the Greysville Quadrant Hospital's very own Dr. Rod Stinguard has unraveled the secrets for the cure for cancer. He has synthesized a lentivirus vector that will carry the genetic code to produce key DNA repair enzymes in humans. These DNA repair enzymes are proteins that will cure the gene mutations causing cancer. In essence, this revolutionary new gene therapy will prevent the onset of cancer. Now humans will also heal from cancer-causing mutations because of the life-saving gene therapy carried in the Stinguard viral vector. A new day has dawned on Earth, for we will be free of cancer. Hence, the Age of Humans will last forever!"

The film's facile conclusions reassured the audience, and they clapped in appreciation. When the thunderous applause had subsided, the video replayed in front of a new audience. Meanwhile, two ominous android security guards who patrolled a door leading to the medical research facility inspected Surina's face and badge with suspicion before allowing her to proceed to her laboratory.

Surina's lab occupied a tiny corner of the twelfth floor next to Stinguard's lab. It did not surprise her when Rex informed her of Stinguard's plans to occupy her vacated space such that his lab would encompass the entire twelfth floor. Without delay, she began the daunting task of sorting through all the accumulated clutter. Despite her reservations, she willed herself to do it while swallowing her disappointment. She was in a pickle, and there was no way out.

As she packed her belongings under Rex's watchful eye, she wondered why she had spent all her time at work instead of traveling to see more of the Earth while she still had a chance. Since there was only one week left, she would go to Gnaritus without seeing many of the wonders of the world. She felt like such a schlemiel. Why had she focused only on producing a body of scientific work that would secure her place on Earth? Even though she had the scientific credentials to succeed in her research, she never got very far because she could not adhere to Stinguard's rules that well.

Despite being sixty-eight years old, Stinguard had managed to ensure his place on Earth. He had exclusive memberships not only in the most prominent committees but also in the same golf club as the medical director. Nevertheless, the real coup propelling Stinguard to the rarefied atmosphere of the elite came with his marriage to the sister of Cuthbert Miller, the vice chair of the World Governing Body. Now, with the imminent release of the viral vector, Stinguard's fame had skyrocketed to superstar status.

The most compelling evidence of the breadth of Stinguard's sphere of influence came from his strategic placement of his research associates in the highly regarded scientific committees of the World Governing Body, shutting out other less well-connected candidates. For example, she knew Stinguard had blackballed her application for membership in the prominent International Scientific Committee on Human Evolution and bestowed the honor on one of his protégés. That had been the eventual outcome of most of her applications for committee membership. A research position at the renowned Greysville Quadrant Hospital guaranteed membership in at least one of the World Governing Body's scientific committees, thereby ensuring a lifelong place on Earth. However, she had never gained Stinguard's blessing. In fact, she had realized that she could never belong in Stinguard's inner circle since it included only those who evinced complete deference to his will and never questioned him. For instance, one of Stinguard's star research associates, Dr. Ed Kadison, had bludgeoned his way through the hospital's political minefield and come out on top unscathed. By achieving Stinguard's complete trust and confidence, he had even secured a promotion to a lifelong appointment on the prestigious International Scientific Committee on Human Evolution.

Just then, Ed Kadison sauntered into Surina's lab like an obsequious sycophant with a pompous air of considerable self-importance. He was a short, bald, paunchy man with a blond mustache. His potbelly forced him to leave his lab coat open. His eyelids did not shut all the way over his protruding eyes either. As a result, he had to instill a few drops of a natural-tears solution into his dry eyes every hour on the hour. Even so, he had the requisite skills to achieve success in the hospital, for he was a master of apple-polishing and wheedling. Since his large contingent of friends included only the most important people who advanced his career, his presence in the lab surprised Surina. In fact, he had never given her the time of day before.

"Just looking at the facilities, Surina," Kadison said with an unmistakable hint of schadenfreude in his tone. "Stinguard's given me this lab."

Flashing a roguish smile, he swaggered up and down the aisles with tremendous relish as he made his plans on how to use the space. Then, standing with legs akimbo, he stared at Surina with his protuberant, unblinking eyes.

"The key point to remember is to play the game better!" the

lickspittle said with a condescending snarl. "Why did you goad Stinguard with the results of your experiments that contradicted his data? Don't keep flogging your opinions to death. Just go along with the flow, Surina, and always choose the path of least resistance. I hope you do that on Gnaritus!"

"Hello, Surina," said a dulcet-toned voice. "I heard you're leaving. Remember to forward all your research files to me by the end of today before you go."

Surina spun around with alarm. After slithering in unseen like a snake in the grass, a man far shorter than even Kadison had planted himself in the middle of the doorway. His fatuous smile made his beady, saurian eyes close shut. His thinning white hair, sparse beard, and permanent scowl added an extra layer of menace to his mealy complexion. It was Stinguard.

To Surina, he was a small man not only in height but also in his aims, for he had a single-minded focus of neutralizing anyone he perceived as challenging his stature on Earth. For this, he had a wide-ranging arsenal at his disposal to intimidate and marginalize anyone he labeled as a threat. This arsenal included not only blocking a promotion or committee membership but also rejecting research for publication in scientific journals. Moreover, he would expedite the offending party's relocation to Gnaritus at the earliest possible time.

In fact, Surina believed only the piecemeal annihilation of a victim, like the slow drip of a faulty faucet, quickened Stinguard's pulse and gave him the impetus to breathe. Owing to his insatiable blood lust, he would search for his next quarry as soon as he finished off one victim. As a result, the surgical precision of his ruthlessness had become legendary at the Greysville Quadrant Hospital and far beyond so that he had acquired the moniker *poison arrow*. However, Surina reckoned that Stinguard had given himself that appellation to sow fear in the hearts of friend and foe alike.

Surina knew Stinguard had used Machiavellian deftness to seal off every avenue available to her so as to drive her into a corner. She stopped packing. "Will it even be necessary to forward my data now, Dr. Stinguard? After all, the World Governing Body's scientific committees discounted my research."

"It's a formality but an essential one so as not to stir up panic if the files get into the wrong hands," the cockalorum said in his haughty, saccharine manner.

Surina decided to propound her theory one last time. "Yes, I'll forward the research files to you. My experiments showed the very real possibility of the viral vector producing lethal gene mutations instead of the hoped-for DNA repair enzymes in about half the patients who receive it. We need much more testing before using it worldwide. There's just no way around it."

She kicked herself because she thought she had mangled the speech. In the meantime, Kadison opened his eyes even wider and raised his eyebrows in shocked disbelief at her defiance.

Stinguard's thin lips twitched, and his eyes hardened. He bristled at her in a petulant manner and spat out his words. "The launch of the viral vector culminates years of research. The tests in mice confirmed the viral vector's safety. Since we can't always extrapolate the mouse model to humans, we also conducted a clinical trial on twenty subjects in Africa. They're all doing well two weeks later. In the final analysis, even this human clinical trial proved the viral vector's safety. Moreover, we are introducing the viral vector worldwide in phases out of an abundance of caution. In fact, in October, two thousand subjects in Africa will receive the first batches of the viral vector before we distribute it to other regions in a stepwise fashion. Due to these definitive results, every scientific committee in the World Governing Body gave their official seal of approval for the project. In any case, I only came to say how sorry I am to see you go. I bid you a heartfelt good-bye."

Surina knew both Stinguard and Kadison had come only to gloat at her relocation to Gnaritus while they basked in the security of their lifelong positions on Earth. After feasting their eyes on her diminished circumstances, they darted out of the room. As the sound of Stinguard and Kadison's cackling laughter receded in the hallway, she returned to clearing her bookshelves in a disconsolate mood. Indeed, she had tried hard, but her research had led nowhere in the end. She sank into the mire of self-doubt. Was she just wasting her time battling against an imaginary threat like the dreamer Don Quixote, who tilted at windmills in the mistaken belief they were giants?

When Vera Ma, her efficient research assistant, returned from her coffee break, Surina breathed a sigh of relief at seeing a friendly face. Although Vera favored climbing the twelve steep flights of stairs to the lab to maintain her robust athletic build, today she had taken the elevator since she also carried two empty boxes. With all due haste, Vera began clearing out her desk in the corner of the lab by the window. As she stuffed the contents of the drawers into her boxes, her complexion appeared wan and anemic.

"Surina, they reassigned me to Stinguard's lab," she said in a brittle voice, as if she was about to cry. "How I will miss you! I enjoyed working with you so much. It's still puzzling why the scientific community glossed over our significant research findings, which flagged potential problems in the Stinguard viral vector. Since I'll be joining you on Gnaritus in a few years, we will meet again. There's nothing to do now but to accept the relocation and make the best of things such as they are."

Thinking the better of saying anything more after glimpsing Rex's sinister form guarding the door, Vera changed the topic. "We must meet for lunch or something before you go, Surina. I'll call you to make the arrangements."

After finishing her packing, Vera embraced Surina before leaving like a morbid ghost with her boxes and the money tree plant that had adorned her desk for the past ten years. Surina remembered all her friends she needed to bid farewell to, including Dr. Mercy Jakande in Keswick and Dr. Heidi Burmann in

London. She rushed through the remainder of her packing, for she yearned to go home. Before she left, she e-mailed her research files to Stinguard and placed her white lab coat on the countertop.

Rex handed her two forms. "Please sign both pages, indicating that you returned all the hospital-issued equipment."

Surina scribbled down her signature. She glanced around the lab one more time with nostalgia as Rex hoisted the four medium-sized brown cardboard boxes containing the sum of her belongings from the past ten years on a cart. In the hallway, three eager cleaning androids waited to wipe clean every trace of her presence in the lab so as to make it ready for Kadison's immediate occupancy.

Amid the excited patients itching to go home, the shrill video about the Stinguard viral vector played again in the main entrance hall. As Surina handed Rex her badge and keys, she regretted not having the opportunity to say good-bye to her patients, all of whom she would miss so much. However, patients had grown accustomed to their doctors' relocation to Gnaritus. Outside the hospital, in the pelting rain, a fleet of electric volitant air cars with teardrop silhouettes lined the driveway of the roundabout. In due time, the long queue of patients and their families waiting to go home whittled down so that soon it was Surina's turn. While she climbed into the backseat of the aerodynamic vehicle with relief, Rex loaded the boxes into the trunk in an expeditious manner.

"Eighty-four Oakdale Avenue," she told her driver.

The car revved up its engines and hovered for a while before flying away without a sound. When Surina glanced back pensively at the hospital for a final time, the dying light had already begun to cast shadows on its austere façade. Oblivious to the rain, Rex remained outside in the crepuscular gloom until Surina's air cab had cleared the perimeter of the Greysville Quadrant Hospital's grounds. Then he strutted back indoors, with a jaunty stride.

3

Mercy

THE AIR CAB wove around other vehicles ferrying passengers home. As it zoomed over the glistening Derwentwater Lake, Surina peered out the window at the bucolic valleys of the Lake District. Soon, a gleaming saucer-like building emerged on the outskirts of Keswick. It was the headquarters of the World Governing Body, which had relocated to Keswick at the end of the twenty-first century since the town had remained an oasis. In fact, the Lake District had been a sanctuary from the prevailing floods due to the rising sea levels and climatic upheavals common at that time. After the seas had receded, the unparalleled beauty and allure of the area had kept the World Governing Body in Keswick. Due to the tumult caused by climate change, a wave of nostalgia for the traditions of simpler times was sweeping the Earth. As a consequence, there was a push for the historic preservation of many towns and cities, including Keswick, so that the buildings retained all the charm of the twentieth century.

Surina thought back to when the World Governing Body first came to power and had to jawbone the governments of individual countries into accepting its authority. However, the threats from climate change had dovetailed with the World Governing Body's ambition for supremacy over all jurisdictions. Soon, the countries had acquiesced. Now the World Governing Body's far-reaching power set the entire agenda for the governments of each of the Earth's one hundred and ninety-six countries to implement. In essence, nothing threatened the hegemony of the World Governing Body, which had ruled unchallenged for the past one hundred years.

As Surina unfurled her tablet computer to check her e-mails, she admired the graphene construction of the device. She recollected how the discovery of the potential of graphene in energy storage had spearheaded the end of the reliance on fossil fuels and had reduced the greenhouse gases to preindustrial levels. At present, graphene was ubiquitous. For example, graphene powered the batteries that lasted a hundred years and recharged in only fifteen minutes. Its malleability allowed the design of paper-thin smartphones and computers that rolled up when not in use. Since graphene was a hundred times stronger than steel, it had become the chief building block of the spaceships traveling across the Milky Way galaxy to Gnaritus. In fact, three-dimensional printing with graphene had built every square inch of the space colony and provided the energy for its operation.

Ten minutes later, the air cab slowed down as it crept along the side of a hill overlooking Keswick and the Derwentwater Lake. They passed rows of quaint cottages with verdant gardens where the residents basked in the setting sun on that somnolent summer day. Surina's pale-yellow cottage was at the head of the cul-de-sac on Oakdale Avenue. The cottage was of graphene construction but had a charming vintage thatched roof and dusky-blue door. An oak picket fence surrounded the garden in which daffodils, bluebells, lilies of the valley, and yellow roses blossomed along the path leading to the door. The driver was a husky youth with a thick mop of wavy chestnut hair and a weather-beaten complexion. He landed the cab in front of the gate with a thud and hauled her boxes into the cottage.

"Are you going to Gnaritus?" he said with a knowing smile. "I often take people home with their boxes on their last day at work. Good luck in the New World!"

After giving him a tip, Surina closed the door to the snake bitten day, which had bruised, beaten, and vanquished her. As she sank into the embrace of a yellow rose-print armchair with a weary sigh, she thought of how she loved her home: her sanctuary against the vagaries of circumstance and chance. Adorning the center of the coffee table was a miniature marble replica of the Taj Mahal, which brought back memories of her holidays in her ancestral home of India with her parents. A curio cabinet in the corner exhibited an eclectic mix of decorative teak sculptures of Masai masks, giraffes, antelopes, and elephants from her best friend Dr. Mercy Jakande's vacation to Africa. There was also an Inuit stone sculpture of a dancing polar bear from Mercy's vacation to Canada.

She mobilized her waning energy and trudged to the kitchen, knowing that piping-hot tea and a warm scone would restore her spirits after a marathon day of backbreaking toil at the hospital. As she slathered raspberry jam and clotted cream on her scone, she knew everything had changed. Her troubles were starting to pyramid. In the past, she had believed there would always be another day to prove her bona fides. Now Jane Woodford's lacerating admonition—"There's no place for you on Earth"—kept ringing in her ears. The memory of the vile smell in the medical director's office prickled her nose as well. She would gain neither acceptance nor approbation from this world. Had there ever been a place for her, or had she been deluding herself all along? It seemed as if the Earth had room only for the Stinguards and Kadisons of this world.

While she nibbled at yesterday's leftover shepherd's pie, she thought of her parents, who had succumbed to cancer years ago, when they were on Gnaritus. She had gone through the highest channels to procure the seal of approval to visit her parents on Gnaritus despite knowing she would be traveling on a one-way ticket. There had been a summary dismissal of her request as expected. The terse letter with a rubber-stamped signature had cited the need to preserve resources as the reason for the rejection of the application.

Surina grimaced as she remembered how she had lost touch with her parents after they had relocated to Gnaritus. The only available communication lines between the two worlds consisted of censored e-mails. Most of the time, e-mails never got through. The World Governing Body pinned the blame for the poor communication on the prohibitive distances separating the two worlds since Gnaritus lay on the fringes of the Milky Way galaxy, ten thousand light-years away. Sad to say, she had received only a single e-mail from her parents, informing her that they both had cancer. She had replied but had received no further response. Many years later, a curt e-mail from the World Governing Body had notified her of the date and time of her parents' deaths and nothing more. It haunted her to this day that, in spite of being a cancer specialist, she had been unable to help her parents with their treatment.

Surina was still reminiscing about her parents when a rat-a-tat-tat on the door roused her. Smiling with relief, she let in her best friend, Dr. Mercy Jakande, who worked at the Greysville Quadrant Hospital in stem-cell engineering. Due to her tall, thin frame, Mercy cut a striking figure as she strode into the room wearing a pale-blue tweed tunic over a crisp white shirt. Her expressive, iridescent eyes, glowed against her skin of midnight black, and her rapier mind gave her a cerebral aura.

Surina knew she had a lot in common with Mercy. Their friendship had begun due to their proximity, for Mercy lived only four doors away on Oakdale Avenue with her husband and two children. However, it had continued to strengthen because, in a way, they were both still outsiders. For even though Britain was their country of birth, the majority of the population still regarded them as foreigners. In spite of her quintessential British accent, Surina remembered the inevitable questions about her country of origin. No one ever seemed to guess that maybe she could be from right there in Keswick. All the explanations became tiresome, for even when she said she was from Britain, the matter never ended there. They would press her on where she was *really* from, which necessitated her to launch into the extensive migration history of her family. After describing her parents' passage from India to London in their youth, she would explain that her birthplace was Keswick because her parents had moved there next.

Whether this explanation satisfied the inquisitors, Surina could never fathom for they still looked at her askance as the "other" and not as one of them. The narrow focus on alterity or otherness seemed to define the stifling society on Earth. In essence, the russet-brown hue of her skin made it necessary for her to explain her humanity, as few recognized it in her. It baffled her as to why she needed to validate her presence because Britain, the country of her birth, was the only home that she had known for her entire existence on Earth.

These thoughts still preoccupied Surina as Mercy flopped down into the rose-chintz sofa and placed a yellow box on the coffee table. "Surina, I just heard what they did! It was their game plan all along. I'm sure of it. I know you probably aren't in the mood to celebrate your birthday after your dreadful day at the hospital, but I bought a cake."

The delicate Victoria sponge cake with raspberry jam filling and a fresh pot of Earl Grey tea brightened up the cheerless day. They decided to forgo the candles. While they savored the melt-in-your-mouth cake along with steaming-hot cups of fresh tea, a shadow descended over Mercy's despondent eyes. She leaned forward on the sofa to commiserate with Surina.

"It doesn't seem fair," Mercy said. "When I reviewed your data, I found nothing amiss whatsoever. Since your results add up, they need to delay the release of the Stinguard viral vector. Then again, even though my experiments are sound, my supervisor discounted the results as well. I'll never forget his bluntness in telling me to explore another avenue of stem-cell biology and abandon my line of investigation altogether! They're shutting me out of all the key committee memberships and leaving me to flounder on the margins. They treat me like an outsider, even though I was born here after my parents migrated to Keswick from Nigeria. My exclusion from committee meetings has become so tiresome that I wonder why I bother even going into work other than for a paycheck. Since they brush off my opinions without the slightest hesitation, I have no input on anything either.

"For instance, that smarmy Ed Kadison, who joined the hospital staff eight years after me, is already in the International Scientific Committee on Human Evolution. He has a lifelong residency on Earth now. That promotion bloated his already insufferable ego even further. Two months ago, I overheard him telling his cronies that Stinguard had promised him your lab space. Kadison is a master snake charmer and knows how to milk the system. I'm not sure I have the appetite to play his game. You're lucky there's no cleaning android here to record everything for the benefit of the all-knowing World Governing Body. I don't think what I just said would go over too well! By the way, how did you avoid having a cleaning android?"

Heaving a sigh of relief after offloading her concerns, Mercy relaxed back into the sofa, with both her hands cradling a hot cup of tea.

Surina pressed a button on the coffee table. "I just said the cottage is small, and there wouldn't be much for a cleaning android to do. Besides, they have many other ways to monitor us. The news today will have more information about the Stinguard viral vector's launch date."

On the wall above the fireplace, a paper-thin graphene screen flickered into life. A slender woman appeared with her platinum-blond hair cascading onto her soigné purple jacket's shoulder pads. Her smug smile revealed a row of perfect white teeth, which glistened all the brighter when contrasted with her brilliant-red glossy lipstick.

"Thank you for joining us," the newscaster said. "This is Stacy Smith, bringing you *Global News* from London. Our top story is a new method of preventing cancer. A world-renowned scientist, Dr. Rod Stinguard of the Greysville Quadrant Hospital, has announced the launch of the Stinguard viral vector in Tanga, Tanzania, in three months."

In the background, images of hospital wards full of emaciated patients lying in despair on cots and mothers bringing their children to a cancer hospital in Tanzania flashed on the screen.

Both the cheeriness of Stacy Smith's voice and her fixed gummy smile belied the tragic images shown, but she continued undeterred in the same manner. "We are lucky to have Dr. Rod Stinguard in the studio. Dr. Stinguard, please explain the benefits of this viral vector to our worldwide audience."

Beside her towering frame sat a short man a quarter of her size, wearing a gray-tweed jacket, an open-collar shirt without a tie, and an immovable mirthless smile. He must have spent considerable time primping and preening himself for the television appearance. Not only had he groomed his sparse white hair but also an intensive makeup session had transformed his ashen skin to a healthy pink glow. Moreover, the close-up view of his hard-boiled face brought into clearer focus his beady eyes, which appeared as lifeless as the androids. From his catbird seat, he bragged with grandiloquence how every Earth citizen would receive the viral vector.

"Tanzania, with one of the highest cancer rates, will receive the earliest benefit from the viral vector," he said in an ostentatious manner. "After three months, the program will shift to the Punjab, the cancer belt of India. The viral vector carries the genetic code for enzymes, which will repair all the cancer-causing mutations. Our goal is to wipe out cancer."

Throughout the broadcast, Stacy Smith's broad smile never dimmed as she fawned over Dr. Stinguard and showered him with thanks for gracing the program with his presence. Next, the news shifted to the centenary anniversary celebrations of the establishment of the colony on Gnaritus. For the most part, the television footage focused on images of elderly Gnaritonians in party hats feasting in rooms full of balloons. The show ended with a brief ceremony on Earth where the World Governing Body's chief executive officer, John Jones-May, and other panjandrums officiated at a solemn twenty-one gun salute.

From the impression given by the news, Surina surmised that the tentacles of the leviathan World Governing Body reached all the way to Gnaritus. Moreover, the sanitized news from Gnaritus and the heavily censored e-mails had left her without a clear impression of life in the New World. As a result, a general air of mystery shrouded Gnaritus, which engendered fear on Earth.

"Did you bring your research files with you?" Mercy asked as the closing credits rolled on the television screen.

Surina muted the sound of the television. "I've always kept a copy of my research files at home, but I'm debating whether to take them to Gnaritus with me. Somehow I think it would be best to make a clean break with the past."

"You must take them with you in case something happens," Mercy said in an ominous tone. "I shudder even thinking about the lethal mutations that could result in half the patients receiving the Stinguard viral vector."

"The scientific community trounced my experiments," Surina replied, still reeling from the barrage of rejection letters.

"Remember, the journals and committees *under* Stinguard's control discredited your studies," Mercy said. "What chance did you have in those circumstances? Who can ever escape from the *poison arrow?* Does the truth have any hope to see the light of day in this world? I don't know anymore. All I know is that I don't want to have this Stinguard viral vector, and I don't want my kids to have it either!"

Nonetheless, they both realized how little choice there was in the matter. Mercy strolled across the room, past a vase of sunflowers, to the window overlooking the front garden. She recoiled in alarm and closed the curtains. "A drone overhead is spying on this house. Why would there be any need for surveillance?"

"The spaceship blasts off in a week," Surina said. "Maybe they want to make sure I get onboard and don't run away."

"No one can hide on Earth anymore," Mercy replied, shivering with a sense of dread. "The World Governing Body stinks with money and controls the levers of power. They can find anyone. In a given year, only one or two families ever protest against the relocation of their relatives to Gnaritus. It's pointless to tangle with the World Governing Body because android security guards will raid the homes of any firebrands and force them to go Gnaritus along with all those family members who dissented. Any level of resistance or even asking too many questions in our unyielding, dogmatic society gets you nowhere but on a one-way trip to Gnaritus. We are under the jackboot of the World Governing Body. No spy drones monitored my parents when they went to Gnaritus. I bet the fear of your research files leaking out triggered their Pavlovian response in spying on you. What's the point of all this snooping, though? They would thwart any leak because they control every avenue of communication. Remember to keep the research files with you as you may need them one day."

Just before leaving, Mercy made a cryptic announcement, "We must meet again this week. I may also have some news to share with you!"

Surina put away the leftover Victoria sponge cake and tidied up. Mercy's visit had raised even more questions than answers. To begin with, why was a drone monitoring her house? The unanswered questions buzzed around her head as she climbed the stairs to go to bed. Before turning the lights out to go to sleep, she glanced out the window. The unmanned aerial spy drone still fluttered like an annoying insect above her front garden. By the next morning, it had not budged one iota from its stakeout.

4

Trafalgar Square

IN MANY WAYS, not having to go to the hospital again filled Surina with enormous relief, for she realized she had ceased to be relevant to the institution a long time ago. A sneaking suspicion niggled at the back of her mind that perhaps she had never mattered in the larger scheme of things either. However, in her final six days on Earth, she had time neither to grovel in self-pity nor to dillydally. Instead, she had to channel all her energies into packing for the space voyage and putting her affairs in order. The only good news was that due to the Relocation Policy to Gnaritus, she had always kept her possessions to the essentials. She had even winnowed through her belongings about a year ago, for she had an inkling of her imminent departure from Earth.

She had only a few items to pack now, such as her prized collection of the miniature Taj Mahal, Masai masks, giraffes, antelopes, elephants, and the dancing polar bear. Since she still needed her essential stainless-steel cooking pots and pans, she decided to pack them on the day before her departure. Remembering Mercy's prudent advice, she would take the disc containing her research files with her to Gnaritus as well.

She also had an appointment today to sign her will at Hargreaves and Thomas, the law firm in London that her parents had always used. Since she was an only child, Surina's parents had left her the cottage when they went to Gnaritus. Now, she would bequeath all her worldly possessions to Mercy in lieu of The Ministry of Housing selling off any abandoned property to the highest bidder.

After breakfast, she went by air cab to Keswick Station to catch an underground vacuum tube train to London. During her ride, she flipped through a magazine about how the world had changed after the development of streamlined vactrains ten years ago. These silver bullet trains had shortened journey times. In fact, magnetic levitation through airless resistance-free underground vacuum tubes propelled vactrains at eight times the speed of sound so that even the trip from New York to Mumbai took only two hours. Despite the lack of a view, underground vactrains became the primary mode of transportation due to the ease and convenience of supersonic travel. After the advent of vactrains and air cabs, personal transportation vehicles became relegated to the heap of relics from the remote past. The vactrains took over the existing subway and railway stations. The air cabs adopted the roads from a bygone era as just another landmark by which to navigate from the sky. Otherwise, pedestrians used the roads at their leisure.

Surina arrived at Charing Cross Station within five minutes and trudged to Trafalgar Square using Nelson's Column to guide her. She passed a "Pedestrians Only" sign since there was an embargo against air cars in the city center for security reasons. Here and there, the hawk-eyed android security guards in their blue uniforms patrolled the square. In a similar way, flocks of pigeons surveyed the crowd from their perches on the giant statues at the four corners of the plaza. In the northeastern corner of Trafalgar Square, a legion of excited tourists swarmed around the fourth plinth, now hosting a riderless horse skeleton statue.

In contrast to the jubilant sightseers, a downhearted homeless couple and their two young children in tatterdemalion clothes enjoyed a brief respite in the summer sunshine on the steps in front of the National Gallery. Two black plastic bags on the ground containing all their worldly possessions attested to their impecunious state. Surina winced when the android security guards pounced on the indigent family like birds of prey. They scuttled them into a waiting white air van, which skedaddled off like a lightning bolt, to deposit its human cargo in one of the many detention centers. The ultimate destination of the homeless masses was Gnaritus, but no one could ever confirm this. The incessant buzz of the miniature drones circling the skies overhead made Surina wonder if the one monitoring her was among them.

After turning right onto Whitcomb Street, she reached her destination: the law offices of Hargreaves and Thomas. The preserved Georgian façade of the building contrasted with the contemporary furnishings inside. In honor of the founding member of the firm, a stately portrait of the bespectacled Justin Hargreaves in his traditional silk robes dominated the waiting room.

After climbing a winding staircase to the second floor, she entered the comfortable corner office of the current senior partner in the firm, Tristan Hargreaves. At once Hargreaves ushered her to a polished circular oak table by the window, which offered a panoramic view of the entire street. While Surina settled into the luxurious brown-leather chair, he gathered a stack of files from a cabinet. He epitomized a pedantic professor, with tousled gray hair and gold-rimmed spectacles on the tip of his aquiline nose. His deep-set eyes matched the color of his gunnery-green tweed suit. The measured cadences of his speech gave the impression that he weighed the meaning of each sentence with care before uttering a word. His fastidious demeanor radiated confidence, reassuring the many anxious clients who sought his help.

"This firm has served your family for generations," Tristan Hargreaves said. "Both my parents are also on Gnaritus. When you see them, please reassure them that the whole family is doing well, including my brother, who is now a banking executive. My three children are just about to graduate in law, political science, and bank management. Even though I send many messages, somehow I fear that most of them disappear into a black hole. I've heard nothing from Gnaritus for many years. I have only eight years left before going to Gnaritus as well. I know how imperative it is for us to preserve Earth's limited resources for future generations. As my father said when he founded this firm, there are rules, regulations, and laws for a reason, and we must obey them to the letter."

He spoke with conviction, but Surina detected a faint flicker of doubt in his eyes and voice.

Hargreaves placed a stash of papers on the table. "Your will is ready for your signature, Dr. Mathew. The transfer of your property to Dr. Mercy Jakande will take effect on the day of your departure for Gnaritus."

She leafed through the papers. "I have to sign all eight documents?"

Tristan nodded. After she had perused the documents and signed in the appropriate places, the certainty of the forthcoming voyage to another world dawned on her. Jane Woodford's excoriating rebuke—"There's no place for you on Earth"—also reverberated in her ears, heightening her sense of impending doom.

Tristan Hargreaves embraced her as she prepared to leave. Later, he stood like a statue at the window to watch as Surina's solitary figure disappeared down Whitcomb Street. A substantial part of his firm's business dealt with property and business transfers at the time of relocation to the space colony. He felt comforted by the knowledge that his son, Sean, would inherit the firm in a few years after his graduation from Oxford University

Law School. He thought with pride how the line of succession in the Hargreaves family would continue uninterrupted since the founding of the firm. However, the loss of a client always affected him on a personal level, especially in cases like Surina, for she was the last member of her family on Earth.

Amid the boisterous clamor of the tourists, Surina waited on the steps of the National Gallery for Dr. Heidi Burmann. She thought of how the History of Art exhibition, followed by dinner, would allow her a fitting opportunity to bid farewell to her best friend from medical school. Most of all, she was glad she had already warned Heidi about the Stinguard viral vector.

Out of nowhere, a stolid android security guard leaped up the steps and cast a menacing shadow over Surina.

"There is no loitering allowed here, madam," he said in his chirpy voice.

Surina's heart quaked. Just then, Heidi Burmann rushed to her side. Her bohemian gypsy dress and leather cowboy boots gave her the overall impression of being a free spirit. Moreover, her flaxen hair hung about her shoulders in loose waves and framed her makeup-free, fresh face. In fact, no amount of makeup could improve her already flawless porcelain skin.

"We're just on our way to see the art exhibition," Heidi said in her mellifluous voice.

Still suspicious of their motives, the android security guard spent an interminable amount of time reappraising the situation. Only after scrutinizing their faces, did he stomp off without a word.

Surina breathed a sigh of relief as she and Heidi entered the cloistered peace of the National Gallery.

Heidi chuckled when they saw an android tour guide. "Tough to escape these omnipresent androids. I'm glad to see you. You look well. It'll be a treat to savor the entire sweep of art history, from the earliest cave paintings to the present Renaissance era."

Due to these events, they shied away from the android-led tour group. Instead, they read the captions accompanying each painting. Beginning in the Stone Age gallery, the haunting cave paintings of ferocious wild beasts such as bears, wooly rhinos, mammoths, and bison swept them to the dawn of humans.

Heidi pointed to murals depicting herds of horses and deer in flight from unknown bloodthirsty hunters. "This painting captures the pulsating fear in the eyes of these animals so well. I can almost hear the stampede across the gallery."

"Oh wow," Surina said. "It seems as if this burnished-ochre human handprint at the bottom corner of the mural is hailing our common humanity across the millennia. Is this palm print the signature of the primeval painter? These bold, confident brushstrokes and colors are so full of promise and still resonate over the ages."

Heidi, an art enthusiast, led the way through the exhibition. "I love the ornate Egyptian gallery, with its florid tomb paintings. These hieroglyphics and golden chariots helped to guide the pharaohs in the afterlife. The Mesopotamian stone sculptures of the fertility goddesses are wonderful too. The idealized perfection of the Greek sculptures and the Doric and Corinthian columns are magnificent. Though, nothing can compare with the tranquil, contemplative art of India and China."

In the Renaissance gallery, celebrating the rebirth of classical art, they joined a gaggle of visitors paying homage to Leonardo Da Vinci's *The Virgin of The Rocks* and Michelangelo's *The Entombment*. Meanwhile, Peter Paul Rubens's *Samson and Delilah* made them nostalgic for the dazzling splendor and opulence of the Baroque period.

Later, the *Water-Lilies, Setting Sun* painting by Claude Monet in the Impressionism gallery mesmerized Surina. She thought of how Monet had accomplished the impossible by capturing the fleeting effects of the setting sun's rays as well as the eternal light. Pulling themselves away from the cubism and futurism of the Picasso gallery, they proceeded to the postmodernism gallery. It spanned a tumultuous era from the 1970s until the end of the twenty-first century. Elegiac, barren landscapes embodied the Zeitgeist of that fatalistic era.

"Earth was in bad shape in the twenty-first century," Heidi said. "Climatic upheavals rocked the Earth, and the sun scorched the land. These pictures of bone dry lakes and rivers break my heart. Look at this painting of smoky factories spewing sludge into foul, swampy water. It reeks with the smell of the polluted air. Ugh! Here are some more apocalyptic paintings. Such thick smog choked most cities at the end of the twenty-first century that people had to don goggles and gas masks just to walk outside. Thank heavens the twenty-second century ushered in the second Renaissance period that's still in effect. Somehow, the lakes and rivers came back to life and teemed with fish once more. I love the idyllic paintings of lush vegetation, extravagant flowers, and cascading waterfalls in the contemporary art gallery. Don't you think they're reminiscent of Gauguin's vibrant paintings of Tahiti? These starship paintings are impressive as well. All the starships are V-shaped. Perhaps, that's the most aerodynamic shape."

"Why are there only a handful of paintings of spaceships?" Surina asked. "They serve as such a powerful testimony to human ingenuity. I wish I had a body of work to leave behind."

Surina was proud of the impressive breadth and scope of human creativity, which the gallery sought to eternize for posterity. The artists had left a timeless legacy; nevertheless, she wished she could also leave something behind, even half as good. Pangs of regret seared her. She would leave no mark on Earth, for her middling research was now only an object of ridicule.

Toward the end of the gallery, the glaring omissions in the History of Art exhibition dawned on her. Conspicuous by their absence were paintings of humans suffering at the hands of other humans, such as Felix Nussbaum's *The Refugee*, Picasso's *Weeping Woman*, and Nikolai Getman's series about the Stalin-era gulags. Paintings of the ravages of famine from the great drought at the end of the twenty-first century were also absent. Nor were there any depictions of the innumerable wars, which had maimed, disfigured, tortured, and butchered humans. In essence, there was a conscious effort to efface artwork showing how humans can be capable of not only sublime creativity but also immense destruction. Moreover, there were no paintings of Gnaritus, not even one.

"Did we miss the Gnaritus collection?" she whispered.

Heidi shrugged her shoulders. "No. It's the end of the exhibition. Oh well, after your rotten day yesterday, you could use some tea and sympathy. The National Café is nearby. I feel a bit peckish."

Soon, they ensconced themselves in the packed National Café. The soft light bounced off the mirrored walls, making the restaurant appear much larger and brighter. An energetic young waiter in a crisp white tailcoat tuxedo served them as he moved like a dancer between the crowded tables. After they had finished one course, the second one materialized before them as if by magic. He showed great assiduousness in replenishing their teapot with perfect, piping-hot water. He even obliged by snapping photos of them enjoying their last sumptuous supper together.

They tucked into a delicious, red-hot spicy curried pumpkin soup and smoked haddock kedgeree. After Surina had topped the soup with crispy curry leaves, the piquant flavor of the nourishing broth revitalized her. However, they needed to bellow to hear each other over the animated conversations filling the National Café.

"I never took my job as seriously as you did," Heidi said halfway through a succulent grilled pork chop, Provençal lentils, sweet corn, and spinach with crème fraîche. "I'm glad to work just part time in the emergency room at the Royal London Hospital. At least, I have time to bring up my three children and set them on the right path for the future before I leave. According to the

Relocation Policy, I can only go to Gnaritus after they turn twenty-one years of age, which gives me more time on Earth. It's going to be hard for me to leave London since I was born here after my parents emigrated from Germany. It seems rather arbitrary as to who goes to Gnaritus. Just look all around you. Many people here are older than sixty years, the so-called mandatory age of relocation. This Relocation Policy makes no sense to me. In any case, I have a wish list of all the sights I want to visit before I go to Gnaritus. We're going to see the antiquities of Greece this year. Have you been?"

Surina stopped eating the flourless gooey chocolate cake and shook her head. "No, I've never been to Greece. Not seeing more of the world is one of my many mistakes. Yes, you're right. My job consumed me. I wasted a lot of valuable time at work. Somehow, one thing always led to another. While life passed me by, I focused on trying to publish just one more research article. At least, your priorities will allow you to make full use of this limited time on Earth—something that always eluded me."

"Remember, I'm only able to work part-time because my husband works full time," Heidi said in between bites of delicious treacle tart with lashings of silky custard. "We'll join you in a few years. Even on Gnaritus, life will carry on! I wonder why so much secrecy shrouds Gnaritus. Imagine, no Gnaritus paintings even! Why is there only a trickle of communication between the two planets? Although they give an introductory session about Gnaritus during the month-long journey to the planet, why not tell us beforehand? Sometimes, I question this Relocation Policy, even though I know how vital it is to preserve Earth's resources for my children's generation. You're so wrong in believing you botched your life on Earth! In fact, one of our mutual patients said you saved his life, and he thanked me for referring him to you. To save a life can leave profound ramifications rippling forever. You've left your mark not just once but many times. Think of all the people you'll help on Gnaritus!"

"Heidi, you always cheer me up!"

"By the way, Surina, thanks for your warning about the Stinguard viral vector. I agree with your assessment of this mealymouthed Stinguard guy. Did you see his disingenuous interview on the *Global News* program the other day? His self-serving platitudes, triteness, and cold, calculating demeanor did not inspire any trust, whatsoever."

After finishing the scrumptious feast, Heidi proposed a toast. "To the New World!"

Surina raised her teacup in a halfhearted manner. "To the New World."

Heidi glanced at her watch. "Oh, it's nearly closing time. Where did the time go? It's already eleven o'clock."

Outside, a dense fog had descended, through which drizzling raindrops glistened in the gloom. Surina and Heidi dashed back to Charing Cross Station. To make matters worse, they had forgotten to bring their umbrellas. The brume permeated every nook and blurred the outlines of the buildings. Surina thought the city resembled one of the hazy paintings hanging in the Impressionism gallery.

Two young violinists sheltering from the rain under an archway at the entrance of Charing Cross Station emerged like specters in the sepulchral miasma. The couple played a duet to uplift the mood of the rain-soaked passengers hurrying to catch their trains. Only a few of the passersby paused for a few seconds to listen to the virtuoso performance. After casting the musicians pitying looks, they scurried away into the bowels of the station. For the most part, the performers were either ignored or treated as nuisances sullying the slick cityscape. Undaunted, they played with such passion that the bows became a blur as they raced across the strings of the violins. The male violinist moved his head back and forth with the music, and his dreadlocks danced in the air. In the inky shadows of the archway, their luminous eyes shone all the brighter against their rich black complexions. For Surina, the otherworldly music evoked images of the stars and planets.

"Bach's 'Gavotte En Rondeaux from the Partita Number Three in E Major' is one of my favorites," Heidi said.

They lingered beside the violinists for a while to hear the mesmerizing sounds of the ethereal music, which was as excellent as from any orchestra in the world. Surina noticed that the nonpareil musicians' matching T-shirts had the words "Soul" and "Mate" set against the vivid colors of the Jamaican flag. On the pavement were two frayed green backpacks and a battered brown violin case with the words "Gabriel and Rafaela" on the inside in shiny gold thread. As Surina and Heidi threw a few coins into the empty violin case, the male violinist glanced at them with haunting eyes. A shy smile lit up his dejected countenance for a fleeting moment.

All of a sudden, the heavens rumbled, and a lightning bolt pierced the night. When the rain pelted down in sheets, Surina and Heidi ran into the elevator.

"That celestial music came at an opportune time as a prelude to my starship voyage," Surina said.

"What a frabjous day," Heidi said. "The music was like the icing on a cake."

As they piled out of the elevator onto the underground platform, Heidi's vactrain to her home in Kent rolled into the station.

"I wish we could go to other art exhibitions at the National Gallery," Surina said. "It's such a shame that it's the last time."

Heidi hopped aboard the vactrain. "Remember, Surina, life will go on even on Gnaritus. There's so much more life to live."

Surina waved goodbye as the vactrain whooshed by into a tunnel. From the entrance of Charing Cross Station, Bach's zephyrean violin concerto wafted down the stairs to the platform until the arrival of the screeching vactrain to Keswick drowned it out. During the journey home, Heidi's sage advice bolstered Surina's morale. Life would go on even on Gnaritus, she thought.

Later, as she glimpsed the spy drone circling her cottage like a hunter lying in wait for its prey, the all too familiar doubts came flooding back.

5

The Setting Sun

THE NEXT MORNING, Mercy surprised Surina by joining her for breakfast on the sunny terrace in the backyard of her cottage. They enjoyed the meal at their leisure to the sound of honeybees buzzing around an assortment of flowers in full bloom. The fragrances of the rhododendrons, chrysanthemums, foxgloves, roses, and lilies of the valley intermingled to create a sublime perfume.

In the past, Surina's kinetic pace had never allowed her enough time for breakfast, other than a hasty granola bar before rushing off to the hospital. In contrast, today she luxuriated in a proper full English breakfast. There was an impressive array of fried eggs; lovely, fat pork sausages; baked beans; crisp fried tomatoes; and crusty toasted brioche with a thick spread of tangy marmalade jam. In fact, she needed to fuel up for an excursion along the Bowder Stone and Watendlath walking path in the Lake District.

"I quit my job," Mercy said with relief. "I'm tired of jockeying for position at work. I'd rather spend more time with my kids while I can. Jari could not have been more supportive of my decision."

Surina remembered Mercy's husband Jari was a well-established cardiologist at the Greysville Quadrant Hospital. Rather than dampening Mercy's ebullience, she tried to suppress her inner pangs of sadness since the unexpected resignation marked a significant loss for the scientific community. For the most part, the departure of a brilliant, industrious physician such as Dr. Mercy Jakande indicated the failure of a system with no investment in her success. Surina knew with hindsight how little commitment the system had toward her advancement either. Was the system just indifferent or biased toward them? In essence, she felt like a supernumerary member of Earth's society who had never had a chance from the beginning despite her years of diligent study and conscientiousness. By focusing on alterity or otherness, the hidebound society on Earth treated her like an outsider and bilked her dreams and hopes. Perhaps, she should also have resigned long ago, knowing the mercenary agenda of the institution. It seemed as if Mercy had already reached the same conclusion.

"Mercy, I wish you hadn't resigned, but I understand how you feel," Surina said. "I'm glad you're happy. We should celebrate! I always hoped to see the antiquities of Athens before leaving Earth. Want to go to Greece? Since it's the summer holidays, why not bring Janet and Darren as well?"

"How about going tomorrow for three days and being back on Saturday evening?" Mercy replied. "The kids will enjoy it! It'll be a good way to end their month-long summer holiday before the new term at school. Kids these days have shorter and shorter vacations. I remember when school restarted in September after the summer break, but now it's the end of July. Don't you have packing to do?"

"Oh, I've already done all my packing, and my seven boxes are ready to load on the starship," Surina said in between bites of brioche. "Let's go tomorrow. There's so little time remaining for me on Earth. I haven't even seen much of the Lake District, so I'm going on a walking tour today to soak up the natural wonders just a stone's throw away."

After finishing the splendid breakfast with fresh orange juice and English breakfast tea, they set off down Oakdale Avenue in high spirits. In the front garden of Mercy's cottage, ten-year-old Janet and twelve-year-old Darren whizzed around on hoverboards.

"Want to go on holiday to Greece?" Mercy asked.

Both children alighted from their hoverboards and stared with shell-shocked wonder.

"When do we leave?" Darren asked.

"Tomorrow morning," Surina said.

A grin beamed across Janet's face. "We'll be ready. I'll begin packing right away."

Janet and Darren rushed inside the cottage with Mercy as Surina left them to go to Keswick, which lay at the end of Oakdale Avenue. The lake of Derwentwater was only a ten-minute walk from Keswick town center. Before long, she was sailing across the pellucid lake on the water bus service to join the walking tour at the Brandelhow landing stage.

The fifteen-member walking tour group included mainly city dwellers from London and Manchester on summer holiday with their children. A knowledgeable tour guide would lead the way and ensure the safety of the entire group. He was a stocky youth with broad shoulders and thickset arms, who looked as if he pumped iron. Due to his extensive time spent outdoors, he had developed a ruddy, sunburnt complexion. He greeted each member of the walking tour and handed out maps of the points of interest along the way.

The Cicerone squinted in the summer sun and spoke in a booming voice. "Welcome to the Lake District. The weather is perfect for us today! By the way, what country are you joining us from?"

"Oh, I'm from right here in Keswick," Surina answered. "This is my home."

He was quite taken aback by her response as if he had considerable trouble picturing her as a native of Britain. "Is this where you are originally from?"

Surina knew that nothing would convince the tour guide of their shared origins and humanity, for he would always see her as an outsider. She was too tired from the hectic week to launch into the migration history of her family. "Since this is my birthplace, this is my home. Before going to Gnaritus in a week, I wanted to see the beautiful scenery on this walking tour."

As soon as she mentioned relocating to Gnaritus, the tour guide lost interest in his line of questioning. Instead, he marched ahead, and the walking tour group raced to keep up with him. It was a typical reaction since most people turned away after hearing of her imminent departure to Gnaritus. She understood how other personae non gratae must be feeling on Earth.

Without delay, the walking tour group went through the ancient woods of Manesty Park to the village of Grange and the Jaws of Borrowdale, the narrow entrance to the valley. Here ancient glaciers had carved the valley that lay between Grange Fell and the rocky Castle Crag. After they had traversed the double-arched stone bridge over the River Derwent, a meandering bridleway led them to a slate quarry and the Bowder Stone, a two-thousand-ton Ice Age boulder. Due to the overwhelming picturesque beauty of the green farmland dotted with grazing sheep, Surina snapped numerous pictures of the dramatic vistas.

Further down the bridleway, at the village of Rosthwaite, the rustic Oak Tree Farm Inn sidewalk café on the main street provided them with an opportunity to enjoy an hour-long lunch amid the splendor of the gilded valley. Given that Surina had worked off her breakfast long ago, her appetite was as voracious as that of other members of the walking group. Even the children cleaned up their plates, overflowing with generous helpings of hearty Wiltshire ham, cheddar cheese, and creamy horseradish-buttered chicken sandwiches. The children jumped with delight as a pair of horses clip-clopped down the street while their riders enjoyed an animated conversation. Surina still managed to have room for a large slice of cinnamon apple pie and vanilla ice cream. As she gulped down a refreshing cup of Darjeeling tea, she noticed a gaunt man with thinning white hair sitting opposite her. His maudlin eyes, which seemed to be almost on the brink of tears, were the most striking aspect of his musty face. His ravenous appetite was incongruous with his skin and bones frame, though.

After gorging on custard tarts and guzzling copious amounts of apple cider, he put down his goblet and spoke in a tired voice. "I'm famished. The fresh air is conducive to a healthy appetite. Lunch never tasted this good before. Coming here today before leaving for Gnaritus next week has gone a long way in pulling me out of the slump I've been in ever since my wife died a year ago. She was my whole world. Unfortunately, we had no children either. This walk has the reputation of being among the loveliest in the world, but nothing could prepare me for such magnificence. I wish I could stay here forever."

"My departure to Gnaritus is next week as well," Surina replied in a cheerless tone. "Despite living in Keswick all my life, this is my first walking tour in the Lake District. In any event, I'm kicking myself for spending so much time at work and not experiencing more of this gorgeous scenery."

While Surina spoke, the man nodded and seemed to understand her disappointment. Just as he was about to respond, the tour guide gathered them together at the front of the inn from where they resumed the trail along the bridleway and climbed to Puddingstone Bank. Lavender and cornflowers stippled the wondrous, verdant valley. Surina relished the exhilaration of the pure, fresh air as if it was the last time. Perhaps, Gnaritus would have an indoor manufactured atmosphere, although of course she could not say this with certainty.

Similar to sparkling champagne, the winsome children's ebullience and effervescence bubbled over into the valley below as they made their descent. After passing through the tiny hamlet of Watendlath, they glimpsed the welcoming sight of the slate-gray castle hotel at High Lodore through the weeping willows and ash trees of Mossmire Coppice. Here they lounged on a golden sunlit terrace overlooking a flowery meadow, where horses chomped on grass. The nearby balsam poplar trees bathed the terrace with a sweet honey, musky perfume. A lavish afternoon cream tea of warm raisin scones with strawberry jam, clotted Cornish cream, and Assam tea fortified the weary sightseers. Petits fours and biscuits provided a fitting accompaniment to this glorious feast. Once again, the vivid beauty of the valley arrested them, and they lingered longer than necessary.

After an hour, they set out again, following a winding footpath around the shores of the Derwentwater Lake. The dark tower of the Greysville Quadrant Hospital loomed across the lake as an aberration in the ineffable beauty of the surroundings, similar to a wart plaguing an otherwise perfect complexion. Soon, they returned to their starting point, the Brandelhow landing stage.

In contrast to the merriment of the children, the forlorn, gaunt man with hunched shoulders gazed with downcast eyes at the mirrored surface of the Derwentwater Lake, which seemed to reflect back the depths of his despair. Surina understood his regret; however, it was far too late for him and, for that matter, even for her. More than anything else, she wanted to tell the children never to be sad or take anything too seriously. Instead, they should grab every minute on Earth with both hands and relish being alive. Why had she placed such a premium on her job and advancement in the hospital? Such shallow goals were irrelevant in the grand scheme of things. Sad to say, life had passed her by. She wondered why she had never found the time for the essential matters in life, such as nurturing her soul.

Overcoming their reluctance to leave, the members of the walking tour boarded the air cabs home. Only the laughter of the children ringing out across the lake awoke the gaunt man from his reverie. After a final, mournful look all around the lake, he hailed an air cab, which whisked him away. Meanwhile, Surina sailed on the water bus past St. Herbert's Island and Lord's Island. The haunting ancient ruins of the Earl of Derwentwater's home from a bygone era decayed among the weeping willows on Lord's Island. The water bus chugged along the placid Derwentwater Lake onward to the northern shore, where Surina disembarked. With the moon and the stars hiding behind the clouds, night had fallen thick and fast by the time she returned to her cottage.

After supper, she packed for the excursion to Greece with gusto, making certain to take the comfortable shoes that had served her so well in the steep hills and valleys of the Lake District. Other than her holidays with her parents in India, she had seldom found the time to travel as an adult because her job had consumed her with a feverish intensity. She longed to see the Taj Mahal again, shining like a perfect teardrop on the landscape. However, the few remaining days allowed her to visit only some of the many sights she had never seen.

• • •

Surina had breakfast on the sun-drenched terrace the next morning. She drowned a stack of fluffy blueberry pancakes with golden maple syrup, buttered her toast, and put a dollop of creamy butter on the pancakes too. When she looked up at the familiar spy drone, she flinched, for it seemed she could never escape from its prying eyes. She brushed aside her apprehension only when Mercy, Janet, and Darren joined her for breakfast.

The children fizzed with excitement. They had dressed in cheerful, summertime attire, in keeping with the mood of the holiday. In particular, Janet's mint-green sundress in a seashell-and-starfish print accentuated the richness of her ebony complexion and cornrow-braided hair. Darren, meanwhile, wore a crisp red and green madras shirt with knee-length khaki shorts. He sported a worry-free buzz cut. Both of them had Mercy's incandescent eyes.

Unable to contain their wanderlust for Greece, they wolfed down their breakfast. Afterward, they flew by air cab to Keswick Station for the five-minute journey by vactrain to London St. Pancras International Station. They stood in a tortuous line of passengers for an hour as it inched through the security gate for international travel. Not even the android security guards, who gawped at their Earth passports and bombarded them with a string of questions, could dampen their enthusiasm. They boarded the vactrain to Greece with relief and arrived at Larissa Station in Athens within twenty minutes. In the center of the platform, a man in a green-felt beret and striped blue nautical shirt carried a sign displaying their names. The children ran toward him as soon as they recognized their names.

"Welcome to Athens!" he said in a lilting voice, bending down to shake their hands. "I'm Theokles, your tour guide."

Theokles, a heavyset man in his late forties, resembled a weight lifter. He had skin the color of golden wheat and thick, curly black hair that fell to his shoulders. Moreover, his sincere smile accentuated the wrinkles covering every inch of his weatherworn face. Walking with considerable assurance in the teeming clamor of the station, he cleaved a path for them through the multitude of passengers milling around on the platform.

Outside Larissa Station, a sleek, teardrop-shaped air van waited for them on the curb. Theokles opened the door of the van, and a middle-aged couple from Stockholm greeted them. Both Liam and Bergitte Lofgren had a studious air that comes from endless hours of scholastic dedication to a discipline. They were lanky, and their knees almost touched their chins in the cramped van. After only a few days in the scorching Greek sun, their dark tans stood out all the more against their blond hair. Both wore loose-fitting white T-shirts, khaki Bermuda shorts, straw hats, and Birkenstock sandals. Due to the sticky, muggy weather, Bergitte had tied her long, ash-blond hair in a simple ponytail. Despite their cheery holiday clothes, an invisible load seemed to be weighing on Liam's mind and lining his craggy face with deep furrows. On occasion, Bergitte shot piercing glances in her husband's direction while wrinkling her forehead and tightening the muscles in her face at the same time.

"Our relocation to Gnaritus is in a year," Liam said. "However, we are just beginning our tour of the great wonders of the world. We should have traveled more, but our jobs at Stockholm University preoccupied us. I'm a professor of history, and my wife is a professor of physics. In the past four days in Athens, we've seen Mount Lycabettus, the Temple of Olympian Zeus, and the wondrous National Garden. Everything is so beautiful. I'll miss Earth when I go to Gnaritus."

Surina thought it best not to mention that she was just now beginning to see a few sights with only four days left on Earth. Why had she left everything so late?

After the van had achieved its flying altitude, Janet and Darren kept their eyes peeled for the Acropolis in the sprawling metropolis of shimmering skyscrapers. Although much of the city had graphene-constructed buildings in the trendy minimalist style most popular now, the Plaka District below the Acropolis Hill was a World Heritage Site. Bustling sidewalk cafés and charming boutiques lined the winding streets of the Plaka District. After twenty minutes, the van landed outside the Ambrosia restaurant, which offered magnificent views of the Acropolis. A bevy of android porters unloaded their luggage.

A hologram of the Greek wine god, Dionysus, holding grapes in one hand and a goblet in the other, greeted them at the entrance in a shrill voice. "Welcome to the Ambrosia restaurant, where the food is fit for the gods themselves."

Theokles led the way along cobblestone walkway to a patio full of rustic wooden tables under a thick canopy of grapevines and bougainvillea in full bloom. Brilliant-red geraniums in clay pots lined the edges of the patio. The sounds of animated conversations and peals of laughter filled the warm, sweet air.

Right away, the efficient waiter regaled the weary travelers with a tasty traditional Greek salad with olives and feta cheese, followed by classic eggplant mousaka. Even Janet and Darren, usually finicky eaters, downed every morsel of the splendiferous meal and helped themselves to baklava with pistachio-mint ice cream for dessert.

After lunch, Theokles explained the history of the Acropolis with a dramatic flourish. "We are in the Plaka District or the neighborhood of the gods. It's a World Heritage Site. The architecture is much the same as in the ancient times, which will provide you with an authentic experience. Today, we will tour the hill of the gods, the Acropolis. The Parthenon and the Erechtheion are on the hilltop. The ancient Greeks built the Parthenon from marble in 447 BCE to honor the patron of Athens, the goddess Athena Parthenos, as a way of thanking her for protecting the city during the Persian Wars. It's a Doric temple with eight columns at the façade and seventeen columns on the flanks. The Parthenon once housed a colossal, forty-foot ivory and gold statue of Athena. However, pilgrims only glimpsed it from the outside since the interiors of the temples in Ancient Greece were off-limits. There is an elevator to the hilltop, but most people want to tread the footsteps of the ancients up the stairs. Are you ready?"

Indeed, the introduction piqued their curiosity. Before they left, Theokles furnished them with broad-brimmed straw hats, similar to those of the Lofgrens for protection against the fierce afternoon sun. The agile Lofgrens led the way up the steep incline, with Janet and Darren following on their heels. Surina, Mercy, and Theokles trailed behind.

On the stony hill, a leafy wood grew with a profusion of grass and wildflowers. The ancient houses in the Plaka District, with their red ceramic-tile roofs, sprawled below them. After passing by the reconstructed smaller temple of Athena Nike, they went through the Propylaea, the entrance to the Acropolis. They stopped in their tracks when the Parthenon materialized before them on the hilltop. Even though Surina knew of the grandeur of the Parthenon from television travel shows, the pharaonic splendor of the building still astounded her. Despite being a ruin, the Parthenon's perfect proportions imparted an unrivaled beauty and grace. She marveled at how it must have been in its heyday. In the background, a contingent of stealthy android security guards monitored the crowd from their posts on the perimeter of the hill. Tourists flocked around the Parthenon and listened to a hologram of a tour guide reciting historical facts.

Mercy whispered in Surina's ear. "I'm glad we have a human tour guide rather than just a hologram."

Surina nodded in agreement.

"The Parthenon has had many lives," Theokles said, peering at them from under his straw hat. "Over the centuries, it was a temple, a church, a mosque, and even an ammunition store. However, the Venetians shelled the city in 1687 with cannonballs and blew up the Parthenon by igniting the stockpile of gunpowder inside it at that time. Looters removed many artifacts as well over the centuries. The restoration began in earnest in 1975. Most of the sculptures here are replicas of the originals in the climate-controlled Acropolis Museum."

"Why is the same story repeated throughout human history?" Liam said, sighing in exasperation. "The mindless thirst for power and dominance usually destroys goodness and beauty."

"Nothing has changed even now, all these millennia later," Bergitte said, out of earshot of the android security guards.

Surina agreed with the Lofgrens about human history repeating itself in a seamless continuum from the past to the present. Overcome with fatigue from the arduous ascent of the Acropolis Hill, she rested on one of the many marble blocks on the ground all around the Parthenon. Despite the stifling heat on the hill, her linen pants and blouse kept her cool. The Parthenon's soul-stirring, marmoreal beauty transfixed her. She wondered how the glorious ancient Greek architects had reached the heights of transcendent purity, even though it lasted for an instant in human history.

Theokles pointed to the Roman theater below the southern wall of the Acropolis, the Odeon of Herodes Atticus, dating from 161 CE. "It still hosts plays and events, but the southeast wall provides the best view of the oldest Greek theater below the Acropolis, the Theater of Dionysus. The stone seating, circa 330 BCE, provided enough room for seventeen thousand people to enjoy plays such as the ancient Greek tragedies of Euripides and Sophocles. In fact, the meaning of tragedy comes from Greek plays, where the fate of mortals was beyond their control."

Then they strolled all around the Parthenon to the back porch.

Theokles wiped off beads of sweat from his forehead with an already soaked handkerchief. He directed their attention to the collapsed roof. "Once a frieze adorned the upper part of the Parthenon, depicting epic battles with justice triumphing over injustice. The depiction of ordinary people and the gods side by side on the frieze was a remarkable feat for an ancient society. The ancient Athenians believed in the significance and value of each citizen. Many parts of the frieze are in the Acropolis Museum, and we will see them later."

Liam winced as if in pain. "Our destiny is at the mercy of forces beyond our control as well. Our fate lies on Gnaritus. Is that our tragedy?"

Surina shared Liam's doubts. She wanted to say something to console Liam in his apparent turmoil, but his candor left her searching for words. By that time, Theokles had steered them to the Erechtheion.

"The Erechtheion is the site of the tomb of the legendary King Erechtheus, who lies underneath the porch of the maidens, or caryatids," he said. "Of course, these six statues of maidens supporting the porch are casts of the original ones kept in the Acropolis Museum. The Erechtheion marks the site where Athena and Poseidon fought over who would be the deity of the city. As a result, it is the most sacred place on the hill, where this olive tree celebrates Athena's victory over Poseidon. The olive tree also symbolizes peace, hope, prosperity, and resurrection."

The indefatigable Janet and Darren danced with fresh legerity all around the Erechtheion. In contrast, the remainder of the tour group admired the gossamer folds in the caryatids' robes from their seats on the marble blocks littering the ground.

Theokles marshaled the weary group close to the edge of the hill. "Below the Acropolis you can see the Agora, the heart of ancient Athens as well as the political, commercial, and cultural center. We will see the well-preserved temple of Hephaestus in the Agora tomorrow. Also in the distance is Mount Lycabettus, the highest point in the city."

They mustered enough energy to dawdle all around the Erechtheion and the Parthenon again before turning their gazes to the sapphire-blue Aegean Sea in the distance. Surina thought perhaps the Parthenon had not withered away with age after all, but rather the loving hands of the winds of time had sculpted and refined its beauty further over the eons.

Tearing themselves away from the Parthenon, they descended the hill to visit the Theater of Dionysus. Sitting on the stone seats, Surina could almost hear the ghosts of the ancient actors reenacting the epic tragedies of hubristic characters with fatal flaws that proved to be their nemeses. During sunset, they returned, bone weary, to the air-conditioned comfort of their hotel in the Plaka District, opposite the Ambrosia restaurant. Out of nowhere, a canopy of a thousand stars speckled the night sky like sequins. Their hotel rooms had a shared balcony offering a commanding view of the Parthenon, now glowing in the darkness. After a light supper, Theokles led them through the swarm of tourists milling around the quaint boutiques and cafés along the labyrinthine lanes of the Plaka. At the doorways of the shops, holograms of historical figures, such as Socrates and Plato, enticed the customers inside. By nightfall, the novel sights and sounds bombarding Surina's senses chased away the horrible gloom engulfing her ever since the meeting with the medical director.

• • •

They woke the next morning to a healthy breakfast on the patio of the Ambrosia restaurant. It was a felicitous name since ambrosia was the food of the Greek gods that conferred immortality. After refreshing themselves with grilled apricots and Greek yogurt garnished with honey and tahini, they set off with enthusiasm for their next great adventure. First, at the Acropolis Museum, they marveled at the caryatids and the remnants of the frieze once surrounding the Parthenon. For the remainder of the afternoon, they meandered along the many footpaths of the Agora, the ancient gathering place of Athens.

"Socrates, Plato, and Aristotle came here to teach and discuss philosophy," Theokles said. "Socrates forged the Socratic principles right here in the Agora. For example, he taught about the need to nurture your soul and to examine your life to make it worth living. Another Socratic tenet says if you have a good soul, then others cannot harm you because no one can injure your soul. He perfected the Socratic method in the Agora, which involves teachers posing a series of questions to elicit answers from the students so that they could learn profound new insights and develop critical thinking."

"Socrates perhaps raised too many questions that the establishment deemed to be threatening, so they sentenced him to death by drinking poisonous hemlock in 399 BCE," the bel esprit Liam said. "Raphael honors Socrates, Aristotle, and Plato along with other ancient Greek philosophers in his masterpiece Renaissance fresco *The School of Athens*, which is in the Vatican City. The magnificent mural honors the Greek ethos of philosophy as the culmination of human achievement because it seeks the knowledge of the causes of all things."

As they rambled along the passageways, the voice of the colossus Socrates still echoed in the Ancient Agora, but Surina knew all too well the ramifications of asking too many questions.

When they approached a two-storied building with a double row of colonnades, Theokles raised his hand to halt their progress. "Here is the Stoa of Attalos, which hails from 150 BCE. Most of what you see is the marble and limestone reconstruction from the 1950s. The original stoa functioned as an ancient shopping mall, but now it is the Museum of the Ancient Agora. This type of public building, with a porch and two rows of columns leading into shops, was common throughout ancient Greece since it allowed many people to gather in the airiness of the colonnades."

The shaded porch and a pleasant zephyr sifting through the colonnades provided them much-needed relief from the fiery midday sun. After admiring the row of ancient statues at the back of the porch, they entered the museum that overflowed with the artifacts from the excavation of the Agora. As Theokles led them through the museum, they witnessed firsthand the heights of human creativity and the depths of destruction from the many wars over the centuries. Surina became acutely aware of the fugaciousness of time as they left the Agora. Since their hotel was only two blocks away from the Agora, they trekked back to pick up their luggage on their way to Larissa Station. They bid farewell to Athens with pangs of regret as they boarded the vactrain.

Within five minutes, they arrived in Oia on the northwest coast of Santorini, a part of the Cyclades islands in the Aegean Sea. Church bells clanged from the belfries. The blue domes of the churches and the square, whitewashed houses contrasted with the starkness of the volcanic scenery.

As they strolled along a cobbled path to their hotel, Theokles explained the turbulent history of Santorini, the largest island in this archipelago. "This semicircular island formed during a catastrophic volcanic eruption circa 1630 BCE. Later, ancient pioneers carved thriving villages out of the volcanic rock. These improbable villages along the inaccessible cliffs have narrow, winding cobbled streets to make them easier to defend in a bygone era when pirates marauded the islands of the Aegean Sea. The village of Oia clings to the red cliffs facing the Caldera Bay."

"Oia seems crowded," Bergitte said. "Is there a festival in the village?"

"Tourists flock to Oia year round to see the acclaimed views of the setting sun," Theokles replied. "Ah, here we are at the Delphinium Hotel. Let's check in."

Their hotel rooms were a series of refurbished caves on multiple levels of the cliff. A profusion of cacti, geraniums, wild fig trees, and bougainvillea lined the footpaths and stairs connecting the cave rooms. The main hotel building contained a spa, an exercise room, a restaurant on the rooftop, and an infinity pool reaching out to the Aegean Sea. As it was suppertime by the time they settled in, they headed to the rooftop terrace restaurant to sample the island's mouth-watering traditional dishes. Surina had Greek salad, crispy fried goat cheese, grilled red snapper, lobster, and zucchini on which she sprinkled lemon olive oil.

Hotels lined the cliff, each with a rooftop terrace bustling with visitors. The fresh food and gentle rays of the sun enveloped Surina with such comfort, warmth, and contentment that it felt as if nothing bad could ever happen again. Unlike the hustle and bustle of Athens, the terrace was quiet despite being full of holidaymakers, with only the screams of the seagulls and the soothing ocean waves breaking the silence. While the heliolaters paid homage in silence, the sky and ocean turned from an aqua blue to blood orange and clinquant violet as the sun sizzled down into the Aegean Sea. All of a sudden, a myriad of twinkling stars and a full moon spangled the cloudless night sky. Surina searched the heavens, wondering where Gnaritus could be in that endless expanse.

After supper, Theokles showed them a map of the village. "Oia has many quaint boutiques selling local arts and crafts. There's a

Naval Maritime Museum as well. Shall we go?"

"Oh, I just want to stay on this terrace in the magical sea breeze and starlight," Mercy said.

Everyone nodded in agreement. Janet and Darren raced to swim in the infinity pool, with Mercy following close behind. By the open-air bar, a band played lyrical Greek folk dancing music. In the corner of the terrace, a pair of gregarious green and yellow parakeets warbled in their cage in tune with the music. Overhead, strings of white paper lanterns swung in the sea breeze. Seagulls soared and glided while sooty ravens rolled and somersaulted in the air.

"This is an enchanting evening!" Liam said, basking in the moonlight. "Such splendor is unrivaled anywhere in the world. I learned an enormous amount about the trajectory of human history today from the edifying sights in Greece. However, I wonder whether our collective consciousness and humanity have evolved much since the ancient times or if we have gone even further backward. The striking remnants of the Parthenon's frieze with ordinary people alongside the gods expressed such a visionary idea of the value of each human that is now more or less consigned to the dustbins of history. Why do they treat us like numbers and banish us to another world when we reach sixty years of age or even sooner in some cases? What is the value of a human life today?"

"I want my three children to enjoy the natural resources here as much as I did," Theokles replied. "Before the Relocation Policy came into effect, we overstretched the Earth's reserves in the twenty-first century. Although I don't want to, I must go to safeguard the Earth for future generations."

Bergitte looked askance at Theokles. "Do you believe everything they tell you? There should be a choice in whether to relocate to Gnaritus. We have no voice and are powerless."

Liam drooped his head and bemoaned. "Not only the Relocation Policy troubles me but also that nothing has changed over the millennia! Human history is larded with inhumanity. For example, the profound cruelty and power plays rampant even in this era can derail the best intentions and highest aspirations. There is still an undue emphasis on skin color to this day in all countries. As a result, origins and connections mean much more than merit. In fact, the extent of melanin pigment in the skin determines, for the most part, the kind of life and opportunities a person will have. God created such beautiful colors in nature, yet humans in many countries stigmatize even a hint of color in the skin."

Sorrow welled up in Bergitte's eyes, and she winced. "It's a tragedy. With so many razor wire fences, barriers, and schisms in our society, how can we ever evolve together to reach our full potential? We forgot Aristotle's concept of entelechy, or actualizing our perfect form, long ago. To say nothing of all the people held back by abject poverty. Why have the homeless fallen off the grid? Our mercenary society gypped them out of a future. Since we are an advanced society in the twenty-second century, we should at least be able to feed, clothe, house, and educate each human being. These are also worthy people with untapped potential. No one even knows where the homeless disappear to all of a sudden."

Mr. and Mrs. Lofgren's sincerity and erudition impressed Surina, and they provided an affirmation of many of her sentiments. She wondered whether their paths had crossed for a reason before she left Earth.

"In three days, I'm going to Gnaritus, leaving everything here behind forever," Surina said in a solemn manner. "Although I dreaded this moment for a long time, my leap into the unknown is almost here. I go in the hope that there is still work for me to do on Gnaritus and patients to help. What luck for me in coming on this great adventure in Greece and meeting all of you! I'll cherish these memories forever."

Surina wanted to discuss the pillars of Earth's society further until she glimpsed an android security guard marching onto the other end of the terrace. Her uneasiness always increased in the presence of androids because they earwigged on conversations. While working in the Greysville Quadrant Hospital, with the eagle-eyed android security guards lurking on every floor, she had learned the pernicious repercussions and ramifications of even an offhand remark. Instead, she asked the Lofgrens about their plans for the remainder of their holiday.

Liam spoke *sotto voce* after glimpsing the android. "We'll go to Crete and India. Our focus will be a grand tour of all the religious sites in India, including the Bodh Gaya to see the bodhi tree where the Buddha gained enlightenment. In particular, we want to go to the Jain Dilwara temples in Rajasthan and meet the ascetics of the Jain sect to learn more about their reverence for the profound value of all life, even insects. Their faith centers on the inherent right of every life form to live without fear and to its full potential."

Mercy, Janet, and Darren returned from their swim just in time to catch Liam's last sentence, which nonetheless stimulated their interest. When a bell rang to mark the midnight hour, the Greek folk band stopped playing and packed away their instruments. The guests trickled out. Surina returned to her cool, refreshing cave room that offered a dramatic view of the moon and stars dancing on the Aegean Sea. She wanted to stay awake all night stargazing, but before long sleep overwhelmed her.

• • •

The next morning they lingered again at breakfast on the heavenly sunlit terrace, still under the enchanting spell of the beguiling sapphire sea. Breaking free of the ocean's magical aura, they navigated through the maze of cobbled footpaths leading to quaint boutiques, where Surina bought a silver spiral brooch. When they wandered inside an innocuous chapel, they gasped at the gruesome walls of countless human skulls and bones. They shivered from the chill piercing their bones, which all too soon could join those on display.

"This is an example of memento mori architecture," Theokles said. "The Latin words *memento mori* mean 'remember that you too have to die' and provide a new perspective on life by reminding us not to squander our time. Everything is transient!"

A spine-tingling shudder went through the tour group, and they scooted out of the macabre scene to warm their bones in the sunshine. After a tour of the Naval Maritime Museum, Theokles led them to a precipitous spiral staircase of a hundred and forty-four steps down the red cliff face to the Ammoudi beach for lunch. In the bay, colorful fishing boats tugged at their moorings as the sea breeze tossed the vessels to and fro. In the distance, the fishermen struggled with their nets as they brought in the catch of the day.

On the patio of a fish tavern overlooking the bay, the group dined alfresco at circular oak tables under the shade of giant, white-linen umbrellas. The delicious repast included fresh sea urchin, artichoke salad, and savory fish stew. They spent the rest of the languid afternoon swimming. Janet and Darren's shrieks of laughter echoed through the air together with the caterwauls of the seagulls gliding in the air. Mercy watched over the two high-spirited youngsters to make sure they remained in the shallow water and avoided entrapment in the fishing nets of the sloops and schooners further offshore. On the precipice, a solitary long-legged buzzard surveyed the bay.

Following a brief swim, Surina floated on the placid waters, gazing up at the cloudless blue sky with her mind empty and her heart at peace for the first time in a long while. In due course, the Lofgrens drifted toward her, and the rolling waves lulled them into a comforting silence. Still, the sense of uneasiness encumbering her ever since the meeting in the medical director's office bubbled up to the surface despite the idyllic scene.

"What do you think about the launch of Stinguard viral vector in Africa?" Surina blurted out.

"Like anything else, what can we do about it?" Bergitte replied. "We are the voiceless masses. Sweden is already making the final preparations to administer it to the entire population."

Surina felt compelled to warn them. "My experiments on this viral vector showed the instability of the viral integration site in the human DNA."

"Please tell us more about these viral vectors because I never understood them," Liam said, looking puzzled. "Is this a cancer vaccine of some type?"

"Vaccines help the body's immune system to fight infection or destroy damaged cells, such as cancer cells," Surina said. "In contrast, the Stinguard viral vector is a gene therapy that prevents the onset of cancer by correcting mutated genes. First, specific modifications make the virus noninfective to humans. Then we put an engineered gene into the viral DNA in the place of a nonessential viral gene. Other names for the DNA are the genome or the building blocks of life. The viral vector carries the engineered gene into other cells.

"For example, once humans receive an intravenous infusion of the viral vector, the viral genome integrates at particular sites along the human cell genome and introduces the new gene. In the case of the Stinguard viral vector, the new gene synthesizes DNA repair enzymes with the potential to reverse the mutations causing cancer in humans. However, the viral genome has to integrate at precise sites in the human genome to produce the DNA repair enzymes. If the viral genome integration site is off by even a little bit, life-threatening mutations could result. In other words, my experiments showed the Stinguard viral vector integration site is not stable and can disrupt the function of adjacent human cellular genes by causing lethal mutations. Although I tried to publish my research, every scientific journal torpedoed it."

Liam stopped floating and swam closer to Surina.

"Wouldn't the preliminary clinical trials have uncovered any danger?" he asked with a grimace. "The hoopla surrounding the Stinguard viral vector is hyping it up to be the salvation of humans by preventing cancer. It's supposed to be a panacea for cancer: a magic bullet."

"My former supervisor, Dr. Rod Stinguard, engineered this viral vector, hoping to seal his personal legacy," Surina replied. "Overnight, his name has rocketed to the top of the list of contenders for the Nobel Prize in Medicine. Stinguard used his formidable connections in the World Governing Body to finagle the approval for the viral vector's worldwide distribution. However, the short follow-ups in only twenty healthy subjects could skew the data on a statistical basis by missing the mutations. For this reason, they are phasing in the launch starting in Africa and later in other countries. Stinguard rushed the viral vector's development, and it's just not ready for distribution.

"I always hesitate to share this information since most people usually dismiss me as just another disgruntled person or a kvetch. Most people pay attention only when something bad happens to them or their families. Otherwise, they seldom acknowledge uncomfortable truths. I'm telling you so you can decide whether to have it. It's impossible to divine why Stinguard would throw caution to the wind!"

Liam's inner turmoil was apparent as he decried the mistakes of human history. "Sad to say, Surina, there are many instances in human history where people have looked the other way. Why do they brush aside uncomfortable truths? Either it may not affect them yet, or they don't want to acknowledge all the darkness in the human heart. Maybe, the grinding economic struggles on Earth distract many people from seeing anything beyond their own lots in life. In my experience, looking the other way leads to even greater trouble in the end. Numerous examples litter human history such as the buildup to the atrocities in Hitler's Nazi Germany. It began with the insidious persecution of the physically challenged, Roma gypsies, Catholic priests, and Jehovah's Witnesses. Later, it spread to the industrialized massacre of the Jews in concentration camps, where physicians such as Dr. Josef Mengele and Dr. Eduard Wirths conducted cruel human experiments. For instance, one study involved inflicting wounds on the prisoners to assess antimicrobial efficacy. In spite of these atrocities, the world remained silent until World War Two erupted in 1939.

"Another egregious example occurred in the 1950s and 1960s when Western Europe and Canada licensed thalidomide as a wonder drug for morning sickness during pregnancy and as a sleeping aid. The tragic side effects of fetal malformations, miscarriages, and stillbirths were unknown at that time because of a total lack of animal testing to assess side effects during pregnancy. In the end, they banned thalidomide, but it was too late for the countless babies who either died at birth or suffered from disabilities such as blindness, deafness, or the absence of limbs.

"I fear the Stinguard viral vector will soon join this regrettable list. When I return to Sweden, I'll see if any news outlet would be willing to publish an article warning the public about the Stinguard viral vector. However, the prospects of newspaper editors sticking their necks out to do the right thing are slim. We know what happened to Socrates when he revealed uncomfortable truths with his probing questions. Your hesitancy in discussing this topic with most people is valid; however, you have indeed found a receptive audience here. After all, as a student of human history, I know it keeps repeating itself."

Surina could see Theokles on the patio of the fish tavern, waving his arms and pointing to his wristwatch. They swam ashore with heavy hearts since it was already five o'clock and almost time to leave Oia. Even though they had made a point of sampling all the local fare in a diverse array of eateries, they went again to their hotel's rooftop terrace restaurant. Each of them craved to see the sunset one more time. While they basked in the last vestiges of the sunlight, they toasted each other with the local Santorini wine.

Mercy raised her glass. "Theokles, thanks for your expert guided tour through the wonders of Greece."

Theokles smiled in appreciation.

"Mom, can't we stay another day?" Janet and Darren asked in unison.

Mercy shook her head. "I wish we could, but remember school starts on Tuesday."

"Here's our e-mail address, Surina," Bergitte said. "Let us know how you fare on Gnaritus."

Liam frowned. "I hope the messages get through."

After bidding farewell to the beautiful turquoise Aegean Sea, Surina, Mercy, Janet, and Darren boarded the last underground vactrain from Oia at seven o'clock in the evening. Overcome with exhaustion, they catnapped during most of the journey. In thirty minutes, they reached London St. Pancras International Station. Five minutes later, they arrived in the rain-soaked Keswick Station, from where an air cab braved the elements to take them home to Oakdale Avenue, just in time to avoid the brunt of the summer thunderstorm.

Surina thought the antiquities of Greece laid bare the impermanence of all things. At least she still had her happy holiday snapshots of the golden sunshine of Greece. As she closed the door of her cottage, the reality of her next journey, this time across the unfathomable cosmos, dawned on her.

6
The Odyssey

SURINA AROSE WITH the sun on her last Sunday on Earth. After breakfast on the brilliant sunlit terrace, she put the finishing touches to her packing. First, she weighed each of the seven standard-issue graphene boxes on the scale so as not to exceed the set limit before sealing them in preparation for collection later that day. Then, she lugged her two carry-on suitcases to the hallway by the front door. Once again, she scrutinized the instructions given to all Earth citizens relocating to Gnaritus and inspected her cottage a final time. Only a single item remained undone on the list: the automatic transfer of her bank account to Gnaritus on the day of departure.

She wondered why going to Gnaritus no longer filled her with as much fear as before. Of course, some level of uncertainty existed due to the possibility of the spaceship never reaching Gnaritus. However, these accidents seldom occurred now, or at least nowhere near the numbers from the start of the relocation program. Had she just accepted the inevitability of the relocation? No, it was much deeper than that. She realized now that Earth's society had hamstrung her and never offered her any real chance to reach her full potential. As unlikely as it seemed, perhaps she might have better prospects in another world.

Later that morning, Surina's former research assistant, Vera Ma, called to apologize for canceling their farewell lunch at the local pub in Keswick. In fact, she was still in the midst of an experiment in Stinguard's lab even on a Sunday. Vera was candid and forthcoming in divulging all the details of Stinguard's unreasonable demands, such as expecting her to work on weekends. He not only carped about her work with an inexhaustible litany of complaints but also made life hell for her at every opportunity with his frequent bouts of tetchiness. Although it had been just a week, it seemed like a lifetime to Surina since she had left the hospital's bare-knuckle political machinations far behind. However, she understood Vera's predicament all too well in playing an unwinnable game.

In the hope of resting for the journey tomorrow, Surina spent the languorous afternoon in her garden, which was redolent with aromatic flowers in full bloom. The gregarious rooks and robin redbreasts, scurrying back and forth on the tree branches, seemed to trill and chirp with so much passion as if each song was their last. Tears prickled her eyes as she realized it was also her last chance to hear the birds sing. Only the mover who came to collect her seven boxes interrupted her dreamy afternoon. He wore a khaki suit, and a deerstalker hat shaded his swarthy face. The left breast of his jacket had an imperious crest depicting a starship and the words "Manchester Space Airport" in gold thread. After scanning and weighing each box with scrupulous care, he schlepped them onto the air van.

Soon, the time came to go to the farewell dinner at Mercy's cottage. Right away, Mercy's husband, Jari, impressed Surina with his kindly countenance and humble demeanor conveying his profound appreciation for even the smallest things in life. From the head of the table, he presided with benevolence over Janet and Darren's antics as they played a game with unfathomable rules.

Mercy had gone out of her way to put on a magnificent Sunday roast with all its trimmings. A sense of well-being enveloped them as they dived into the steaming, puffy Yorkshire pudding with succulent roast chicken and thick gravy. The bubbling vivaciousness of Mercy's family made Surina kick herself for not marrying or having any children. On the contrary, her work had defined her, even though it had led nowhere in the end. Why had so little gone according to plan?

Jari raised his glass with a flourish to propose a toast. "To new beginnings! When I immigrated to Britain with my parents from Tanzania, I had a new beginning here with countless possibilities. Despite my Dickensian childhood, I studied hard and won a scholarship to Oxford University to study medicine. On this momentous occasion, we must remember how the explorers who discovered Gnaritus had the courage to leave their homes on Earth a hundred years ago to journey into the unknown. Here's a toast to the endless possibilities awaiting us in the New World."

"Mom, I want to go to Gnaritus as well," Janet said, much to Surina's surprise. "The only problem is I'll miss you too much. I'll miss the Earth as well."

"We have a class on climate change at school," Darren said. "The Relocation Policy to Gnaritus helped to heal the Earth."

"We must all make this journey in due time," Mercy said with a hint of uncertainty creeping into her voice. "The voyage will lead to many new prospects. Surina, here's a gift from all of us."

Surina held the pink box in the palm of her hand and opened the green velvet ribbon.

"It's a St. Christopher pendant necklace, the patron saint of travelers," Mercy said.

Surina put on the necklace. "It's just what I need for my journey. I love it."

During the rest of the evening, they immersed themselves in

the photographs of their holiday in Athens and Santorini, recounting their many adventures in Greece. When the grandfather cuckoo clock in the hallway cuckooed nine o'clock, Surina thought her time on Earth had just about run out, but at least she would have some more time on Gnaritus. Even those with nothing else, still have time. It was as perfect an evening as anyone could have spent, and she wished for many more such occasions but knew it was the last time. Before leaving, she embraced all the members of the Jakande family. While Mercy and Jari waved good-bye from the doorway, Surina closed the front gate and slunk back to her cottage with a heavy heart.

• • •

Monday, July 28, 2200, Surina's final morning on Earth, dawned as a rainy day. The booming bursts of thunder punctuating the torrential downpour in the early hours of the morning gave way to a continuous drizzle for the remainder of the day. The sun was nowhere in sight. Much to her surprise, she had slept like a log even through the growls of thunder. Despite the unappealing breakfast, she forced herself to eat a bowl of Greek yogurt with honey. Heaving a sigh of relief as she let Mercy in, Surina was thankful to have her best friend's company in her final moments on Earth. She prayed for the air cab to arrive late as it usually did, so she could tarry a little longer in her cottage or maybe miss the spaceflight altogether. However, on that morning it was punctual, dashing her hopes.

The driver, a burly young man in his twenties, hardly broke a sweat as he muscled the two suitcases into the boot before returning to his seat in the air cab to finish drinking his coffee. Just before exiting for the last time, Surina stood in the hallway, picturing all the good times in the cottage with her parents. Her hands shook, and the keys jangled as she locked the front door. After settling in the air cab, she gave the keys to Mercy, who accepted them with reluctance. As the cab flew along Oakdale

Avenue, the ubiquitous spy drone retreated from its continuous surveillance. Even through the mizzle, the heart-achingly beautiful Keswick, the Derwentwater, and the verdant valleys of the Lake District filled Surina with awe. Despite her attempts at being stoic, her tears gushed out when the stark reality of never seeing the Earth again overwhelmed her.

Mercy handed her a handkerchief. "None of this is fair, Surina. I wish you didn't have to go."

Before long, the countryside of the Lake District National Park gave way to the suburbs of Manchester. The air cab navigated around the gleaming spires of the graphene skyscrapers and landed on the eastern edge of the city, at Manchester Space Airport.

"I don't much feel like getting out," Surina said. "But, I guess I must."

Mercy climbed out of the cab. "I wish you didn't have to go. Nothing seems fair. Oh well, I'll help to take one of the suitcases inside."

The driver hoisted the two suitcases onto the sidewalk. "Have a safe journey to Gnaritus."

Surina gave him a tip. She remembered the imposing airport well, for she had been there once before when her parents had left for Gnaritus. The space airport and general airport for earthbound destinations were miles apart on the eastern and western outskirts of Manchester, respectively. Despite Manchester Space Airport being almost twenty times larger than the general airport, it had only a single departure and arrival gate for flights to and from Gnaritus.

Upon entering the single-story terminal building, Surina and Mercy saw the monolithic starship *Odyssey* on the tarmac, dwarfing everything around it. The steely color of the *Odyssey* burnished even through the drizzling rain. Each spaceflight carried twenty passengers from the United Kingdom, leaving on the dot once a month at nine o'clock in the morning. Saturnine countenances readily identified the passengers among the small clusters of people in the terminal. A bevy of family members consoled the lachrymose passengers to ease the strain of departure. In contrast, other travelers had chosen to come alone, or perhaps they had no one to accompany them. Surina thought the relocation to Gnaritus had leached all hope from the lives of the passengers.

Surina and Mercy galumphed with the suitcases to the android security guard staffing the check-in counter. With his blank, lifeless eyes, he scanned Surina's face and her Earth passport.

"This Gnaritus passport will replace your Earth passport," the android said, putting away the blue document and handing Surina a new green one. "You will need it to pass through the scanner at the boarding gate. Place any luggage on the conveyer belt now. The departure time is in an hour from gate one, with boarding to begin in thirty minutes."

Surveillance cameras with x-ray vision to detect even a microscopic incendiary device dotted the ceiling of the terminal. Android security guards flanked a gigantic, dome-shaped scanner that stood before the departure gate as an additional layer of security. The entire terminal reminded Surina of a sterile surgery theater with a cathedral ceiling from which bright lights glared on humans, who stood out like anomalous specimens. She felt lighter without the encumbrance of her two heavy suitcases as she searched for a comfortable area to rest before boarding time. The airport's only tea shop, overlooking the departure gate, provided some measure of relaxation despite the lack of cushions on the chairs around the polished chromium tables. A few bites of the delicious rock cake made Surina forget the uncomfortable seating. In due time, other passengers and their relatives piled into the tea shop to cheer themselves for the arduous voyage ahead.

"Surina, all of us will miss you so much!" Mercy said. "Please tell my parents when you see them on Gnaritus how much I want to visit. I've heard nothing from them for a long time. Why is there so little information about Gnaritus? Aren't some of these travelers rather young?"

Mercy referred to several youthful passengers standing by the gate without any relatives to make a fuss over them. Most striking was a couple with two small children that Surina remembered from somewhere but could not quite place. The desolate family in threadbare clothes had haunting, mistrustful gazes, as conspicuous as their young age. At the same time, their wounded demeanor bore none of the sentimentality of the other passengers, who agonized over their relocation to Gnaritus. On the contrary, these travelers had accepted their departure from Earth in a matter-of-fact sort of way, without any expression of happiness or sadness.

"I can't be sure, but they could be some of the homeless," Surina replied. "It seems as if they are not wanted on Earth either."

Surina and Mercy fell into a somber silence for a while. Then knowing how little time remained, Surina bid farewell. "Mercy, you're the best friend ever! I'll be all right. After all, I have the protection of the patron saint of travelers. I'll always wear this St. Christopher pendant, even on Gnaritus!"

All of a sudden, a giant walkway connecting the airport terminal to the starship's open hatch creaked into place. The V-shaped, two-deck spacecraft provided enough room for the crew on the upper deck and the passengers on the lower deck. Numerous portholes lined the arms of the *Odyssey* at regular intervals. Multiple layers of graphene formed the framework, which was lightweight yet resilient enough to withstand not only the space debris but also the harsh temperatures of deep space. On the upper deck's bow, the captain's bridge had a giant window. On the lower level, the observation deck's 360-degree window offered panoramic views. Three legs with gigantic wheels supported the entire spaceship on the ground. An airstrip for acceleration and ascent into space stretched for three kilometers from the terminal gate. Picturesque countryside clinging to the horizon surrounded the airport.

A hatchet-faced woman in a gray pantsuit scurried to the podium in the midst of the blue-clad android security guards. She was the lone human among the airport staff. Her chignon of battleship-gray hair emphasized her long face and pencil-like lips even more. Moreover, her firmly pressed-together lips, with the corners down, and her furrowed brow imparted an air of fretful uneasiness.

The airport terminal soon reverberated with the echoes of her stentorian voice. "Ladies and gentlemen, welcome to flight number seventeen to Gnaritus. We will now begin boarding. For general boarding, I would remind you to have your Gnaritus passports ready as you go through the scanner. First, the space tourists will board with their Earth passports."

A young, well-dressed couple, most likely members of the elite jeunesse dorée on a round-trip vacation to Gnaritus, brimmed with confidence as they sauntered through the scanner and onto the walkway leading to the *Odyssey*. After that, the general boarding began in alphabetical order. The fainthearted passengers boohooed as they tore themselves away from their grieving relatives to join the ponderous procession through the scanner on their one-way journey to Gnaritus.

At the sound of her name, Surina embraced her best friend, thanking her for all her kindness. Gulping back her tears, Mercy said she would stay until liftoff. After glancing at her Saint Christopher pendant, Surina girded herself for the arduous voyage into the unknown and plodded toward the boarding gate. For a moment, she blenched as she placed her Gnaritus passport on the screen until the green light flashed to allow her to proceed through the scanner. Uncontrollable fear prickled her skin with goosebumps. Turning around one last time, she waved to Mercy before taking a few tentative steps onto the gangway and joining the desultory queue creeping toward the hatch on the lower deck of the *Odyssey*.

Wearing crisp, olive-green army fatigues and berets over their buzz cuts, the senior crew officers greeted the passengers with smiles from ear to ear. The captain, a Herculean man with an urbane manner, towered over his crew and shook Surina's hand with sincerity.

"Welcome aboard Dr. Mathew," the stately man said. "I'm Captain Spero. I'd like to introduce Chief Engineer Manus and Chief Steward Pars."

When the crew clicked their heels to salute in unison, Surina's fading courage received a much-needed boost. She then followed a steward to the flatbed seats in the main cabin, which were each next to a porthole and arranged in a single file. After strapping on her three-point safety belt, she placed her purse in the storage cabinet adjoining the seat. Wearing broad grins, two young, energetic stewards gamboled up and down the cabin to help the passengers with their bags. Without a doubt, the welcome from the crew contrasted with the acerbity of the airport's staff. The crew's unexpected level of concern went even further to hearten Surina, but she saw many of the passengers remained distraught.

After all the travelers had taken their seats, Chief Steward Pars arrived to review the safety instructions. He had thick auburn hair and a handsome face that reminded Surina of the idealized ancient Greek statues in the Acropolis Museum.

"Welcome, ladies and gentlemen!" Pars said with a genial smile. "We hope to make this journey as comfortable as possible for each of you. Please don't hesitate to ask any questions and tell us if you need anything. During the liftoff and landing, please remain seated with your safety belts on securely. Once we are in space, you may move around the cabin on this deck only. The upper deck, containing the captain's bridge and machinery department, is for the crew only. If we engage in evasive maneuvers to bypass asteroids, comets, or other space debris, then the overhead speakers and your wristwatches will warn you to fasten your seatbelts. Another message alert by both systems will signal when it is safe to walk on the deck again. Please put away your personal wristwatches, and use only the ones in the storage cabinet next to you. You must wear these watches at all times during this journey since this is the primary method of communication onboard. In case of turbulence, both the dining compartment and the observation deck have chairs with seat belts also."

The mention of turbulence stirred anxiety among the passengers. Trying to hearten them, Pars added some flourish to the mundane instructions. "After liftoff, we will begin a tour of this deck and your individual sleeping berths. Sleeping bags in your compartments as well as here in the main cabin will secure you in place safely for the night. Meals will be in the dining compartment next to the observation deck three times a day; nevertheless, snacks are available at all times. Each afternoon, you'll receive an hour of instruction about life on Gnaritus. Our most popular venue, the observation deck, will offer a chance to see the sweeping vistas of space, the planets, and the stars!"

After glancing around the cabin and seeing no one had any questions, he settled into his seat at the front in preparation for liftoff. Surina put on the wristwatch right away, which already alerted her to the imminent launch. She longed to see the fantastic views of space from the observation deck; however, she also felt anxious about Chief Steward Pars's obvious omission in his instructions. Why had there been no mention of the protocols to follow during an emergency, such as evacuating in space lifeboats? Maybe Pars was reluctant to alarm them, especially if the space lifeboats could accommodate only a few passengers. A far more likely scenario, though, was that no way station or sanctuary awaited them since only communication towers on extraterrestrial planets punctuated the expanse between Earth and Gnaritus. With no one to help them, there would be no way out of a crash or another emergency! She could only pray now for an uneventful journey.

The starship's engines roared and thundered. Surina stared out of the porthole while the *Odyssey* went full tilt on the airstrip until the countryside became a blur, and they catapulted to greater heights in a seamless arc. First, Manchester's city center came into view, followed in rapid succession by the landmasses of Britain, Europe, Africa, Russia, China, and India. Soft, wooly clouds broke up the brilliant blue expanse of the ocean. Owing to the reliance on underground vactrains as the primary mode of transportation, she had never seen the Earth from this perspective before.

At four hundred kilometers above sea level, the *Odyssey* began an orbit around Earth while the crew made final checks for the interstellar flight. The vivid, magical views of the Earth contrasting against the dark matter of space bewitched Surina and held her spellbound in her seat. She knew a billion souls lived on the blue and green orb in the security of the importance of their jobs, positions in society, incomes, and institutions. From the vastness of space, such preoccupations hardly mattered at all.

7
Stardust

ONCE THE *ODYSSEY* had entered an orbit around Earth, Chief Steward Pars stood at the front of the cabin to make another announcement. "Ladies and gentlemen, we will begin our tour. Please follow me."

The passengers proceeded in single file from the main cabin through a manhole and into the dining compartment, containing orderly rows of slate-gray tables and chairs. On the starboard side, they could hear the clanging of pots and pans from the kitchen. The lambent light throughout the *Odyssey* was neither glaring nor menacing in any way, but rather it mimicked natural sunlight, which had a salutary effect on the passengers. Through the portholes, they caught brief, reassuring glimpses of their home planet, Earth.

After exiting the dining compartment, many of the passengers gasped upon entering the observation deck. A magnificent view from the floor-to-ceiling window encircling the observation deck greeted them. The entire globe of the Earth seemed close enough to be within their reach. Even the two curly haired moppets lurched toward the window with outstretched hands, all the while trying to wrestle free from their parents' holds. Since the greater speed of the *Odyssey* outpaced the spinning of the Earth on its axis, they saw daylight and nightfall on the planet surface within moments of each other. The dayglow over the brilliant, sapphire-blue ocean yielded to the twinkling lights of the cities and roads in the night that spread out like the threads of a giant spider web across the planet. The astounding view riveted the passengers to the spot, but Pars marshaled them through another door at the end of the deck, which opened onto a narrow corridor with a row of green doors on both sides.

After they had all assembled in the hallway, Pars explained the daily routine onboard. "Ladies and gentlemen, your suitcases are in the cupboards of your sleeping compartments. The standard attire onboard the *Odyssey* is a green jumpsuit uniform instead of your civilian clothing from Earth. Only stewards staff the waterless laundry facility on the upper deck, which is off limits for passengers. So, place your laundry bag in the container at the end of the hall by eleven o'clock in the evening for pickup daily. There is only a twelve-hour turnaround time for the laundry. The bathroom and showering facilities are at the end of this hallway. Due to the onboard recycling of the finite amount of water available for this journey, each passenger can shower only once a day. You have twenty minutes now to change into your uniforms and settle in before we meet again in the main cabin."

They quickly identified their assigned compartments by their names on the doors. Despite its small size, Surina was glad to have space for herself in the bustling colossal starship. The narrow room contained a cupboard as well as a table and chair, which were fixed to the deck like all the furniture onboard. Beneath a circular porthole at the end of the room was a sleeping berth.

As she opened the cupboard door, she found her suitcases inside as well as two long-sleeved, green jumpsuits and a pair of lightweight black clogs. As she changed into the starship uniform and tucked the Saint Christopher necklace under the jumpsuit, she thought the garment seemed tailor-made for her. Of note, it had plenty of room in the pockets, which also zipped closed to safeguard her wallet and Gnaritus passport. The right breast of the green jumpsuit bore her name in embroidered brown italic letters.

She knelt on the bed to peer through the porthole. The familiar sight of the Earth boosted her flagging courage. To be sure, the hardest part would come when the *Odyssey* lost sight of Earth forever. Although her day had begun in Keswick at five o'clock in the morning, she was in orbit around the Earth by noon! With five minutes to spare, she sank into the comfortable bed, thankful to close her heavy eyelids, and snoozed until woken from her repose by the chatter of the passengers gathering in the hallway. Even though she wished to rest, she forced herself up from the bed to join them.

Surina thought the starship uniforms seemed to shift most of the attention onto the apprehensive faces of the passengers. Only the two children in their smart new green jumpsuits appeared overjoyed and full of expectation for the journey ahead. Pars led the passengers back through the observation deck, much to the delight of the two winsome children, who left only when their parents tore them away from the window. In the dining hall, a short, bald man with a rotund face and a ballooning waistline rushed out from the kitchen, brandishing a megawatt smile. He wore a spotless white bib apron over his battle fatigues. Pars introduced the affable Chief Cook Grenier.

"Welcome!" Grenier said with cheerful bonhomie. "Please have some refreshments!"

Two young, stick-thin stewards, whose names were Charlie and Henry, staffed the serving area of the kitchen. The sight of the impressive array of hearty sandwiches, McVitie's milk chocolate digestive biscuits, biscotti, rock cakes, oranges, and apples cheered the travelers. With their trays overflowing with the tasty treats, the weary passengers sat down at the tables while greetings and salutations hummed throughout the entire dining compartment. Much to Surina's surprise, the gaunt man from the walking tour around the Derwentwater Lake was sitting opposite her. Instead of his previous air of melancholy, he stared at the passengers and crew with wide-eyed wonder.

"I'm glad to see you again," he said, smiling at her in recognition. "I'm Stefan Stohl. I was a journalist on Earth. I'm hoping to write a book about our voyage. I never received such an enthusiastic welcome as this anywhere on Earth. The crew seems a little bit too happy. Could something be wrong with them?"

"I'm Surina Mathew," she said. "The crew's effervescence seems inexplicable."

The man sitting next to Surina shook her hand. "Hello, I'm David Ellison. This is my wife Mary and my two kids: two-year-old Elizabeth and three-year-old George. Android security guards caught us sitting on the steps of the National Gallery last week and sent us here."

Surina wondered if the Ellisons were the homeless family that she had seen at Trafalgar Square. She was uncertain, for she had noticed only their tattered clothing at the time. In the end, she concluded they were probably that same indigent family. Both David and Mary Ellison had bony, angular, gritty faces, with steely gazes as a result of suffering the harshest privations on Earth. Moreover, they had a defeated demeanor as if they no longer expected anything much from life. They had matted, oily, and roughly hewn hair, for they had shorn their locks themselves. In contrast, the giggles and ebullience of their children enlivened the mood at the table.

"Our kids are happier now than I've seen them in ages," Mary said with bewilderment. "Instead of their usual crankiness, they seem to have been jumping for joy ever since they went to that observation deck showing the views of the Earth and all that endless space. Seeing that puts a different spin on things, doesn't it?"

Both children had finished their lunches and raced back for second helpings of the sandwiches. The baby-faced children had shoulder-length, curly, caramel-colored hair and humungous hazel eyes that viewed the entire room with great interest and, in particular, the portholes showing the Earth and outer space. However, Surina noted the children were much thinner and shorter than their ages would have suggested.

Surina perked up at the sight of the wide assortment of teas available on the starship, including her favorite, Scottish breakfast tea. She dunked a chocolate biscuit into her tea and savored the taste of home. The enjoyable meal ended when a message overhead advised them to return to their seats since the starship would begin its voyage out of the solar system. After placing their trays in the serving area, the passengers dashed to the main cabin with their unfinished desserts just as the *Odyssey* left the Earth's orbit without a sound in the vacuum of space. While sipping her tea and nibbling a biscuit, Surina peered through the porthole as the Earth receded into the distance, and the moon loomed straight ahead. After a while, Chief Steward Pars clapped to gain the attention of the passengers, who remained hypnotized by the views of outer space.

Pointing to a chart of the known universe, he launched the lecture series with great gusto. "Welcome to our daily lecture on our incredible voyage to Gnaritus in the outermost regions of the Milky Way galaxy. First, to put everything in perspective, we must return to the dawn of our universe. In the beginning, around fourteen billion years ago, the big bang created time and space from an infinitesimal point that exploded and released tremendous energy causing the universe to expand as it still does today. In particular, the energy was in the form of electrons, protons, and neutrons. Protons and neutrons later clumped together to form the nucleus around which electrons orbited to produce the first atoms, such as hydrogen. In other words, atoms make up the building blocks of all matter. The electrons, protons, and neutrons are the subatomic particles.

"Hydrogen, the lightest atom, has one proton in its nucleus around which an electron orbits. Clouds of hydrogen atoms formed the primordial nebulae. When the nebulae became thick enough, the hydrogen atoms clumped together, amassing gravity and even more hydrogen atoms to form the core of the stars over the millennia. After two hydrogen nuclei collided and fused at the high temperatures in the core, the element helium formed in a process called nuclear fusion. Nuclear fusion in stars releases tremendous energy in the form of light and heat. Our sun shines due to nuclear fusion. In fact, stars first appeared twenty million years after the big bang, making them among the oldest objects in the universe. Galaxies are a collection of stars, which are held together by gravity and orbit around the galactic core at the center of a galaxy. Let me pause now to see if there are any questions."

In the front row, a lanky youth with a mop of curly black hair was sitting bolt upright, taking profuse notes on his computer. Often he would furrow his brow, bringing his bushy eyebrows together, and stare at Pars with piercing large, brown eyes. His hand shot up. "Sir, I'm Alfonso Diaz. All this is fascinating, but what caused the big bang? What was there before the big bang?"

Pars remained silent, deep in thought, for a protracted length of time before answering. "That's a thought-provoking question, much like a Cinderella problem where no solution quite fits. Is it possible that the universe materialized out of nothing? No one to this day can be sure of what triggered the big bang or what came before it. As a result, we only know a little something about what followed the big bang. Many aspects of the universe's provenance and fate are unknown."

"Chief Steward Pars, would you mind explaining the concept of nuclear fusion again?" Stefan Stohl asked in a clear, forthright voice from the middle of the cabin.

"Yes, let me clarify," Pars said, pointing to a diagram of the constituent parts of an atom. "Nuclear fusion results when the nuclei of two atoms fuse into a heavier nucleus, and this process releases energy. In fact, nuclear fusion can occur with many types of atoms, but when the nuclei of heavier atoms fuse instead of releasing energy, there is energy absorption. Of note, hydrogen, the lightest atom, releases the most energy when it fuses with another hydrogen nucleus. When a star's hydrogen atoms run out, then the second-lightest atom helium combines by nuclear fusion to form carbon. After the helium runs out, then carbon nuclei can combine to form oxygen, again by nuclear fusion.

"As the star begins to fuse heavier and heavier atoms, there is less energy release. In due time, when the sun has converted most of its atoms to the heaviest atom, iron, by nuclear fusion, then further energy production ceases altogether. When there is no more nuclear fusion to counterbalance the tremendous force of gravity, the star collapses inward. After the shock wave of this implosion reaches the iron core, the star explodes in a supernova, releasing a nebula cloud of billions of atoms such as carbon, oxygen, nitrogen, silicon, and iron. A part of this nebula can form another star, and the leftover atoms in the cloud can coalesce into a planet with the heavy iron atoms in the core. The lighter atoms, such as hydrogen, helium, carbon, and oxygen, are on the surface of planets. Thus, new planets arise around many stars every day. In our solar system, the smaller planets closer to the sun, such as Mercury, Venus, Earth, and Mars, have iron cores. In contrast, those farther away, such as Jupiter, Saturn, Uranus, and Neptune, are icy gas giants of mainly hydrogen without solid surfaces. The planets in our solar system orbiting the sun formed about four and a half billion years ago. In other words, the atoms of old, dying stars created not only the planets but also humans!"

Stefan, wearing a quizzical expression on his face, stood up with some urgency. "How can we be made of dying stars?"

Although many passengers scoffed and raised their eyebrows with skepticism, others listened openmouthed with rapt attention.

Undeterred by the incredulity in the cabin, Pars answered with confidence. "An excellent question! Elements such hydrogen, carbon, oxygen, and iron forged humans. The big bang formed hydrogen, whereas the other elements such as carbon in the universe come from the nuclear furnaces of stars. Since all the elements in the periodic table except hydrogen are stardust, the majority of the human body mass is stardust."

A rhapsodic murmur rippled through the audience. "Are you saying we are stardust?"

Pars's eyes danced with merriment. "Yes, we are stardust!"

A stunned silence fell over the cabin as they stared at Pars without blinking. Pars pointed to an infinitesimal blue speck on a diagram of the ungraspable universe. "This is Earth. However, there is much more than our universe, for there may be additional universes or multiverses coexisting now. Perhaps, there was even a past universe. Not only are there more than a hundred billion galaxies in our universe but also a big galaxy can have trillions of stars. Moreover, our Milky Way galaxy has four hundred billion stars and enough dust to make billions more. Since each star has at least one planet, there are hundreds of billions of planets in the Milky Way alone. What, then, is our place in the universe? We are also stardust!"

He waited for more questions from the passengers. Seeing no hands up, he decided to conclude the lecture. "Next we will see the moon. Forty-five million years after the Earth formed, a collision with another celestial body tore off a chunk to create the moon. In other words, the moon is a piece of the ancient Earth and has a rocky surface of silica, which is a combination of silicon and oxygen. Since the moon is too small to have sufficient gravity to hold onto lighter molecules like oxygen and hydrogen, it lacks an atmosphere. Even the footprints of the first man on the moon, Neil Armstrong, have been preserved unchanged since 1969 due to the absence of an atmosphere."

Out of the blue, deafening applause erupted in the cabin. While

Stefan and Alfonso ran up to quiz Pars some more, the majority of the passengers remained seated, gaping through the portholes and digesting the momentous events of the day. In due time, some dozed off to sleep, whereas others distracted themselves by watching movies on the miniature computers that were resting on top of the storage cabinets by their seats.

As she watched the news from Earth on a twelve-hour time delay, Surina learned about the feverish anticipation for the release of the Stinguard viral vector. Surreal videos of Stinguard grandstanding at a string of world-renowned universities, where he was lionized in tributes and pretentious ceremonies, flashed in rapid succession on the screen. He continued to bang the drum for the viral vector. After that, the usual hackneyed news focused on business moguls, mergers of corporate giants, outings of underperforming chief operating officers, and the investiture of even more hard-nosed bureaucrats. The vapid newscaster imbued each announcement with such solemn gravitas that seemed alien and irrelevant from the new perspective of the infinite universe. Surina wondered how other intelligent life in the universe would perceive the insipid news from Earth. Before she could answer her question, Chief Steward Pars beckoned them to supper.

As expected, the two space tourists sat in positions of honor at the captain's table with the crew. Surina had not seen them since the start of the voyage as they occupied a master suite on the upper deck. They appeared ill at ease in their new surroundings, for they fidgeted in their seats and shuffled their feet. They wore civilian clothes and had tall, slender frames with glorious crowns of thick, golden hair. However, the expressions of ennui on their pallid faces marred their overall striking patrician appearances. They regarded the passengers with an aristocratic hauteur and callous indifference. Chief Cook Grenier served them their meals personally, but they crinkled their noses and tasted the food in a tentative manner. All of a sudden, they ducked out of the dining room in a hurry.

In contrast, the other passengers thanked Grenier for a first-class supper. The variety of fresh produce reminded Surina of home, including the crisp lettuce and delicious fruit. The tasty Irish stew and crusty brown soda bread with plump raisins, caraway seeds, and creamy butter stuck to her ribs like glue. For dessert, there were cupcakes with four-leaf clover frosting. They would need good fortune to reach Gnaritus safely, thought Surina. For the most part, reticence reigned in the dining compartment as they all hunkered down and braced themselves resolutely for the voyage into the unknown expanse of the Milky Way galaxy.

Surina spent the rest of the evening on the observation deck, which had a homey feel with comfortable beige lounge chairs and side tables. She stared in wonder at the commanding views of the sun, Earth, moon, and distant stars flung in the blackness of space. On occasion, a solar storm burst on the surface of the sun and sent flaming showers close to the *Odyssey*. The blithesome Ellison children danced without fear all around the edge of the observation deck, trying to reach out through the windows to the celestial spheres. Stefan contemplated the imponderable vistas of space as he wrote his novel about the extraordinary interstellar expedition on his tablet computer. In the meantime, Chief Steward Pars meandered through the observation deck and asked the passengers whether they needed anything to make their journey more comfortable.

Surina introduced herself to a couple in their sixties who were sitting beside her. They had almost identical, lived-in faces, with prominent Romanesque noses and healthy, rugged complexions framed by short-cropped gray hair.

"Hello, I'm Linda Cavacecci," the woman said in a charming, lilting Italian accent. "This is my husband, Giuseppe. We're retired accountants from Blackpool. We were Italian immigrants to Britain."

"I miss our three children already," Giuseppe said. "Even though they are adults now, I worry about them. I wish we could have stayed on Earth."

Linda waved her hand to get Pars's attention. "Chief Steward Pars, how do we send messages to Earth?"

Pars sat down and used the computer resting on the side table to teach them. "Only the starship computers can link to Earth, so your personal computers are redundant."

By the time Surina learned the intricacies of the onboard computers, it was well past eleven o'clock in the evening. The historical import of her day more than matched the vastitude of the universe, for the memorable events ensured that nothing would ever be the same again. However, she felt knackered to the bone.

After a quick shower, she cocooned herself in the blissful warmth of the sleeping bag on the bed in her room, still thinking about the unbelievable roller coaster of a week. It had begun with the gut-wrenching meeting in the medical director's office where they had told her that she had no place on Earth. Only a week later, in the depths of space, she learned that she had a place not only on Earth but also in the universe. Moreover, the universe had room for all humans, irrespective of their lineage. As a matter of fact, the oxygen, nitrogen, carbon, and iron atoms in the human body originated from the nuclear furnaces of hundreds of different stars. As the *Odyssey* drifted past the crater-riddled surface of the moon, she peered through the porthole, feeling a kinship to the ancient rocks as well as to all the millennia before and the millennia still to come. We are all stardust, she thought.

Seeing the blue orb of the Earth in the darkness of space overwhelmed her with inexplicable sorrow. So many questions raced through her mind. What purpose did all the wars, slavery, colonial conquests, poaching of wildlife, pillage, and plunder of the environment on Earth serve in the grand design of the universe? On a daily basis, those thirsty for power and domination denied many others their rightful place in the universe, either by exploiting them or by subjugating them into submission. From the vastness of outer space, the immeasurable suffering of humans at the hands of other humans seemed senseless and pointless. Would humans on Earth ever acknowledge their unity with one another and with all the matter in the universe? After all, the nuclear furnaces of the stars supplied the elements coursing through the veins of all life and matter, including humans. Still with a sense of foreboding, she fell fast asleep.

8

The Golden Spiral

SLEEPLESS NIGHTS SPENT ruminating and regurgitating past events, all the while ruing their aftermath, often drained Surina the next morning; nonetheless, on the first full day in space, she awoke restored. Her restful sleep was not just due to the profound physical exhaustion from the liftoff. Rather, after her consciousness had roamed among the stars, she had gained a fresh perspective that allowed her to rest from the burden of her sorrows for the first time in many years. Of course, there was no night any longer since the sun never set in outer space.

The green jumpsuit had many advantages, including how easy dressing became in the morning without any decisions to make on what to wear. Another benefit of the jumpsuits occurred to Surina while sitting opposite the Ellison children at breakfast. Without the distraction from either shabby or chic clothing, the utilitarian garment shifted the focus to the quiddity of the individual. When she had first spotted the children on the steps of the National Gallery in London, their threadbare clothing had distracted her from noticing the wonder in their eyes at just being alive. Even today, George and Elizabeth Ellison bounced up and down with glee as they glimpsed Mars through the portholes. After breakfast, all the passengers rushed to the observation deck to take front-row seats to a view of a lifetime.

Alfonso, the young man in his twenties with otherworldly eyes, shared a list of facts about Mars from the *Odyssey's* computer with Surina and the Cavaceccis. A toothy smile dimpled his round cheeks as he spoke with gusto. "Mars, also known as the Roman god of war, is the fourth planet from the sun. The Earth means 'ground' in Anglo-Saxon, whereas all the other planets have names from the Roman or Greek gods. Mars formed four and a half billion years ago just like the Earth. The rusty-red color of the planet comes from iron oxide. Since it's much farther away from the sun, the Martian year is twice as long as the Earth's year. Similar to Earth, it spins on its axis and rotates once every twenty-four and a half hours. However, Mars is only half the Earth's size, which means it has much less gravity and a hundred times thinner atmosphere of primarily carbon dioxide, with a small amount of water vapor. Like Earth, Mars has different seasons with a mean temperature of minus sixty-five degrees Celsius. During summer, the surface temperature is as high as thirty degrees Celsius, but it drops to minus a hundred and forty-three degrees Celsius in the winter. Any liquid water would evaporate due to the thin atmosphere, although there are polar ice caps. Of note, Mars is home to the Olympus Mons, an extinct volcano three times the height of Mount Everest. Two moons orbit Mars: Phobos and Deimos. Despite extensive exploration, we never found any life on Mars. Still, we considered Mars to be the most habitable planet for humans until the discovery of Gnaritus. About a hundred years ago, we abandoned the fledgling space colony on Mars in favor of Gnaritus."

Without warning, a massive red-ochre dust storm stirred on Mars and spread across the rocky, crater-riddled surface. Surina's mind roamed in the raging sandstorm on the planet until Giuseppe

Cavacecci's rambunctious voice pulled her back to the *Odyssey*.

"Young man, why are you on this ship?" Giuseppe asked with bemusement. "I thought only people my age went to Gnaritus."

The bluntness of the question startled Alfonso at first, but then, seeing the earnest faces of Surina and the Cavaceccis, he decided to tell them about his life on Earth. "It's a long story, but I'll try to make it brief. As a child, I emigrated from Guatemala to Britain with my parents. I majored in computer engineering and later received a PhD from the University of Manchester, graduating with honors. I considered it a blessing to land a job as a computer specialist at the Rochester Manninghouse Corporation, the largest computer firm in the world. However, the company had a strict hierarchical structure, with a code of never questioning your superiors about any of their decisions. In the event of anyone breaking this cardinal rule, bad evaluations followed, to derail any chance of promotion within the system.

"In short, I broke the code of silence. I slogged away at my job, even on weekends, but I never kept my big mouth shut. I meant no harm by it. My far more compliant colleagues soon joined the upper echelons by showing deference to the hierarchy. My tragic flaw was that something beyond my control made me speak up and ask questions. For example, when I learned that the Rochester Manninghouse Corporation also constructed the computer system on Gnaritus, one of my fatal mistakes was asking why a firewall existed between the two planets. Tongues began wagging, and the administration pigeonholed me as a troublemaker. Pretty soon, even my colleagues shunned me, so I had no one in my corner to advocate for me. They said I didn't fit into the corporate culture and gave me a choice of either going to Gnaritus or remaining on Earth in another job. It's well known that if the Rochester Manninghouse Corporation gets rid of anyone, they make it virtually impossible to find any other employment on Earth. In effect, I would have been homeless without any work. Under those circumstances, I jumped at the chance of going to

Gnaritus. I believe advantages exist in every situation because I can't wait to see my parents, who are also on Ganritus!"

Afterward, his eyes searched their faces to gauge their reactions to his revelations. While listening to Alfonso's forthright presentation, Surina had realized more than half of the passengers were far younger than the usual age of relocation of sixty years. Did they qualify for the one-way trip to Gnaritus by virtue of not fitting into the system? Surina felt a bond with Alfonso since in many ways she too had not gone with the flow, as Ed Kadison had noted.

"Earth is ruthless," Giuseppe said, gesticulating in an animated manner. "I just kept my head down. Since taking care of my family was my priority, I kept silent even when I saw things that were not right. I kick myself now for being too chickenhearted to set things right. Of course, I never got far in the accounting firm where I worked. I could sense their relief when I left because for some reason I never became part of the in-crowd so to speak. The laws of the jungle still rule on Earth, with a definite pecking order."

While Giuseppe was speaking, his wife, Linda, put aside her knitting and listened with sympathy.

"Why even aspire to fit into a system like that, Alfonso?" Surina asked. "I ran into a similar situation. I asked too many questions, which is why I'm on this ship. Alfonso, don't feel bad. Certain things are just not worth it, and in a way, you're lucky to find out early. On the other hand, I wasted my time trying to play a game with rules that made no sense to me. As the time allotted to us is finite, we have to find something more useful to do."

"My journey is written in the stars!" Alfonso replied, smiling and pointing to space. "Maybe it's my karma, destiny, or fate. Call it what you will! Everything happens for a reason. I stopped seeing anything new on Earth long ago, and every banal day droned on the same as before without ever changing. Everything is new again now, with endless possibilities, similar to the universe itself. I feel like an Argonaut on a great adventure! Nothing can compare with that view. I feel freer here in space than ever before. I was only a puppet on Earth, whereas it's almost as if I have free will in space."

After that, they fell silent, meditating on the infinity of space. Surina had almost come to believe in the uniqueness of her experiences; however, on the *Odyssey* she had learned about many other narratives comparable to hers.

In the afternoon, they gathered again in the main cabin for their daily lecture by Chief Steward Pars. He arrived exuding goodwill and warmth. This time, he showed slides of the Milky Way galaxy on a screen at the front of the cabin to explain the relative positions of Earth and Gnaritus.

"Ladies and gentlemen, I hope you're settling in and finding everything to your liking," he said to a roar of prolonged applause from the audience. "Today, we have seen Mars. Tomorrow evening, Jupiter will be on the horizon. The gas giant Jupiter, whose name comes from the Roman king of gods, Zeus, is the largest planet in the solar system. In fact, Jupiter is twice the size of all the other planets in our solar system en masse. It's four and a half billion years old, similar to Earth.

"Jupiter orbits the sun every twelve years, and its day is only ten hours long. The temperatures are frigid. The mean temperature is minus one hundred and ten degrees Celsius! Brrr! I can't even imagine that. Jupiter has an enormous amount of gravity due to its large size. Seventy-five percent of its mass is hydrogen, and the remainder is helium gas for the most part. In other words, it's a gas giant, without a solid surface. These gases move in thick bands across the planet's surface, and when they intersect one another, giant storms occur. For example, the largest cyclone on Jupiter is the Great Red Spot, which is twice the size of Earth. Of note, the astronomer Galileo in 1610 discovered four of Jupiter's moons: Io, Europa, Ganymede, and Callisto. Since then, we have seen sixty-three other moons for a whopping sixty-seven moons in total! Until now, we have not found life on any of the moons, even on those that contain ice. Any questions so far?"

In the front row, Linda Cavacecci lay down her knitting. "How far away is Gnaritus?"

Pars pointed to the vast swathes of space on the diagram of the Milky Way galaxy. "Gnaritus is at a formidable distance of ten thousand light-years from the Earth. In fact, light travels at about three hundred thousand kilometers per second, so a light-year is the distance that light travels in a year. The Milky Way galaxy is a hundred thousand light-years across. Look at the spirals of the Milk Way. The Earth is in a small spur called Orion that lies between the two major spiral arms of Perseus and Carina-Sagittarius. We will travel to the outskirts of the Perseus arm to reach our destination. Beyond the Milky Way is the intergalactic space leading to our next-door larger galaxy, Andromeda, which contains a trillion stars. Yes, Alfonso, you have a question?"

"Sir, aren't the spirals of the Milky Way similar to those of nautilus shells and snail shells?" Alfonso asked in astonishment. "The spiral pattern seems to be a common theme throughout the universe."

"Another intriguing question," Pars said. "Some believe in the existence of a golden ratio throughout the grand design of the cosmos. What is the golden ratio? First, let me explain the Fibonacci series or nature's numbering system. The Fibonacci sequence is, for example, zero, one, one, two, three, five, eight, thirteen, twenty-one, thirty-four, fifty-five and so on until infinity. In essence, each number is the sum of the two numbers that precede it, and the ratio of two consecutive Fibonacci numbers corresponds to the golden ratio or one point six one eight. The golden ratio also goes by other names, such as Phi, after Phidias, the Greek sculptor of the Parthenon in Athens.

"On Earth, sunflowers have seeds totaling a Fibonacci number: for example, thirty-four, fifty-five, eighty-nine, or a hundred and forty-four. Buttercups have five petals, and daisies have twenty-one petals: all Fibonacci numbers. Even our DNA molecule, providing the building blocks of life, measures thirty-four angstroms in length by twenty-one angstroms wide for each cycle of the double-helix spiral. Both of these numbers are in the Fibonacci series, and their ratio approximates Phi.

"In the cosmos, the ratio of the orbits of Earth around the sun, three hundred and sixty-five days, and Venus, two hundred twenty-four days, is the golden ratio. Now, when you analyze a nautilus shell, the spiral gets wider by Phi every quarter turn it makes, and this is a logarithmic or golden spiral. The cochlea in our inner ear, the sensory organ of hearing, is also a golden spiral. The spiral galaxies like the Milky Way also approximate the golden spiral. Is there a grand design in the cosmos, or is it much messier than that? Then again, everything seems connected."

"If the universe has a grand design, could the architect be God?" Alfonso asked, hoping for an answer.

Pars paused and marshaled his thoughts. "Only faith can answer this question. What I can say is that the spiral is present throughout ancient mythology as a symbol of infinity and represents the journey from our outer world to our center or inner soul."

The stunning revelations struck a chord among the passengers. No sooner had he paused than an enthusiastic murmur burst out in the cabin as they debated whether the universe had a grand design. Realizing the near impossibility of regaining their attention, Pars decided to leave the rest of the lecture till another day. "Thanks for your attention. Remember, we're introducing the universe to you in all its complexities. There are still many unknowns that perhaps future generations will answer."

Of course, Pars had seen this reaction many times before among the passengers that he ferried across the galaxy to Gnaritus. He knew the space voyage had turned the passengers' lives upside down, in a literal and figurative sense. Their predictable, quotidian routines on Earth in the daily grind of survival had bogged them down on terra firma. Other than aspiring to have secure jobs to pay their bills, they had seldom concerned themselves with what lay beyond the clouds. Now, the firmament, in all its infinite variety and possibilities, had jump-started their dimming aspirations, for they realized the enormous potential that lay not only in the sempiternal universe but also in them.

Surina gazed through the porthole as the fiery-red Mars receded in the distance. The azure Earth was now only the size of a tennis ball, whereas the sun was still a fireball. Before going to supper, she sent her daily message to Mercy, Heidi, and the Lofgrens on the *Odyssey* computer. She wrote: "Incredible journey! Just saw Mars, and next is Jupiter. It's one wonder after another. The Captain and crew are fantastic. By the way, we are all stardust! All is well. Surina." Even so, she wondered whether the message would reach them. She had no way of finding out.

As customary at supper, most of the crew assembled at the captain's table. The space tourists also enthroned themselves at the Captain's table. Contrary to the surly space tourists, the entire crew radiated a festive cheerfulness to add to the raillery and peals of laughter ringing out from every corner of the dining compartment.

Surina joined Stefan, Alfonso, the Cavaceccis, and the Ellison family at a table in the center of the room. In between mouthfuls of scrumptious rhubarb crumble with lashings of custard, a vivacious Stefan regaled the Ellisons with tales about his life as a journalist. Meanwhile, Alfonso discussed his job at the Rochester Manninghouse Corporation with the Cavaceccis, punctuating the narrative with frequent giggles. The laughter was about nothing in particular and seemed to have no object at all. However, for Surina, it expressed the joy felt when an arduous, perpetual journey through a circuitous dark, damp tunnel ends unexpectedly in triumph by reaching dazzling sunshine and sweet, fresh air. It had been ages since she had exercised her risible muscles, and it was most refreshing, even though she became weak with laughter.

After supper, the Ellison children raced to the observation deck and arrived first. Their imaginations never ran out of games to play, for the endless vistas of space inspired them even more. Soon, most of the passengers settled in for the evening to admire the grand design of the universe from the comfort of the lounge chairs on the observation deck. Many of them chronicled every step of their journey, with numerous snapshots for their burgeoning digital albums that included unsurpassed images of the sun, planets, and all their friends onboard. The spontaneous fellowship among the passengers mystified Surina. She wondered how the celestial spaces had succeeded in blurring the insurmountable thorny borders that had separated them on Earth.

While Linda knitted a shawl, she paused on occasion as she tried to match the rusty-red color of the craggy Martian surface to one of the threads in her basket. In the meantime, Stefan mulled over his book. For the most part, he mused on the harmony in the cosmos, but at periodic intervals he would type away in a frenzy as if overcome by a bout of inspiration.

Opposite Surina, an amiable, portly woman in her fifties painted a flamboyant watercolor of Mars in her sketchpad. Her silvery-white hair was in a braided ponytail. Black-rimmed Wayfarer glasses adorned her upturned nose. She stared at Mars with dreamy eyes as she tried to capture its spirit on paper. Both Linda and Alfonso marveled at her artistry as well.

"What a lovely painting!" Surina said. "I like the colors. I'm Surina Mathew."

"Francesca Lenzi from Liverpool," she replied, putting down the painting on the table. "Pleased to meet you. I love art but never had much time for it. This one is Mars, god of war, although perhaps that should refer to Earth instead."

They all nodded in agreement with her somber assessment. She showed them her sui generis collection, beginning with a watercolor of her husband, who had died a year ago, and her adult son still on Earth. Her more recent Impressionist-styled paintings of the moon, Earth, sun, and even the *Odyssey* were innovative, for they crystallized the ephemeral essence of her subjects.

"I should have majored in art, but my parents insisted I become a lawyer, and I always listened to them," Francesca said in a faltering voice, perhaps due to regret. "The judicial system never appealed to me, but I hammered away at my job and never wavered from my duty for over thirty years. The plethora of subject matter on this voyage is as endless as the universe. I can hardly wait to paint Jupiter next! Then, in interstellar space, there will be a myriad of stars, nebulae, and supernovas. I hope to continue painting on Gnaritus, this time as my profession. The landscapes on Gnaritus are a mystery, though. Maybe Pars will tell us more about our new home planet tomorrow."

"Do you hold exhibitions of your artwork?" Alfonso asked.

"Oh, no, I only dabbled in art on the weekends," Francesca said with surprise at the compliment. "Maybe when I accumulate a body of work, I'll start to exhibit."

"There needs to be more outer-space art, in particular from Gnaritus," Alfonso said. "Your paintings would show Earth the wonders of the universe and broaden their horizons."

"At the National Gallery in London last week, I saw no Gnaritus paintings whatsoever," Surina added. "Francesca, you could start a much-needed new genre of Gnaritus art."

Francesca's smile widened. "I can't wait to paint Gnaritus, but everything hinges on whether we get through the asteroid and comet minefields. I heard even a collision with a small meteoroid could damage the spaceship enough to end the voyage in an instant."

Surina's heart thumped in her ears. "Are there any space lifeboats onboard?"

Alfonso shrugged. "I'll see if I can find out. We reach the asteroid belt tomorrow."

Francesca resumed painting, contemplating the enigma of the universe. Surina gazed at the celestial spaces. The dark matter of space seemed so serene, at least for now.

9

The Asteroid Belt

AS THE PASSENGERS flocked to the main cabin the next afternoon, an alert on their wristwatches warned them of the impending arrival of the asteroid belt in another two hours. They listened with rapt attention as Pars gave a timely lecture on the perilous asteroid field.

"This evening we'll see Jupiter and in the next few days, Saturn, Uranus, and Neptune, the final planet in our solar system," he said. "Before arriving at Jupiter, we need to cross the asteroid belt that also contains the dwarf planet Ceres. First, we'll discuss the origins of the space debris orbiting our sun such as comets, asteroids, and meteoroids. In fact, comets are the frozen leftover gases, rock, and dust from a dying star's supernova explosion that did not form a planet. In other words, comets are giant space snowballs! When comets fly by the sun, the ice melts and leaves just the rocky parts, which form asteroids over time.

"Meteoroids are the smallest chunks of rocks in space. Upon entering another planet's gravitational field, meteoroids become meteors or shooting stars as they heat up and disintegrate due to friction with the atmosphere. Meteorites are the pieces of the meteors that land on the planet. Beyond Neptune is the donut-shaped Kuiper Belt, containing short-period comets that orbit once around the sun in less than two hundred years. In contrast, the spherical Oort cloud in the farthest reaches of our solar system is the home of long-period comets with orbital laps of more than two hundred years. Pluto and Eris are two dwarf planets in the Kuiper Belt. Just to clarify, these dwarf planets are unable to forge clear paths around the sun, unlike the other eight planets in our solar system. Instead, dwarf planets orbit with other space debris, such as asteroids or comets. Beyond the Oort cloud is interstellar space or the space between the stars."

Alfonso shot up his hand. "Sir, please tell us more about Halley's Comet."

"Halley's Comet is one of the most famous short-period comets originating in the Kuiper Belt," Pars replied. "When a comet nears the sun, the surface ionizes, releasing a comet tail of gas and dust even visible to the naked eye from Earth. Although comets are ten to a hundred kilometers across, their iridescent-blue tails are millions of kilometers long. In fact, there are records of Halley's Comet throughout human history since it is visible from Earth every seventy-six years. For example, Halley's Comet is present in the famous Bayeux Tapestry commemorating William the Conqueror's victory at the Battle of Hastings in 1066.

"During its journey, Halley's Comet sheds dust particles that accumulate over the centuries in its orbital path. When the Earth's orbit intersects this trail of dust particles every October, they appear as the Orionid meteor showers. Through the ages, any sighting of a comet has foretold of pivotal, far-reaching changes or calamitous events coming to our world. There are a trillion comets in the Kuiper Belt, so we'll see plenty of them!"

Surina remembered her dream about riding on a comet. Could comets be nothing more than space junk, or did they prophesy doom? Could they portend a long journey, transformative change, or personal expansion instead? Perhaps as the inscrutable universe unfolded before them in the coming days, the answer would as well.

Then, Pars warned them of the dangers lying ahead. "As we enter the asteroid belt, please remain in the main cabin, with seat belts on. The *Odyssey* has a force field that can deflect the smallest meteoroids; however, evasive maneuvers may be necessary to navigate through the field of larger asteroids. Brace yourself for sudden, sharp, three hundred and sixty degree turns, with the *Odyssey* spinning all the way around. Rest assured that our pilots are familiar with maneuvering through the asteroid and comet minefields. The conglomerate mass of all the asteroids in the sparsely populated belt is much less than the Earth's moon; nonetheless, the peril is significant, for any impact with an asteroid could be catastrophic."

All of a sudden, the overhead speakers and their wristwatches cautioned them of their arrival in the asteroid belt.

Pars dashed to his seat at the front of the main cabin. "Please strap on your safety belts."

The *Odyssey* navigated with precision through a field of spinning boulders and the smaller meteoroids. In the beginning, the spacecraft tilted at a slight angle, causing the passengers to jostle gently back and forth. Through the portholes, Surina could see massive gray rocks with varying shapes. Some were spheroidal, whereas others were rectangular, with pockmarks from the impact with other asteroids that left jagged edges and craters on the surface. Further into the belt, the asteroids became charcoal black in color as the silicate content diminished, and the carbon increased.

Knowing the tenuous circumstances, Chief Steward Pars tried to distract the anxious passengers by pointing out the multitude of unique features of the asteroid belt. "Oh, there's the rocky dwarf planet Ceres, which is nine hundred and fifty kilometers across but with enough gravity to assume a spherical shape. Look to your right at the rectangular asteroid Ida with its moonlet, Dactyl."

Although Surina marveled at the moonlet orbiting around the asteroid, her heart pounded in her chest. Before long, the jarring roller coaster ride started as the *Odyssey* rotated a full 360 degrees followed by a series of precipitous descents and ascents. Surina's heart leaped into her throat, even though she remained transfixed by the view of the ancient boulders hurtling past. Stealing a quick glance at the other passengers, she noticed many of them kept their eyes shut while clutching the armrests of their chairs. Giuseppe Cavacecci, suffering from motion sickness, retched into a bag. Linda mouthed a silent prayer. Stefan wiped off rivulets of sweat from his forehead. Only the Ellison children continued to stare out of the portholes at the asteroids whizzing past the *Odyssey*.

As the starship clawed its way forward, it came within a hair's breadth of several potential collisions. When Surina peered out the window, a fearsome asteroid resembling a human skull hurtled toward the *Odyssey*. The minatory asteroid, which had two hollow eyes and an open mouth, gaped at her and threatened to swallow the starship whole. By a miracle, the starship's force field deflected the boulder, which veered off into space. Fear of impending doom forced her to close her eyes just to avoid the sight of the barrage raging outside.

When there was a temporary lull, Surina built up her courage and sneaked a peek out the porthole only to see a fresh onslaught of asteroids catapulting toward them. The starship's roller coaster ride resumed for what seemed like an hour before emerging from the treacherous, ancient rocky sea into the tranquility of space. The storm had passed. Somehow, they had scraped through the asteroid minefield by a whisker. The passengers clapped in unison with rapturous hurrahs as the all-clear announcement boomed throughout the cabin. They celebrated not only in honor of the crew's skill but also for still being alive.

Only the Ellison children remained glued to their seats in the main cabin, hoping to continue the white-knuckle roller coaster ride until their parents pulled them away to dinner. Despite their jolting ride, most of the passengers' morale rebounded as they settled in for supper. Soon, animated conversations filled the dining compartment. Few could match the ebullience of the Ellison children, who reminded Surina of birds singing after a harsh storm. Even though many passengers wanted to thank the pilots, Captain Spero said they remained hard at work on the bridge. The two space tourists were also absent from the captain's table. The heartwarming Lancashire hotpot, pickled red cabbage, and tangy gooseberry tart with whipped cream restored Surina's waning spirits.

Soon Surina immersed herself in the expansive vistas of space on the observation deck. Out of nowhere, the jaw-dropping view of Jupiter, with its colorful bands and Great Red Spot, floated into her perspective. The Brobdingnagian gas giant left no doubt in her mind that she beheld the king of the gods. Francesca Lenzi wasted no time in setting out to explore the soul of the Jovian world with bold, colorful brushstrokes on her canvas.

Alfonso enlightened the passengers by reading aloud facts about Jupiter from an online encyclopedia. "The brilliant red, orange, yellow, and brown on the planet surface are a result of the reactions of sulfur-containing gases. The white and blue colors are due to frozen water and carbon dioxide. Of the many moons of Jupiter, Callisto is the most cratered moon, Io has the most volcanoes, and Europa is icy. Wow! The close-up view is even better. I never knew about the faint rings around Jupiter. The rings are the dust particles resulting from the impact of thousands of micrometeors on the moons. In fact, all the four gas giants, not only Saturn but also Jupiter, Uranus, and Neptune, have rings."

After that, Surina contemplated the stunning Jovian planet as it approached ever nearer. Next to her, a young couple in their early thirties twanged the strings of their violins and tuned them to perfection. Tumultuous gale-force winds and unknown battles had etched haunting lines on their faces, although softened now by the serenity of space. Despite wearing green jumpsuit uniforms, they retained the air of flamboyance common to musicians. Gabriel wore his long dreadlocks in a ponytail at the nape of his neck. He had incandescent eyes, swimming with multilayered depth. On the spur of the moment, they stood up and played Bach's "Gavotte En Rondeaux from the Partita Number Three in E Major" with great flair and panache. The beautiful, multicolored beads at the ends of Rafaela's cornrows danced in tune with the supernal music in the same fashion as the sixty-seven moons rollicking around Jupiter. Elizabeth and George sashayed around the deck to the tempo of the music. Finishing with a flourish, the musicians bowed as the audience gave them a standing ovation for their bravura performance.

The haunting violin concerto from Bach transported Surina back to Charing Cross Station, where she had first seen Gabriel and Rafaela after her visit to the National Gallery with Heidi Burmann. The melodious sounds tapped into the remote memory of the primordial times after the big bang had created the hydrogen of the Jovian world. She wondered if Bach had composed the music in honor of the celestial bodies of Jupiter and its sixty-seven moons. Of course, he could not have known of their existence at that time. Perhaps part of Bach's genius was his uncanny connection with the universe, or maybe music was the language of the universe. She understood why Bach's empyreal music was on the probes bearing messages of goodwill to extraterrestrial life.

"The music of the heavens!" Giuseppe said. "I don't mean to pry, but why are you going to Gnaritus at such a young age?"

"We don't mind the question," Gabriel replied. "In a nutshell, our orchestra in London didn't think we played in step with their music or kept up with their beat, so they let us go. In spite of busking on the streets, in parks, and in the underground vactrain stations, our inability to earn a living from our classical music recitals led to our homelessness. After the android security guards had detained us on a rainy, foggy London night outside Charing Cross Station, we went first to a detention center, followed by this spaceship. To begin with, we dreaded this journey, fearing that we had lost everything, but look at what we found instead!"

With a dramatic flourish, he spread both his arms apart while smiling from ear to ear as he pointed to space. Both Francesca and Linda put away their artwork to listen to the musicians' plight.

"This journey is a priceless affirmation of something we always felt but could never put a finger on," Rafaela said in a dreamy voice. "In a sense, we recognized the absence of something essential in our lives. On Earth, they treated us as if we never quite belonged due to an endless variety of reasons. For example, we didn't keep in step with the music, we never wore the right fashions, or our Jamaican accents set us apart. We grew up in London after moving there from Jamaica as children. The primary focus was on reminding us how we didn't fit in. They treated us as if we came from Pluto. Rather than emphasizing all that unites us, they put the spotlight on magnifying the differences. It made me wonder where we fitted in if not on our home planet, Earth. As soon as we became homeless, passersby hurled comments at us such as: 'Why are you here? What are you doing here? You don't belong here. There's no room for you here.' They dehumanized us and made us feel so small that we became invisible in the end.

"After learning we are stardust from Chief Steward Pars and seeing all the infinite variety in the universe, I understood that I also have a home. Even though space is vast, it doesn't make us feel as small as Earth did. Instead, we feel as big as the universe! We are made of stardust from hundreds of stars, so we are children of the universe! In other words, I fit in and belong in the universe. I don't feel like an outsider anymore as I did on Earth because the universe has enough room for all its creation. Since the Earth is in the cosmos, I belong on Earth as well. My place in the universe is the affirmation I have looked for all my life. After the asteroid belt today, I know there's a distinct possibility we may not make it to Gnaritus. Still, I'm grateful for the privilege of these precious days in space to see a part of the grand design of the universe. Of course, I hope and pray we land on Gnaritus in one piece."

"I feel more accepted in space as well," Alfonso said. "I've also been looking for this acceptance all my life."

Everyone nodded in agreement. Gabriel and Rafaela returned to simply being in the moment as they enjoyed the panoramic vistas of space. In due time, Elizabeth and George stopped playing and came to rest at their parents' feet, for the nail-biting day through the asteroid belt had drained even their inexhaustible energy. David Ellison felt an affinity with Gabriel and Rafaela because the Earth's society had shunned him and muted his hope as well. He remembered he had no home on Earth either. However, the voyage across the Milky Way revealed to him how everyone has a home in the universe that none could deny or take away. Instead of his usual uncertainty, he found surer footing now with this knowledge of his place in the universe. The Ellison family retired to their sleeping berths when George and Elizabeth began yawning.

Alfonso trawled through the online design details of the *Odyssey*. Then, he stared into the deep recesses of space as he made his grim announcement. "We've hit a snag. This website makes no mention of any space lifeboats onboard! As Rafaela said, we need to pray for our safe arrival on Gnaritus. We scraped through the asteroid belt somehow. Whether we make it through the treacherous comet minefields, which are even more populated than the asteroid belt, seems like a role of the dice. Let's keep our fingers crossed. Hopefully, the force field and the superb crew will get us through."

Giuseppe held his head in his hands and groaned. "We're trapped, and there nothing we can do. What a lonely place to die, where no one will ever find us."

Linda and Francesca exchanged looks of concern at the sobering news. Surina thought the journey to Gnaritus seemed even more precarious, without any space lifeboats. If there was a silver lining to the voyage, at least she had discovered the bounty of the universe and even more about herself in the most unexpected of places: the rarefied atmosphere of deep space. However, many pressing questions plagued her. To begin with, would they ever reach Gnaritus?

10
A Voice

THE PANOPLY OF Saturn's colorful rings greeted Surina the next morning. Many dazzled passengers also packed the observation deck to admire the fresco of shimmering pastel pinks, browns, and yellows: the handiwork of the most prolific artist of all, the creator of the universe. Surina read from the online encyclopedia that icy rocks in Saturn's ringlets from the blown-up remnants of the ancient moons reflected the sunlight to produce the glittering pastel colors. Similar to Jupiter, Saturn was a gas giant without a solid surface, on which fierce winds, lightning storms, and freezing temperatures raged. Titan, the biggest of the sixty-two moons, was even larger than Mercury and shrouded in the yellow haze of an opaque atmosphere of nitrogen and methane clouds. Below the clouds, lakes and rivers of liquid methane peppered the surface.

The passengers had worked themselves into a lather of anticipation for Chief Steward Pars's didactic lecture that day because they would learn more about life on Gnaritus, at long last. Pars, a cultivated citizen of the universe, had a calming influence in allaying their dreaded fears whenever he entered the room, perhaps due to his considerable knowledge of the forces at play in the cosmos. Moreover, his inherent good nature, pragmatism, and sagaciousness inspired confidence in his complete reliability even during the most challenging circumstances.

"Welcome," Pars said with a flourish. "We saw Saturn today, which is named after the Roman god of agriculture. Tomorrow, we will see the last two planets in our solar system. First, will be Uranus, or the Greek god of the sky and later Neptune, or the Roman god of the sea. These ice giants of frozen water, ammonia, and methane have much fainter rings than Saturn's dramatic ones. From their far-flung locations at the edge of the solar system, it takes eighty-four years for Uranus to orbit once around the sun and a hundred and sixty-four years for Neptune. Neptune is not visible from Earth without a telescope, unlike the other planets in our solar system.

"Both planets have frozen landscapes, with mean temperatures of minus a hundred and forty degrees Celsius for Uranus and minus a hundred and ninety-five degrees Celsius for Neptune. The two planets appear blue due to the reflection of blue light by methane, a primary component in their atmosphere. Also, the twenty-seven moons of Uranus have names from characters of William Shakespeare's plays, such as Juliet, Ophelia, and Puck. In contrast, Neptune's fourteen moons have names from the Greek sea gods and mythical beings, such as Triton and Larissa."

In the front row, Alfonso stopped taking notes on his computer. He scratched his shaggy head and frowned. "Sir, is there life anywhere else in the universe?"

"We launched many unmanned probes into space, bearing messages of goodwill," Pars answered, showing them a diagram with the location of the probes in the distant Andromeda galaxy. "The probes carry music from composers such as Bach, Mozart, and Beethoven in the hope of communicating with extraterrestrial civilizations. Up to now, we detected no signal from sentient beings elsewhere. It's unlikely that the conditions on planets like Uranus and Neptune could sustain life as we know it. Since there are about nine billion Earthlike planets in the Milky Way alone, including Gnaritus, it's hard to imagine the complete absence of other intelligent life in the hundred billion galaxies of the universe.

"Despite the enthusiasm for searching for extraterrestrial life, perhaps it's just as well to remember the fate of the Native American Indians when settlers from Europe landed on their shores. Close to fifty million indigenous people died from the contagious diseases that the Europeans brought to the pristine New World. In a similar way, an influx of migrants from the Western Hemisphere subjected the aborigines of Australia to extreme degradation. Somehow, the same story keeps repeating itself throughout human history. We may wonder if these native populations benefited from their encounters with the colonists."

A somber silence reigned in the cabin.

Next, Pars pointed to a photograph of the heliopause. "This line at the edge of the solar system is the heliopause and demarcates the end of our sun's influence. Beyond the heliopause lies interstellar space. The interstellar medium is of lower density than some of the best vacuums on Earth. However, it's not a total void as it contains an interstellar gas of hydrogen, helium, and heavier elements at one atom per ten cubic centimeters. Dust from exploding stars with elements such as carbon, nitrogen, and iron also permeates interstellar space. When portions of the interstellar medium clump together due to the inherent gravity of the particles, nebulae clouds result that have the potential to create new stars. Nebulae contain molecules as well. For example, when the atoms of elements such as carbon link together, they form complex branched-chain molecules. In fact, these branched carbon chains are the building blocks of life and seem to be widespread in the galaxy. We will see magnificent nebulae as well as supernovae—explosions of dying stars—and perhaps even the birth of new stars on our way to Gnaritus! What will we discover when we reach our destination, Gnaritus?"

"Is it like Earth?" Stefan said.

The passengers were all ears to learn about their prospective home.

"Gnaritus is about the same size as Earth," Pars replied, directing their attention to a dramatic photograph of their new home planet's solar system. "It's also at a similar distance from its larger parent sun, about a hundred and sixty million kilometers. This orbital distance is not quite the same as for the Earth, which is a hundred and fifty million kilometers from the sun. However, Gnaritus orbits around two other smaller daughter stars that are, in fact, a hundred and fifty million kilometers away. With three stars in the solar system, there is at least one sun in the skies over Gnaritus at all times, resulting in perpetual daylight. In essence, the sun never sets on Gnaritus!

"Although Gnaritus's moon, Clementia, can eclipse one sun on occasion, a total eclipse of all three suns is impossible. So, no total solar eclipses occur on Gnaritus either! Don't be too surprised if you cast more than one shadow when all three suns are in the sky. There could even be up to three shadows! The largest sun is Clotho, whereas the two smaller stars are Lachesis and Atropos. These names are from the three Fates in Greek mythology that oversee the allegorical strands of life. For instance, Clotho spins our lifelines, whereas Lachesis weaves the thread into the tapestry of our lives, and Atropos cuts the strings.

"Gnaritus is a Goldilocks planet in that it is just right for human habitation due to being the right distance from its suns and the right size to have an atmosphere. Since both planets have a similar spin axis of twenty-three and a half degrees, we use Earth time on Gnaritus. However, with a solar orbit of three hundred and seventy-four days, Gnaritus celebrates New Year on a different day than on Earth! Gnaritus has the privilege of hosting the first human space colony due to its remarkable resemblance to Earth, more so than any other known exoplanet. All these benefits of Gnaritus as a second home for humans far outweigh the hazards of the voyage through the comet belts and the expanse of ten thousand light-years. There are two other planets in the solar system orbiting with Gnaritus: Spes and Fiducia. Who knows the meaning of these names?"

Alfonso impressed everyone when he rattled off the meanings. "In Latin, Spes means hope; Fiducia is faith, and Clementia stands for mercy. Gnaritus means knowledge. Is there other life on Gnaritus?"

Pars applauded. "You're right! However, the hope of finding life on Gnaritus never materialized even after a hundred years of searching, which continues to this day in the department of cryptozoology at Gnaritus University. The first theory to explain the absence of life is that Gnaritus is only three million years of age and too young to harbor life. For example, although the Earth is four and a half billion years old, the most ancient fossils are from a billion years later. In other words, life emerged on Earth only after a billion years. Dinosaurs appeared around two hundred and forty-five million years ago, whereas modern *Homo sapiens* arose only about two hundred thousand years ago. Thus, the evolution of life takes a long time.

"Another theory is that a giant asteroid crashed on Gnaritus a million years ago, resulting in the monolithic crater in the south as well as either a mass extinction or a cessation of the evolution of life. This scenario is reminiscent of the massive asteroid striking Earth about sixty-five million years ago in Mexico's Yucatan Peninsula, with a force of more than a billion atomic bombs that sparked colossal earthquakes and tsunamis. The dust and debris from the impact of the asteroid remained in the atmosphere and blocked the sunlight. The ensuing Ice Age darkness caused the mass extinction of the dinosaurs along with more than half of the world's species, including plants. In fact, Earth required nearly two million years to recover before the dawn of mammals that gave rise to the current Age of Humans. The Age of Humans, which is also known as the Anthropocene epoch, is only a flash in the geological history of the Earth when you consider all the species that have come and gone before us."

He searched the cabin to see if there were any questions. After taking a sip of water, he resumed. "Our hope in colonizing other planets such as Gnaritus is that the Age of Humans will prevail in *saecula saeculorum*; however, the universe offers no guarantees whatsoever. We have found no fossils of even single-celled organisms anywhere on Gnaritus to suggest that life existed before the impact of the asteroid, if indeed there was such an occurrence.

"The Earth has seven continents, innumerable islands, and a hundred and ninety-six countries. On the other hand, Gnaritus has a single landmass spanning half the planet from the North to the South Pole and no islands in the vast unfathomable ocean of liquid water. Since the gravity and atmosphere are similar to Earth's, you'll be able to walk on terra firma in the open air on Gnaritus, rather than just float around. Water vapor and dust forming clouds are in the troposphere, the layer closest to Gnaritus's surface. Just as on Earth, nitrogen constitutes seventy-eight percent, oxygen twenty-one percent, and carbon dioxide less than one percent of the atmosphere on Gnaritus."

"Are you saying we'll be able to walk outside without any oxygen masks or space suits?" Alfonso asked with surprise.

"Yes and no," Pars answered. "Since the layer above the troposphere, the stratosphere, has a thinner ozone layer than on Earth, there is less absorption of the harmful radiation from the three suns. Although you'll be able to walk without the need for oxygen tanks, it would be advisable to wear protective clothing to cover exposed skin. Gnaritonians wear garments and broad-brimmed hats of an opaque fabric containing chemical ultraviolet absorbers that block out the ultraviolet radiation."

A spontaneous cheer rang out in the cabin. Pars had seen a

similar reaction among the many passengers that the *Odyssey* had shuttled across the galaxy. He thought maybe the exuberance signified a collective sigh of relief, for somewhere from primordial times humans had a biological need to walk in the natural world instead of living in a sterile, manufactured environment. In other words, stepping out from the darkness into the sunshine was hardwired in the human DNA.

"Sir, since there is no life on Gnaritus, what is the land surface like then?" Alfonso asked with some anxiety.

"Very similar to the Patagonian Desert of Argentina on the South American continent," Pars answered. "However, a desert has an annual precipitation of less than two hundred and fifty millimeters, whereas Gnaritus has an average rainfall of fifteen hundred millimeters every year. By this definition, Gnaritus is not a desert, even though there is an absence of life. Red clay plains and gravel plateaus surround the space colony. Mountain ranges, canyons, and volcanoes are in the south. In fact, the space colony is in the comparative safety of the north, far away from the remaining active volcanoes by the South Pole.

"Brooks, streams, rivers, lakes, and even waterfalls spring like oases in the barren landscape. The coast has vivid-yellow or white sandy beaches along which dunes form a type of sand sea. The ocean is reminiscent of the Aegean Sea of the Greek islands, with the same crystalline turquoise waters. The climate is not typical of a desert either, for there are no wide temperature fluctuations between day and nighttime. Instead, the climate is mild, with four seasons, since Gnaritus also spins on its axis at an angle similar to Earth's. Winter has snow, whereas spring has more rainfall than in any other season. However, the three suns soon thaw the snow, so it seldom lasts long. The weather in the north is much like that of Dorset on the southern coast of Britain, with an average temperature of eight degrees Celsius in the winter and twenty-two degrees Celsius in the summer."

"Since the atmospheric conditions, soil, and abundant water

seem ripe for planting seeds and letting vegetation flourish on the planet, why is the planet still uncultivated?" Stefan asked.

"The introduction of an ecosystem and interference with nature on another planet can have profound ethical ramifications," Pars answered. "The consequences of terraforming are unknown. For example, the rampant, feckless pillage of the Earth's environment in the twenty-first century caused catastrophic climatic upheavals, such as global warming and rising sea levels. Who can even predict the damage resulting from our interference in an alien environment? For now, the consensus opinion on Gnaritus is set against terraforming."

"Terraforming would not cause that much interference since there is no life on the planet," Stefan said.

"We've been on Gnaritus for only a hundred years," Pars replied. "Can we be sure of the absence of life? We have explored most regions on Gnaritus, although not every square inch of the myriad of caves, canyons, rivers, and lakes. Even the ocean floor is uncharted, and this venture alone will take centuries since it lies twelve thousand meters below sea level on average. In fact, the sea is far deeper than the nethermost depths of the Earth's oceans: the Pacific Ocean's Challenger Deep in the southern part of Mariana Trench. If one day we discover single-cell organisms somewhere on Gnaritus, they would have to coexist with the flora and fauna from Earth, raising further ethical concerns. Most of the population on Gnaritus denounced terraforming and defeated the measure in a vote. The prevailing viewpoint is that any alien life has the right to evolve to its full potential in its natural ecosystem without human interference."

"Then how are fruits and vegetables produced?" Alfonso asked. "Is there any animal farming?"

"All agriculture occurs in greenhouses that provide contained environments for plant growth," Pars said. "There is no cross contamination of the natural ecosystem on Gnaritus with this method of cultivation since the self-contained space colony recycles everything. The main horticultural methods are hydroponics using mineral nutrients in water and aeroponics, where mists of a nourishing solution bathe the roots of plants. Just as on Earth, the molecular structure of water on Gnaritus consists of two hydrogen atoms and a single oxygen atom. The fresh taste of the water from the natural springs surrounding the space colony is incomparable. With a few essential ingredients, a three-dimensional printer can replicate the appearance, taste, texture, and nutrient value of meat. This meat is indistinguishable from the natural product, so there is no need for animal farming. In fact, Chief Cook Grenier is also preparing meat dishes with a three-dimensional printer on this spacecraft. Please raise your hands if you consider the meat dishes to be unlike the natural products on Earth."

Seeing no objections, Pars continued. "Three-dimensional printers manufacture butter, salt, pepper, spices, and other staples. Earth has the advantage of the traditional agricultural methods; however, chefs on Gnaritus rely on the three-dimensional printing of many of the ingredients. Dr. Mathew, you have a question?"

"Sir, since Gnaritus disapproved of terraforming, what position did the Earth's World Governing Body have, and did it factor into the final decision?" she asked.

Pars fast-forwarded the slides to an illustration of the timeline of the founding of the space colony. "I'll try to explain the history of Gnaritus in brief. At the dawn of the space colony a hundred years ago, the World Governing Body named the planet Earth Colony and dispatched a governor to oversee it. The governors from Earth never lasted more than two or three years at a time. Some fifty years later, as the space colony matured, it became apparent that these rotating governors could never appreciate all the events shaping Gnaritus or be that much invested in its future. At the behest of the New World settlers, Earth divested itself from governing Gnaritus. Once free from the colonial tutelage, the space colonists changed the planet's name to Gnaritus by a vote.

"In fact, the current laws on Gnaritus assure each citizen over sixteen years of age a voice and a vote on every issue. A group of five council members representing the five boroughs of Gnaritus implements the outcomes of the elections. No autocrat presides over the decision-making. All eligible citizens cast their ballots on Gnaritus, unlike the prevalent voter apathy on Earth. On my many visits, I have come to understand that every Gnaritonian has a sincere commitment to the advancement of the colony. Of course, Gnaritonians are still ironing out the many wrinkles in the system and even rewriting the laws on a regular basis. The overall goal is to create a just society for the benefit of all the citizens and the planet. Even though the World Governing Body on Earth promoted terraforming, they never convinced Gnaritus to implement the measure. In essence, Gnaritus determines its own future. Gnaritus is far from being a closed society since it welcomes Earth's citizens to help grow this new frontier."

Alfonso lobbed another question. "How many cities and villages are there on Gnaritus?"

"Good question," replied Pars, pointing to a map of a city. "Gnaritus has no separate countries, cities, or villages. At the start of the space colony, five main roads, like the spokes of a wheel, spread out from the city center and divided the area into five main districts. The housing for the population grew outward from the city center, which now contains the commercial buildings. So far, each district has a population of about one million inhabitants. These boroughs are named Terra, Ignis, Acqua, Aeris, and Spatium. Who knows what these mean?"

"These are the Latin names for the five elements of nature: earth, fire, water, air, and space," Alfonso answered with great gusto.

Pars congratulated him. "Well done! In fact, the number five has played a prominent role throughout human history. The five fundamental virtues in the ancient world were wisdom, love, truth, goodness, and justice. Another example is the Hindu god Shiva's cosmic dance, which is an allegory of the five forces of cosmic energy: creation, destruction, preservation, illusion, and grace."

"CERN has a statue of a dancing Shiva," Stefan said.

Pars nodded. "Yes, CERN is the European Organization for Nuclear Research in Geneva, Switzerland. They study particle physics or the components of matter. In fact, CERN is responsible for many advances in our understanding of the fundamental forces in the universe. A plaque next to the statue commemorates how Shiva's cosmic dance is a metaphor for the dance of subatomic particles, such as the electrons orbiting around the nucleus. In essence, the cosmic dance symbolizes the harmony of the universe. Any other questions?"

Seeing no hands up, he continued. "Now I'll return to Alfonso's question about the space colony that lies in a valley in the north. Mountains surrounding the colony protect it from the harsh coastal winds. The nearby beach on the west coast is a hundred kilometers away, whereas the volcano fields are much farther south. Graphene is the chief building block of the entire colony. For example, three-dimensional printers made the graphene buildings, furniture, appliances, air cabs, and computers. In addition, graphene batteries can power the colony for a hundred years and recharge in only fifteen minutes. An enclosed system of water mains, sewers, and drains allows efficient recycling to avoid cross contamination of the environment.

"Each new settler will have lodging. As on Earth, flying air cabs are the primary mode of transportation. Though many of you have jobs on Gnaritus in fields similar to your positions on Earth, there is no shortage of work in building all aspects of the colony. Each borough has a hospital; however, the Spatium Borough Hospital is the major medical facility, with an affiliation to Gnaritus University as well. Enrollment in the universities is soaring as more inhabitants embark on their studies in a diverse array of subjects.

The schools and universities are not only for adults but also for the growing population of children born on Gnaritus, who know no other world."

"What type of a computer system does Gnaritus have?" Alfonso asked.

"There is an internal computer network connecting all of Gnaritus," Pars explained. "However, only the communal computers in the public squares have links to Earth with a time delay of a week or more since communication towers on extraterrestrial planets relay the messages across ten thousand light-years of space. The time is up for today!"

Across the aisle from Surina, Gabriel stared into space as he brooded about Pars's revelations. Then, turning to Surina, he spoke in a glum tone. "There never seemed to be enough room for us on Earth. I find it difficult to imagine being welcomed anywhere, let alone in another world. Do you believe that each of us will have a voice on Gnaritus when we never did even on our home planet?"

Surina tried to hearten the dispirited youth. "Pars is a fine, upstanding citizen of the universe. I believe he would give reliable information. Gnaritus may indeed turn out to be an interesting and refreshing change from the past. We'll soon find out! It's time for supper."

"Then Gnaritus sounds like a planet I would want to live on," Gabriel said.

He grinned as he sprang from his seat and joined a steady stream of passengers filing into the dining compartment. The sheer volume of information overwhelmed many, but they were glad to learn more about Gnaritus at last. In fact, Pars's presentation had set the passengers agog and given them considerable hope that perhaps life on Gnaritus would not be as bad as they had envisioned.

At supper, Surina sat opposite Stefan, who discussed his journalism career on Earth with refreshing candor. However, he had to shout over the uproarious din in the dining compartment. "We'll have a voice on Gnaritus! I became a journalist to have a voice and to give others a voice by telling their stories. I soon discovered that the news outlet I worked for censored certain contentious stories to varying degrees and published only the official doctrine. For example, they turned thumbs down to my article about Dr. Rod Stinguard, who synthesized the viral vector to prevent cancer. In spite of the legitimate questions I asked during the interview, Stinguard waffled and lacked the sincerity and gusto of someone trying to save the world from the terrible scourge of cancer. My article recommended greater caution and further testing of the virus before distributing it to the general population. The editor ditched my entire column, whereas he only bowdlerized it in the past. He told me point-blank to stop muckraking.

"I don't believe in censoring information in any way, which is most likely why they never promoted me to be an editor. As a journalist, I always searched for my voice and never found it. Even though I was not yet at the usual age of resettlement, I received my relocation notice to Gnaritus soon afterward. On the most fundamental level, to quash someone's voice is to deny them their very existence. On Earth, I lost my voice long ago, or maybe I never had it in the first place."

Despite the emotive subject matter, Stefan's rational analysis lacked any bitterness as if he had accepted the past with unflinching resolve. After helping himself to more apple crumble, he continued with an enigmatic smile. "Even though a glut of news bombards us, who knows what the real story is? The World Governing Body spins many tales to soften the harsh reality of life on Earth. One of the most baffling things is why Earth censors information from Gnaritus since it would offer so much reassurance to know that it's not as bad there as imagined. Is it because the governance of Gnaritus is no longer in the Earth's hands? Could people having a voice on Gnaritus be a threat? The

World Governing Body muzzles the voices of the population on Earth. In a similar way, they are repressing the voices from Gnaritus to prevent them from reaching Earth."

Stefan's conversation rekindled the dying embers of Surina's evanescent memory about the Stinguard viral vector. She wondered if she should burden him with the grim knowledge she had carried all the way from Earth. "Stefan, I did research on the Stinguard viral vector. I also suggested more testing before offering it to the general population. The viral vector has to integrate into the human genome at a specific site to produce the essential enzymes to repair the DNA mutations causing cancer. However, my research showed that the integration site of the viral vector into human DNA could vary and result in lethal mutations. All the scientific committees repudiated my data with such fervor that I never published it in any medical journal. So, they censored my experiments too. Stinguard's powerful connections in the World Governing Body paved the way for him to lobby the scientific committees to approve the launch of the viral vector."

"I wish I could have interviewed you for my article," he stammered in alarm. "I never found anyone who contradicted Stinguard's opinion during my investigation. No one expressed any doubts about the viral vector whatsoever. In fact, they praised Stinguard as a Promethean scientist and dubbed the viral vector 'the magic bullet to cure cancer.' I found it difficult to trust Stinguard due to his chest-thumping, shifty gaze, and condescending voice. He ducked most of my questions and gave me the runaround, but I saw through his rigmarole.

"When I sniffed around, I uncovered some interesting information that could explain the rush to launch this viral vector. Stinguard is on the board of directors of the Rochester Manninghouse Pharmaceutical Company, which will manufacture the viral vector! What's more, the chief executive officer of this multinational pharmaceutical company is none other than Dr. Robert Hurpan, the medical director of the Greysville Quadrant

Hospital. That nostrum-monger Stinguard and the pharmaceutical company stand to make record profits as a result. Even if I had interviewed you, my editor would have nixed it and replaced it with the usual empty prattle."

"The viral vector story is not unheard of since there have been many other instances of dubious medical interventions in human history," Surina said. "For example, millions of women took diethylstilbestrol between 1930 and 1971 to prevent miscarriages and preterm births, but it also caused breast, ovarian, and uterine cancer in the mothers. Even worse, their daughters developed cervical and breast cancer at early ages. Later, they found that diethylstilbestrol didn't prevent miscarriages or preterm births in the first place!"

Stefan winced. "With the Stinguard viral vector, the horse left the barn long ago. They will launch the viral vector in Africa in a few months before its worldwide distribution. We did everything we could! Even if we sent messages back to Earth now, the World Governing Body would squelch them all. The only truths on Earth are the versions acceptable to the World Governing Body and their self-serving, mendacious propaganda. Let's not tell the other passengers about this viral vector. They just managed to pick themselves up by the bootstraps. How can we shatter their newfound optimism for the future?"

In a pensive mood, he glanced at the other passengers, who were oblivious to the ominous news of the Stinguard viral vector. The animated voices and laughter of the passengers rang out from every table. Then, he spoke in a lower voice. "Will this Stinguard viral vector come to Gnaritus as well?"

Surina shook her head. "I never heard them mention anything about dispensing it on Gnaritus, although they kept me out of the loop of their real agenda. They're targeting every Earth citizen to prevent the high rates of cancer. It's unlikely that the World Governing Body has any interest in Gnaritus since we never mattered to them in the first place."

Stefan stopped eating as if gripped by a new sense of foreboding. "Perhaps, the real question is the fate of the innocent citizens of Earth. Do you still have your research files? Maybe the best bet is to hand them over to those five council representatives on Gnaritus and ask them how to proceed. We've exhausted all possible options on Earth already!"

With supper over, the passengers poured onto the observation deck to marvel at Saturn once more. Stefan appeared resolute as he settled himself in for the evening to pen the next chapter of his book about the starship's voyage to Gnaritus. Alfonso wrote an indecipherable code for a mysterious computer program, which he divulged to no one in spite of the many questions from curious onlookers. Meanwhile, Francesca turned to a fresh page in her sketchpad to paint Saturn in all its finery, whereas Gabriel and Rafaela composed music using the celestial bodies waltzing in space as their inspiration. Linda Cavacecci knitted a multicolored scarf with a pastel pink yarn to match the color of one of Saturn's ringlets. In their usual place by the window, both Elizabeth and George Ellison were sketching Saturn's rings with crayons in a dazzling array of colors as their parents watched with pride. For the first time, Surina spotted a glimmer of hope for the future shining through the bleak shadow hanging over David and Mary Ellison.

Happy to leave her usual frenzied, kinetic pace on Earth behind, Surina stretched back in the lounge chair, with her head resting on the cushion. She thought their prospects still held some promise, even in the depths of space! In fact, the journey on the *Odyssey* had taken her from doubt to belief. She swiveled around in the chair to see the vanishing Earth, now only a blue speck shining in the noiseless vacuum of space. Beyond Saturn, they would lose sight of their home planet forever. Even though the unpropitious Stinguard viral vector still haunted her, she reminded herself that looking back would lead nowhere. The only path for her in this uncharted expanse would be to soldier on without wavering, even through the comet minefields looming ahead.

All of a sudden, she had an inkling of another universe existing within her as well. Far from being static, even that inner universe continued to change and expand. Acting on an impulse, she glanced back one more time after the *Odyssey* had sailed past Saturn. The Earth had disappeared without a trace.

11
The Nanobots

THE *ODYSSEY* CRUISED past two ice giants the next day, Uranus and Neptune. Linda Cavacecci spent most of the morning trying to find the right color in her yarn basket to replicate the subtle indigo-green of Uranus and the gelid blue of Neptune. Over time, Linda had transformed the scarf into a giant tapestry, with the apt name of *The Colors of the Universe*. It portrayed a multitude of celestial bodies in a breathtaking blend of crimson, gold, silver, peacock green, turquoise, iridescent pink, black, brown, and copper. Giuseppe helped Linda to unfold the tapestry and spread it out for the benefit of the admiring onlookers. Surina contemplated the unfinished tapestry, which was already a masterful tribute to the creativity of the universe. As the magical, glowing hues leaped out, she could not help but think how the universe must love the entire color spectrum indiscriminately. Out of the blue, a message flashed on her wristwatch, summoning her to Pars's lecture earlier that morning to discuss the fast approaching Kuiper Belt. Linda and Giuseppe folded the tapestry and hastened to the main cabin too.

Pars was already waiting in the main cabin, and he began the lecture without delay. "Today, we saw the last planet of our solar system, Neptune. Later this afternoon, we will reach the Kuiper Belt, which is thirty to fifty-five astronomical units from the sun. In contrast, the Oort cloud stretches over a distance of five thousand to one hundred thousand astronomical units. Just to clarify, one astronomical unit measures one hundred and fifty million kilometers, which is the distance from the sun to the Earth. In other words, the Kuiper Belt is thirty to fifty-five times Earth's distance from the sun.

"Populating the Kuiper Belt are the trans-Neptunian objects, including the reddish-tinted dwarf planets, such as Pluto, Makemake, Haumea, and Eris as well as the short-period comets. For example, the dwarf planet Pluto has an orbital lap of two hundred and forty-eight years since it is about six billion kilometers from the sun. It is mainly rock as well as nitrogen ice and has four moons. In ancient mythology, Pluto was the Roman god of the underworld. In the Kuiper Belt, the comets will appear as irregularly shaped giant snowballs with icy coatings covering charred black rocks that are ten to a hundred kilometers across. On the other hand, when comets approach the sun, the surface ionizes, releasing an iridescent-blue tail of gas and dust. Comets may have bashed into the Earth billions of years ago, bringing organic molecules and water with them to jump-start the birth of life. The Kuiper Belt is twenty times wider than the asteroid belt and is the origin of a trillion short-period comets with orbital laps of less than two hundred years.

"For these reasons, our journey through the Kuiper Belt will be longer and more taxing than in the asteroid belt. Please keep your safety belts on during our entire transit through the comet belt. Meals will be served right here in the main cabin. The pilots have charted a clear passage through the comet minefield. We prepared for any contingency; however, in case of unforeseen events, the force field around the *Odyssey* will deflect away any potential collisions. We'll have to continue this lecture another day. Fasten your seat belts now!"

A shrill announcement of the arrival of the Kuiper Belt rang out overhead. Their wristwatches beeped and cautioned them to remain seated. Pars, Charlie, and Henry scooted to their seats at the front of the main cabin while innumerable charred icy rocks stampeded past. The *Odyssey* wove around the mercurial sea of comets as if performing a series of intricate dance steps with a partner. On occasion, the spaceship tilted 180 degrees before snapping back to its original position.

A deathly silence gripped the cabin. The *Odyssey* crawled like a tortoise through the Kuiper Belt, on occasion careening right, other times twisting to the left, and sometimes tottering in a zigzag motion. Only the Ellison children's chatter punctuated the stillness whenever they glimpsed another comet, which pirouetted like a spinning-top toy. The ongoing threat from the jagged, icy rocks flying toward the *Odyssey* drained most of the passengers' energy. Many of them wrapped themselves in the security of their sleeping bags on the flatbed seats to escape from the harshness of the comet field outside. Nevertheless, there were a few stalwarts like Linda and Francesca, who sketched the fantastic shapes of the comets. Stefan logged the day's dramatic events in his forthcoming book. Meanwhile, Alfonso rubbernecked with reverential awe at the primordial space detritus that was still unable to escape the clutches of the sun.

Chief Steward Pars meditated with his eyes closed. Now and then, he surveyed the cabin to ascertain if the two junior stewards had everything under control before he resumed meditating. In the meantime, Surina burrowed herself into the velvety warmth of her sleeping bag. She tossed and turned, fearing the worst. Then, she realized she was powerless to change the outcome of the voyage. Overcome with exhaustion, she dozed off until a soft hand patted her shoulder and roused her from her nap. It was Charlie, the lanky steward, who handed her a menu.

"Dr. Mathew, it's suppertime," he said. "Would you like a sandwich? We have many varieties."

Groggy and bleary-eyed with sleep, Surina needed a few owlish blinks to regain her bearings as she sluggishly raised the head of the flatbed. She lingered over the menu.

"Scottish breakfast tea, a chicken sandwich, and blackberry cake for dessert please," she said.

Similar to an acrobat balancing on a tightrope, Charlie bent and straightened his long legs at the knees as he went to the kitchen. In a few moments, he returned to the main cabin, carrying a heavy tray from the kitchen with skill and dexterity.

He laid the heartwarming spread in front of Surina. "Enjoy your meal, Dr. Mathew. Henry will bring your tea."

Before she knew it, Henry, the attentive junior steward, emerged from the kitchen. He swayed back and forth like a funambulist with as much alacrity as Charlie. His crew cut revealed an earnest face with large, floppy ears that stuck out. Despite the sudden rotations of the starship through the comet field, his great mirth continued to flow throughout the cabin without any sign of ebbing.

He placed the tea in a spill-free cup on her tray. "Dr. Mathew, is there anything else you need?"

"How much longer before we clear the Kuiper Belt?" Surina asked.

"It depends on our progress, but it could be another seven hours," Henry answered.

Surina's heart sank. Anything could happen in another seven hours. The sheer implausibility of her portentous dream about riding on a comet struck her as another icy rock zipped past her window. Moreover, the relentless onslaught of comets only heightened her awareness of the absence of a nearby port of call to drop anchor for even a brief respite. Since the comet belt became denser with time, the starship's evasive maneuvers intensified.

The sight of the two assiduous stewards whirling about the cabin and attending to even the minutest details of the passengers' requests provided a rudder for Surina. After supper, she attempted to forget the treacherous comets by watching online movies or listening to soothing music. All of a sudden, an intense screeching noise jolted the passengers back to reality. Even the two stewards careered to their seats at the front of the cabin.

Oh no, a comet thwacked the *Odyssey*, Surina thought. She sat bolt upright while the starship gyrated out of control. The engine sputtered and coughed. Frenzied panic permeated the cabin, and the Ellison children hollered. Even their parents could not console them.

Captain Spero's announcement boomed overhead. "Ladies and gentlemen, we've pinpointed the cause of the *Odyssey*'s rotations. A comet broke through the deflector shield and rammed into the *Odyssey* on the starboard side. The comet gouged out a small piece of the outermost layer of the ship, but the nanobots will save the day. The minuscule nanobots not only repair any damage but also sense the starship's position in space and make the hairbreadth adjustments in its bearing to ensure a safe passage through the comet fields. Expect the *Odyssey* to continue spinning in the meantime. Please remain seated for now."

Surina squeezed her eyes shut in terror as the stricken starship spun like a whirling dervish in a trance, even blurring the outlines of the ship. She almost swooned with fright. Only the sound of the Ellison children's wails and Giuseppe Cavacecci's dry heaves filled the eerie stillness.

Chief Steward Pars's wristwatch flashed with a message. He made another announcement. "I've just received more information about the collision. Chief Engineer Manus calculated the size and depth of the hole in the ship's outer shell. It will take an hour or more for the nanobots to repair the defect."

As the nanobots swarmed in to repair the gaping hole from the comet's collision, the rattling and spinning slowed down by incremental degrees over the next hour until the starship ground to a halt. Then the *Odyssey* shuddered, and its engines sprang into life. Surina sighed with relief and opened her eyes again when the starship plowed forward through the Kuiper Belt again. Soon, the Ellison children stopped crying as well. After an hour of snaillike progress, Captain Spero announced that the repairs had been successful. However, he did not have the heart to tell them how close the call had been. For if the comet had breached the next layer of the ship's shell, then the voyage would have ended in an instant.

While the *Odyssey* hopscotched through the Kuiper Belt, each of the passengers recognized the potential for another more destructive encounter with a comet just around the corner. In other words, they knew without anyone telling them that each moment could be their last. Surina stopped dwelling on the sorrows of her past on Earth or dreaming about her future on Gnaritus. Without the encumbrance of the past or the illusion of the future, she focused her entire being in the present moment instead, and time stopped. When she shed all her disappointments and expectations, which had hung around her neck like an albatross, she felt lighter. In essence, she realized only the present moment existed to find happiness and nothing more than that.

In due time, the comets petered out, and the *Odyssey* resumed its cruising speed. A jubilant Chief Steward Pars sprang up from his chair and stood at the front of the cabin. "The Kuiper Belt is behind us, but we will reach the Oort cloud, home of the long-period comets, by tomorrow evening. Until then, you can resume your normal activities. Refreshments are waiting in the dining compartment!"

The passengers erupted in a prolonged round of ecstatic cheers. When they staggered into the dining room in a shell-shocked daze, an unexpected late night feast greeted them and helped to create a party-like atmosphere. Chief Cook Grenier had pulled out all the stops in preparing a splendid banquet of delicious bite-sized nibbles, including sausage rolls, marinated chicken skewers, miniature meat pies, and fish and chips. As Surina indulged in the mouth-watering delicacies, her memory of the spine-chilling comet collision receded, just a little. After spending the majority of the day seated, she was glad to mingle around the room and enjoy the finger foods. Although she had few close friends on Earth, all the passengers greeted her like a lifelong acquaintance by the end of that evening.

The most extraordinary part of the celebration for Surina came when she met Bob and Betina Pagett for the first time, even though they had also lived on Oakdale Avenue in Keswick. Despite being neighbors on Earth for many years, they had never even spoken to one another. Betina had a round-shouldered slump and a slight build. She had a habit of brushing back her spiky bangs of gunmetal hair that fell over her blue eyes. Bob was a thickset, bull-necked man with a round belly.

"I remember seeing you gardening on the weekends," Surina said.

Betina's eyes welled up with tears, and her pale lips quivered. "I wish we hadn't come on this dangerous flight. At least, we were safe on Earth. I miss my kids so much. We had a thriving family business, The Lake District Water Bus Company, on Earth, which we left to our son and daughter. Our youngest son had cancer as a teenager. He was such a talented lad and died so young."

Bob frowned and stroked his wiry beard. "Surina, I wished we had talked with you on Earth while our youngest son was sick. A cancer specialist lived opposite us all that time, and we never even saw you once!"

Surina wondered why people like herself had been invisible on Earth. Why had it taken a journey to the outer reaches of the solar system among the trans-Neptunian objects for them to acknowledge one another for the first time? Perhaps, the merciless gas giants and comets in the rarefied atmosphere of space forced them to recognize their common humanity rather than only their perceived differences.

In the meantime, a much-relieved Chief Steward Pars circulated among the passengers, making sure to talk to each of them in turn. He soon caught up with Surina.

"We overcame this hurdle, but there are many more to go," Surina said in a weary voice. "The Oort cloud comets are ahead. I pray there isn't another collision."

Pars tried to allay her concerns. "We seldom encounter incidences like the comet collision. In fact, this is only the second such occurrence in my thirty years of space travel, but errant comets with unpredictable orbits can throw a monkey wrench into our best-laid plans. I must say I'm looking forward to my holiday on Gnaritus! In fact, the entire crew will have a well-deserved two-week vacation on Gnaritus before we embark on another voyage across the galaxy."

Several other members of the crew also joined the party, including Captain Spero. Once again, the space tourists were absent from the festivities. The passengers raised their glasses scores of times to toast Captain Spero and the pilots. Meanwhile, Surina met Chief Engineer Manus at the buffet table that was resplendent with a cornucopia of tasty finger foods. His battle fatigues suited his beefy build. Freckles peppered his square-jawed face, and he had a crown of flaming red hair in a precision crew cut under a green beret.

With an effusive smile, Manus told Surina about the *guardians* of ship: the nanobots. "Invention of the nanobots a hundred and fifty years ago made space travel possible. Nanobots work together in harmony to build molecule by molecule and repair the starship's shell, engines, and internal wiring. We can squeak through these treacherous comet belts only because the nanobots configure minute positional changes in the ship's bearings. Despite being the smallest members of the crew at one billionth of a meter in size, they are integral to the safety of the ship and are responsible for saving countless lives. These tiny things are true giants!"

Surina turned her gaze to the jamboree that overflowed with effervescent energy and brio, like a newly opened bottle of champagne. However, she realized they had made an inadvertent faux pas in not toasting the nanobots as well. The littlest things can have profound ramifications, and, in reality, nothing was small. For example, she remembered from her biology class that the microscopic plankton in the Earth's oceans produces half of the oxygen in the atmosphere, without which other life would cease to exist. Even a butterfly flapping its wings in Brazil could set off a chain of events leading to even larger scale cataclysms, such as a hurricane in China, on the other side of the world. In fact, everyone had a place and an integral role to play in the scheme of things.

12

The Oort Cloud

FOR MOST OF the next day, the passengers prepared themselves for the four-day jaunt through the Oort cloud. To make matters worse, they woke up late as the party had lasted until one o'clock in the morning.

Chief Steward Pars rushed through an abbreviated lecture that afternoon. "Ladies and gentlemen, once we cross the Oort cloud, we'll escape the sun's sphere of influence, or the heliopause, and enter interstellar space. The Oort cloud is larger than the Kuiper Belt, stretching five thousand to a hundred thousand astronomical units or five thousand to a hundred thousand times Earth's distance from the sun. Trillions of long-period comets with solar orbits of more than two hundred years originate in the Oort cloud. In fact, some comets orbit the sun once every thirty million Earth years.

"It will take four days to navigate through this vast Oort cloud depending, of course, on our progress. The safety precautions are similar to those on our journey through the Kuiper Belt. Please remain in the main cabin with seat belts on at all times. You will also dine here in the main cabin and no longer in the dining compartment. If you need to walk around or go to the bathroom, a steward will accompany you for your safety. Instead of showering, you will find cleaning scepters in your storage cabinets. We hope we can make you as comfortable as possible during the next phase of our voyage across the Milky Way. Further lectures will resume once we reach interstellar space."

He then hurried out of the main cabin to join the flurry of activity on the upper deck. Chief Engineer Manus tinkered with the force field so as to bolster it against any other potential collision with the space detritus. In the hope of avoiding an errant comet, Captain Spero plotted computer simulations of every conceivable flight path through the Oort cloud to account for any contingency.

Meanwhile, Philip and Anne Jones-May, the space tourists, had cloistered themselves in a spacious luxury suite where their personal steward, Russell, catered to them. Russell attended to the space tourists because he was the most experienced steward after Pars, with some twenty years of interstellar flight under his belt. Even though he had grizzled sideburns, his unlined face appeared youthful for his age of forty-eight years. Both Philip and Anne had a bland, pasty appearance as if they did not get much sun exposure. Each was tall and slender, with flaxen hair. Their overall fainéant demeanor reeked with a sense of entitlement, which came from a lifetime of being coddled and cosseted.

Today, Philip thought with pride how he had landed a job with the Rochester Manninghouse Corporation after graduating from a three-month computer course in high school. He relished his meteoric rise through the ranks of the company, for he had leapfrogged into the board of trustees as the youngest member ever. Even his sainted father, the chief executive officer of the World Governing Body, John Jones-May, had said he was proud of him.

However, Philip had a sinking feeling that maybe he should not have embarked on the space voyage, for its novelty had worn off for him after seeing Mars. After prancing about the commodious cabin like a coxcomb, he peeked through the porthole at the monotonous scenery, in which he saw no redeeming features. Overcome with weariness, he collapsed on a lounge chair. He thought he had never heard of anything so preposterous as when Russell proclaimed that all humanity was one. After all, he could not help but notice the disparity between the gauche passengers onboard and his family, which mingled only with globe-trotting gadabouts and glitterati.

What, then, had been his motivation in convincing his wife to take so daring a flight into fantasy? Well, he wanted to join the exclusive club of the handful of privileged Earth citizens, such as his parents, who had made the round trip to Gnaritus. In fact, high-society space tourists returning with adventurous tales about the interstellar expedition were always the center of attention on the wealthy sybarite party circuit. However, this rationale for embarking on the voyage did not sustain him through the difficult passage. At the start of the voyage, the tediousness of the trip had irked him, but now it crippled him with homesickness for Earth. He itched to indulge his predilection for the high life.

As Russell reviewed the safety procedures for the chancy trek across the Oort cloud, Philip rolled his eyes while Anne yawned. Their lassitude soon turned to horror when Russell showed them the cleaning scepter.

"The cleaning scepter clears away germs and dead skin cells from the body by using a short burst of ultraviolet light that is harmless," Russell said. "Keep it at least two centimeters away from the skin surface, and you can use it while clothed. The cleaning scepter has helped make our space flights easier, and the crew even prefers this to a traditional shower. Would you like to try it, Mr. and Mrs. Jones-May, or do you have any other questions?"

"I think we understand the mechanics," Philip replied with nonchalance, wrinkling his nose and dismissing the steward with a wave of his hand. "We'll just rest for now."

Russell tried to cheer them up. "Sir, have you been on the observation deck? It gives a magnificent, three hundred and sixty degree panoramic view of space. You can also meet some of the other passengers there, such as the two violinists who often give spectacular concerts! It's such a merry, lively place."

"We're far too busy now with more pressing concerns," Anne said in her plummy voice. "We haven't even recuperated from the Kuiper Belt, and now we need to brace ourselves for another onslaught in the Oort cloud! It seems as if we're playing Russian roulette by even going there."

Sensing nothing would enliven the aggrieved couple or ease their doldrums, Russell left. He thought it was a moot point. He knew these splenetic, shiftless space tourists would never deign to consider joining the other passengers on the observation deck. In fact, they had demanded to have all their meals in their cabin after complaining about the noisy passengers in the dining compartment on the lower deck. Of course, he had seen this same reaction among many other pampered space tourists throughout his career. In spite of boarding the starship with bravado, they became despondent and restive soon afterward. Even their sojourn in Gnaritus failed to lift their spirits despite the warm reception given to them. They rallied only on the journey back to Earth. In contrast, the passengers on the deck below impressed him because they became even more upbeat and optimistic as the voyage progressed.

In her sleeping compartment on the lower deck, Surina followed Pars's instructions to the letter and locked any loose items safely in the table drawers. Then, she squirreled away extra snacks in her storage cabinet in the main cabin. After updating Mercy, Heidi, and the Lofgrens about the comet fields, she joined the other passengers on the observation deck. The murky haze of the Oort cloud loomed in the distance. The sun was only the size of a pinhead now, thirteen and half billion kilometers away.

As they approached the reddish dwarf planet Sedna, Alfonso shared some facts and figures from an online encyclopedia. "Sedna received its name from a mythological Inuit goddess who protects all the sea creatures in the Arctic Ocean. Although once a mortal, Sedna became immortal after she drowned in the sea. In contrast with the spherical orbits of the eight planets in the solar system, it has a unique elliptical orbit with an orbital period of about once every eleven thousand years. Needless to say, this frozen dwarf planet has a surface temperature of minus two hundred and forty degrees Celsius. Although Sedna doesn't benefit much from the warmth of sunlight, it remains unable to escape from the grip of the sun's gravitational field. Wow, what a view!"

While the *Odyssey* sailed past Sedna's glacial world, Gabriel and Rafaela played one of their original celestial compositions. As usual, the beehive of activity on the observation deck came to a halt at the sound of the music. Even the rambunctious Ellison children paused to enjoy the lilting melody. For Surina, the multidimensional violin concerto throbbed with hope for it captured all the grandeur, opulence, and mystery of the polymorphous universe. She detected the simplicity, purity, and enormous promise of the big bang's primordial force of creation throughout the soul-stirring harmony as well. The comforting, melodious sounds were promissory of the magnanimity of the universe, which had enough room for everyone. She had no doubt the music belonged in the space probes exploring the farthest reaches of the universe as a personification of the noblest creativity of humans.

Surina wondered why such gifted musicians had suffered grinding poverty and homelessness on Earth. Despite their prodigious talent, they went unnoticed on an indifferent Earth. She knew Gabriel and Rafaela's violin concerto, similar to Bach's timeless classical music, would endure for eternity in the universe. She could have listened to the music for an eon if the announcement of the Oort cloud's arrival had not broken the spell. All of a sudden, the concert wound to a halt in the middle of a stirring movement, and Gabriel and Rafaela locked up their violins while the passengers bolted to the main cabin.

An anxious Chief Steward Pars greeted the passengers as Charlie and Henry guided them to their seats. They arrived just as the *Odyssey* nosedived to avert a ferocious comet careering headlong toward them. That first near miss presaged the ensuing four days through the Oort cloud, for they had several close shaves. Only the Ellison children's chatter interrupted the somber silence in the main cabin. Many exhausted passengers decided to hibernate, but not before the stewards had cajoled them into having an evening snack. To Surina, the Oort cloud seemed more populated with comets than the Kuiper Belt. The relentless barrage of comets targeted the starship from all directions and impeded their progress. There was no end in sight.

The wide aisle made it difficult to talk without either shouting or walking over. However, walking was fraught with inherent danger due to the frequent sharp turns made by the *Odyssey* as it ducked the blows from the comets. The stewards served their meals on time in sealed packages and nonspill cups. Several passengers suffering from motion sickness needed prophylactic tablets to prevent the mal de mer induced by the *Odyssey*'s undulating movements in the choppy sea of comets. Before going to sleep for the night, Surina used the efficient cleaning scepter, which was even more refreshing than a traditional shower.

For the next four days, the strenuous journey stripped all the distractions from their lives. The inescapable blitz of comets ratcheted up the tension by adding an element of uncertainty that did not lend itself to frittering away time. The heightened sense of urgency forced Surina to live each moment to the fullest. Even the Zen-like silence of the main cabin did not bore her. She remembered how she had grasped at a multitude of things on Earth that had caused nothing but needless worry and insecurity.

She had wasted precious time by complicating everything to such a degree that it had achieved little except to blur reality even further. During the journey to Gnaritus, she had let go of all the clinging and grasping. She recollected a documentary film on nautical vessels where the lighter boats were the swiftest and reached their destinations sooner. After discarding all the unnecessary cargo that had anchored her in place, she also felt liberated. As a result, she was no longer tormented by convoluted thoughts but rather began to admire the simple laws of the universe. Although the laws of the universe applied even on Earth, she only appreciated their simplicity for the first time now.

On the fourth day through the sea of comets, the *Odyssey's* plunging turns lessened by degrees so that the stewards no longer needed to tiptoe on thin ice. Surina also had to wait for a considerable length of time before seeing another comet whiz past. Even the passengers stirred again in eager anticipation of the end of the comet field.

At last, Chief Steward Pars stood at the front of the cabin to make the long-awaited announcement. "Ladies and gentlemen, we have completed our voyage through the Oort cloud and our solar system! You can resume your regular activities. The sun is two light years away. Welcome to interstellar space, where we will travel at above the speed of light by releasing the tachyon particles."

"What are tachyons?" Stefan asked with interest.

Pars pointed to a diagrammatic cross section of the auroras at Earth's magnetic poles as he spoke. "Tachyons are subatomic particles that travel not only at the speed of light but also all the way up to infinity. The breakthrough came when we detected the tachyon particles in the northern Aurora Borealis and southern Aurora Australis. Just to clarify, the solar storms shed plasma containing many charged particles, such as electrons and protons, which collect in the north and south of the Earth's magnetic field. These charged particles in the plasma excite the gases in Earth's atmosphere, producing glowing auroras as well as tachyons in the process. The auroras originate in the thermosphere, between a hundred and six hundred kilometers above the Earth.

"We can harvest the tachyons in the auroras and store them in magnetic rings. In fact, the ejection of tachyons can provide sufficient thrust to propel spacecraft to faster than the speed of light. A one-way journey to Gnaritus uses only eight hundred grams of tachyons. Now that we are in interstellar space, we'll deploy the tachyon propulsion system. Travel at above the speed of light leads to a time warp. In other words, time will speed up. Even though it will take us about nineteen Earth days to reach Gnaritus, it will feel more like three days for us. In other words, flying at above the speed of light, the *Odyssey* will cross ten thousand light-years of space and reach Gnaritus in three days, but in that time nineteen days will have passed on Earth!"

"Oh wow!" Alfonso said. "Will the views of space be blurred at that speed?"

Pars shook his head. "Chief Engineer Manus has already turned on the tachyon propulsion system. You can check out the magnificent view from the observation deck."

As the engine went at full throttle, elation and joy spread through the main cabin like the ripples from a pebble plunging into a previously still lake. Similar to the other passengers, Surina sprinted to the observation deck to recalibrate her bearings. Unlike the tunnel view through the portholes, the observation deck furnished a sweeping panorama of space. Surina looked behind. The sun had vanished, and the comet minefield was receding as well. Ahead lay the delicate, colorful wisps of clouds in whimsical shapes, resembling creatures such as eagles with enormous wingspans, balletic swans, and even giant crabs. Some of the diaphanous nebulae glowed reddish pink in color, whereas others were garlands of silver and gold tinsel that flashed like neon lights. They stretched across the vastitude of space for many trillions of kilometers and even light-years. She remembered from

Pars's lectures that the stardust in these nebulae nurseries had the potential to form millions of new stars and planets and gave birth to all humans as well. Amazement rooted her to the spot, for she was standing before the genesis and creation of all things.

13
Black Holes and White Holes

THAT NIGHT SURINA slept once again in the blissful comfort of her sleeping berth, thankful to leave the merciless icy comet belts far behind. When she woke the next morning, the psychedelic eddies of the nebulae and the scintillating light from the massive supernovae explosions of dying stars remained visible in the distance. Her gaze lingered on a mysterious black void in the farthest reaches of the vast expanse of space that was incongruent with the kaleidoscopic display of nebulae clouds. Hoping for a better view of this anomaly, she threw on her green jumpsuit. She tucked her lucky charm, the St. Christopher pendant necklace, inside the jumpsuit. After pinning the spiral brooch, which she had purchased in Santorini, to her lapel, she dashed to the observation deck.

She joined the other habitual early birds, such as Linda Cavacecci, who knitted a crab nebula with a fluorescent blue thread. Meanwhile, Francesca painted a nebula cloud in the shape of four giant pillars by splashing whorls of glittering color in broad, vigorous brush strokes. Surina paused to marvel at the captivating composition.

"I named this *The Heavenly Pillars of Creation*," Francesca said with a gentle smile. "I love the infinite variety of colors in the universe. A monochrome universe would be bland and uninspiring."

"I can almost feel myself swimming in the fantastic primordial stardust and floating in the clouds," Surina replied in awe.

Francesca pointed to the window with her paintbrush. "Surina, take a look at the Ellison children's artwork. They have precocious talent."

Both children lay sprawled on the floor by the window and pored over a picture of a black hole amid the whirling clouds of prismatic nebulae and supernovae explosions. They were oblivious to Surina as she approached. Elizabeth filled in the center of the drawing with a black crayon while George used a rapid succession of vivid, iridescent crayons to color the swirling nebulae at the edges of the painting. Surina thought that the emptiness of the black void in the center of the painting provided a paradoxical oasis of calm amid the clamor of the nebulae and supernovae. Although she had a vague understanding of black holes, she never understood how they formed.

That afternoon, Pars gave an opportune lecture on the significance of black holes. Hoping for yet another enlightening session, the passengers listened with bated breath as he spoke. "Ladies and gentlemen, today we will explore the inner workings of black holes. Here in interstellar space, our journey should be much smoother than before. Captain Spero has charted the safest course to bypass the supernovae explosions of dying stars and the gravitational pull of black holes. If you recall the lecture from the start of our voyage, stars can run out of hydrogen atoms for nuclear fusion after several billion years. When this happens to our sun, for example, it will become a red giant, which is larger but emits less heat than before.

"In a red giant, nuclear fusion changes helium atoms to carbon, followed by carbon to oxygen and so on until iron forms. At that point, no further nuclear fusion can occur. In fact, nuclear fusion provides the energy to counterbalance the force of gravity from the mass of the star. The star collapses inward without nuclear fusion to offset the tremendous force of gravity. When the shock wave from this implosion reaches the iron core, a massive supernova explosion occurs, releasing a nebula cloud of billions of atoms, such as carbon, oxygen, nitrogen, silicon, and iron. After tens of thousands of years, part of this nebula can form another star, thereby recycling the atoms of the old star. The leftover atoms in the nebula can coalesce to form a planet as well, with the heavy iron atoms in the core and the lighter atoms such as hydrogen and oxygen, on the surface. Remember, we are also stardust.

"When a red giant explodes, it leaves behind a miniature high-density star, or a white dwarf, which emits no energy. When gigantic stars many times the size of our sun undergo supernova explosions, they also leave behind remnant cores. If a remnant core is about three times the mass of our sun, the immense force of gravity overcomes other forces, and the core collapses inward to form a black hole. In essence, a black hole is an enormous amount of mass in an infinitesimal area with an immense gravitational pull.

"The gravitational singularity in the center of a black hole is an infinitely small space that contains an infinite amount of mass. At this singularity, in particular, gravity is infinite, and space-time curves infinitely as well. Even light cannot escape from the gravitational forces of a black hole, resulting in darkness. Black holes occur throughout the galaxy. Ultra-massive black holes even exist in the centers of some gigantic galaxies that contain the masses of more than twenty billion suns. Spanning a hundred and twenty astronomical units across, the galactic-core of the Milky Way galaxy is also a supermassive black hole containing about four million solar masses. Who can tell me what an astronomical unit is?"

"It's about a hundred and fifty million kilometers, which is the distance from the Earth to the sun," Alfonso replied with a flourish.

"Yes, well done," Pars said, smiling with apparent satisfaction that the passengers were retaining the information in his lectures. "The sun is about thirty thousand light-years away from the galactic-core in the Milky Way. In a similar fashion to planets orbiting stars, our sun revolves around the galactic-core black hole every two hundred and fifty million years. Whenever a black hole's gravitational force sucks in any matter, such as the nebulae or other stars, it rips them apart into subatomic particles, forming an even larger black hole. You can now understand why we would want to make a detour around these gluttonous black holes."

"I once read about advanced extraterrestrial life living in black holes," Stefan said.

Giggles and guffaws reverberated through the cabin.

"Yes, Stefan, that's one hypothesis," replied Pars. "A theory suggests that aliens don't explore outer space because their only goal is to develop their inner space further. As a result of evolution, they are no longer restricted to the biological confines of physical bodies. Instead, they may exist in black holes outside the space-time continuum. These advanced alien civilizations are Type Three at least. Perhaps, the goal of evolution is to become infinitesimally small or to achieve a state of nothingness and become a pure collective consciousness. Alas, civilizations unable to do this may not survive in the future. The spiral symbol abounds in the ancient iconography on Earth and represents the journey from the outer spaces to our inner soul and from the individual to a collective consciousness."

Alfonso paused in his customary copious note-taking to lob another question. "Chief Steward Pars, please explain more about a Type Three civilization."

"We can determine a civilization's level of technological

advancement by how much energy it has available to use," Pars said. "A special classification categorizes these stages of evolution for hypothetical civilizations. For example, on this evolutionary scale, a Type Zero civilization can harvest some of the energy of the home planet. On the other hand, a Type One civilization can use all the energy of their home planet, which would even lead to mastery over nature, such as controlling volcanoes and earthquakes. A Type Two interstellar civilization can harness all the power of a star such that they could manipulate the orbits of planets and mine the resources of celestial bodies. A Type Three galactic civilization can reap the energy of all the stars in an entire galaxy. They can accomplish feats such as moving planets from one solar system to another and even creating stars. A Type Four universal civilization can use the power from all the galaxies in the entire universe. A Type Five multiverse civilization will have all the energy from multiple universes available at its disposal. A Type Six celestial civilization can exist outside of time and space and even create universes. Therefore, they could escape from dying universes and be immortal, much like a divinity.

"Needless to say progression on this scale would require tremendous advancements in our knowledge and understanding of the outer and inner universes. However, many mysteries remain. For example, is it conceivable to advance beyond the Type Six civilization, or is that the pinnacle? Is it possible to have the knowledge of all things, or is knowledge limitless?"

"Where are humans on this evolutionary scale?" asked a chorus of passengers.

"Humans are still Type Zero and have yet to advance to Type One," Pars replied, much to everyone's disappointment. "Yes, we are a juvenile culture. It seems our quest has just started! To achieve our full potential, we will need to shift our focus toward developing our inner space rather than continuing our emphasis on the materialistic outer world. An exponential increase in our knowledge will be necessary as well. In my opinion, we would need to temper this knowledge with our humanity and wisdom."

The lecture came to a sudden standstill. The passengers wrestled with the reality of belonging to a Type Zero civilization, for it did not augur well for them.

"What are wormholes?" Surina asked, hoping to move the stalled lecture along.

"The theory of general relativity postulates that wormholes exist in the center of black holes," Pars replied. "According to these calculations, black holes could serve as entrances to space-time conduits or wormholes with white holes as exits. The white hole will eject matter in another part of the universe or perhaps in a different universe. In other words, there could be a way out of a black hole! In fact, the big bang may be an example of such a phenomenon. Due to our limited technological resources, we are unable to detect a wormhole."

Chief Steward Pars paused to ascertain the mood in the main cabin. The sobering revelations of Earth being a Type Zero civilization had stunned most of the passengers into a reflective silence. Meanwhile, the white dwarfs, red giants, black holes, white holes, and wormholes orbited around their heads. Seeing that the passengers had had more than enough to digest for one day, Pars decided to end the lecture. Straight away, a throng of enthusiastic passengers swarmed around Pars and inundated him with questions.

Across the aisle from Surina, Gabriel was in a pensive mood. Even though he had railed against relocating to Gnaritus at first, he was thankful now not to waste his entire youth on Earth. He remembered his homeless days on the unforgiving streets of Earth. Now, in just ten days, as the distance from the Earth grew ever greater, he no longer felt uncertain or fearful. What a relief to leave the indignities and inhumanity far behind on Earth, he thought. He marveled at his renascent hope for the future, which came from a newfound understanding of his place in the universe.

Above all, he no longer yearned, like before, to belong to the society that had forsaken him. For him, Earth's tattered humanity cut a poor figure, without any real stature in the universe. He cringed as he thought of the misguided culture of grabbing and clinging to possessions and power, which resulted in the marginalization of the majority of the population to the fringes of society. Why had humanity forgotten to celebrate the value of every life, he wondered. Every life mattered since the actual goal of evolution was to achieve a collective consciousness with the contributions from not only the well-heeled, privileged few but also from everyone.

"Surina, will humanity ever find its way back to its rightful purpose?" he asked with a grimace. "The pell-mell wanderings of humans on Earth are aimless. Can humans on Earth prevail with only a simplistic goal of hoarding even more materialistic possessions for the coffers of the privileged few to the exclusion of everyone else? Instead of the here and now, we should be aiming for eternity."

"The powers that be on Earth have shaped a one-dimensional society when the universe is multidimensional," Surina replied. "I shudder to think what is happening or will happen on Earth. Why is so much valuable time wasted on useless, convoluted endeavors leading nowhere? I'm also guilty of squandering time in these dead-end pursuits. I hope the aspirations of the society on Gnaritus are more in synchrony and harmony with the forces at play in the universe."

Soon, they joined the other passengers in the dining compartment. Chief Cook Grenier had prepared yet another splendiferous feast to mark their arrival in interstellar space. As usual, Surina sat with Alfonso, Stefan, Gabriel, and Rafaela. However, they had to holler over the rollicking merriment in the dining compartment just to hear one another across the table.

Alfonso surveyed the entire room as if he was searching for someone. Then he scrunched his forehead in bewilderment. "What happened to the space tourists? They've just disappeared since the start of the journey. Maybe, they want to confine themselves to the upper deck. I know Philip Jones-May from my time at the Rochester Manninghouse Corporation."

"Where you friends with him?" Gabriel asked.

"Well, not really," Alfonso replied. "Our careers were diametrical opposites, but then he is the son of John Jones-May, the chief executive officer of the World Governing Body. Philip had a meteoric rise through the ranks and leapfrogged into the board of trustees. The company earmarked him for promotion from day one. When Philip joined the company, he worked for a few weeks in the same department as I did. Although I tried to say hello, he would just walk by with a cursory nod in my direction, so I never got to know him. Rather, I should say I know of him."

"I haven't seen any androids either, although they could be on the upper deck," Surina said.

"There are no androids onboard the *Odyssey*," Stefan said. "Since I worked in an office where the omnipresent androids eavesdropped on and recorded all the conversations, I became conditioned to being vigilant and wary twenty-four seven. I felt their absence right away after boarding the *Odyssey*. When I asked Captain Spero about it, he said there were no androids onboard out of respect for the wishes of the citizens of Gnaritus. In fact, the Gnaritonians voted against having any androids, even on the vessels landing on Gnaritus!"

"That shows exceptional foresight on their part," Alfonso said in astonishment. "Did Spero mention any reasons that led them to abolish androids on Gnaritus?"

"Gnaritonians believe androids to be the antithesis of humanity," Stefan replied.

Smiles of relief wreathed Gabriel and Rafaela's faces as they welcomed the news. Alfonso laid down his fork halfway through a delicious rhubarb pie and stared through the portholes, hoping to see Gnaritus soon. In the distance, the majestic, polychromatic nebulae and the celestial fireworks from the supernovae curled and coiled as far as the eye could see. While chewing on a melt-in-your-mouth Battenberg cake, Surina became even more intrigued by the heterodox views of the citizens of Gnaritus that bucked the conventional practices on Earth.

"Who are these courageous people of Gnaritus?" Gabriel asked, echoing all of their sentiments. "I can't wait to meet them!"

14
The Colors of the Universe

THE NEXT DAY, the *Odyssey* navigated through a dazzling array of nebulae as they left the Orion spur and entered the Perseus arm of the Milky Way galaxy. In one area, in particular, the spiral nebulae reminded Surina of Vincent Van Gogh's *The Starry Night* painting. On another occasion, an electrifying nebula cloud in the shape of a cat's neon-green eye glared at her from a distance. In fact, the serpentine arms of the nebulae stretched throughout interstellar space, providing nests to incubate baby stars and planets. Moments later, the kaleidoscope of shimmering, evanescent colors and configurations would morph into new apparitions as if the ephemeral nebulae were alive.

From the telescope on the observation deck, Surina even glimpsed distant spiral galaxies that resembled iridescent, rose-colored pinwheels and whirlpools from afar. Elsewhere, the supernovae from exploding stars coruscated like sequins in the jeweled tableau of nebulae, stars, planets, and black holes. When the *Odyssey* skirted around the edge of innumerable solar systems, Surina beheld the breathtaking sight of exoplanets of every size and hue orbiting around exotic suns. Some of the planets were globular, whereas others spun so fast around their axes that they were elliptical.

During the voyage, the observation deck had become a beehive of artistic endeavors. The avant-garde artworks were impressive and astounded Surina.

"All these paintings and photographs are spectacular," she said.

"I only discovered photography here in space," Bob Pagett said. "I love chronicling all the stages of the journey. The colors of the universe are awe-inspiring in their variety and majesty. It would be a deadly dull place with just one color. It's a shame most people on Earth will never see these photos."

"Many passengers are spellbound by the creative process, even those who have never considered themselves as artists before," Francesca said. "The endless variety of the sublime celestial images provides me with unlimited inspiration, and I'm sure to all the burgeoning painters, writers, photographers, and musicians onboard as well."

"Maybe all humans are artists, for life is art," Surina said.

"Although I knitted sweaters and baby bonnets for my grandchildren, I never set out to produce any *art* before," Linda said. "I've finished *The Colors of the Universe* and started a new *Arrival on Gnaritus* tapestry. Tomorrow, we arrive at our new home planet's ternary solar system."

Francesca's eyes lit up. "We need to celebrate our arrival. It's been a life-changing voyage for me. Due to the exponential blossoming of artistic endeavors, we could have a party with a *Journey to Gnaritus* art exhibition. Gabriel and Rafaela, your music could add some zing to the party."

Rafaela grinned. "We'll play one of our compositions about our journey from the murkiness of the foggy London night at Charing Cross Station all the way to the exhilarating clarity of the Perseus arm in the Milky Way galaxy."

"Knowing Chief Cook Grenier, he'll be only too glad to arrange a celebratory feast," Linda said. "We should be able to organize the exhibition by tomorrow."

· · ·

The next afternoon, the two passageways on the opposite sides of the observation deck leading to the dining and sleeping compartments were awash with paintings, sketches, and photographs. In the center of the observation deck, Linda displayed *The Colors of the Universe* tapestry opposite Francesca's series of paintings chronicling the voyage through the Milky Way. Surina noticed Francesca's confidence as an artist had bloomed, for her galvanizing canvases were bolder than before. The Ellison children also exhibited their vibrant crayon drawings next to Francesca's watercolors and oil paintings. Most of the artists remained beside their art pieces to answer any questions. However, the Ellison children were absent from their collection, for they were busy playing elsewhere on the observation deck. Instead, their parents showed off the mesmerizing drawings to the admiring crew and passengers.

The new forms, patterns, and ideas in the art exposition impressed Surina. The exhibit was a heart-wrenching celebration of both the outer and the inner spaces of the universe. She wondered why there were only three paintings of Earth. Was it because most of the passengers discovered their creative talents only much later in the voyage when the Earth was a fading memory? Then, she realized that at the start of the journey, their worldly cares drowned their dreams about anything beyond the Earth, so they clung to terra firma with doggedness. After the distances from the Earth had grown insuperable, they found the courage to sever the umbilical cord tying them to their former prosaic lives. Once they had freed their crushed souls from the confines and conventions of the Earth, their imaginations soared into space.

Surina squeezed through the throng congregating around

Francesca's collection to view one of the few paintings of Earth. She gazed at Francesca's rendition of their former home planet during nightfall, with a surprising dearth of lights shining on the landmasses of Europe and Britain. It looked like a musty and tired world. Even though the *Odyssey* had left Earth recently, the blighted planet seemed alien to her. In fact, she was more at home in the immaculate, liberating refinement of space yet untouched by the stain of much of human history. She no longer felt as small as she had on Earth. Instead, she seemed to be expanding and becoming almost as big as the universe!

Gabriel and Rafaela commanded a view of the entire observation deck from their positions by the window. The phantasmagoria of supernovae amid the intertwining helices of the blue, yellow, and red nebulae made an apt backdrop for their celestial violin concertos. The harmonious melody not only suffused the observation deck but also diffused outside the starship into the soundless vacuum of space, carrying the passengers on a blissful cosmic dance.

The space tourists continued their obstinate policy of avoiding the lower deck. In contrast, the members of the crew, including Captain Spero, reveled in the festivities. Chief Steward Pars paused to admire Bob Pagett's photographs of the colossal mosaic Crab Nebula for a considerable length of time before he continued meandering through the exhibition. Meanwhile, Charlie and Henry weaved through the convivial gathering with trays that were resplendent with a surfeit of tasty treats and managed to be everywhere at once. In particular, Surina enjoyed the delectable English cucumber and smoked salmon sandwiches with horseradish butter on pumpernickel bread. The savory fish fingers and chips with tartar sauce and vinegar were scrumptious as well.

"Potato samosas with tamarind chutney, Dr. Mathew?" the nimble Charlie asked.

"Thank you," Surina said. "Chief Cook Grenier is an artist!"

Surina caught up with Stefan, who contemplated Linda

Cavacecci's *The Colors of the Universe* tapestry while polishing off the decadent mixture of cream, meringue, and strawberries known as the Eton mess. *The Colors of the Universe* tapestry attracted the largest audience, perhaps because it dominated the observation deck by sheer size alone. Linda's waifish frame and pixie hair gave her the appearance of an ephemeral elf in a green jumpsuit as she flitted back and forth in front of the tapestry, answering the rapt audience's questions. Although she seemed bemused by the interest in her work, her husband, Giuseppe, swelled with pride at her accomplishments.

In the meantime, Bob Pagett snapped numerous photographs of the tapestry and other artworks to chronicle the *Journey to Gnaritus* art collection. Surina and Stefan joined Alfonso by the window, and they scoured every inch of *The Colors of the Universe* tapestry for its meaning.

"It's clearer from this distance," Alfonso said. "On close-up, the tapestry is an abstract pastiche of ethereal colors reflecting all the emotional upheavals during the journey. From a distance, you can see the big bang in the center, which unlocks a door to the primordial nebulae. Then, moving outward, another door unveils a magnificent star. From there, a portal opens to the solar system with its eight planets, including the Earth. Beyond the next entryway is the spiral Milky Way galaxy with stars, planets, supernovae, nebulae, black holes, and white dwarfs. At the edge of the tapestry, the final door shows the many galaxies in our known universe and harkens to the multiverses."

Surina thought, in many ways, their journey through the outer and inner spaces was akin to opening locked doors leading to the endless possibilities in unexpected New Worlds.

"It seems as if Linda, an unassuming accountant from Blackpool, has knitted a masterpiece while sitting in the front row during Chief Steward Pars's lectures and on the observation deck," Stefan said.

"No one can begin to guess the unfathomable protean

universes that exist within each of us," Surina said.

"Petits fours or Banbury cakes?" Henry asked.

Surina indulged in the delectable delicacies with relish. Gabriel and Rafaela's music permeated every corner of the *Odyssey* and beguiled the passengers.

All of a sudden, Captain Spero's announcement echoed overhead to rouse them from their musings. "Ladies and gentleman, we are now approaching the planet Spes on the outskirts of the space colony's solar system! We will turn the tachyon stream off."

Gabriel and Rafaela stopped playing the music in midstream and swiveled around to stare at the riveting scene. Everyone dashed to join them at the window to behold the heart-stopping view of the triple-star solar system for the first time. A vast ring system of every shade of phosphorescent blue, yellow, pink, and bronze encircled the colossal planet.

"Spes is four times larger than Jupiter, the biggest planet in the Earth's solar system," Chief Steward Pars said. "Those icy rocks in the rings reflect the sunlight to produce the vivid colors. Saturn's rings span two hundred and eighty-two thousand kilometers, whereas Spes's rings stretch five hundred and fifty thousand kilometers across. The immense size of these rings is due to the planet's relative youth of three million years in contrast to Saturn's age of four and a half billion years. Over time, the icy rocks in outer rings of Spes will coalesce to form moons, similar to the sixty-two moons of Saturn. In other words, the ring system will whittle away over the millennia, leaving only the inner bands. At present, Spes has a single moon on the periphery of the ring system. Oh, you can see the three radiant suns in the distance!"

"Is Spes visible from Gnaritus?" asked Alfonso.

Pars nodded. "Yes, you can see the rings of Spes with the naked eye. In fact, the sky above Gnaritus offers a dazzling panoply of Spes, Fiducia, Clementia, and the three suns. Spes's orbital period is twenty-five Earth years, whereas its day is twelve hours long.

However, it's improbable there is life on this icy gas giant due to the inhospitable average temperature of minus a hundred and ten degrees Celsius."

The *Odyssey* tiptoed around the titanic planet Spes to avoid becoming embroiled in the ferocious maze of icy boulders in the rings.

"We have crossed ten thousand light-years of space to the edge of the Milky Way," Pars said. "Looming ahead is the even greater intergalactic space leading to the billions of other galaxies in the universe. In the distance, you can see Andromeda, our next-door neighbor spiral galaxy. It is two and a half million light-years away and larger than the Milky Way. For example, the Andromeda galaxy is two hundred and sixty thousand light-years across, whereas the Milky Way spans a hundred thousand light-years. It contains more than a trillion stars, whereas the Milky Way has about four hundred billion stars.

"In four billion years, the Andromeda and Milky Way galaxies will merge, according to the predictions in astrophysical texts. I hope that the distances separating the stars will be great enough to avoid collisions, but most of the stars will either collide or enter into unfamiliar orbits around the brand-new galactic center of the supersized elliptical galaxy. The new cosmic address of either Earth or Gnaritus in the mega galaxy is unpredictable. In any case, the cosmic fireworks in the skies above Earth and Gnaritus will be a sight to behold and last more than a billion years!"

"I hope humans can avoid annihilation from this or other causes by advancing on the evolutionary scale," Alfonso said. "It doesn't bode well for us since we're only a Type Zero civilization now, and it would take a big leap for us to become even a Type One."

"There are many unpredictable physical threats to human existence," Pars replied in a somber tone. "Alas, if civilizations can't evolve to an infinitesimal state of nothingness as a pure collective consciousness, they may not endure in an ever-changing, transitory universe."

Surina riveted her eyes on the desolate intergalactic space, now shrinking as the Andromeda and Milky Way galaxies hurtled toward one another for a probable head-on collision in four billion years. Her giddy, jubilant mood gave way to somber reflection. She thought of how much longer she had to travel to reach her full potential. Well, at least she had embarked on her quest to the outer and inner spaces. Tomorrow, the landing on Gnaritus would mark a significant milestone for her. Above all, it would bring a fresh world of possibilities, although only a stepping-stone to yet more doors leading one day perhaps to her ultimate destination. Despite every door slamming shut on Earth forever, she still needed to rejoice for the open door welcoming her to Gnaritus!

15
The New World

ON THE UPPER deck, as on the lower deck, the elation at the prospect of landing on Gnaritus later that day was palpable. Captain Spero stood at the helm, surveying his seasoned crew with immense pride. Whenever the starship entered the tristar solar system, he always felt a sense of quiet satisfaction coupled with enormous relief. Indeed, they had steered the *Odyssey* through ten thousand light-years of space and emerged unscathed from all the perils that lay between Earth and Gnaritus. In fact, many brushes with near catastrophe had occurred during the voyage, unbeknownst to the passengers. A frenzy of activity ensued as the crew made their final preparations for the landing. The pilots checked the space weather and scoured the surface of the three suns for solar storms, especially those of the larger parent sun, Clotho. During the night, they had skirted around Spes with extreme caution to avoid entanglement in its rings of icy rocks.

From the bright cheeriness in the rest of the *Odyssey*, Russell entered into the mournful, spiritless gloom of Philip and Anne Jones-May's cabin. Onboard the *Odyssey*, only the space tourists refrained from celebrating. Instead, their melancholia deepened after learning the next starship would leave Gnaritus no sooner than two weeks. Although they had planned a month-long vacation on Gnaritus, the monotony and dreariness in the expedition had impelled them to hightail it home to Earth upon landing. That thought alone sustained them until the stark realization of living as maroons on the godforsaken exoplanet for another two weeks sent them into paroxysms of grief and anxiety.

"Why are we stranded on Gnaritus for two weeks?" Philip asked in exasperation.

"It takes two weeks to repair and restock the starship for a safe journey back to Earth," Russell replied.

Russell realized this explanation fell on deaf ears, so he tried to cheer them up. "Through the porthole, you'll see the planet Fiducia, otherwise known as the diamond-in-the-sky since crystallized carbon, or diamond, forms a third of its mass. However, Fiducia lacks sparkle because a dark graphite surface overlies the thick diamond layer. No life exists on Fiducia, for it has no water. Still, it's a magnificent diamond-in-the-sky. We'll be landing this evening in the fresh air and sunshine of Gnaritus. Have you packed, Mr. and Mrs. Jones-May?"

As if severely ill, Philip hid under a woolen blanket while he slouched on a lounge chair. His petulant wife, Anne, doted on him and ministered to his every need. He glared at Russell and spoke in a lackadaisical drawl. "We managed to pack our suitcases this morning. By the way, it was impossible to sleep last night with that awful din coming from the lower deck until the early hours of this morning. I'm so surprised that you allow such disruptive, blaring music onboard!"

Russell wheeled a trolley with towers of food to the table and served them a deluxe breakfast. "It's customary for us to have a party when the voyage nears its end, Mr. and Mrs. Jones-May. Yesterday's bash was extra special because it celebrated the artwork of all the passengers on this voyage, to the accompaniment of the original violin music from two talented musicians onboard. It's such a pity you missed the *Journey to Gnaritus* art exhibition. *The Colors of the Universe* tapestry is a masterpiece that everyone should see."

Philip yawned and glowered at Russell with dissatisfied eyes. He remained unconvinced by Russell's mawkish, sentimental account of his fellow passengers. From his frame of reference, it seemed implausible that the ragamuffin, motley scraps of humanity on the lower deck could be capable of anything relevant. After all, how could such inconsequential, ostracized people who contributed so little on Earth produce something worthwhile out of the blue?

Philip remembered his father, John Jones-May, the chief executive officer of the World Governing Body, often referring to that undesirable segment of the population as disposable misfits, wastrels, and troublemakers. The party sounded like an utter waste of his time. In fact, the entire tedious voyage offered little more than the opportunity to stare into the void. Only the thought of never having to go on another space voyage after returning to Earth consoled him in his misery. Despite having lost his appetite at the start of the journey, he turned his attention to the unpalatable food on the table and snubbed Russell.

Russell exited the cabin double-quick, thankful for a reprieve from the claustrophobic sinkhole that threatened to swallow all those who entered. All of a sudden, he decided to tell Pars at the earliest opportunity that perhaps the time had come for someone younger, like Charlie or Henry, to take over his role of serving the space tourists. He found it baffling that successive generations of callow space tourists showed such utter disdain toward both the passengers on the lower deck and the entire crew. Their perpetual complaints, histrionics, and lack of appreciation for the small blessings in life had exacted a visible toll on Russell. He wondered why they even quibbled over the food, which was always delicious. In fact, their malcontented opinions sapped every ounce of his strength. Their insouciance, slothfulness, and flippant attitudes rankled him most of all.

Once again, Russell reflected on yesterday's extraordinary party. Despite their constrained circumstances, the industrious passengers had the grit and gumption to exhibit their lyrical artwork as an ode to their faith in the promise of the future. In a fit of exasperation, Russell made a firm resolution to serve only the passengers on the lower deck in the future.

Meanwhile, the lower deck was abuzz with eager passengers packing their suitcases for collection by Charlie and Henry at noon that day. Although Surina sent daily missives to her friends on Earth via the onboard computer system, she became concerned by the lack of any replies. In spite of that, she sent Mercy, Heidi, and the Lofgrens another message reading: "Landing on Gnaritus today! Astonishing to see it has three suns. We celebrated with a party last night!"

As they left the diamond-in-the-sky Fiducia behind, Gnaritus's moon Clementia, approached. Craters pockmarked Clementia's surface and reminded Surina of Earth's moon. Clotho, the larger parent sun was in the center of the solar system around which the two smaller daughter suns orbited. Now and then, dark sunspots appeared along the equator of the suns. At periodic intervals, the *Odyssey* swerved to avoid the solar storms that leaped out into space from the suns.

That afternoon, Chief Steward Pars explained more about the significance of having a troika of suns in the solar system. "Ladies and gentlemen, welcome to our final lecture since later today we'll be landing on Gnaritus! Remember, we are back on Earth time now that Chief Engineer Manus has turned the tachyon stream off. When we used the tachyon stream to travel at above the speed of light, we were in a time warp. Although it feels as if we traveled across interstellar space in three days, on Earth nineteen days have passed. It'll be useful for you to understand more about Gnaritus's three suns. Let me begin by summarizing the background information from the beginning of this lecture series. The three suns of this solar system are stars, which contain hydrogen gases with a lesser amount of helium. Due to the intense force of gravity, the proximity of the hydrogen atoms in the centers of these suns results in their nuclei fusing to form helium atoms. This nuclear fusion releases heat and sunlight that reaches Gnaritus and the other planets in this solar system.

"Hydrogen gas on the sun's surface is in the form of plasma in general. Plasma is ionized gas. For example, the heating of solids produces liquids, and then gases, and later plasma, which is the fourth state of matter. This plasma can escape the sun's gravity to become the solar wind that blows through the solar system. In fact, ninety-nine percent of the universe is plasma!

"You can sometimes see dark sunspots on the surfaces of the suns in regions that are cooler than the surrounding areas. Solar storms also rage on the surface consisting of massive solar flares and coronal mass ejections. Solar flares occur as flashes of bright light on the sun's surface, similar to millions of hydrogen bombs detonating at once. On the other hand, coronal mass ejections result when the magnetic field fractures, hurling billions of tons of plasma into space. Then, Gnaritus's magnetic field guides the charged particles in the plasma to the polar caps, where phenomenal auroras can occur. Auroras form when the charged particles in the plasma excite the gases in the planet's upper atmosphere, causing them to glow. Green is the predominant color, but just about every shade of red, yellow, blue, and purple can occur. Since this solar system has three suns, each with occasional solar storms, the auroral glow on Gnaritus is on a much grander scale than on Earth."

"Does the plasma from these solar storms pose any danger to space travel or Gnaritus?" Alfonso asked from his usual spot in the front row, across the aisle from Linda Cavacecci, who was busy knitting her next project, *Arrival on Gnaritus.*

"Important question, Alfonso," Pars replied. "In space it's best to avoid coronal mass ejections since they can damage a starship's electronics. As we near Gnaritus, the pilots may engage in evasive maneuvers to dodge any coronal mass ejections. The solar wind poses less of a threat since this continuous stream of plasma is far weaker than the coronal mass ejections. Gnaritus has a protective magnetic field to deflect most of the ionized particles in the plasma, but it has a thin ozone layer. For these reasons, you will continue to wear your starship jumpsuits and broad-brimmed, sand-colored hats on Gnaritus due to the special ultraviolet radiation absorbers ingrained into the opaque fabric. As we enter Gnaritus's atmosphere, there could be turbulence and jarring of the spaceship. Please keep your seat belts on throughout the descent."

Chief Steward Pars glanced around the main cabin. "Well, ladies and gentlemen, that concludes the lecture series. Although we discussed many aspects of the universe, there is much more to learn. Thanks for all your excellent questions. Now, let me ask you to provide some feedback for future lectures. Thinking back on our discussions, what particular topic made the journey more understandable and the future less uncertain?"

"We are stardust!" Alfonso said.

Gabriel nodded. "It was an epiphany to learn we are made of stardust. It changed me forever. I have a sense of belonging and having a home in the universe—something I had never experienced before. I no longer feel like an outsider."

All of a sudden, wild cheering filled the main cabin as they caught their initial glimpses of Gnaritus through the portholes!

Captain Spero's euphoric voice from the overhead speaker drowned out the hurrahs. "Ladies and gentlemen, we will make final preparations for landing on Gnaritus in an hour!"

Pars suggested that they go to the observation deck for a better view. As usual, George and Elizabeth Ellison scampered ahead of everyone to arrive first. What a heart-stirring sight greeted them! About half of the planet was a turquoise ocean, and the remainder was a single golden-yellow landmass. Flecks of red and brown interlaced the golden soil. Fleecy white clouds floated across the New World. As the *Odyssey* approached closer, the white sandy dunes of the beaches along the coast came into view. Surina scanned the planet's surface in the hope of seeing the space colony, but they were still too far away. Without a doubt, Gnaritus lived up to its name as a Goldilocks planet, for it could have been the Earth but for the absence of green.

However, Surina sensed the aura surrounding Gnaritus was distinct from the Earth's. After traveling thousands of light-years across the cosmos, she had come to believe in energy fields with a consciousness interconnecting all the celestial bodies. In essence, the whole universe was a single living consciousness. Similar to the electromagnetic fields or auras around the planets, humans had auras as well. Energy fields not only surrounded but also existed within all living beings and inanimate objects on Earth. These energy fields connected humans on Earth to each other as well as to the celestial bodies throughout the universe. For that reason, the thoughts, ideas, and actions of every human being had an impact on the mosaic of the Earth's aura. Indigenous cultures knew this long ago and valued the Earth as a living consciousness. Since each person's aura contributes to the fabric of the whole, everyone and everything matters.

Surina thought it seemed paradoxical that her half-forgotten memories of the Earth came flooding back with their imminent arrival on Gnaritus. Flashbacks of the fateful meeting in the medical director's office inundated her. Jane Woodford's eviscerating comment—"There's no place for you on Earth"—echoed in her ears. In fact, all the negative thoughts and actions, such as the marginalization and abuse of large swathes of people, only diminished the Earth's aura further.

As Surina gazed in wonderment at the awe-inspiring New World, she felt its aura waxed strong in harmony with the cosmos. Gnaritus filled her with hope for the future that, sad to say, the

Earth never had. What elements in the cultural and social milieu on Gnaritus led to its expanding aura, she wondered. However, it was impossible to know without living on Gnaritus, since so little news ever reached Earth. Well, she would soon find out!

The wayworn passengers' elation in their safe arrival knew no bounds. Bob Pagett's snapshots captured all their hugs, handshakes, and euphoria for posterity. Linda and Francesca wasted no time in sketching their first impressions of Gnaritus. Meanwhile, Surina, Gabriel, Rafaela, Alfonso, and Stefan stood riveted by the view.

"There's one more obstacle left," Gabriel said. "I hope the landing is smooth. We're personae non gratae on Earth, so there's no turning back now."

"No matter," Surina replied. "At least Gnaritus has offered us a sanctuary."

"It's a breathtaking view," Alfonso said. "What a beautiful planet."

"It's the cynosure of our hopes and dreams," Stefan said.

Captain Spero's long-awaited message rang throughout the *Odyssey* on the overhead system. "Please return to your seats in the main cabin as we will begin our descent to the planet's surface in ten minutes."

They were happy to oblige and returned lickety-split to the main cabin. With heat shields up to protect the starship from igniting on entry into Gnaritus's atmosphere, the *Odyssey's* propulsion engine rumbled as it decelerated in measured increments during descent. Surina gazed out of the porthole openmouthed as the starship burst through the cloud cover, and Gnaritus came into closer view. The *Odyssey* flew with seamless fluidity over the vast turquoise ocean. When it reached the white sandy beaches, the starship's engines hiccuped and emitted a grating sound that startled Surina. She closed her eyes as the *Odyssey* bounced and rattled when it landed on a gigantic, gleaming airport runway in the middle of an inland desert. The passengers swayed back and forth in their seats as the starship screeched across the runway. After the *Odyssey* had come to a complete standstill, exultant applause broke out in the main cabin to mark the conclusion of the life-changing voyage across ten thousand light-years of space to the new frontier!

16
The Welcoming Ceremony

AN EXPECTANT SILENCE filled the main cabin. Through the porthole, Surina scoured the desert terrain, stretching far into the horizon, for any signs of the inhabitants of the New World but saw none. An enormous Gnaritus Airport sign on the gently sloping hip roof of the single-story airport terminal glinted in the sunshine. The first passengers off the starship, Philip and Anne Jones-May, were already boarding an air van waiting on the tarmac. Rather than fearing this alien world, Surina was eager to disembark as well. More than anything she hoped to learn how the populace had managed to expand the aura around the planet.

The passengers were all ears as Captain Spero's historic announcement rang throughout the cabin. "Ladies and gentlemen, welcome to Gnaritus. The *Odyssey* has landed. It is two o'clock in the afternoon local time on Tuesday, the twenty-sixth of August. The temperature is a balmy twenty-eight degrees Celsius, with rain expected later this evening. An air van is waiting to transport you to the space colony just a short distance away. In addition, we will deliver your luggage to your new homes later today. On behalf of the crew, I thank you for your extraordinary level of cooperation in understanding and adhering to our protocols on the *Odyssey*, which ensured the safety of this flight. Welcome to Gnaritus!"

Deafening cheers and two-handed whistles erupted. Some passengers even threw their hats into the air. The triumphant celebration lacked only confetti, streamers, champagne, and the tantara of trumpets! Still giddy with relief and happiness, the passengers grabbed their belongings and hastened toward the exit hatch. Captain Spero, Chief Steward Pars, and Chief Engineer Manus had stationed themselves at the exit to bid each passenger farewell.

"It was a pleasure to have you onboard, Dr. Mathew," Captain Spero said as he shook her hand with both his hands. "I hope the journey was not too turbulent for you. You'll soon find Gnaritus to be a second home for humanity!"

"Thanks for everything, Captain Spero," Surina replied in gratitude. "Even though the journey scared me in the beginning, I've understood more than I ever could have by staying on Earth!"

Captain Spero agreed, for in his experience most of the passengers soon appreciated that the limitless freedom offered by the universe more than compensated for anything forfeited on Earth. He knew his crew looked forward to dropping anchor in the tranquility of Gnaritus. Pars even wanted to relocate to Gnaritus permanently. In an ironic twist, the World Governing Body frowned upon voluntary requests for relocation and left them languishing in mountains of bureaucracy on purpose.

Putting on her hat, Surina stepped out of the *Odyssey* and paused before descending the airstairs. While a warm breeze caressed her face and tossed up her curly hair, she filled her lungs with the sweet, fresh air. The light seemed brighter than on Earth, for up above were three dazzling suns. In the east, the giant rings of Spes added delicate wisps of blue, yellow, and pink to the sky. As she squinted in the glittering light, she could discern the faint outline of Gnaritus's moon, Clementia, and the diamond in the sky, Fiducia. After she had come to the end of the airstairs, she paused again before trotting across the runway with aplomb and a spring in her step just as on Earth, owing to the similar gravity. On either side of the tarmac, the golden soil of Gnaritus clung to the skyline.

Standing in the shade of the van's three shadows was the striking figure of a tall, lean elderly man with thick pearly white shoulder-length hair. His flowing green cape fluttered in the light breeze. Seeing a native of Gnaritus for the first time astounded Surina, but she noticed only his large eyes, which glistened even brighter than the three suns of Gnaritus and blurred the other features of his face. She remembered from medical school that the eyes attained their full size at around the age of thirteen; therefore, in reality the physical dimensions of his eyes could not be larger. Perhaps the intensity of his eyes not only gave them the impression of a greater size but also obscured his other facial characteristics. As he ushered Surina into the van, his sympathetic hazel eyes seemed to smile at her with a wholehearted acceptance and graciousness that she had seldom known on Earth.

He read her name badge on her starship uniform and clasped her hand in a vigorous handshake. "Welcome to Gnaritus, Dr. Mathew! I'm Somerled Knightly, the council member of the Spatium borough. We're glad to see you! Please take a seat in the van. Our first stop will be the General Assembly Hall in the heart of the space colony for a welcoming ceremony before you settle into your new home."

Surina bounded onto the spacious van and glimpsed an empty seat beside Francesca in the back.

"Oh gosh, the light is perfect for painting," Francesca said as she moved her painter's tool bag from the seat to the floor to make more room for Surina. "It's similar to the vivid, silvery sunshine of the Mediterranean on Earth."

A partition in the front of the van separated the driver from the passengers and shielded him from view. The two curmudgeonly space tourists had enthroned themselves in the first row. Not that the distinction meant much to them for it seemed as if they were about to implode with misery. Philip and Anne regarded each new citizen of Gnaritus climbing aboard the van with antipathy. However, nothing, not even the space tourists, could douse the celebratory mood in the van.

Surina watched as the eager new settlers emerged from the *Odyssey* into the sunlit haven. Linda and Giuseppe gaped at the golden soil as they strode onto the airport runway not only without any hesitation but also with firm, assured steps. George and Elizabeth Ellison veered off the tarmac to scout out a trail across the desert terrain until carried back by their parents onto the van. As was his custom now, Bob Pagett photographed his wife, Betina, shaking hands with Somerled Knightly. Meanwhile, Gabriel and Rafaela sat down across the aisle from Surina in a shell-shocked daze.

Rafaela's voice shook with emotion as she flicked away the tears in her eyes. "I still can't believe we are light-years away from that rainy night when the hawk-eyed android security guards besieged us under the archway of Charing Cross Station in London."

From the seat in front of Surina, Stefan turned around with a grin from ear to ear. Relief filled his eyes. "Gnaritus doesn't seem as bad as I imagined. Have you noticed Somerled Knightly's eyes?"

Both Surina and Francesca nodded without knowing quite how to describe Somerled Knightly's eyes in words. As the front doors closed with all eighteen new Gnaritus citizens and two Earth citizens onboard the van, Somerled took his seat across the aisle from Philip and Anne Jones-May. Surina wondered why he cast the space tourists a look akin to pity.

Right away, the van's engine burred and whirred into life for the flight at a low altitude across the desert to the space colony. First, they circled the Gnaritus Airport, past the air terminal with its labyrinth of runways before flying north into the desert. From overhead, Surina saw dramatic swirls of red, orange, and brown soil crisscrossing the yellow ground that enlivened the arid terrain despite the absence of vegetation. However, she remembered Gnaritus was not a desert since it received more than 250 millimeters of precipitation every year. After fifteen minutes, the van climbed to a higher altitude as it floated up the side of a snow-capped mountain chain of craggy red rocks and black lava soil. From the summit, she glimpsed the sprawling space colony and its environs in the effulgent valley below. The mountain chain acted as a bulwark against the occasional fierce winds that blew in from the coast. A prodigious waterfall at the foot of the mountain fed a river flowing from the Terra borough in the south to the Spatium borough in the north. A glistening lake on the cloudless, blue horizon served as the potable water supply for the space colony.

A magnificent, stately building reminiscent of a circular Parthenon stood on the shore of the river. From the heart of the colony, five roads like spokes of a wheel divided the community into the five boroughs of Terra, Ignis, Acqua, Aeris, and Spatium. Surina recollected that these meant earth, fire, water, air, and space in Latin. Amid the desert on the outskirts of the Terra borough, the lush, leafy-green crops in a mammoth network of greenhouses were a reassuring sight.

The standard square bungalows in the suburbs soon gave way to multistory commercial buildings in the city center. The air van skimmed over the skyscrapers and glided toward the crossroads. Down below in the bustling metropolis, air cars meandered in and out of the narrow spaces between the towers while pedestrians strolled on the ground. All at once the van screeched to a halt and descended in a sheer vertical drop to land softly in the park surrounding the Parthenon-like General Assembly Hall. Music began playing as soon as the van's door opened.

"That's the 'Four Seasons, Violin Concerto Number One in E major, La Primavera' by Antonio Vivaldi," Gabriel told Surina from across the aisle. "This springtime music seems an apt choice to greet us."

Somerled Knightly alighted from the van first. Then each successive row followed him in an orderly fashion into the park to the welcoming sounds of the enchanting music of spring, awakening, and rebirth. However, the space tourists at the front remained seated, wallowing in self-pity. The sight of the two malcontents caught the driver by surprise when he emerged from behind the partition. He wore a green jumpsuit and, like Somerled Knightly, had piercing, benevolent eyes that went unnoticed by the space tourists.

"I'm leaving to go to the bus depot," he said. "Then, I'm going home for the day. Why don't you join the festivities in the park? There will be a wonderful feast to celebrate your arrival."

After much coaxing, the two recalcitrants relented. With slumped shoulders and wary gazes, Philip and Anne joined the new settlers, who sat in rows facing the lofty General Assembly Hall and the orchestra. A banner proclaiming "Welcome" bridged two of the Doric columns that encircled the building.

In front of the General Assembly Hall, Somerled Knightly stood with the four other council members, also clad in the same green jumpsuits and capes. A dramatic fountain behind the orchestra had a monumental sculpture of Gnaritus in its center. From this globe, five oscillating torrents of water spurted upward before collapsing into a circular pool of water. Behind the audience, an artificial waterfall cascaded down a miniature rocky cliff. The tranquil sounds of the fountain and waterfall melded with Vivaldi's springtime music to create a sublime harmony.

Mohawk Park, surrounding the General Assembly Hall, had numerous circuitous cobblestone footpaths and rock gardens in every color of the visible spectrum. These polychromatic rocks, from the nearby mountains, formed intricate geometric designs along the paths that converged from all directions onto the omphalos of the space colony: the General Assembly Hall. The winding Omaha River at the northern edge of the park provided a glimmering backdrop to the General Assembly Hall. In the distance, a ring of five totem poles on the shore of the river soared skyward. A crescent-shaped street formed the remaining borders of the park, beyond which lay the multistory commercial buildings.

Surina noticed the orchestra, and everyone else for that matter, wore the same green jumpsuits and hats as the new settlers but without the floor-length capes of the council members. All the male Gnaritonians had shoulder-length hair as well. Well, Alfonso and Gabriel will fit right in, she thought. When the conductor ended Vivaldi's "La Primavera" with a masterful flourish of his baton, the orchestra bowed and received a prolonged standing ovation.

Then Somerled stepped forward to address the audience. "Welcome to Gnaritus! Thank you for coming. We look forward to your invaluable contributions. Commendations also go to the masterful skills of the Gnaritus Orchestra and Maestro Muireach. Since you've had a long journey across the Milky Way, I'll keep this introduction as brief as possible! Joining me are the council members of each of the boroughs."

As Somerled introduced them, the four council members waved at the audience in an earnest manner. They appeared to be of comparable age, in their late sixties. Similar to the other Gnaritonians, their glittering eyes dimmed their other facial features. First Somerled introduced Cinead Adaire, the council member for the Ignis borough, who was a willowy, dignified woman with an elegant chignon of gunmetal hair. As she stepped back, Bruce Artair, the council member for the Terra borough came forward. He was a barrel-chested man with the physique of a marathoner and towered above the rest, even Somerled Knightly. Although Eoin Dunbar, the council member of the Aeris borough, appeared to be a wisp of a woman with a shimmering nimbus of braided silver hair, she had an imposing air. A contagious, toothy grin lit up the face of Greer Irvine, the council member of the Acqua borough, who was a vigorous woman with a steely gray pageboy hairstyle and rosy cheeks.

"We'll send the locations of your new homes to your wristwatch message system shortly," Somerled said in an orotund voice. "Air cabs at the edge of the park will ferry you to your new homes. Your neighbors will tell you more about the daily life on Gnaritus, such as where to get your supplies. First, a welcoming feast awaits us in the dining room of the General Assembly Hall. Please follow me!"

A tall, strapping youth, Neilan Trahern leaped into action from his position next to the band to guide the audience to the dining hall. Although he was handsome with lustrous, shoulder-length dark-toffee hair, he did not have quite the same piercing, large eyes as Somerled Knightly. The enthusiastic new settlers followed him in single file up the steps leading to the General Assembly Hall, whereas the space tourists skulked in the back of the line.

They ambled past the Doric columns into the cool, shaded portico and through an ornate door, which featured a spiral motif. The General Assembly Hall reminded Surina of a Parthenon that was unscathed by cataclysmic manmade wars and human nature. They entered the dining hall through the last door on the right of an endless corridor. By the far wall of the regal room, next to the kitchen, was a buffet with towers of food. Alongside the cornucopia of tasty treats, four waiters wearing white aprons over their green jumpsuit uniforms stood poised with trays. Elaborate crystal chandeliers, hanging in the four corners of the ceiling around a massive central one, seemed superfluous since natural sunshine flooded through the skylights all day long. Seven circular tables filled the dining hall. Already Gnaritonians, including the five council members, occupied seats at each of the tables to welcome the new settlers personally.

After the orchestra had reassembled on a podium in the middle of the great hall, they entertained the crowd with musical selections from Bach, Mozart, and Beethoven. As Surina joined Alfonso, Stefan, Francesca, Gabriel, Rafaela, and the Cavaceccis at a table, the group's Gnaritonian host for the evening, Davina Graeme, stood up from her chair to greet her. They felt at ease right away and gave their Gnaritonian host their undivided attention except for Francesca, who was admiring a giant mural of Gnaritus's tristar solar system decorating the wall next to the kitchen.

Davina was an imperious dame in her seventies and sported a halo of curly, snowy-white hair in a poodle cut. Similar to most of the other Gnaritonians, the abundant light from her enormous eyes clouded all her other facial features. Although Davina gave them a cordial reception and inquired about their expedition across the Milky Way, she did not dwell on their country of origin, unlike the custom on Earth. She seemed to recognize their common humanity at once, even though they came from a different planet.

Without a sound, the waiters spread out to the four corners of the room. Before the weary travelers knew it, the first course of the tantalizing feast materialized before them.

A beaming youth placed a tureen in the center of the table and ladled the soup into warm bowls for each of them. "Hello, friends, I'm Ronan. I'll be your waiter for the evening."

The delicious tarragon cream of tomato soup, crusty French bread with garlic butter, and traditional Greek salad were on par with the best London restaurants. The freshness of the ingredients and the crispness of the lettuce impressed Surina maybe because it was entirely unexpected so far away from Earth. The meal and the music revitalized her to such a degree that she felt at home already.

Ronan was fastidious without even a scintilla of obtrusiveness. He cleared away any empty plates with great efficiency, refilled their glasses, and replenished the breadbasket with warm, fresh French baguettes. He was a skinny youth wearing an infectious smile as he waltzed on the floor while carrying the trays laden with food. In fact, Surina could not recall seeing a downcast Gnaritonian anywhere. Ronan's eyes gleamed with merriment, but they did not have quite the luminosity of the council members or of Davina

Graeme for that matter.

"Here's the main course of savory roast lamb with mint jelly, crispy roasted new potatoes, and savoy cabbage with caramelized shallots," Ronan said. "The chef brined the lamb in water, salt, rosemary, and garlic before roasting. Enjoy!"

As they dived into the lavish banquet, Davina spoke about her arrival on Gnaritus. "I came twenty years ago full of trepidation. I was a widow with two adult children, who I had to leave behind on Earth. During the voyage, I soon realized how privileged I was to see even a small part of the universe with all its stars, supernovae, nebulae, and planets. I've never looked back, although I wish my children could join me here, away from the discord on Earth. Gnaritus is my home now. It's the only real home I've ever had. I live in the Terra borough that lies at the foot of the mountain chain. You'll like living here too."

Alfonso slathered another piece of the warm French bread with a generous layer of the melt-in-your-mouth creamy, garlic butter. He dunked the bread into the tomato soup. "The food is so fresh and aromatic. I hope I can afford more meals like this, but I didn't have much money in my Earth bank account to transfer here."

Davina seemed mystified for a while as she studied him with her keen eyes. "Haven't you heard that we voted to do away with a monetary system? Money has no currency here. Of course, Chief Steward Pars would not have known to tell you this in his lectures since we adopted this measure only three weeks ago. It's also a near impossibility to send messages to the Earth."

Everyone at the table stared at Davina. Alfonso's eyes lit up at this jaw-dropping revelation. Gabriel's furrowed forehead attested to his utter disbelief in the veracity of this announcement since the lack of money had defined most of his life. As former accountants on Earth whose entire livelihoods revolved around finding tax loopholes to preserve their clients' personal wealth, Linda and Giuseppe Cavacecci wondered if they had been improvident and misspent their careers.

"Yes, it was time to do away with money, for our society has undergone a transformation," Davina said. "Since money has no value here, there is no ownership of property or profits from commercial enterprises. In one of the series of community debates before this vote, a recent arrival to Gnaritus reminded us how the privileged few consolidate all the power and wealth in their hands alone on Earth. Therefore, leaving the vast majority of the population marginalized by intractable poverty. Only personal wealth defines a human being's value on Earth; however, it seems as if the worst elements of society accumulate the most money, power, and respect. Even the laws of Earth's society serve only to safeguard all the wealth and power in the hands of the plutocrats without any regard for the smallest measure of justice for anyone else.

"The insatiable desire to accumulate money fuels mindless pursuits such as avarice, corruption, thefts, crime, power grabs, inutile wars, exploitation, and injustice. Money trumps everything on Earth. In fact, the motivating force behind systems such as slavery, colonialism, and segregation was to reap bumper cash profits for the populations in the Western Hemisphere of the Earth. These systems still pervade Earth's society today, although in more covert forms. They spend so much time in pointless, convoluted schemes to preserve their personal wealth that they neglect the real meaning of life and happiness. The great desideratum on Earth is money. Instead of the model of scarcity that pervades the thinking of Earth's society, we operate on the principles of abundance here on Gnaritus. We avoid shortages because everything is for the common good. We can meet everyone's needs. We leave no one behind."

"Does anyone here work?" Stefan stammered in amazement. "What if someone needs a plumber? Who keeps the grocery store shelves stocked, so we can pick up our food? I don't understand! Does anyone have a reason to get out of bed in the morning as gratuitous volunteers?"

Davina regarded him with some amusement since most new arrivals asked the same questions. "Money is an impediment to true industry and happiness, Stefan. Without money motivating our actions and thoughts, we are free to pursue our genuine interests. Some choose to be plumbers or farmers, whereas others are teachers or librarians. For example, I'm one of the newscasters of the *Gnaritus News* on television. Since there is no hierarchy here, no role is more or less important than another. Everyone works in some capacity and contributes happily to the smooth functioning of the day-to-day activities of the space colony. Although there are no formal requirements to perform a particular role, everyone gravitates toward their niche in the end. Everyone on Gnaritus has an important part to play.

"Although the motivation of working for money is no longer present, we have pride in doing our jobs well because that is the ultimate reward. Since there is no pursuit of money or materialistic possessions, there is no crime or corruption either. Instead, our quest is to seek knowledge. In fact, Gnaritus University runs seven days a week to accommodate the high volume of students of all ages. Individuals with professional degrees from Earth also study a diverse array of subjects to expand their horizons. Thus, we have more reasons than ever before to get out of bed in the morning since our quest is to gain the knowledge of all things!"

Davina emphasized each word of *the knowledge of all things*. Surina wondered how it could be possible to have the knowledge of all things. Where would you even start or end? By that time, Ronan had brought them a sumptuous raspberry and blueberry sherry trifle: a dainty confection of heavenly flavors.

"Why is everyone on Gnaritus wearing these green jumpsuits?" Alfonso asked in between bites of the luscious dessert. "Is it to cut down on expense?"

"Our ozone layer is thinner than on Earth, so we need special clothing to protect us from the ultraviolet radiation from our three suns," Davina said. "These loose-fitting jumpsuits, with high collars and double yokes, are a necessity since they provide more efficient total body protection from ultraviolet radiation than other styles of clothing. In fact, the opaque fabric with built-in chemicals absorbs the ultraviolet radiation from our three suns. Green became the most popular color because the early settlers missed the grassy-green hues of the trees and plants on Earth. Now, some hundred years later, we continue to wear green, not seeing a good reason to change. Appearance and fashion are just not a priority here."

The attire was so comfortable and functional that Surina did not mind wearing the green jumpsuits at all. When Alfonso asked Ronan for more of the delicious trifle, everyone around the table decided to have second helpings too.

Ronan laid the tea tray before them. "Tea anyone? I have Scottish breakfast, English breakfast, Earl Grey, and rooibos teas."

While the velvety rooibos tea steeped, Surina noticed the two space tourists at the end of the dining hall, sitting with David, Mary, George, and Elizabeth Ellison. Philip and Anne rebuffed Eoin Dunbar, the council member of the Aeris borough, who then turned her entire attention to the Ellison family. The children, who usually spent most of their mealtime playing, listened instead with interest to Eoin Dunbar, as did their parents. Meanwhile, Philip and Anne played with their food and even turned over the lettuce leaves for closer inspection since they were squeamish about eating anything from Gnaritus. Well, it's their loss because the food is fantastic, thought Surina.

The orchestra stopped playing when Somerled Knightly arose from his table in the center of the room and raised his champagne glass into the air. "Ladies and gentlemen, to new beginnings!"

The elated passengers cheered as they clinked their glasses together. "To new beginnings!"

The music, sincere laughter, and spirited conversations started up again. Surina pinched herself to make sure that she was not dreaming of receiving such an exuberant welcome to the New World. On Earth, she believed she had lost everything, but here she was celebrating a propitious new beginning. Gnaritus had steamed light-years ahead of Earth and no longer even resembled the mother planet. To begin with, they eschewed the worship of money. Without the lust for lucre, could there *really* be no corruption or treachery on Gnaritus? The dreams of utopian societies without a monetary system also existed on Earth but were handicapped by human nature. Instead, through the millennia, time and time again, the same history kept repeating itself on Earth, as Liam Lofgren always said.

At the birth of the space colony, the diaspora was adrift and alone at the edge of the Milky Way galaxy after being cast off by a broken world on Earth. Surina wondered if the pioneers had learned the many hard lessons of Earth's history and vowed never to repeat those mistakes on Gnaritus. Or had they understood the imperative to unite rather than to bicker about petty ethnic or cultural differences so as to flourish on their new planet? Had they shifted gears from the blind pursuit of money to the goal of attaining a collective consciousness in the hope of giving *Homo sapiens* a fighting chance to survive and thrive in the universe for eternity?

17

Huron Square

THE UNEXPECTED WELCOMING feast was a far cry from the send-off on Earth. Some four hours later at eight o'clock in the evening as the frabjous festivities ended, the wristwatch messaging system alerted the newcomers of their home addresses. As they scurried to search a map to orient themselves, they learned with interest how the founding pioneers had started the tradition of naming all the streets after the Earth's flora. Surina was overjoyed to learn her new home at number eight Juniper Tree Lane was only a five-minute walk to the hospital, close to the city center in the Spatium borough. Even more reassurance came in knowing her good friends, Gabriel and Rafaela, were her neighbors.

The new settlers followed Neilan Trahern out of the General Assembly Hall into the park, where the gentle sunshine from one of the smaller suns greeted them despite the lateness of the hour. Marching in single file, they charted a course along one of the many anfractuous footpaths to the edge of the park, where the air cabs waited in a row along the curb. Unlike the custom on Earth, the taxi drivers did not jostle for customers, instead choosing to proceed in an orderly fashion. Soon, the cabs fanned out across the space colony, carrying the new settlers to their homes.

Surina, Gabriel, and Rafaela decided to share an air cab since they lived on the same square. Their driver, Norval Gilmer, a gangling youth with an effusive smile and raven hair, welcomed them. His immense, vivid eyes offered layers of understanding that seemed unusual for such a young person. Soon they were flying away from Mohawk Park, over the glistening Omaha River to the Spatium borough in the northern part of the space colony.

"I'm grateful to have a house to live in," Rafaela said. "It's a relief not to have to sleep under bleak bridges or in derelict, dilapidated buildings! In London, we had to move to a new place every day to escape from the android security guards. Somehow no blanket could ever keep out the dampness of the rainy season in London, which seemed to last all year round. The city council even placed steel spikes under the bridges and around the buildings to ward us off, which only added to our misery by restricting our options in finding a place to rest.

"The sole bright spot in our day came when we received our daily hot meal from the altruistic local Sikh temple. The Sikh faith's founding member, Guru Nanak, started the tradition of serving the *langar*: a daily meal to the whole community of donated food. In this way, Guru Nanak championed the principle of equality by bringing together people from all faiths and social classes to share a meal together. In fact, most of our homeless friends benefited from the generosity of the Sikh temples. The healthy Punjabi cuisine of curried lentil *dahls* with either rice or unleavened flatbread *chapatis* tasted like the food of the gods and filled us up like magic until the next day. The Sikh temple kept us going, or we would have starved to death. Our other saving grace was that we had each other, but countless of our friends suffered alone, bereft of hope and loathed by society."

Gabriel put his arms around Rafaela and tried to sound

optimistic. "Yes, that's true. The long queues at the Sikh temple wrapped around the street corner, but the Punjabi food was well worth the wait. We have to remember what Somerled Knightly said about starting afresh on Gnaritus. We have a new beginning here."

As Surina's eyes moistened, she understood how the ghosts of their impoverished and dispossessed past lived on in the haunting threads of their musical compositions.

When the air cab reached a cruising speed, Norval spoke, trying to buoy them up. "I couldn't help overhearing. I have nothing to compare Gnaritus with since I was born here, but most settlers say nothing here is the same as on Earth. For example, the founding pioneers chose the name of the Omaha River because it means 'people who go against the current' in the Native American dialect. I think you'll like it here a lot more."

As the cab flew at a low altitude, Surina noticed that numerous squares for public gatherings and recreation dotted the residential area of the Spatium borough. For instance, her house on Juniper Tree Lane was on Huron Square. When the air cab alighted on Silver Birch Street on the other side of Huron Square, the single-story homes came into closer view. Sleek, minimalist lines and large one-way windows characterized each home. Before disembarking, Surina tried to pay the fare.

"There's no need for that here on Gnaritus," Norval said, grinning.

She chuckled as she put her Earth money back into her purse. "Just a force of habit, I guess."

Norval sprang out of the air cab and led them to the middle of Huron Square, where the residents had gathered under a festive canopy of multicolored pennant streamers. A simple fountain with a single jettison of water falling into a rectangular pool dominated the center of the square. Benches lined the footpaths at strategic vantage points to allow the residents of the square a chance to admire the lava-rock sculptures of the Earth's flora and fauna from the best angles. In fact, Gnaritonian artists had created lifelike sculptures of rose bushes, sunflowers, daffodils, bluebells, snowdrops, ferns, squirrels, rabbits, and even a row of ducklings following their mother. On one side of the fountain stood an octagonal gazebo containing eight chessboard tables and a communal computer with a communication link to Earth. On the other side of the fountain, jolly children frolicked in a playground abounding with multicolored swings, a merry-go-round, a seesaw, and a giant sandbox.

The weary travelers entered a cheery red and white striped party tent, where a table was resplendent with a heartwarming assortment of dainty petits fours and macaroons. A man in his late eighties stood up from the table. Since one leg was shorter, he wore orthotic shoes and limped toward them with a cane. A spinal curvature curbed his height even more. He had the unmistakable air of a Gnaritonian, with a leonine mane of wiry white hair and huge, incandescent eyes that shrouded his other facial features. Moreover, his sprightly energy gave him the impression of relishing each second of being alive with every fiber in his body.

"Welcome to Gnaritus," he said in a mellow, agreeable voice. "I'm Gowan Carney."

"I'd like to introduce Gabriel and Rafaela Higgins as well as Surina Mathew," Norval said.

"Surina, I'm your next-door neighbor," Gowan said. "I'll show you your house later."

A graceful woman, who had blue-gray hair in a precision wedge cut, offered them a tray of refreshments. She appeared to be in her seventies. Similar to many other Gnaritonians, her immense, incandescent eyes blinded one to the rest of her facial features. "Welcome. I'm Berenice Ainsley. Would you like some petits fours or macaroons?"

Surina helped herself to the delectable treats. Each of the residents of Huron Square greeted the newcomers with goodwill and generosity. Since the scale of the welcoming reception seemed appropriate for only very important people, the newcomers wondered if it was all a mistake. However, *they* were indeed the reason for the celebration. Of course, the party attire was still the simple green jumpsuits and broad-brimmed, sand-colored hats that were essential on the planet. The fête exuded genuine warmth without any of the artifice or pretentious airs of the parties that Surina usually attended. She remembered feeling awkward at most social gatherings, for the inevitable questions about her country of birth, occupation, and years of education peppered the persiflage. In contrast, today she felt at ease talking with her new neighbors.

The residents of the square hailed from every country on Earth, and their faces were every shade of brown, black, olive, white, and yellow. However, the country of her birth, occupation, or socioeconomic status seemed of little interest to the Gnaritonians, for they did not press her on these issues. They had accepted her right away just as she was. Even though she had just arrived in the New World a few hours ago, she did not feel like a stranger. In other words, it had taken a journey of ten thousand light-years to another planet for humans of diverse backgrounds to recognize their common humanity without the necessity for a lengthy explanation or analysis.

Once again Surina's thoughts returned to that ominous day in the medical director's office when Jane Woodford had asserted that there was no place for her on Earth. Without a doubt, the common theme of fitting in pervaded all aspects of life on Earth. What, then, did fitting in mean? For the most part, the emphasis on fitting in was nothing more than a method of exclusion. Wouldn't the creator of the universe have designed all human beings to fit in on their home planet, Earth?

She wondered why her memories of Earth popped up again on the glorious, auspicious day of her arrival on Gnaritus. Maybe the stark physical contrast between the two planets underscored the differences in their philosophical approaches to living life. In general, the lush vegetation on Earth imparted a far greater physical beauty than the desert terrain of Gnaritus ever could. However, the magnanimous spirit of the Gnaritonians put the merciless society on Earth to shame. The heart and the mind were in a state of equilibrium on Gnaritus, whereas the mind had raced ahead and abandoned the heart on the wayside on Earth.

All of a sudden, fatigue overcame Surina, and she took a seat at the table in the party tent. Moments later, Gowan joined her. "Surina, your furnished house is that one on the street corner. It's in move-in condition, with all the necessities. All the buildings in the space colony meet the stringent specifications necessary to withstand the periodic high winds that can come in from the sea. You'll also find just about every item available on Earth in the shops on Mohave Square. They delivered your two suitcases and seven boxes from the airport this afternoon. Don't worry, none of your luggage got lost in space! You can even walk to work since the hospital is only a block away on Cypress Tree Lane."

"Who lived there before?" Surina asked, unable to contain her curiosity. "How are these house assignments made?"

"It was a delightful couple," he replied with a wistful smile. "I think they were a hundred and fifty years of age when they died just within a few days of each other. The transfer of houses occurs following events such as marriage or death."

"I can't even imagine being a hundred and fifty years old!" Surina said. "How is that even possible?"

"It's not that unusual," Gowan said. "When I was last on Earth, bowhead whales in the Arctic lived up to two hundred years. There must also have been considerable advances in human longevity over the years on Earth."

"Bowhead whales became extinct when the sea temperatures rose with climate change," Surina said. "The average life span of humans on Earth is still about eighty years, the same as in the twenty-first century. Most people succumb to cancer in the end. Some regions have a much shorter life expectancy due to the rampant wars, poverty, and infectious diseases. It's a reportable event on Earth for anyone to be over a hundred years old. Were they even ambulatory and able to perform their activities of daily living at that age? Did they have full possession of their mental faculties?"

"They were not only functional but also they kept their wits about them right until the end," Gowan said, grinning. "In fact, they were both writers who composed beautiful poems throughout their lives, even in their final days. I'm still functional, despite being a hundred and twenty-two years old! Just before I came here from France, my wife died of cancer on Earth. It was traumatic for me to leave my two children behind on Earth. I sent many messages encouraging them to get out of the strife on Earth and come to Gnaritus, but I think the messages never got through. I was so relieved when my kids joined me on Gnaritus a few years ago. They said I hadn't aged that much."

"You do look decades younger than your chronological age," she said, unable to conceal her disbelief. "Are there others here who are more than a hundred and twenty years?"

With a sweep of his arms, Gowan directed her attention to the partygoers. "Many of us are. For example, the five council members are well into their hundred and forty- something years. They are hale and hearty even in their so-called old age. Even so, a few die at much younger ages from the common ailments, like cancer and heart disease. The average life expectancy on Gnaritus is about a hundred and thirty years of age. This leap in longevity is a recent phenomenon of the past fifty years and may be attributable to the unpolluted air or the healthy, uncontaminated food from the greenhouses of the Terra borough. There is much less social and political strife here as well. All these reasons could contribute to the dramatic fall in the rates of diseases such as cancer, obesity, anxiety, and depression. No one can fathom all the reasons; however, you, as a physician recently from Earth, could bring another dimension to our understanding of this phenomenon."

"It seems impossible to predict anyone's age on Gnaritus

without them telling you first," Surina said. "Even the five council members appear to be only in their sixties."

Gowan poured himself another glass of pineapple juice and took a few sips. "Well, what difference does it make knowing someone's actual age anyhow? Let me ask you a question now. If, for whatever reason, you forgot your age, then how old would you feel?"

Surina felt timeworn, even more so than the venerable Gowan. She could not escape from the conditioned reflex of thinking that anyone over the age of relocation of sixty years was as ancient as Methuselah. In essence, only her chronological age had defined her identity in the youth-obsessed culture on Earth.

Gowan guessed her answer. "On Gnaritus our primary concern is our inner space rather than our outer shells. You will come to understand how the inner space within us expands with knowledge daily, even as our bones grow brittle, and our bodies crumble. In fact, knowledge is our fountain of youth and elixir of life. Every experience and insight adds to our understanding of the universe all around us and within us. In reality, we grow old only when we stop learning and just stagnate. I'm still studying and working at the Algonquin Beach Meditation Center. I feel as if I'm in my salad days rather than in my dotage or decrepitude."

While Gowan spoke, Surina munched on a macaroon and thought about Earth, where education was a privilege and not a right. Due to the exorbitant prices, universities were difficult to access so that many people on Earth remained uneducated. All at once, she realized that her fortuitous arrival on Gnaritus had come just in time to save her life and her sense of self-worth. Without a doubt, Gnaritus had thrown her a lifeline and rescued her from the sinkhole engulfing her on Earth.

"Gowan, did you know my parents, Ravi and Priya Mathew, when they were alive?" Surina asked.

"Not that well," Gowan replied. "I saw them on occasion at the Algonquin Beach Meditation Center. You should ask Toben and Diola Okafor, who were their good friends."

Surina smiled. "Oh, the Okafors are Mercy's parents. Mercy was one of my best friends on Earth. Do you know where my parents are buried?"

"Our custom on Gnaritus is to scatter the ashes into the wind over the ocean," Gowan replied. "We are made of stardust and will one day return to our origins in the stardust."

It was ten o'clock and long past the children's bedtime, even though daylight still flooded Huron Square. Most of the parents had to drag their offspring from the swings and merry-go-round or pull them out of the sandbox. The crowd thinned as the parents commandeered their children home despite their protestations. In due course, Gabriel and Rafaela rejoined Surina and Gowan under the party tent, bringing Norval Gilmer with them.

"I enjoy these welcoming parties," Norval said. "Gabriel and Rafaela, I'll take you on a tour of your new house at number twenty-four Silver Birch Street, just two doors from mine."

Meanwhile, Surina followed Gowan to her house on Juniper Tree Lane on the other side of Huron Square. With their departure, an eerie silence engulfed the empty square. The small rock gardens in the front of each house showcased elaborate displays of unique terra cotta boulders and multicolored gravel mulch from the mountains. The sprightly Gowan ambled up the path to the front door of the house.

As Surina stepped gingerly across the threshold, she saw that similar to the exterior, the aesthetic design of the indoor furnishings had sleek minimalist lines to create a sense of lightness and airiness. The neutral-color furniture and the open floor plans maximized functionality and durability. The light toast-colored flooring throughout the house, along with the chartreuse-yellow walls accentuated the breezy, uncluttered atmosphere. They strolled from the entryway to the spacious living room, then the kitchen and the dining area, from where French doors opened onto a veranda.

A two-tiered pond, reminiscent of terraced rice paddies, dominated the backyard oasis. Square, flat stones overhanging the edge of one level of the pond created a miniature waterfall. In fact, the terraced pond gave the tiny backyard the illusion of spaciousness. Smooth, round stepping-stones in the middle of the pond led to the gardens of the adjacent Seneca Square houses. Multicolored gravel mulch and a few rough volcanic boulders surrounded the terraced pond. No fences separated any of the homes along Juniper Tree Lane, and each backyard had an olio of distinctive water features. These included a variety of statuesque sea horse fountains with water spouting out of their mouths, disappearing fountains sprouting from colorful amphorae, or just trickles of water from ornate taps. The gravel crunched underneath Surina's feet as she explored the garden.

"Do you like your new home?" Gowan asked. "The yard is serene."

"It's just perfect," Surina replied in awe. "I'm fortunate in finding such a sublime sanctum in an unfamiliar corner of the universe! The thoughtful design of the houses and the yards allows them to function together. Despite the absence of flora or fauna, the flowing water makes the yards come alive."

As Surina searched for the lone sun now hiding behind the dark clouds, a few raindrops fell on her face, followed by a torrential downpour. Gowan made a hasty retreat, seeking shelter from the pounding rain in his house next door. The large raindrops vanished into the terraced pool, creating ringlets that rippled out on the surface. The miniature waterfall became a gushing torrent, racing down to the lower pool and erasing all the ripples in its path before flowing over the edge into the thirsty golden soil. Surina turned her face to the heavens to taste the fresh, shiny raindrops from the New World. As she took off her hat with joy, the warm rain droplets soaked into her hair and bathed her face. The merciful rain loosened the ground-in dirt that no amount of bathing could remove. Bit by bit the thick grime and blemishes from all the yesterdays washed away. Then as the rain petered out, a second sun climbed to its zenith, carrying with it a rainbow.

18

The Easter Rose Tea Shop

WHEN SURINA AWOKE on her first morning in the New World, she saw all three suns together in the sky. The splendor of the auroral light seemed as if it hailed from the primordial big bang's first untainted rays shining with so much promise. Although the house had indoor lights, she would seldom need them except on those rare occasions in the late evening when the clouds covered the lone smaller sun in the sky. However, the window shades blocking the light were a necessity for a good night's sleep. She was glad to have the day free to explore her new home before her meeting tomorrow with the medical director of Spatium Borough Hospital to discuss her new position.

The well-stocked kitchen astounded Surina, for it had everything on hand to make an excellent breakfast, except tea. She rustled up a fluffy omelet and whole-wheat toast, which she smothered with tangy marmalade jam. She ate in the living room, for she was curious to watch the *Gnaritus News* program on television. In an instant, a paper-thin screen emerged from the cabinet in the center of the living room. Davina Graeme was the newscaster; however, the camera did not capture the full luminosity of her eyes so that her facial features came into clearer view. Indeed, she had a high forehead, prominent cheekbones, a Roman nose, and thin lips. She wore the wrinkles on her craggy face with pride. Even though her average-sized eyes had droopy, hooded eyelids, they still sparkled. In contrast to most of the newscasters on Earth, she did not showboat for the cameras with a fixed, unnatural smile or a shrill, false tone. She delivered the factual elements of the news in a dignified manner without rendering her opinion at the end of each story.

It was a welcome change not to hear about raging wars, civil strife, and riots on the news. Nor were there any stories of redrawn borders, poverty indices, kidnappings, robberies, cybercrimes, murders, job layoffs, sackings, bankruptcies, company closures, or mergers. Instead the main story focused on the grand opening of a new art gallery in the Spatium borough, specializing in children's art. Next came a list of the latest courses on offer by Gnaritus University, including How to Think Outside the Box and How to Walk on the Razor's Edge Between the Stable and Unstable Universe.

When Surina learned about the opening of a brand-new meditation center on the limestone cliffs overlooking a beach, she decided to visit it at the first available opportunity. The newscast closed with images of yesterday's welcoming celebration at the General Assembly Hall for the new arrivals from the Earth. It was telling that there was a dearth of other news about Earth. Due to the remoteness of Earth, perhaps the stories from there had little resonance on Gnaritus anymore. Surina wondered whether the communal computers on the squares offered more news about Earth.

Later she decided to go to the Mohave Square shops to remedy the momentary lack of her favorite brew. When she opened her two suitcases, she realized how flimsy the fabric of her clothing from Earth was to provide any protection from the ultraviolet radiation on Gnaritus. Five green jumpsuits and an all-weather beige trench coat with a removable woolen lining were already hanging in the cupboard much to her surprise. While changing into a new green jumpsuit, she thought how easy dressing was without any decisions to make on what to wear. However, something in Gnaritus's atmosphere made her hair even curlier and harder to constrain, so she wore it loose. Before she left, she arranged her prized collection of the miniature Inuit dancing polar bear, Taj Mahal, Masai masks, giraffes, antelopes, and elephants in a curio cabinet in the sitting room. She decided to tackle the rest of the unpacking later.

Since her personal computer could access only the local Internet on Gnaritus, she went to the communal computer in the gazebo outside to apprise her friends on Earth of her safe arrival. On Huron Square, no vestiges of the party from yesterday remained after the removal of the red and white striped party tent as well as the multicolored pennant banners earlier that morning. Young mothers strolled around the square at their leisure, pushing their infants in prams. Due to the older children being in school, the playground stood deserted. A few of the residents lounged on the benches and basked in the languorous rays of the troika of suns.

In the gazebo by the fountain, Gowan played a chess duel with a graceful woman. As Surina sat down at the communal computer, she remembered meeting Berenice Ainsley at the Huron Square welcoming party yesterday.

Gowan paused in pondering his next move on the chessboard. "The access code to log in is written on the lower right of the keyboard."

"It's impossible to communicate with Earth!" Berenice said in exasperation. "When my son joined me here, I stopped even trying. He said no one on Earth even receives any messages from Gnaritus."

Surina nodded. "Yes, it's probably futile. In any case, I'll try and see what happens."

As soon as she logged in, the computer screen opened to the Earth Page, which contained links only for e-mail messages and the news. No search box existed, which meant the communal computers had only the one Earth Page. Her heart sank at finding not a single reply to all the ones she had sent to Mercy, Heidi, and the Lofgrens almost on a daily basis since the start of the voyage. Nonetheless, with unwavering determination, she told her only friends on Earth about the incredible welcoming reception on her arrival in the New World. She recounted her conversations with all the extraordinary characters on Gnaritus, who had already made her feel at home.

When she opened the link to the news, it seemed as if the events were the same as before. As usual, stories of company mergers, bumper corporate profits, and a spate of job layoffs riddled the news. The headlines blared that the Rochester Manninghouse Corporation had halved its workforce to triple its profits. As she scrolled down further to the Health Section, a picture of Stinguard leaped out from the screen. He had a supercilious expression with a toothy smirk under the headline "Virus Will Cure Cancer!" The Rochester Manninghouse Pharmaceutical Company intended to ramp up the production of the viral vector to meet the launch date in Africa in a week. The article exalted the virtues of the viral vector and praised Stinguard for his brilliance in engineering a medical marvel.

The sudden rush to distribute the viral vector ahead of the previous launch date in October perplexed Surina. She reread the article, hoping to understand why but to no avail. In particular, it worried her that limited data about any undue side effects in the trial subjects would be available due to the even shorter follow-up. Perhaps, the earlier launch had dovetailed with Stinguard's ambition to win the Nobel Prize in October of this year. The only good news was there were no plans to administer the viral vector on Gnaritus, at least not yet. After comprehending her utter powerlessness in having her voice of caution heard from ten thousand light-years away, she tried to forget the matter, although it still gnawed away at her.

Before Surina left Huron Square, Gowan gave her the directions to the main shopping thoroughfare on Mohave Square, which was only two blocks away and well within walking distance. Passing by the adjoining Seneca Square, she noted the similarity of the houses to those on Huron Square. However, a distinctive carousel with multicolored horses monopolized the children's playground on Seneca Square. Otherwise, in much the same fashion, the square had a prominent fountain in the center and a gazebo with chess tables. A menagerie of abstract, red and gray lava-rock sculptures dotted the square.

Every passerby acknowledged her by saying hello with an effusive smile. At first she assumed they had mistaken her for someone else. After realizing it was the custom, she adopted the practice as well. She remembered the little toddlers on Earth who insisted on greeting every stranger on the street, perhaps in recognition of their common humanity. She wondered what events had transpired in the ensuing years to condition these children to retreat into their shells and walk by in silence, with their eyes inverted inward, as adults.

As soon as Surina left the peaceful residential enclave, the bustling activity in Mohave Square accosted her. Grocery, hardware, clothing, hiking, and arts and crafts stores lined both sides of Mohave Square, on Cottonwood Lane and Hickory Street. A tea shop offered outdoor seating for its patrons under the shade of a blue and white striped awning. Upon entering the gargantuan Food Emporium, she saw the comforting sight of stalls full of fresh fruits and vegetables.

While the other Gnaritonians hummed around the store, Surina checked the authenticity of the produce. When she realized the produce was as edible as the natural products on Earth, she rummaged through her handbag for her shopping list. She soon stocked up on many victuals such as apples, blueberries, onions, potatoes, garlic, butter lettuce, and cauliflower. At the end of the produce section, a profusion of colorful fruit startled her. At first she believed them to be unique to Gnaritus until a cheerful, lanky grocery clerk, noticing her bewilderment, told her about the origins and healing powers of each one.

"You must have just arrived on Gnaritus," the youth said. "The greenhouses of the Terra borough harvest these rare fruits hailing from Earth due to their juicy sweetness and medicinal properties. For example, the grapelike jaboticabas from Brazil, hairy pink rambutans from Southeast Asia, and purple mangosteen fruit from Indonesia boost the immune system. The orange-colored cupuacu from the Amazon rainforest prevents heart disease while the knobby green cherimoya fruit removes toxic elements from the body."

"What about these?" she asked, pointing to small, red berries.

"That's the miracle fruit from the tropical rainforests of West Africa," he replied. "It's ever so good for stimulating the appetite."

The miracle fruit is just what patients suffering from cancer-related cachexia need to whet their appetites, she thought. The sight of the spunky Gnaritonians sampling the rare fruits emboldened her to try some rambutans. Her worries about not finding fresh produce on Gnaritus proved to be unfounded, for she would lack nothing also available on Earth.

The impressive galenical medicines section had rare Korean mint to treat headaches as well as the even rarer *Barosma betulina* from South Africa for healing kidney stones, heartburn, and fluid retention. The tea collection more than lived up to her expectations, for it included every variety imaginable. For example, the black teas included Scottish breakfast, Irish breakfast, English breakfast, black dragon pearls, golden monkey, Earl Grey, Darjeeling, Ceylon, Lapsang souchong, and Keemun. The diverse array of green, oolong, white, rooibos, and tulsi teas filled her with wonder as well. In fact, some of the brands were new to her, such as the puer-aged black tea from China. After much deliberation, she helped herself to a generous amount of some of her favorite teas, such as Scottish breakfast and rooibos.

The meats had the same appearance, texture, taste, and nutrient value as the premium cuts on Earth. However, she balked at getting any as she had yet to come to terms with the three-dimensional printing of the meat. The plethora of cooking oils on display flabbergasted her, but in the end, she selected olive oil. After lingering over the hearty bread and delectable pastries, she settled on some madeleines.

The Gnaritonians continued the custom of acknowledging one another as they roamed the aisles of the grocery store so that by the end of the shopping trip, Surina had about forty new acquaintances. After hunting for the elusive checkout stands, she decided to ask directions from an aged grocery clerk, who was restocking the lowest shelf of the cookie aisle with shortbread and biscotti.

"Have you just arrived from Earth?" the elderly soul asked, straightening up and scrutinizing Surina with his effulgent eyes. "You won't hear the jingle of cash registers since there is no need for spondulicks here on Gnaritus!"

Surina rolled her eyes in frustration. "Oh, of course. No spondulicks! No money! Why would I forget that?"

He grinned and tried to reassure her. "Don't worry. Everything is new here on Gnaritus for you. Still, it takes the majority of new citizens the most time to get used to the glaring reality that money has no value here, and there is no need to work for a paycheck. On the other hand, it's a breeze to adjust to having three suns and no nightfall. Even living in a desert and the need to wear these jumpsuits for protection from the ultraviolet radiation doesn't faze most people as much as acclimating to a money-free society. Give yourself more time to adapt!"

Taking leave of him, Surina found the exit door, where two efficient youths transferred the goods from the baskets into bags. With each customer, they asked only one question: "Did you find everything you needed?" Surina gave a resounding yes before leaving with her arms overflowing with packages. She wanted to explore the other intriguing shops on Mohave Square, but it was lunchtime, and her hands were already full.

She joined the throngs on the mazy footpaths of Mohave Square, which was resplendent with the vivid, polychromatic lava-rock sculptures of flowers. Similar to the other squares, there was a central, two-tiered fountain as well as a gazebo with chess tables and a communal computer. After crossing Hickory Street, she reached her destination, the Easter Rose Tea Shop. Hungry patrons packed the outdoor seating, so she entered the tea shop in search of an empty table. The décor inside reminded her of a rustic English farmhouse, with a vaulted ceiling and red-brick fireplace, albeit with electric logs. The haphazard arrangement of the blue and pink rose-chintz armchairs surrounding circular, oak-colored tables imparted a homey feel. The imitation bamboo floor and mint-green walls rounded out the idyllic scene.

As she sank into the embrace of an armchair by the artificial fireplace, she goggled at an elaborate display of scrumptious cakes and pastries in the middle of the bay window. Merry conversations and periodic peals of laughter filled the tea shop. The customers were of all complexions but had the unifying feature of enormous, incandescent eyes. Surina thought it was refreshing that no one had the bombastic pomposity or the scheming machinations common to Stinguard and his ilk. Nor did they seem oppressed or beset with troubles. Instead, an unburdened lightness radiated from them as if they just lived in the moment.

When the kind proprietor came to greet Surina, she recognized Justin Hargreaves right away: her parents' former solicitor and the founder of the Hargreaves and Thomas law firm on Whitcomb Street in London. He had shoulder-length, wispy white hair, in keeping with the custom on Gnaritus, and no longer even resembled his staid portrait hanging in the foyer of Hargreaves and Thomas. Even more striking was the shiny, smooth bald patch on the top of his scalp, much like the tonsure of a monk. Owing to his habit of discarding his hat outdoors, he had a russet-brown tan. His corpulent habitus and rosy, chubby cheeks came, for the most part, from the overabundance of irresistible tasty treats in the tea shop. As soon as he glimpsed Surina, his candescent eyes shone with merriment through his black horn-rimmed spectacles.

"Surina, I'm so glad to see you again!" Justin said in an avuncular manner. "How are you? My wife, Torree, our head chef, is in the kitchen, and you must meet her as well. First and foremost, may I bring you a beverage? We've just revamped the menu to include an expanded list of lunch items."

"I'm glad to see you too, Justin," Surina said. "You look well. Everything on the menu sounds delicious. It's a tough decision, but I'll have rooibos tea, roasted eggplant lasagna, and sweet potato soup with a sprinkling of chives. For dessert, the Italian cream cake on display in the bay window seems too good to resist."

Without delay, Justin disappeared through the swinging doors into the kitchen. In a trice, he brought the rooibos tea as well as some warm Italian bread with olive oil and balsamic vinegar dipping sauce. Leaving the rest of the tea shop in the care of two energetic waiters, he plopped down opposite Surina, cradling a cup of rose hibiscus tulsi tea in his hands.

"I've already had lunch, and this tea is just what I need now," he said.

"Do you know what happened to my parents?" Surina asked with some anxiety.

"Your parents were our neighbors on Seneca Square," Justin said. "We had many good times together. It seems they developed cancer only a year after arriving on Gnaritus. Your mom had multiple myeloma, and your dad had lymphoma. They died about five years ago. They wanted me to tell you never to be sad about anything, least of all them. They were happy here. They often said they were much happier here than on Earth, and they wished you could have come to Gnaritus as soon as possible. I'll send you your dad's digital photo album. He wanted me to give it to you. Did you see my son, Tristan, before you left Earth?"

"I'm glad to hear my parents were happy here," Surina said with relief. "Not knowing anything about them for so long has been difficult. It was impossible to find out anything on Earth either. Yes, I saw Tristan when I made my will. He wanted me to tell you not to worry. The law firm is doing well. Also, your younger son is a bank executive, whereas your three grandchildren will be graduating soon in law, political science, and banking management. Did you ever receive any of Tristan's messages?"

"They seem to be doing well," he said. "Funny, despite my umpteen e-mails, I haven't received any word from him for several years. Communication between Earth and Gnaritus is almost nonexistent. I should be proud my children and grandchildren are in the most influential professions on Earth such as banking, law, and political science. However, these jobs are obsolete now on Gnaritus, whereas teachers, artists, writers, and philosophers are in greater demand. Of course, we'll always need certain professions, such as doctors, computer scientists, engineers, and astronauts. If only they had received my messages telling them to go into more worthwhile occupations."

Surina agreed with many of his sentiments. As the steam from the cup of rooibos tea wafted into the air, carrying the fragrant aroma to her nose, she eyed the comfortable, cozy décor with admiration. "This is a charming tea shop, Justin. When did you decide to open it?"

"There is no personal property or profit from commercial enterprises on Gnaritus," he replied. "Nor is there any money or bartering. The laws here are few, such as registering all births and deaths. There are also laws recognizing education and healthcare as human rights. After my lengthy career as a solicitor, I concluded that as long as there is a monetary system, justice could never prevail since the antiquated laws on Earth favor those with greater personal wealth. The venal justice system functions to protect and serve the interests of the wealthy and does nothing for the poor other than oppress them. Without money to corrupt society and justice, there is little for the lawyers and politicians to do on Gnaritus. Although we ratified the money-free laws about a month ago, the debate brewed for many years. In any event, since my law firm had so few clients due to the paucity of crimes, disputes, and grievances on Gnaritus, I closed my practice about four years ago. Instead, Torree and I made a radical change in direction and indulged in our lifelong passion for fine tea and dining. Even the former courts and prisons from a hundred years ago at the founding of the colony now house more rewarding enterprises such as art galleries and libraries."

Surina had polished off the delicious eggplant lasagna in no time and was waiting for her dessert. "I'm amazed you have no politicians here. You said money corrupts justice in laws and governments. Then what type of government is there on Gnaritus after the elimination of money?"

As if arguing a case in court, he selected his words with care and modulated the tone of his silvery voice. "Each Gnaritonian over the age of sixteen years has a vote. We put everything that affects the functioning of the colony to a vote, such as where to build a new university or the rules governing landing areas for air cabs. Since everyone is equal, every vote counts. Unlike the political cul-de-sac on Earth, where the voter turnout is about twenty or thirty percent, here everyone casts their ballots. Then the five council members from each of the boroughs enact the results of the vote. However, they don't influence the vote or manipulate public opinion. Nor do they launch campaigns in favor of one side over another or engage in bunkum.

"You won't hear lengthy political harangues here. Instead, civilized debates provide a forum to voice opinions without the threat of censure. People vote according to their consciences in the end, and no single individual oversees the governing of the space colony. Everyone is part of the government, so everyone has a stake in its success. Lengthy acrimonious political campaigns, elbowing for power, or lobbying for a position are obsolete now. There are no puerile political grandees or chest-thumping demagogues here. The infrastructure and goals of our society ensure everyone benefits, not just the privileged few. The *commonwealth* is our founding principle."

His voice trailed off as a nimble waiter brought Surina an enormous slice of the Italian cream cake, which consumed her entire attention. Meanwhile, Justin Hargreaves withdrew into himself as he cogitated about his life on Earth, where he had acted on a conditioned reflex without forethought or vision. Coming to Gnaritus had increased his awareness of the profound ramifications of his thoughts and actions on the invisible threads linking all matter in the cosmos. He awoke from his trance only when his wife, Torree, patted his shoulder. She wore a tall chef's hat over her cotton candy white hair. Gravy and soup stains had splattered on her red-gingham bib apron. The rivulets of sweat glistening on her forehead from her labors in the kitchen seemed not to perturb her, for she exuded contentment and even blissfulness. Her eyes opened wide as she glimpsed Surina, and a megawatt smile lit up her face.

"I'm glad to see you after so long," she said in amazement. "How are you?"

"I'm well," Surina replied. "The food is fantastic. I love this perfect Italian cream cake!"

Torree settled into the comfort of the armchair beside Surina. Since she had never worked for a living on Earth, she had discovered her calling as a chef late in life. However, she compensated for lost time by becoming even more adventurous in creating new textures and flavors for the evolving menu. In other words, she hoped to push the limits of her creativity. Her ultimate reward was a satisfied customer who experienced the nuances of the mouth-watering, fulsome flavors, aromas, and textures. She wore a sweet smile as she heard the news about her family on Earth but later wrinkled her forehead, furrowed her eyebrows in a frown, and winced as if in pain.

"We wanted to give our children a sound foundation more than anything else," Torree said. "That other world on Earth seems so distant not only in space but also in time. In reality, we were only in our infancy on Earth and ill equipped to put our children on the proper path for a meaningful future. Instead, we steered them to the fields of banking, law, and politics, which went by the way of the dinosaurs here on Gnaritus. I fear that following those hollow careers will serve only to quell their even more vital inner development. I wish they could join us on Gnaritus as soon as possible. We sent our children so many messages to encourage them to write to the Relocation Council for a transfer to Gnaritus, but I think they never received any of them."

Justin guffawed. "Yes, the bellicose World Governing Body would need to intercept those types of messages. If the population on Earth learned how vacuous and barren their world is, there would be little reason to stay there. Then the floodgates would open with an exodus to Gnaritus."

Surina wished she had come to Gnaritus long ago to escape from the pitiless society on Earth. Would everyone on Earth want to relocate to the desert planet Gnaritus, though? She thought the scenic beauty of the Earth could never compensate for a society with such blatant disregard for the value of every life in favor of the privileged few. Even without a mass exodus, perhaps the news about the revolutionary advancements on Gnaritus could lead to the adoption of similar changes on Earth. Maybe she was too optimistic in her assessment, for the World Governing Body had anesthetized the minds of the global population and kept them in such a state of nescience that any change in society would take years to accomplish. Moreover, it would be unlikely for the hardcore ideologues in the World Governing Body to devolve their powers to the population without a showdown.

"I wish we could communicate with Earth and tell them there are more reasonable ways of living and being," Torree said. "We asked the starship crew members once if they could take a message back to our family on Earth. Imagine our shock when we learned their employment contract forbids them from discussing or dispersing any information about Gnaritus. I wish we knew a computer engineer who was willing to crack the firewall."

Surina brightened up as she saw a ray of hope. "I met a savvy, crackerjack computer scientist during the voyage here. If anyone can help us, Alfonso Diaz will! I'll ask him. I agree with you. We need to get through to Earth before it's too late."

As Torree poured herself another cup of tea, her eyes sparkled. "It would be such a godsend if this computer whiz, Alfonso, could restore communication between the two planets! A long time ago, several computer scientists tried to bypass the impregnable security on Earth's computers, but they gave up saying it was futile. It's going to take someone thinking way outside the box, like a creative artist, to succeed."

After finishing their meals, a steady stream of patrons inundated Torree with lavish praise and applauded her gastronomic skills. A beaming youth shook Torree's hand. "Felicitations on another memorable taste sensation, Mrs. Hargreaves. The food was fit for the gods themselves. It was like an ambrosial symphony playing a perfect harmony of zesty flavors."

Customers waiting in line outside soon filled the empty seats. As Surina donned her hat and gathered her belongings, the coins in her purse jingled. She had to control her compulsion to pay for the meal and tip the waiter. She decided to pack away the money from Earth as soon as she returned home. Maybe it would be better to donate the money to the Gnaritus Museum's historical oddities wing.

Justin and Torree strolled outside with Surina.

"We're so glad you came to Gnaritus," Justin said. "Thanks for bringing us news about our family on Earth."

Surina hugged them bye. "Congratulations, Justin and Torree, on your amazing tea shop. You've created a culinary Elysium! See you soon."

Then she sallied forth, parcels in hand, merging with the bevy of shoppers on Hickory Street before turning right toward Huron Square. She wondered how the punctilious Tristan Hargreaves, Esquire would cope with his parents' transformation on Gnaritus, in view of his staunch belief in rules, regulations, and laws. However, Justin's insights about the social malaise on Earth had an unusual acuity. Humans were making life hell for each other on Earth. All the unnecessary wars, power plays, servitude, indignities, hunger, strife, and misery on Earth served only to detract time from more fruitful endeavors such as attaining a collective consciousness. There had to be a way of contacting Mercy, Heidi, and the Lofgrens to let them know about Gnaritus as a way out of the nightmarish daily grind on Earth. She would need to find Alfonso as soon as possible.

19

The Totem Pole

AFTER SURINA HAD put away her groceries in her new kitchen, she searched online for Alfonso's street and electronic address. In fact, Alfonso lived with his parents only minutes away in neighboring Seneca Square, on Maple Street. He responded to her message right away, and they agreed to meet at his house the next afternoon for lunch.

Then, she pored over her dad's digital photo album that Justin Hargreaves had e-mailed. She could hardly contain her curiosity, for the album of the Gnaritus chapter of her parents' lives contained twenty years worth of photographs. As she turned the pages, tears welled up in her eyes. *Mom and Dad's smiles light up the pages*, she thought with relief. They had powder-white hair and appeared thinner than before. She noticed her Dad's fingers were gnarled and spindly, and her Mom walked with a cane. Even so, they had celebrated life with countless friends and pastimes. As the years progressed, their eyes had become even more luminescent and hopeful. Then on the last page, she read an uplifting message from her parents: "Surina, we wished you could have joined us here, away from the dissension on Earth. If you are reading this, you must be on Gnaritus now. Be happy always. If you connect to cosmic consciousness, we will also be there." Their message bolstered her spirits, but what did they mean? She was still wondering how to connect with cosmic consciousness as she puttered around the house and unpacked her seven boxes from Earth for the rest of the day.

• • •

Surina's second morning on Gnaritus dawned as both a rainy and foggy day that together added an extra layer of vigor to the cold, brisk air. Just a few hazy rays from the three suns peeped through the thick stratum of clouds that blotted out even the rings of Spes. An unearthly silence shrouded Huron Square as she left for the Spatium Borough Hospital. Due to the indelible mark left by her previous encounter with a medical director on Earth, she regarded her forthcoming meeting with the medical director of the Spatium Borough Hospital with circumspection. She passed other Gnaritonians who emerged wraithlike in their trench coats from the thick fog that blanketed the space colony. Despite the inclement weather, their good-natured salutations warmed up the chill in the air.

At Seneca Square, she turned right onto Cypress Tree Lane, along which were the gleaming buildings of the Spatium Borough Hospital. Unlike the residential areas, a central square was absent in the hospital complex, similar to the rest of the commercial district. After passing a row of air ambulances in front of a monolithic emergency room entrance, she glimpsed the five-story main hospital wing looming through the fog at the end of Cypress Tree Lane. Automatic sliding glass doors at the entrance led into the spacious hospital lobby. To her surprise, a red and brown lava-rock totem pole in a blue-tiled circular pond soared up to the glass cathedral ceiling. Its foundation was a petroglyph depicting a row of spirals. On closer inspection of the totem pole, she observed bright-green butterflies at the base, angelic white doves in the middle, and a tan giraffe with dark-chestnut spots at the top. Behind the totem pole, two corridors led to the interior of the hospital.

Surina's black clogs clacked on the faux-marble flooring as she headed to the information kiosk next to the totem pole. A timeworn man directed her to the medical director's office next to a waiting room in front of the totem pole. Only a few early birds populated the lobby at that hour. After going through another set of sliding glass doors, she checked in with a septuagenarian at the front desk for her seven o'clock appointment with Dr. Ailbeart Ross, the medical director.

His hoary, cobwebby face lit up in recognition. "Welcome to Gnaritus, Dr. Mathew! I'm Munro Barclay, the medical director's assistant. Please follow me."

Munro Barclay supported his willowy frame on a cane resembling the branch of a tree. He tottered on his scrawny legs with such precariousness that Surina thought he would topple over. Sometimes he would stretch out his hand to balance himself against the wall before he resumed wobbling down the short, narrow passageway. He stopped at an unpretentious door and knocked.

"Come in," a voice said from behind the door.

Munro led the way inside. The snug room had no space even to swing a cat due to five floor-to-ceiling bookcases, spilling over with volumes in every size and color. In a corner of the tiny closet-like room, by the light of a bay window, was a simple desk with a smooth surface and no drawers. A venerable nonagenarian in a crumpled white lab coat leafed through a stack of papers. He put down his pen and motioned Surina to the comfortable, button-tufted mahogany leather armchair on the other side of the desk. He had a glistening, brown bare scalp at the vertex of his head; however, he wore his few remaining wisps of shoulder-length, salt-and-pepper hair in a tiny ponytail. His gold-rimmed spectacles could not curb the prodigious light emanating from his massive eyes. To Surina, he resembled a bronze statue of Benjamin Franklin. He thanked Munro, who retreated into the hallway in silence.

"Welcome, Surina!" Ailbeart said in a pleasing, silvery voice. "I'm glad to see you. I hope your journey here was as amazing as mine. The adventurous voyage across the galaxy changed my life forever. For me, the apotheosis was learning we are connected to the entire universe because we are made of stardust from hundreds of stars!"

"Stardust is magical," Surina said. "The sheer beauty of the universe is breathtaking."

Ailbeart's smile widened. "I hope you're acclimating to life on Gnaritus. Mohave Square is a one-stop shopping paradise, which stocks almost every item also available on Earth. Would you like a cranberry or blueberry scone?"

Pushing aside his tablet computer and a stack of papers, he turned his full attention to the tea tray. He lifted the sunflower tea cozy off a large English Rose teapot on his desk. With as much precision as in an ancient tea ceremony, he poured the steaming, fragrant brew into dainty teacups bearing the same red and pink English Rose design. Surina helped herself to a blueberry scone with thick clotted cream. It was similar to Cornish clotted cream, although nothing could ever quite compare. After adding milk and two lumps of sugar to her tea, she gave Ailbeart her undivided attention while munching on the crumbly scone. She felt at ease in the medical director's office right away, much to her surprise.

"I enjoy meeting with all the new doctors from Earth," he said after a few swigs of tea. "The Spatium Borough Hospital is for adults over the age of eighteen years, whereas the pediatric hospital is in the Ignis borough. Both hospitals are affiliated with Gnaritus University. The adult cancer ward is on the fifth floor of this hospital. In the past fifty years, there was a precipitous decline in the incidence of most types of cancer, in particular in long-term residents. The reasons for the body healing itself from the effects of cancer-causing mutations are a mystery. Can we ascribe this to the pure salubrious air, the water free of industrial chemicals, or the fresh produce from the greenhouses of the agrarian Terra borough?

"However, the recent arrivals from Earth are still prone to this deadly disease and comprise the majority of the patients on the cancer ward. The most common malignancy in long-term residents is skin cancer, which occurs in those who forget to wear their hats. So, I dare say that you will be busy enough."

"Are there other diseases like infection on Gnaritus?" Surina asked.

"Since Gnaritus is free from pathogens, patients are not prone to external viral, bacterial, or fungal infections to any degree," Ailbeart replied. "Any pathogens from human secretions never survive more than a few minutes in the atmosphere, again due to unknown mechanisms. The leading theory is that the ultraviolet radiation in the atmosphere destroys the pathogens. Since we have much to learn about Gnaritus, there are many active research laboratories with enough space for you as well if you wish. In fact, many of our physicians engage in research, trying to push the limits of our knowledge about the subatomic biological processes, whereas others focus on studying the conventional mechanisms of the physical body. More tea, Surina?"

"Yes, please," she replied. "Subatomic biology is a new field for me."

Ailbeart performed the ritualistic ceremony again to yield yet another perfect cup of tea. Sinking back in his chair, he cradled his teacup with both hands and spoke. "Our research focus shifted over time. A hundred years ago, our investigations centered on the visible macroscopic human body existing in the physical universe. Our initial goal in the pioneering days was to colonize the universe. However, we switched to studying how we can transcend to a smaller, denser level so as to use space, time, energy, and matter with greater efficiency. If we accomplish our goal, we will be able to move outside of the space-time continuum and leave the physical universe forever. In other words, this branch of research is about space, time, energy, and matter compression. As an analogy, think of the dawn of technological development when computers filled entire rooms, and how they shrank to the nanoscale while becoming more complex."

Surina opened her eyes wide and raised her eyebrows in amazement. "Is the goal of this research for us to disappear from the physical universe?"

"Yes, that is the developmental singularity hypothesis," Ailbeart answered. "If we achieve the developmental singularity, it will allow us to exist in black holes, for example, or maybe somewhere different altogether. This is a nascent field for us with a vast chasm in our knowledge to bridge before it becomes a reality. Our library stopped subscribing to the medical journals from Earth long ago because our research efforts no longer coincide. Our foremost publication about the state of the science in the space, time, energy, and matter compression hypothesis is the *Entelechy Journal*, which could be a useful reference for you as well. Would you be interested in joining our research efforts?"

"Yes!" Surina said. "I first heard about the developmental singularity hypothesis during Chief Steward Pars's mind-boggling lectures about the forces at play in the universe. I'm impressed you're already embarking on the systematic scientific analysis of this concept."

"We have to begin somewhere and see where it leads us," he replied with a new sense of urgency. "I don't think the research is an unachievable chimera. Alas, civilizations unable to evolve to the developmental singularity will not endure in a changeable universe facing a blitz of external physical threats. I'll assign you a research lab by the time you begin so that you can join us in realizing our entelechy: the developmental singularity. Dr. Nieves MacIver will orient you to the hospital on Monday morning at eight o'clock. Here's your badge, which will act as a key fob to give you access to the computers, wards, clinics, and research labs."

Surina examined the rectangular badge, which showed her specialty of cancer and her name. Its simplicity was in stark contrast to her badge from the Earth's Greysville Quadrant Hospital, portraying her photograph, twelve-digit number, and fingerprints. When Ailbeart Ross offered her another scone, she had to decline since she felt stuffed from the hearty breakfast at home.

"There is an additional matter," he said. "The letter of introduction from your supervisor at the Greysville Quadrant Hospital on Earth, Dr. Rod Stinguard, alluded to your relentless pursuit of a faulty line of research despite all evidence to the contrary. From the tone of his writing, I believe he harbors a deep resentment toward you. As a general rule, these letters of introduction have negative things to say. I have yet to find a positive assessment. The World Governing Body blabbers on about the Earth's dwindling natural resources and age over sixty years as the reason for relocation. However, it's well known that the Earth bundles off only people who it brands as troublemakers or as misfits to Gnaritus. I'm in that category myself. I don't give much credence to these letters. In fact, I prefer having no introductory letters whatsoever.

"Here, you'll have no supervisor. There are no bosses on Gnaritus. The absence of a hierarchy empowers everyone to flourish as leaders. The emphasis on self-responsibility, self-reliance, and teamwork allows us to be even more productive than ever. Each of us sets our own pace, but we always work together to assist and help each other. The foundation of the system is trust. Everyone's voice is important. My role as the medical director is to implement the consensus opinion as voted on by the hospital staff."

"Dr. Ross, the results of my research clashed with those of Dr. Stinguard's," she said with a sinking feeling. "I did my best and harbored only good intentions."

Surina winced as she imagined all the other negative comments in the obnoxious epistle. Would Stinguard bedevil her forever? His adverse opinion of her dogged her even across the Milky Way galaxy, all the way to Gnaritus. In fact, his mean-spiritedness was reminiscent of the implacable Inspector Javert's relentless pursuit of Jean Valjean in Victor Hugo's *Les Miserables*. Then, she decided to forget the picayune matter. Why make such a foofaraw about it? After seeing the unfathomable universe on the journey to Gnaritus, she knew Stinguard's opinion of her was not the only one that counted in the grand scheme of things. Even now, in hindsight, she never had any other choice but to present the results of her experiments in their entirety, regardless of the consequences.

Ailbeart scrutinized Surina's face, and his eyes brightened as soon as he discerned she had resolved her concerns about Stinguard.

"You will like it here," he said. "My old bones sense we are on the cusp of a significant breakthrough in working toward our goal of attaining the developmental singularity. Is Earth studying the developmental singularity as well? Since the communication links with Earth are less than optimal, we lost track of events there long ago. It would still be useful to collaborate on this complicated research with as many people as possible."

"No, not to my knowledge," she replied with relief at the change of the topic away from Stinguard. "Of course, they could be conducting that research in secrecy, but I doubt it. As far as I can tell, Earth's main objective is to colonize the universe. The emphasis is on developing the outer spaces rather than the inner spaces."

All of a sudden, Munro popped his head in the door. "Your first patient has arrived at the clinic, Dr. Ross."

Ailbeart reached for his cane and strolled with Surina into the lobby, now teeming with patients and visitors. Seeing Surina's fascination with the totem pole, Ailbeart explained the symbolism of the carvings. "Our hospital's totem pole is our guardian spirit in our quest to achieve the developmental singularity. The spirals on the foundation represent our journey from the outer world to our inner spaces. The butterflies symbolize transformation and transfiguration. Those white doves are cross-world messengers, whereas the giraffe at the top of the totem pole personifies reaching for and attaining the unachievable. In other words, it evokes the concept of our entelechy or actualizing our perfect form."

"It's a magnificent guardian spirit," she said. "Thank you, Dr. Ross. It was a pleasure to meet you."

"See you Monday," he replied, grinning.

He sidestepped the pool gingerly and disappeared down a corridor leading to his clinic. Surina buzzed with enthusiasm about starting her new job on Monday, even though she would embark on this extraordinary developmental singularity research as a novitiate. Nothing could be more urgent than attaining the developmental singularity, she thought. To begin with, she would need to learn about the advances in the field by reading the *Entelechy Journal*. Another great boon was working without a supervisor! What happiness it was not to have to deal with another Stinguard trying to blindside and derail her at every opportunity. Meeting certain people can be so ruinous that the only solution is never to encounter them in the first place. Alas, even the most assiduous efforts to avoid these pernicious individuals and malign forces could fail due to their pervasiveness on Earth. However, she did not sense the same degree of malevolence and hostility on Gnaritus so that even with a supervisor perhaps the outcome would not be so calamitous.

As Surina fumbled around in her handbag for her umbrella, the dignified totem pole commanded her attention again. All at once, the enormity of the tragedy that had befallen the Native American Indians on Earth overwhelmed her: in particular, the decimation of their culture and land by the settlers from Europe. The indigenous population must also rue that inauspicious day they first encountered the migrants. History kept repeating itself on Earth, though. Even the aborigines of Australia were casualties of a stream of migrants from Europe who failed to acknowledge any element of their common humanity with the indigenous population.

Although the rain continued, the fog had lifted to reveal a dusky day as the three suns hid behind feathery clouds the color of black tar. The warm rain droplets pummeling down reminded Surina of a soothing shower. At least there were no puddles to sidestep, for the yellow soil of Gnaritus swallowed the rain whole. As soon as she returned home, the busy past few days caught up with her, and fatigue overwhelmed her. The pitter-patter of the soporific rain pelting down on the terraced pond put her to sleep in a second.

When she woke at noon, the lateness of the hour startled her, for there was barely enough time to get ready for lunch. She grabbed her trench coat and raced to Alfonso's home on Maple Street in the pouring rain. His mother opened the door. Her lush auburn hair was in an ear-length bob. She brandished a piano-key smile that reached all the way to her luminescent eyes and dimpled her cheeks. Her wholehearted smile advertised her contentment in having everything she needed.

"Welcome, Surina!" Agata Diaz said with her voice ringing out over familiar-sounding violin music in the background. "I'll take your raincoat. Pity, it's still raining cats and dogs with no end in sight. The inclement weather forced us to move the barbecue inside. Alfonso did all the cooking. He's a self-taught gourmet chef."

Then she led the way to the capacious living room, which had the minimalist décor popular on Gnaritus. Gabriel and Rafaela stood by the electric fireplace and played one of their original celestial compositions. Meanwhile, Stefan nestled on a chaise longue. Alfonso rushed in from the kitchen, wearing a blue-gingham bib apron, and greeted Surina.

After they had finished the virtuoso violin concerto, both Gabriel and Rafaela flopped down into the sleek tan sofa next to Surina. Their shared journey on the *Odyssey* had brought them together from disparate backgrounds and solidified their friendship. So, the conversation soon flowed with refreshing candor.

Gabriel bubbled with excitement. "We found jobs in the Gnaritus Orchestra! Maestro Muireach put our compositions on the program for all the welcoming ceremonies from next week onward. I never imagined that our music would follow Vivaldi's masterpiece!"

"It's not so hard to imagine," Stefan said. "Your concertos are out of this world! I decided to finish my book before looking for a job. Since there's a great deal to say about all the changes in our lives, writing is a full-time venture for me. Have you been to the hospital yet, Surina?"

"Yes, it's going to be a welcome change," she replied. "I'll be seeing patients of a unique demographic since the average lifespan is a hundred and thirty years. Somehow, the body is healing itself on Gnaritus because there's a low incidence of cancer in the long-term residents, although the newcomers are still prone to it. I'll also have some lab space to study the developmental singularity and the space, time, energy, and matter compression hypothesis."

"The *what*?" Alfonso asked.

He appeared perplexed as he laid out the dishes of spicy satay chicken skewers and fluffy, fragrant saffron basmati rice on the coffee table. Agata garnished the rice with crunchy roasted almond slivers and filled their glasses with fresh lemonade.

While they helped themselves to the delicious lunch, Surina explained the science behind the developmental singularity. "The research here focuses on transcending to a smaller, denser level so as to use space, time, energy, and matter with greater efficiency. In fact, the goal on Gnaritus is to leave the physical universe altogether. I also saw a remarkable talismanic totem pole in the hospital lobby with a giraffe on top, signifying reaching for and attaining the unachievable."

After his busy day in the kitchen, Alfonso flung himself on the sofa with exhaustion. "Have you noticed the extent of the Native American Indian iconography here?" he said. "For example, Mohave Square, Seneca Square, and Huron Square are the names of tribes. I've seen a couple of totem poles in the park by the Omaha River. In fact, Omaha means 'people who go against the current' in the Native American Indian language."

"Gnaritus espouses many of the mores and conventions of the Native American Indians," Stefan said. "The Native Americans Indians maintained no boundaries to their villages or any concept of land ownership either. They considered the Earth a living consciousness with connections binding everything together in a whole. However, Christopher Columbus's arrival in the Americas in 1492 ushered in a new era. Soon the settlers claimed ownership of the land and carved fortified boundaries, borders, and divisions in stone and blood. They severed the threads that connected people to each other and the land. The new boundaries served only to separate and isolate individuals even more. In essence, these immigrants failed to acknowledge their common humanity with the Native American Indians and thought of them as inferior. The settlers flimflammed the tribes out of their ancestral land and gutted the indigenous culture. I agree with the Native American Indian ethos that no person can own the land when it is there for everyone. This concept of doing away with land ownership is the first step in understanding the fundamental equality, interconnectedness, and shared humanity of all peoples. To put in another way, who owns the universe?"

"It's reassuring that the lionhearted pioneers on Gnaritus chose not to tread the same slippery path as the fifteenth-century New

World settlers in the Americas by pillaging and plundering this planet," Alfonso said. "We all know it led nowhere. Why would they honor the spirit of the Native American Indians and disavow the deeply entrenched, mercenary policies on Earth of land ownership, divisions, boundaries, and borders?"

"Did the people who Earth banished have a greater awareness of these types of issues to begin with?" Gabriel asked. "Perhaps their understanding of their place in the universe matured even further after all the sights they saw during the life-changing journey on the starship. I know it did for me. Only the other day, when we went shopping at the Food Emporium in Mohave Square, we bumped into our former benefactor, Garban Singh, who organized the langar at the local Sikh temple in London."

"What does langar mean?" Agata asked.

"The langar promotes the concept of equality by bringing together people from all social strata to enjoy a meal together," Gabriel replied. "In fact, the langar was our one hot meal a day on Earth. Since Garban Singh's community kitchen threw a lifeline to countless destitute people, why did they cast him out of Earth instead of allowing him to carry on his good works? It seems he posed a threat to the powers that be by setting an example of ethical behavior."

Rafaela nodded. "I agree. Maybe, the indomitable pioneers decided to conduct themselves by new standards after they saw the universe unfolding before them on the journey here. If that doesn't change you forever, then nothing will! How can anyone be the same after knowing stardust, from hundreds of stars, flows through our veins as well? Perhaps, when the Earth cast them off, they knew they couldn't afford to repeat the same mistakes of human history if they wanted to survive and flourish. By building a money-free society, they shifted the emphasis from the worship of money to the celebration of the priceless value of each human life. We are now free to actualize our full potential rather than being consumed by the senseless pursuit of money. Even more exciting is the incredible quest for the developmental singularity, the Holy Grail of evolution."

"If only we could send word to Earth about all the exciting developments on Gnaritus," Surina said. "It would offer so much hope to the innumerable marginalized and disenfranchised people on the fringes of Earth's society. The major hurdle is breaking through the fortified wall around Earth, which blue-pencils most messages from Gnaritus."

Alfonso searched the room as he deliberated whether to broach the subject of the computer code he was writing. Then, he decided to use his friends as a sounding board. "Yesterday, I went on an introductory tour of my new job at the Gnaritus Computer Firm. It used to be a subsidiary of the Rochester Manninghouse Corporation from Earth, but it's an independent company now. It handles the entire computer system here, including the communal computers with a communications link to Earth. No one at the firm is trying to find a way to get unedited messages back to Earth or even thinks it's worthwhile to try. Even though many computer engineers attempted to crack the interplanetary firewall in the beginning, they gave up after years of failure. Since nothing gets through, most of my neighbors on Seneca Square also abandoned sending messages back to Earth long ago. I want to lift this iron curtain. Although I began writing this computer program onboard the *Odyssey*, it'll be a formidable challenge to override the code censoring information between the two planets."

Agata frowned. "Will it even be a good thing to send messages back? It's best to let sleeping dogs lie. Think of the tumult and upheaval on Earth if they knew more about Gnaritus. It goes without saying that the ruling elite would not be receptive to any messages from Gnaritus. The tyrants in the World Governing Body will never relinquish their control over the edifices of Earth's society that function only to serve and nurture their interests. On the contrary, they will preserve their way of life at any cost. We are dreaming if we think the Earth will ever emulate the fundamental principles of our society on Gnaritus."

"Mom, it would be a shock to the system on Earth at first but not in the long run," Alfonso replied. "The truth prevails, even though it takes a long time. Perhaps the truth can spur changes on Earth. Without truth, there can be no justice. Dad agrees with me."

"Where's your dad?" Gabriel asked.

"He's at work at the Gnaritus Museum of Fine Arts," Alfonso said.

Stefan creased his brow in bewilderment. "Your mom is right, Alfonso. Remember what Chief Steward Pars told us about life having the right to evolve in its natural habitat, without interference from external sources? We should not meddle either."

"I think Pars was talking about humans not interfering with alien life forms," Surina said. "In contrast, we'll be helping our fellow humans!"

"Are you so sure that Gnaritonians are still comparable to the humans on Earth?" Stefan said. "I don't mean to berate the point, but nothing here is the same. To begin with, they have much bigger eyes than anyone does on Earth. These eyes just look right through you as if they're speaking to your soul. Perhaps, their eyes reflect the depth of their enormous humanity. Even the lifespan on Gnaritus is longer for unknown reasons. Could these changes be due to the common practice of meditation and mindfulness here? The one good thing about the Earth not caring about any of us is that they left Gnaritonians alone to evolve naturally in this habitat. In a similar way, we should not infringe on the natural course of human evolution on Earth."

Alfonso continued to plead his case. "The situation on Earth is dire. I think the World Governing Body wants to suppress any information about the transformation on Gnaritus from leaking out because everything on Earth would change forever, including their cushy jobs. The ruling elite fleeced the population of their dignity and damned them to the fringes. The marginalized need a helping hand out of the quagmire paralyzing them. If we don't help them, then there is no one else who can."

"I'm with Alfonso," Gabriel said. "I'm not sure how the Earth will survive as it hurtles along its current dead-end path. Maybe, it's already too late since things have a way of catching up with people. We have to let the Earth know about Gnaritus as soon as possible, so they can pursue a more promising direction and perhaps save themselves!"

"Shall we vote on whether to crack the firewall?" Agata asked.

Stefan and Agata cast the only two dissenting votes against this motion, so Alfonso felt justified in trying to establish an uncensored link to Earth.

"I have no doubt, Alfonso, if anyone can find a way to free up the communication between the two planets, then you will," Stefan said, trying to sound conciliatory. "Let the council members also know before sending any messages to Earth."

Alfonso agreed right away. "It was always my intention to apprise the council members of my efforts in establishing a communications link between the two planets."

Everyone was happy with that. After the raspberry ripple dessert, they refreshed themselves with more lemonade and gave thanks for their safe arrival on Gnaritus. In sharp contrast with the once-gloomy man in the Lake District walking tour whose biggest bugbear was traveling to Gnaritus, a jocund and rident Stefan declared he never wanted to go back to Earth. They talked awhile longer, exchanging more stories about their first few days on Gnaritus before they returned home. Within a few hours, the incessant rain pouring down in buckets had saturated the ground, resulting in large puddles. Surina traced a zigzag path all the way home, skirting around the shallow pools. If the rain stopped tomorrow, she hoped to visit the meditation center on Algonquin Beach. After such a hectic month, a sunny, idyllic day at the seaside felt long overdue.

20
The Volcano Fields

THE STORM HAD passed. Norval Gilmer careened the air cab to skim along the craggy mountain range, past the Terra borough's greenhouses in the south. He drew Surina's attention to the unusual topography in the picturesque hinterland on the way to Algonquin Beach. Through the sunroof of the air cab, she glimpsed the congregation of Clementia, Spes's rings, Fiducia, and the three suns in the endless turquoise sky. As they moved farther south, the jaw-dropping view of the rainbow mountain materialized with its dazzling stripes of gold, black, green, orange, red, blue, and purple. A soft alpenglow shrouded the snowy peaks as well.

"I learned in my geology classes at Gnaritus University that the higher moisture content of the air from the torrential downpour yesterday makes the colors even more vivid than usual!" Norval said, overflowing with enthusiasm. "We're lucky to come at just the right time."

The mountain range ended in painted hills of glowing yellow, red, blue, and purple hues that contrasted with the smoldering, jet-black lava fields stretching far beyond into the horizon.

"The volcanoes in this section are either dormant or extinct," he said with a reassuring grin. "We won't collide with lava plumes or ash clouds since there haven't been any recent eruptions, at least in this region! There is a cluster of active volcanoes in the ring of fire much closer to the South Pole. The frequent volcanic eruptions and brilliant auroras there make the ring of fire an apt name. Ripples of green, pink, yellow, and blue from the auroras dance in the sky near the South Pole."

An eerie silence enveloped the blighted terrain, which was reminiscent of a ravaged and scarred battlefield. Only the three shadows from the air cab floated like teardrops on the rugged landscape. Gigantic boulders and rocky pillars jutted out from the ground like menacing trolls.

Directing Surina's attention to the right, Norval revealed more of his encyclopedic knowledge of Gnaritus's geology. "That circular-shaped lava dome rising like a cake from the plane is a torta lava dome. These lava domes develop when the lava is too thick to flow very far unlike the much more fluid lava flows. Volcanoes form when the magma extrudes onto the surface as lava. Magma is molten rock in the upper crust of the planet. Oh gosh, on your left is a great example of a coulee, or a hybrid between a lava dome and a lava flow, which can form those wrinkles when it travels a few kilometers. Wow, a coulee also made that formation, resembling a perfectly coiled pahoehoe rope! Do you see that mound to the right? Well, that's the cryptodome, where the magma has yet to rupture through the surface. The variety in this volcano field is endless!"

All of a sudden, Norval swooped the air cab down like an eagle. The cab almost skidded along a warm crater lake where the groundwater and magma mixed to produce a psychedelic array of vivid yellows, neon greens, and fluorescent pinks. On occasion, sulfuric gas belched up from the bubbles that ruptured on the crater's surface. Steam hissed through the fissures and clefts along the edge of the crater, which had red tinges from the iron deposits. Surina winced as the sharp, rank smell of sulfur wafted into the cab.

"It smells like rotten eggs but look at the beautiful colors," he said. "Those colors are from elements such as sulfur and iron oxide. It would be such a boring world with only one color. On Gnaritus, there are many colorful rainbows not only in the sky but also on the land!"

They reached a lava dome, around which were piles of tan pumice rocks as well as monolithic gray, red, and black blocks of rock. A sprawling factory and a fleet of air vans stood at the edge of the rocky field in a clearing.

"All our pumice stones come from this area," Norval said. "When magma erupts, the dissolved gases expand to produce volcanic foam. Then, the magma cools into a vesicular network around these trapped gases, much like a sponge. The blocks of lava rock for all the sculptures and totem poles in the colony come from this field as well."

In front of them, out of nowhere, a geyser jetted straight up a hundred meters into the air and disappeared almost as fast.

"The volcanic heat from the magma warms the groundwater, which must be somewhere nearby," Norval said. "Some of the heated groundwater emerges only as puffs of steam or fumaroles, whereas others are boiling water or geysers that swoosh out from the ground at all angles. Likewise, bubbling mud pots or mud pools form when the boiling water mixes with thick mud."

In an adjacent area, a puff of steam heralded yet another geyser, gushing out at a forty-five-degree angle. He skirted around the geyser basin with impressive adroitness and into a vast network of hot springs. Thick fumes shrouded this rocky landscape of interconnecting pools of neon-turquoise water. In the distance, steaming waterfalls sculpted gently sloping terraces as they tumbled down from the volcanic springs to replenish the pools.

Norval spoke as the cab hovered over a massive, limpid thermal lake, from which steam wafted up into the air. "These hot springs are perfect for swimming as well as rich in minerals such as calcium, sulfur, and iron. On Earth, hot springs can act as a nourishing broth for thermophilic organisms to grow in. Some of them are even harmful like the brain-eating ameba, *Naegleria fowleri*, which enters through the noses of bathers and causes fatal meningoencephalitis. Of course, Gnaritus has no bacteria or other harmful organisms. That's another benefit of living on Gnaritus! I guess there are advantages to every situation if you think about it. Here, we are in the hot springs of the meditation center, where the ambient temperature of the water is thirty-eight degrees Celsius. Volcanic springs replenish the thermal lakes and pools every four hours. These mineral-rich pools provide external healing and detoxifying properties for bathers. We harvest this mineral-rich water for internal healing as well. The meditation center's thermal lake is set in a white limestone basin."

They were approaching a massive glass building sprawling over ten acres, through which Surina spotted bathers splashing in a vivid sapphire thermal lake. A spectacular cataract tumbling down the chalky white limestone terraces fed the lake, from which a stream drained into an estuary of the Omaha River that met the sea. In the sedimentary rock surrounding the periphery of the lake were an additional ten smaller hot-spring pools.

The cab headed past the roundabout outside the entrance to the meditation center on the beach and landed in the adjoining parking lot. Stretching far to the horizon and beyond was the endless ocean, glinting in the sunshine. Another meditation center stood on top of the white limestone cliffs that hugged the coastline and soared to the vertiginous height of a hundred meters above the beach. They reminded Surina of the White Cliffs of Dover, without the grassy cap. Both of the meditation centers were single-story, circular buildings with floor-to-ceiling one-way glass walls. In contrast to Earth, the lashing of the waves on the beach was even more distinct due to the absence of any screaming seagulls to drown the sound. Surina could taste the tangy freshness of the salty breeze that caressed her face and played with her hair.

"The building on the cliff is for the most advanced mindfulness meditation practitioners," Norval said. "It opened this month to accommodate the people graduating from the beginners' lessons. The majority of us still go to this one down on the beach, including me. As a neophyte to meditation, I need to learn a tremendous amount before progressing to the next stage."

An engraved apothegm on a monolithic, red volcanic boulder at the entrance to the Algonquin Beach Meditation Center and Spa caught Surina's attention. The ornate calligraphy read: "The universe is everywhere, even within you. No one can own the universe."

"That quote from Somerled Knightly just about sums everything up," Norval said.

He led the way into the lobby of the meditation center, beyond which the unspoiled golden beach gleamed in the brilliant light of the three suns. In the distance, the cerulean ocean reflected the boundless indigo sky. Surina did a double take at the sight of Gnaritonians wearing their green jumpsuits and hats as they lollygagged in the shade of multicolored beach umbrellas. Clusters of children played ring-around-the-rosy on the beach and roared with laughter at the end of the rhyme when they collapsed onto the soft sand. However, other children just stood on the shoreline. Sometimes they tried to run into the foamy surf until their parents thwarted them. Under the protection of the umbrellas, giggling toddlers with buckets and spades in hand made sand castles, albeit with little success, for the grains were so fine that the precarious structures soon collapsed. The most striking aspect of the beach was the absence of any swimmers in the ocean.

"I know what you're thinking!" Norval said with a winsome smile. "No swimsuits on the beach! Well, we have to continue wearing our usual gear, including our hats, to protect ourselves from the ultraviolet radiation. Only a few cryptozoologists ever venture out to swim in the ocean because it's too cumbersome to dress in the head-to-toe bathing suits, which are similar to scuba wetsuits with frog shoes and skullcaps. Besides, swimming in the thermal lake in traditional bathing trunks is far more relaxing, as well as safer, with the added benefit of the glass shielding the harmful rays of the three suns. On the other hand, swimming in the sea is similar to plunging into the unknown since we haven't yet explored every square inch as we have the thermal pools. Although this section of the ocean harbors no organisms, no one knows if anything lurks in its nethermost depths. Let's check-in."

Gowan bobbed up from beneath the check-in counter, where he had been searching for some files, and greeted them. "Welcome, Surina and Norval. Are you here for the meditation classes or the spa?"

"Gowan, I think both," Surina replied. "Is there a beginners class I can join?"

She was in awe of his proficiency in operating the front desk at the age of a hundred and twenty-two years. Age has not enfeebled him but rather made him stronger, she thought.

"There is indeed an introductory class but only this afternoon," he said in his soft, lilting voice. "The lesson is in the thermal lake. First, I'll take you to the welcoming tea ceremony. Please follow me."

Gowan balanced on his cane, with a slight rotation of the hip to the longer leg, as he limped toward the door, which opened to the veranda outside. On a green padded mat, they knelt on the floor, facing the ocean. Without delay, Berenice Ainsley, the host of the tea ceremony, arrived and bowed humbly to the guests. Kneeling on the mat, she folded her legs underneath her thighs and leaned forward as she prepared the utensils. Next, she offered each of them delectable Japanese confectionery treats in decorative, colorful paper wrappings, which were reminiscent of edible works of art. Then, with delicate fluid movements, she poured three scoops of the powdered matcha green tea into each tea bowl.

From an iron kettle simmering on a brazier, she ladled boiling water to make each tea bowl one-fifth full. Next, she whisked the tea with a vigorous side-to-side motion to achieve the right degree of frothiness. Holding a bowl in her right hand, with her other hand underneath to support it, she offered each guest the tea in turn. In essence, Berenice poured every ounce of her being into creating a perfect cup of tea for each of them.

After Surina had drunk the full-bodied brew, she admired the natural, rough-hewn imperfection of the asymmetrical tea bowl. A sweet taste lingered in her mouth. Even though the serenity and refinement of the dignified tea ceremony contrasted with the clamor of the waves thrashing on the beach, it harmonized with nature. In due time, all the sounds receded into the background as Surina concentrated on Berenice's delicate hand movements. With scrupulous attention, Berenice cleaned the used tea bowls, scoop, and whisk before putting them away in their original places. Even the cleaning portion of the ceremony resembled a ballet. Surina realized only toward the end that the fluidity and restraint of the intricate movements aided meditation.

"The primary goal of the tea ceremony is to empty the unnecessary clutter in your life," Norval whispered to Surina. "Understand what emptiness is by letting go of all your burdens. Relish emptiness! Just focus on taking deep, slow breaths. In fact, the simplicity of the tea ceremony helps to discipline the mind in finding a new harmony between the outer world and the inner world."

"Berenice, that was a masterful performance," Surina said.

"I'm still learning about the tea ceremony," Berenice replied. "One day, I hope to embody the four principles of the tea ceremony: namely, harmony, purity, tranquility, and respect. The sequential steps in the tea ceremony have taught me a tremendous deal about doing things one step at a time in my life."

Gowan helped Berenice to carry the tea ceremony utensils back into the meditation center. Since another two hours remained before the start of the meditation class, Norval and Surina explored the beach. Of course, the well-founded concern about the harmful ultraviolet radiation from the three suns' rays had curbed any practice of heliolatry. On that languid summer day, Gnaritonians lolled on beach recliners under the shade of umbrellas, enjoying an unrivaled ocean view, listening to music, or devouring good books. At the same time, parents watched over their rambunctious offspring to ensure they did not stray into the ocean. The gusts of wind carried the children's merriment across the sandy shore and far out to sea.

Surina and Norval slogged through the mealy sand and a maze of beach umbrellas to the shore's edge, where the waves lapped around and licked their black clogs. The wet sand squished beneath their feet. After traveling ten thousand light-years across the Milky Way galaxy, Surina had to pinch herself to make sure she was indeed standing at the shoreline of the New World. She sifted a handful of the fine sand through her fingers. She felt like a grain of sand that the powerful energy of the vast, capricious ocean could swallow in an instant. However, the undulating waves and the salty breeze whispered sweet messages of welcome and swept her into the ocean of endless possibilities. The foamy surf breathed promises onto the beach as well that any grain of sand could become a pearl.

Out of the corner of her eye, Surina spied two children sprinting toward her, with their hair flying in the wind. Their parents trailed far behind. As they approached closer, she recognized George and Elizabeth Ellison, who were racing to swim in the ocean. Just before George darted into the sea, Surina managed to pick him up. Norval held onto Elizabeth, even though she tried to squirm free until he handed her over to Mary Ellison, who arrived in the nick of time. Surina had trouble recognizing David and Mary Ellison at first, for they looked so rejuvenated. The sea breeze had flushed their cheeks, and their mirth frequently erupted into risibility.

"Thank you!" David said. "It's impossible to keep up with them. They love this beach, but they don't understand why they can't go swimming. On the way to Gnaritus, I worried about my kids not finding many friends of their age to play with, but look at all the children on this beach alone!"

Mary had such a broad smile that crows feet appeared outside her eyes. She cradled Elizabeth in her arms. "We're happy here. We have a lovely house in the Ignis borough. You can't even begin to imagine how grateful we are to have a roof over our heads. We found jobs in the library as well. We had been librarians on Earth before they laid us off and hired androids instead. These two are both going to school on Monday. Children here get a head start on their education since they begin at two years old rather than the customary age of five. Education is a human right on Gnaritus, whereas it's a privilege on Earth. The core curriculum here centers on teaching each child to become a citizen of the universe who embraces and loves all life and matter in the cosmos. The school syllabus on Earth emphasizes geography, countries, borders, and divisions. No wonder the adults on Earth see through the distorted prism of fear and otherness. I'm also taking a fine arts course at the Gnaritus University in the evenings. We have so much to do here! We feel as if we belong. The society on Earth treated us as if we were from Pluto."

Surina and Norval strolled away from the water's edge with the Ellisons to join them under their beach brolly. To Surina's surprise, the two space tourists were loafing nearby. Philip Jones-May frowned, with his brows drawn together and the corner of his lips in a perpetual sneer. He tapped his feet on the reclining chair in boredom. Meanwhile, Anne gawked at the ocean in a listless, torpid state. Gowan brought them fresh juice with a pink parasol adorning each glass.

"What type of beach is this?" Philip asked in his gruff, adenoidal voice. "It has no bathing suits, no sunbathing, and no swimming!

Gnaritus is such a bare-bones planet. What can we do here other than lie down under beach umbrellas?"

Anne pursed her lips in distaste. "Don't make such a fuss, Philip. We're only stuck here for another week and a half. Imagine, how happy we'll be to lift off in that spaceship out of here. As soon as we get back home to Earth, we'll go to a proper beach in Tahiti."

"There's a charming trail along the beach to those white cliffs," Gowan said. "You'll see fantastic rock formations that the wind and ocean chiseled over time, including an archway, which is reminiscent of a grand entrance to a Gothic church. Oh, Chief Steward Pars is walking that way. Just follow him. He'll show you the way. If you want to swim, the mineral-rich thermal lake is refreshing, with extraordinary healing powers for conditions such as rheumatism. The meditation classes could zap away the stresses and strains of your long journey across the Milky Way."

Anne guffawed and rolled her eyes.

"We'll pass on those," Philip said in a shrill voice, scrunching up his nose in dismay. "Taking a dip in a communal pool is not my cup of tea. Meditation classes are a real chore, and I never found them to be of any use whatsoever. Anne, we should get back to our room."

Both Philip and Anne heaved themselves up from the beach recliners in unison without finishing their drinks and decamped to the main building. Surina's gaze drifted to the solitary figure of Chief Steward Pars strolling along the edge of the ocean toward the white cliffs on a pilgrimage to nature's cathedral. Deciding to take a breather from all his labors, Gowan flopped into an empty chair beside Surina.

"I'm impressed you're doubling as a lobby attendant and a waiter," Surina said. "Isn't it a lot of work?"

"I usually spend the morning in the lobby and the afternoon attending to the space tourists," Gowan answered. "I like meeting people, but it's hard to accommodate all the demands of the space tourists. This spa doubles as a four-room hotel for space tourists since the beach is such a scenic area. In recent times, fewer and fewer Earth citizens are holidaying in Gnaritus. I suppose the strenuous voyage across the galaxy can be a daunting prospect for anyone."

All of a sudden, Francesca grabbed a chair from the ones vacated by the space tourists and joined them. She laid down her armamentarium of a folded easel, a painter's tool bag, and an artist's portfolio on the sand as she collapsed into her chair after a busy day painting the seashore.

Francesca turned her face toward the three suns in the cloudless sky. "The light is so pure and crystalline that it's ideal for painting! You look well, Surina! I love Gnaritus. Imagine my relief at hearing there were no law offices, courts, or lawyers on Gnaritus. My art is my focus now. Hooray! The Gnaritus Museum of Fine Arts offered me an artist's residency. I hope you can come to my first exhibition next month!"

Francesca opened her portfolio to show them her burgeoning collection of Gnaritus art. She was a prolific painter, for she had chronicled every milestone from the landing at the Gnaritus Airport to the celebrations at the General Assembly Hall. For example, there were several watercolors of her house in the Terra borough and the totem poles in Mohawk Park by the Omaha River. In particular, Surina liked the spirited paintings of the vibrant umbrellas on the beach and the striking rock formation resembling the archway of a Gothic church. Such was Francesca's skill that the souls of her subjects came to life. As the fingers of the sea wind rustled through the paintings, threatening to carry them away, she shut her portfolio in a hurry.

"Are you going to the meditation class?" Francesca asked with eagerness. "I'm in the beginners' group. Meditation helps me to paint even better!"

"We can only go to the spa," David Ellison said. "It would be hard to meditate with our two kids running around."

Meanwhile, George and Elizabeth had resumed building a

network of sand castles with the help of a large contingent of enthusiastic children. Elsewhere, children of all ages, full of vim and vigor, bounced in and out of the rows of beach umbrellas. Since Gnaritus was the birthplace of many of these children and in view of the nonexistent lines of communication, they would know little if anything about Earth. Maybe it's just as well, Surina thought. She remembered her childhood on Earth, where her spirit withered away in a claustrophobic system that hedged her in and never failed to put her in her place if she ventured too far. Needless to say, she soon learned her place. The society on Earth had clipped her wings and chipped away at her self-esteem so that she had become a mere silhouette of her former self over time. In contrast, these children, even the older ones, brimmed with joy and confidence by retaining their sense of the endless possibilities existing not only around them but also within themselves.

Surina, Norval, and Francesca left Gowan and the Ellisons lounging on the beach recliners and went to the thermal lake. After changing into their bathing suits and flip-flops in the locker room, they followed Norval onto a glass-covered bridge spanning a thermal stream that fed into an estuary of the Omaha River.

"There's no need for hats," he said. "The glass absorbs the harmful ultraviolet radiation."

From the bridge, they entered the hot springs spa, echoing with the exultation of hundreds of Gnaritonians swimming in the massive thermal lake and pools. Several bathers sat on the edge of the lake to catch their breath before plunging into the pellucid water once again. Meanwhile, parents instructed their jubilant children on the finer points of swimming and diving. By the waterfall, a row of Gnaritonians awaited their turns to dive off the springboard into the deep end of the thermal lake.

Norval led Surina and Francesca to a limestone terrace from where they vaulted into the turquoise lake. As the warm water enveloped Surina, the weight fell off her shoulders in an instant, and her niggling aches and pains melted away. After a brief swim, she floated on cloud nine in the embrace of the mineral-rich waters, which seemed to nourish every sinew and bone of her body. All of a sudden, the thick wafts of steam drifting on the lake parted as the Cavaceccis caught Surina unawares by tugging on her shoulder and waking her up from her reverie.

Linda splashed in the water. "This thermal lake is the best, Surina. Ever since I began swimming here three days ago, my back feels limber. My lumbago and the crick in my neck went away. We have many blessings on Gnaritus, such as a charming house in the Acqua borough. It's just as well that there are no accountants on Gnaritus because we needed a change from money mongering. My new position as an artist in residence at the Gnaritus Museum of Fine Arts is a dream job in comparison. The best news is that the Universe Wing of the museum will exhibit *The Colors of the Universe* tapestry as part of its permanent collection!"

"I'll be a tour guide at the Gnaritus Museum of Fine Arts," Giuseppe said with aplomb. "I'm also taking an art history immersion course at Gnaritus University in preparation for my job. I never imagined going back to school again! However, education is so popular here that the university is as crowded as a beehive."

"Oh good, the meditation lecture is starting," Linda said.

They swam back to the lakefront to be closer to the instructor, who stood on an overhanging limestone ledge, wearing a green cape over her jumpsuit. In a flash, Surina recognized the diminutive figure of Eoin Dunbar, the council member of the Aeris borough whose silver hair and eyes sparkled in the sunlight. She assumed that Eoin's blurred outline was due to the thick steam rising from the thermal lake. Stefan and Alfonso joined the fifteen-member class as well. Much like travelers quenching their thirst after languishing in a parched desert, the captivated audience listened with rapturous attention to every word of the lesson. Even the other revelers, who were not participating in the lesson, toned down their jocularity and allowed the class to proceed without interruption.

"Welcome, ladies and gentlemen," Eoin said in a mellifluous voice as clear as the crystalline waters of the thermal lake. "Today we will start our journey to attain cosmic consciousness. First, let us remember the privilege of seeing the wondrous sights of the stars, planets, and nebulae during the journey here across the Milky Way galaxy. In essence, cosmic consciousness is an awareness of the connections between all matter in the universe. Also, it is a state of achieving the pure knowledge of everything in the universe here and now, without having to travel anywhere. There is no separation into distinct celestial bodies or human bodies, for we are the same. Divisions, borders, boundaries, fences, and walls will all disappear after you achieve cosmic consciousness.

"For example, Earth defines and segregates humans according to skin color, race, gender, language, and socioeconomic status. On the other hand, cosmic consciousness would allow these arbitrary divisions to fade away, for we are all one and the same. Even so, cosmic consciousness is not a priority on Earth, and few are trying to achieve it.

"According to astrophysics, all the matter existing in the universe today came from a single dense point that expanded after the big bang explosion. Although the atoms that make up all matter are being flung farther apart in an ever-expanding universe, they were a single point once upon a time: the singularity before the big bang. The intrinsic primordial memory or consciousness of all the atoms in the universe is aware of their unity in the singularity long ago; however, humans have forgotten this. In contrast to the self-consciousness level attained by most people, where each human feels distinct, there is the much harder to achieve cosmic consciousness. With cosmic consciousness, we are one and the same with everything in the universe as we were in the singularity before the big bang."

Alfonso shot his hand up through the water and lobbed a question. "If the universe has a consciousness and all matter existing today formed in the big bang, are you saying we are immortal?"

"Cosmic consciousness is being one with all matter in the universe," Eoin replied with a Mona Lisa smile. "We are in the universe. The universe is also within us. Thus, we are the universe as well. If our consciousness expands to experience the entire universe within us, we have everything within us, and we will lack nothing not just today or tomorrow but forever. In essence, when our consciousness unites with the cosmos, it is immortal."

"These ideas sound complicated," Stefan said. "Are there some straightforward steps we can take to achieve cosmic consciousness?"

An excited murmur of anticipation rippled through the class.

"Today we will start our exercises to restore our connection with the cosmic consciousness," Eoin answered. "I say *restore* because it was always there inside us from the beginning, but we forgot. Let me begin with an example. Instead of thinking of yourself as scaling a mountain, feel the ground as part of you, lifting you up and helping you to conquer the peak. Even when you walk, the ground bears you up. In other words, everything is inseparable and integrated. The road does always rise to meet you and help you along on your journey.

"The entire universe is indivisible and working together in harmony for the benefit and happiness of all. Our first exercise to demonstrate this is to float on the water. Think of the water as part of you and not as a separate entity. Not only is your body floating but also the water is buoying you up since it is an integral part of you. While you are doing this, use your respiratory muscles to inhale and exhale deeply. Then also imagine the air moving in and out of your lungs by itself."

Surina swam to the middle of the thermal lake and floated side by side with the rest of the class. Meanwhile, Eoin remained at her perch on the ledge to answer questions or redirect any class members still in the self-consciousness mode. To their credit, each of them made a concerted effort to carry out Eoin's instructions.

In fact, many stayed afloat even an hour later, unwilling to throw in the towel quite yet.

The floating battalion thinned as several members bowed out, pledging to try another day. However, a few hardy souls like Alfonso, Stefan, Norval, Francesca, and Surina carried on drifting in unison in the ghostly, oneiric mists of the center of the lake. Surina closed her eyes, trying to feel being one with the water. Try as she might, she viewed the water as a separate entity from her. Almost on the verge of giving up, she opened her eyes in exasperation and stared through the glass ceiling at Spes's colorful rings in a cloudless blue sky. For some reason, she heard Chief Steward Pars saying, "We are stardust!" over and over again.

Out of the blue, she felt herself skating on Spes's rings, which she used as a springboard to dive off and glide with complete abandonment across the intergalactic space toward the Andromeda galaxy. She was comfortable roaming among her brothers and sisters, the celestial bodies. Above all else, she sensed her parents' reassuring presence in the intergalactic plasma, helping her along her journey, and she knew that this was home. How could she ever feel alone again when the whole universe was within her?

The nagging question of her place in the world had always haunted her during her time on Earth and in particular since the snake bitten day in the medical director's office. Her insides churned as Jane Woodford's begrudging barb—"There's no place for you on Earth"—echoed in her ears. She was certain now that everyone had a home in the universe forever, from before the first recorded second of time until beyond the last recorded second of time. In fact, her home was within her as well as all around her, and it came fully furnished, with the universe providing her with everything she needed.

Since no words could quite describe her life-changing moment of clarity, Surina was unable to share her experience with anyone else. Was it the cosmic consciousness that Eoin had described?

Even though the illumination lasted for only an instant, it stayed with her, for somehow she no longer felt as alone in the world as before. Nor did anyone else feel the compulsion to share their insights as they headed home, overcome with exhaustion from their meditation and ablutions. As Surina waited on the curb in front of the meditation center for Norval to bring the air cab from the parking lot, Stefan caught up with her.

"There's time set aside every Sunday morning at the General Assembly Hall to discuss any concerns with the five council members," he said. "Maybe we should hand over your research files to them to see if they can foil the launch of the Stinguard viral vector."

Since Surina had buckled under the onslaught of rejection letters from scientific journals long ago, she demurred. "We're powerless to change anything on Earth from this distance. Is there any point? All my previous attempts were ineffectual. Besides, didn't you say we should leave the Earth alone?"

Stefan stood his ground. "This is different, though. If the five council members could influence the World Governing Body and preempt the launch of the viral vector, it could be our only chance to prevent a probable disaster on Earth. What will happen if people who got this viral vector relocate to Gnaritus? Even though it's an uphill battle with everything against us, at least we have to try! Giving up is tantamount to accepting failure."

"Oh all right, I'll meet you at ten o'clock tomorrow morning on the front steps of the General Assembly Hall," she conceded before getting into the cab to fly home.

She hoped this was not just a quixotic endeavor. Then she realized they were no longer on the Earth that would dismiss them as frivolous dreamers tilting at windmills. They lived on Gnaritus now, where their voices would receive a fair and equitable hearing, and that was all she had ever wanted.

21

The Firewall

THE NEXT MORNING on that brilliant, lucid Sunday, Surina leaned against a Doric column in the shaded portico of the General Assembly Hall and gazed at Mohawk Park. The waterfall drizzled over the rocks. In front of the gushing fountain, Neilan Trahern laid out rows of chairs in preparation for the welcoming ceremony, which was held every week on Monday and Tuesday.

A lone air cab landed in the park. Stefan rushed out and bounded up the steps of the General Assembly Hall. "Good to see you, Surina. I hope we can resolve this matter of the viral vector somehow."

"I wish someone could help us," Surina said with a weary sigh.

They entered the building and wandered down the main corridor to the third door on the right, leading straight into a cramped waiting room. The centenarian attendant was so tiny that he almost disappeared into his burgundy-leather swivel chair; nevertheless, he illuminated the entire room with his incandescent eyes. Surina could not help but notice his bald, freckled scalp.

He pointed to an enormous register that was almost as large as he was and spoke in a squeaking voice. "Please sign in. You're next, but the five council members have just started to hear a case."

After checking in, they flopped down onto a comfy sofa. Surina flipped through the Gnaritus Gazette. Stefan closed his eyes and catnapped. He woke up again moments later when the waiting room's door banged open, and the space tourists burst in wearing mortified expressions. Much to Philip and Anne's chagrin, the homunculus attendant instructed them to take a seat and wait their turn. After shooting baleful glances all around the room to register their displeasure, they retreated into the corner in exasperation.

Two hours later, Surina and Stefan heard their names. Although the Lilliputian attendant barely reached the height of the door handle, he opened the creaking door with a brisk motion and led them into a mammoth hall. Skylights shone a spotlight on the luminaries, who huddled together around a circular table that occupied most of the room. The Apollonian Somerled Knightly presided in the middle of the group. Flanking him on the left were the council members of the Ignis and Terra boroughs, whereas to his right sat the council members of the Acqua and Aeris borough. Eoin Dunbar of the Aeris borough asked Surina and Stefan to join her, leaving twenty seats around the table empty.

Surina tried to focus on the five council members faces but saw only their iridescent eyes. However, the painting at the farthest end of the room depicting a beach remained in sharp focus, as did Stefan sitting next to her. She stared at the council members in disbelief at their ages of a hundred and forty-something years old! Without a doubt, Gnaritus placed a premium on the nuance and subtlety of insights that only comes with age.

"Welcome, Surina and Stefan," Somerled said in a melodious voice. "I hope you're settling in and acclimating well to Gnaritus. You'll find the shops on Mohave Square have everything available on Earth as well as a few things found only on Gnaritus. In this venue, there's an opportunity to voice any concerns."

Surina was a little unsure about where to start in retelling the tangled tale of the Stinguard viral vector. With Stefan nudging her along, she spoke in a wobbly voice. "Thanks for giving us this chance to discuss the viral vector that my former supervisor, Rod Stinguard, synthesized. Although his viral vector carries the genetic code for DNA repair enzymes to mend cancer-causing genetic mutations in humans, it has to integrate at precise sites on the human genome first. If the integration site is off by even by a little bit, lethal mutations can result. In essence, my experiments showed that the viral vector integration site in human DNA varies and causes life-threatening mutations in half of the patients.

"In spite of my results, the World Governing Body decided to launch this viral vector next week. No scientific journals would publish my research either. In fact, they pilloried me. When I shared my opinion with the medical director of the Greysville Quadrant Hospital, he skewered it. Stinguard based the viral vector's safety and feasibility data on a small preliminary clinical trial in Africa, with a short two-week follow-up. Since he's a prominent member of many scientific committees, he had no trouble in securing the World Governing Body's official stamp of approval to launch the viral vector. We would appreciate your help in halting the global distribution of the Stinguard viral vector. Here's a disc containing all my research files and a detailed account of my scientific methodology."

From her handbag, Surina fished out the quarter-inch disc and slid it across the table to Somerled. Without delay, he loaded it on his wristwatch.

"I'm forwarding the files to Dr. Ailbeart Ross for peer review," Somerled said.

"I was a journalist for a newspaper on Earth and interviewed Stinguard," Stefan said. "During my investigation, I discovered Stinguard is on the board of directors of the Rochester Manninghouse Pharmaceutical Company. Of course, Stinguard's motivations remain uncertain, but both he and the pharmaceutical company stand to make windfall profits from this viral vector. They're marketing it as an elixir to stamp out cancer. Even though I tried to publish my story, my editor trashed it. No news outlet would touch the article."

"The prime motivating factor on Earth is money, even paltry sums," Bruce Artair of the Terra borough said in a bleak tone. "Itchy palms have wreaked havoc on Earth. It seems you have gone through all the proper channels available on Earth."

"The Earth Page on the communal computers only masquerades as news," Greer Irvine of the Acqua borough said. "The only news about Earth we trust is from newcomers such as you. Earth severed all communication with Gnaritus fifty years ago after we requested a change of our planet's name from Earth Colony to Gnaritus. In fact, the Earth censored all communication from the beginning. Even the emergency channel to the World Governing Body is no longer extant after they closed it fifty years ago, leaving us alone in this corner of the universe. Perhaps, we were always alone. The inability of the only two planets of *Homo sapiens* in the universe to unite as one is a tragedy of unfathomable proportions. Human behavior on Earth tells us this is history redux as shown by the endless wars, racial strife, and marginalization of people. The communal computers on the squares have so many filters that most messages never get through. For the most part, the communal computers exist only to provide the illusion of the ability to communicate so as not to create a sense of panic among family members."

"Are you saying there's no way to warn Earth about this viral vector?" Stefan stammered in shock.

"Yes, I'm sorry, but we are as powerless as you are in this matter," the stately Cinead Adaire of the Ignis borough replied with a hint of regret in her voice. "At first, when we lost the emergency channel to the World Governing Body, we tried to restore it but to no avail. Later, our best computer engineers attempted to remove the filters from the communal computers in the squares, also without success. After being held incommunicado for so long, our will to communicate with Earth has faded. In reality, it's clear Earth wants nothing to do with us. The newcomers who arrive on our shores are the outcasts and exiles from Earth. In a similar way, Earth has cast Gnaritus out of the human family, for they abhor us. Perhaps, there are advantages in every situation since they're making no attempts to peddle the viral vector on Gnaritus."

"Is there still any enthusiasm in cracking the firewall?" Surina asked, wondering whether to tell them about Alfonso.

"Yes, there's significant interest in free and open communication with Earth in the council, at least," Cinead replied while the other council members nodded in agreement.

"Alfonso Diaz, a brilliant computer engineer, is writing a program to bypass the filters blocking communication with Earth," Surina said.

"Yes, Alfonso told us earlier this morning," Somerled answered, much to Surina's surprise. "However, he embarks on this endeavor alone. Since Alfonso's chances of success are unknown in light of our previous failed attempts, let me share with you other possibilities, albeit equally uncertain of a favorable outcome. One option stems from our quest for cosmic consciousness to allow communication with the entire universe. Three of us so far can transmit messages by telepathy across long distances, although only on Gnaritus. Even if we had the ability for telepathic transmission to Earth, receptive recipients are a prerequisite. That's unlikely since connecting with cosmic consciousness is not a priority on Earth.

"There's another option that may be worth a try. The *Odyssey* leaves for Earth in ten days after completing its repairs. Captain Spero and Chief Steward Pars could deliver a letter from us to the World Governing Body warning them about the viral vector. Even though the crew signed an employment contract forbidding them to disseminate information about Gnaritus, I believe they will agree to take the letter in view of the urgency. Whether or not the World Governing Body acts on our recommendations is another question. Just as they disregarded your warning, I'm certain they will ignore our letter since our opinion carries no weight on Earth either. At least, we will register our concerns for the sake of posterity."

Somerled paused to check a message on his wristwatch. "By the way, Surina, Dr. Ailbeart Ross validated your research, and he shares your grave concerns. He said you outlined your scientific methodology in such detail that it was obvious right away that your research is sound."

The council members exchanged worried glances with each other while Surina felt like crying. After so much derision, the subsequent vindication of her research played only a minor part since deep inside she knew that the rigor of her scientific method would stand up to any forthright scrutiny. Rather, the prospect of the looming catastrophe on Earth petrified her. The tragic plight of the unsuspecting inhabitants of Earth filled her with dread. She sat motionless in despair. Then, it occurred to her that she should have done more to stop Stinguard.

Somerled read her mind. "Surina, you did everything possible to warn them. After all, an insatiable greed for money and power stirs up overwhelming, unstoppable forces on Earth, which can turn any truth into a lie. Both of you had no voice on Earth, and neither do we. Even if we send a letter with Captain Spero and Chief Steward Pars, it takes a month for the *Odyssey* to reach Earth. It'll be too late for the majority of the population by then. Earth neither values Gnaritus nor sees us as equals, so I have no confidence in them paying any attention to our letter. Then again, as people of conscience, we must act on even the remote possibility of the World Governing Body heeding our message and saving at least a part of the population from this viral vector."

Even though he ended on an optimistic note, Surina had a

sinking feeling that the World Governing Body would toss the letter in the bin. She could do nothing more except hope that her worst fears would turn out to be unfounded.

"If the new settlers get this viral vector before relocating here, the disaster could reach Gnaritus as well," Stefan said.

"I don't think the World Governing Body would bother giving the viral vector to the outcasts and undesirables who they exile here," Surina said. "The only good news in all of this is that the viral vector is noncommunicable as shown by my data that I submitted earlier today."

"Yes, Dr. Ailbeart Ross also confirmed there is no possibility of person-to-person transmission," Somerled said. "I agree with you, Surina. The chances are slim that the new settlers would have received the viral vector, but we'll start asking them on arrival. This afternoon, we'll meet with Ailbeart Ross to discuss the best methods to monitor any recipients of the viral vector."

"Should we disclose the risks of this viral vector to the population on Gnaritus?" Stephan asked.

"For now, it's best not to alarm other Gnaritonians since we are powerless to affect the outcome," Somerled replied. "The fate of the Earth lies in its own hands now. We can only pray that the bell is not tolling the final knell for the Anthropocene epoch on Earth."

"Would it be useful to talk to the two space tourists waiting outside?" Surina asked. "Philip is the son of John Jones-May, the chief executive officer of the World Governing Body. Perhaps, he could give his father our message if we can convince him to raise the alarm about the Stinguard viral vector when he returns to Earth. Although I'm not that optimistic, it's worth a try."

"All right," Somerled said. "We have so few other options available to us."

Over the intercom, Somerled directed the attendant to bring in the space tourists. Entering in a state of vexation, Philip and Anne sat at the opposite end of the table, creating a gulf between themselves and the council members.

Dispensing with the formality of any introductions, Philip whined with a peeved expression on his face. "Can the *Odyssey* leave sooner than in ten days? We need to go home. Since there's nothing to do here, we're just holed up in our hotel rooms. Everything is so uncomfortable that it's impossible to get a good night's rest!"

"The crucial repairs of the *Odyssey* prevent an earlier departure," Cinead replied, much to their consternation.

"We would also like to discuss some new information about the Stinguard viral vector with you," Somerled said. "Dr. Surina Mathew's research proved that lethal mutations could occur in half the patients who receive the viral vector. Earth is in grave danger. We have to do something before the disaster spirals out of control. When you go home, would you please make a personal plea to your father to halt the distribution of the Stinguard viral vector?"

The unexpected question unhinged Philip. His face flushed with anger, and he slapped his hand on the table. He unleashed a stinging rebuke. "What balderdash! My father would never make such a gross error in judgment."

"In no way did I mean to impugn your dad's character," Somerled said.

Anne sniggered in disdain. Philip scoffed and spoke in a huff. "World-renowned experts on Earth vetted the science behind the viral vector. My dad is an astute judge of character, and he said Rod Stinguard is a selfless, honorable man who will save humanity from the terrible scourge of cancer. All of your scurrilous suppositions are ludicrous and nonsensical! There is no credible threat to Earth. Stop wasting our time with this gibberish. Let's get out of here, Anne."

With that, they stormed out in an apoplectic fit and banged the door shut. The hostility of Philip's outburst caught Surina by surprise. For a while, the five council members remained silent before Somerled concluded the meeting. "We'll talk with Captain

Spero and Chief Steward Pars tomorrow."

Taking a cue from the finality in his voice, Surina and Stefan dragged themselves out of the General Assembly Hall with heavy hearts. Just as they entered the bright sunshine from the shaded portico, Stefan stopped in midstride as if seized by a new inspiration.

"There's one more thing we can do!" he said. "We must tell Alfonso about the dangers of the viral vector, so he can redouble his efforts in tearing down the firewall! The World Governing Body may not be receptive to us, but I'm sure at least some of the general public on Earth would be if only we could reach them."

"Yes!" Surina said.

They made a beeline to the edge of Mohawk Park to catch a cab straight to Alfonso's house.

"You look as if you're in a hurry," the weatherworn driver said. "Where are you heading?"

"Number five Maple Street on Seneca Square," Stefan said.

The cab jetted off. Ten minutes later, it landed on Seneca Square. After thanking the driver, Surina and Stephan spilled out of the cab and sprinted to Alfonso's house.

Still wearing his blue-gingham apron, Alfonso opened the door and led them to the kitchen, where he was preparing lunch. He was alone as his parents were shopping. A yeasty smell of rising bread greeted them. Sensing the urgency on their faces, Alfonso left the chicken stew to simmer on the stove and took out a fresh loaf of rosemary bread from the oven. First, they made him promise not to divulge the details of their conversation to anyone else. He listened openmouthed, on the edge of his seat at the kitchen table, to the startling revelations about the Stinguard viral vector, which left him befuddled and speechless for a moment.

"I know this viral vector story is overwhelming," Surina said.

Alfonso's voice shook with emotion. "How sad it all is! Strange, we were the lucky ones in getting away in the nick of time. Do you think Stinguard is a psychopath? He sounds like a twisted, bumptious oaf. How could the World Governing Body's thinking be so warped and slipshod? I'm flabbergasted they would see Gnaritus only as a dumping ground for human detritus and sever all ties with us! While the Gnaritonians are aspiring for cosmic consciousness, the World Governing Body on Earth is aiming for the gutter. Nothing good can ever happen when their only goal is to make even more money and sweep aside anyone standing in their way."

"How close are you to bringing down the firewall?" Stefan asked, hoping for at least a single piece of good news that day. "If we could reach the general public, I'm sure at least some of them would heed our warning about the Stinguard viral vector."

"I'm glad you told me about how imperative it is because I'll intensify my efforts to complete the job as fast as possible," Alfonso replied in a hesitant voice. "So far, I've found layers of filters that seem to evolve and become even more resistant each time I attempt to bypass them. They designed this diabolical firewall with malicious intent. When I worked for the Rochester Manninghouse Corporation, I found these same filters intercepting communication on Earth as well. During my meeting earlier today with the five council members, they told me about the many computer engineers who had attempted to disable these filters without success. There's no one I can enlist for help because none of the computer engineers here are interested in this anymore. The general feeling is that since Earth wants nothing to do with Gnaritus, why bother trying to open the communication channels? Cracking this firewall could be a Herculean task."

"I know you're trying your best, Alfonso," Surina said. "We're counting on you. I hesitate in saying this, but you may well be the Earth's last hope."

Surina tried to cheer up by eating the hearty stew but still went home with a sense of dread. She felt drained and exhausted by the morning's events. Nevertheless, she was glad to meet with the council members and explore every option available to halt the distribution of the Stinguard viral vector. At least someone else now shared the grim knowledge that she had carried by herself for so long all the way from Earth.

The cloudless sky outside was resplendent with the three suns shining their benevolent rays on that peaceful, restful Sunday. The laughter of the toddlers riding on the carousel filled Seneca Square. On the playground swings, jubilant children urged their parents to push them higher. Under the shade of the gazebo, chess aficionados engaged in an intricate battle of wills. In the distance, an enthusiastic instructor cheered on a group of agile elderly residents performing brisk calisthenics.

Surina agreed with Somerled's prudent advice that they would achieve little by shattering this idyll under the suns of Gnaritus with an announcement of the probable disaster on Earth from the viral vector. In reality, everyone on Gnaritus understood they had no control over any events on Earth. Even though there was no possibility of averting the implementation of the Stinguard viral vector, her heart yearned for a miracle on Earth despite the odds. The sun never set on Gnaritus. She wondered if the sun was about to set on the Age of Humans on Earth.

22
The Spatium Borough Hospital

ON MONDAY, SURINA arrived on time at eight o'clock in the morning on the fifth floor of the Spatium Borough Hospital. She breathed easier after noting the absence of the Argus-eyed android security guards whose usual modus operandi was to lurk in the shadows so as to pounce on even a stray remark made in jest. The gleaming floor reflected the three suns' rays flooding through the skylights. Four hallways, with thirty beds each, extended from the central nursing station at ninety-degree intervals. The ward was a beehive of activity as the nurses combed through the patient rooms to dispense medications. Staffing the nursing station was a silver-haired octogenarian, or perhaps even older, wearing a short, white lab coat over her green jumpsuit, similar to ones worn by the nurses. Her bushy eyebrows jutted out perpendicular to her face at an improbable angle, shading her deep-set, iridescent eyes from the bright light in the ward. She had such a broad grin that prominent laugh lines appeared around her mouth.

"You must be Dr. Surina Mathew," the receptionist said. "Welcome! I'm Fiona. Dr. Nieves MacIver called to say she is on her way to meet you. Please make yourself comfortable in the nursing station. Here's your lab coat. Just hand it to me at the end of the week, and I'll exchange it for a fresh one. There's tea and coffee if you would like some."

While Surina waited at the nursing station sipping a steaming-hot cup of tea with honey, she reminded herself of the many patients she could still help on Gnaritus despite her powerlessness to change events on Earth. All of a sudden, a portly lady in her middle years approached at breakneck speed, wearing a spotless white, knee-length lab coat over her green jumpsuit. She had coiffed her raven hair in an elegant French twist that showed off her dangling pearl earrings and a matching double-strand pearl necklace and bracelet. Her iridescent green eyes lit up her good-natured face as she gave Surina a vigorous handshake and sat down next to her. "Surina, I am so glad to meet you. I'm Nieves MacIver. We can really use your help since we're always busy. Are you settling in and able to find everything you need?"

Before Surina could answer, Nieves stood up and pointed to each of the corridors in turn. "These four hallways are the wards for solid tumors, leukemias, lymphomas, and multiple myelomas. The call schedule in the hospital begins with inpatient rounds at six o'clock in the morning until the nocturnist physician arrives on duty at five o'clock in the evening. Sometimes, medical students or interns join us for a one-month rotation as part of their training curriculum because the Spatium Borough Hospital is the main teaching hospital for Gnaritus University's medical school. Today is the first of September, and the new term is starting. Since part of our responsibilities include training doctors, we have dual appointments as professors at Gnaritus University. I'll show you the sunroom, which provides a welcome respite for patients on each ward."

Dashing past the patient rooms to the end of the ward, they

entered a large sunroom with glass walls and ceiling. All around was a spectacular view of the entire space colony, including the suburbs, the bustling commercial center, the stately General Assembly Hall, Mohawk Park, and the Omaha River in the distance. Several venerable patients in pale-blue hospital robes reclined in the languid sunshine as they listened to the entrancing music filtering in from the direction of the General Assembly Hall. Right away, Surina recognized the piece as one of Gabriel and Rafaela's celestial compositions.

Nieves stood by the window. "The music for the welcoming ceremony is a joy to listen to from the sunroom. Somehow, the music speeds up healing, so no wonder the patients love it. I like Vivaldi's springtime music as well, but this new violin concerto is the best! Let me show you the cancer clinic."

Surina grinned. "I think the music captures the soul of the heavens."

Making a hasty exit from the sunroom, Surina scrambled to keep up with Nieves as they zoomed down a flight of stairs to the floor below. It had only a single long corridor containing innumerable examination rooms on both sides. Wasting no time, Nieves hotfooted it down the hallway toward the reception desk in front of a large waiting room overflowing with timeworn patients in their declining years.

"Dr. MacIver, your clinic starts in another half hour, at nine o'clock in the morning," the receptionist said.

"Thanks for reminding me," Nieves replied. "Surina, let me show you the computer system. It's quite straightforward. For instance, just swipe your identification badge in front of this sensor to access the medical records. Here's the ordering section for radiological studies and laboratory tests. In the examination rooms, pocket-sized body scanners can provide vital signs and high-quality images of the internal organs. If you place a drop of blood in this slot in the scanner, it will furnish a full set of laboratory values. Just place a buccal swab in this aperture, and the scanner will churn out a complete genetic analysis in ten minutes.

"For the first two months, I thought you might want to begin with a clinic in the afternoons. Two patients have already requested to see you today in clinic! After settling in, you can do the inpatient rounds on the cancer ward, but this is only a suggestion since you can arrange your schedule as you see fit. By and large, it depends on how you want to split your time between research and clinical care. Shall we go to your new lab?"

As they sprinted back down the long corridor, they flew past nurses putting patients into the examination rooms. Before going down the stairs to the third floor, Nieves showed Surina an empty examination room and handed her a standard pocket-sized body scanner. Natural sunshine flooded each room through a large window, obviating the need for additional lighting.

Surina scrutinized the ergonomic device. "I worked with similar types of body scanners on Earth, but analyzing any lab test from a single drop of blood is new to me."

"It's one of many homegrown innovations from a prolific group of computer engineers at Gnaritus University," Nieves said with pride. "They're inventing new gadgets at a dizzying pace, far exceeding anything I can remember on Earth. Most of these novel gizmos are for studying the developmental singularity. Ailbeart Ross mentioned you would be doing research in how to attain the developmental singularity."

"Yes, it's a new field for me," Surina replied. "I still have trouble understanding cosmic consciousness and the developmental singularity."

Nieves nodded. "I came to Gnaritus about twenty-five years ago from Spain, and these terms still confuse me. Perhaps, I can explain it to you by saying cosmic consciousness and the developmental singularity are part of a continuum on the evolutionary path. Oh, look at the time. My clinic begins in fifteen minutes, so let me show you your laboratory."

Forthwith, Nieves set a blistering pace down another flight of stairs to the third floor of the hospital, where a skyway led to the research building. They scampered across the skyway and through a maze of corridors to Surina's new lab. It was a generous space with four workbenches containing state-of-the-art scientific equipment.

Nieves huffed and puffed for a while before she caught her breath. Then she showed Surina her corner office in the lab. "There's a nice view of Mohawk Park from this office. Your identification badge will let you through any locked door in the hospital, Surina. Most, if not all, the rooms are accessible as there is little need to lock any doors or bar any windows on Gnaritus. This lab's equipment will give you the tools to study both the developmental singularity and cancer. Since my primary focus is patient care, I don't know much about laboratories. A useful resource for you will be Bruce Artair in the next-door lab."

"You mean Bruce Artair, the council member of the Terra borough, is also a physician conducting developmental singularity research?" Surina asked.

"Yes," Nieves answered in a matter-of-fact voice. "Bruce is at the welcoming ceremony in the General Assembly Hall today, but you'll probably see him later in the week. Surina, I'll show you the doctors' lounge, which offers a secluded place for meditation far away from the clamor of the clinic. Best of all, there's also a snack bar of delicious fruit, cakes, and cookies. I remember the contentious conversations in the doctors' lounge at the hospital where I worked on Earth. Rest assured, there is none of that backstabbing maliciousness here among our confreres. Let me show you what I mean."

At a galloping pace, they tore across the skyway leading to the hospital. This time, Nieves mounted a flight of stairs in what seemed like a single leap back to the fourth-floor cancer clinic. Surina ran after her as she disappeared into a sunroom at the end of the corridor with a "Doctors Only" sign in green italic letters on the door. After entering the sunroom that doubled as the doctors' lounge, she chose a seat next to Nieves in a lounge chair by the window. Soothing sounds of babbling brooks permeated the sunroom. Opposite Surina, an elderly lady doctor wore a peaceful smile as she meditated in the full lotus position. Similar to the pose of the Buddha, her hands rested on her knees with the palms facing outward, and the thumbs opposed to the index fingers.

"The triangular shape of the lotus position symbolizes knowledge, among many other virtues, and can channel energy from the universe while still being grounded in the here and now," Nieves whispered. "The triangle is present throughout human history, such as the Egyptian pyramids. Even in fluctuating water currents, the lotus flower never loses its bearings since its roots are secure in the lake's muddy floor. Likewise, the lotus position in meditation can provide harmony in a shifting and changing world."

All around the doctors' lounge, physicians either meditated in the lotus position or just rested for a few minutes with their feet up. Surina heard someone calling her name in a soft Scots burr. As she wheeled around in the direction of the sound, her memory drifted back to her medical school days in London. After a while, the owner of the voice emerged from behind a recliner and cantered toward her with outstretched arms and embraced her. It was Tamarind Crutchley, her mentor at the University of London Medical School. Even though they last met almost twenty years ago, Tamarind appeared ageless. She still resembled a wise owl with large, all-knowing eyes, ready to furnish solutions to any question or problem.

"Surina, you look well," Tamarind said in a hushed voice. "You'll soon be as thankful as I am to be on Gnaritus if you aren't already. My children joined me here last year, so my family is now complete. I've spent the happiest years of my life on Gnaritus. How can anyone be nostalgic for the rat race on the Earth?"

"It's easy to fall into a rut on Earth as I was," Surina said. "I'm glad to escape that dead-end life."

Tamarind strolled to the refreshment table beside the window. "Want some biscuits? There's tea as well. Oh, Surina, you'll love it here. Only after coming here, did I understand the real meaning of gaining knowledge without an ulterior motive, such as money or fame. I can also assure you the Spatium Borough Hospital far exceeds every conceivable quality measure due to their unsurpassed attention to detail. In effect, patients in this hospital are lucky to get the best care in the universe!"

Nieves sprang up from her chair and darted toward the door. "Surina, my first patient is waiting for me. See you this afternoon!"

"My clinic will begin in another hour as well, but we can talk a little longer," Tamarind said. "By the way Surina, I organize the lectures at Gnaritus University's medical school. May I add you to the roster of lecturers? These medical students possess a genuine thirst for knowledge and are such a delight to teach! Oh, Fergus Wittenberg is over there! You two were my brightest students at the University of London Medical School."

Surina recognized her former classmate right away. After graduating from their subspecialty training in cancer, both of them had secured positions at the prestigious Greysville Quadrant Hospital. Although Fergus had established an innovative and productive research laboratory, he had offended Stinguard by challenging his research methods. She remembered Stinguard had orchestrated Fergus's relocation to Gnaritus ten years ago, thereby nipping a promising career in the bud.

Wearing a smile like a sphinx, Fergus was meditating by the window in the full lotus position. He stirred when Tamarind touched his shoulder. As soon as he saw Surina, he jumped to his feet and gave her a bear hug. Similar to Tamarind, Fergus was ageless. In fact, he seemed as youthful as the last time Surina had seen him ten years ago, toting his boxes out of his lab under the hawkish supervision of Rex, the chief android security guard. Neither wrinkles nor sagging jowls marred his bookish face. Even so, there were changes in his appearance, for he no longer resembled a deer that was permanently in the crosshairs of a rifle. Gone too was his tendency to keep looking over his shoulder for any unexpected threat sneaking up on him. In contrast to his former hunted demeanor, a blissful smile wreathed his face, and his eyes were bigger and more radiant. Also, his coal-black hair was much longer than she remembered.

"Surina, you'll like it here," Fergus said. "Although I cursed my old nemesis Stinguard at first, I'm grateful to him now, for he is the primary reason for my awakened new life. In the beginning, I wished I hadn't locked horns with Stinguard over his research methods. However, if I hadn't come to Gnaritus ten years ago at the age of thirty, I would have wasted my youth on Earth, scampering around like a caged animal on a pet wheel. Gnaritus saved my life since my soul was dying a slow death on Earth. Instead, this is a much more humane society that encourages everyone to live without fear and actualize their full potential. Everyone matters here."

"Everyone matters here," Tamarind said with deep reverence.

"We all know exile to Gnaritus is another tactic to segregate the population on Earth, according to an arbitrary perceived value," Fergus said. "However, the diaspora used their exile to reorganize their priorities and create a more just, generous society where every person counts and has opportunities to engage in meaningful activities. They replaced the blind pursuit of vain, primitive impulses to procure more money and power with a search for knowledge to connect with the essence of the universe: cosmic consciousness and the developmental singularity."

"I'm grateful to be here," Surina said with relief. "There's no question about it. What's happening on Earth is a travesty of unimaginable proportions."

Tamarind agreed. "Yes, it's best we got away. Our lives are but a momentary flash in the history of the universe. Even though the lifespan on Gnaritus is about a hundred and thirty years, it's too short to waste by staying on Earth. Memento mori! Remember we have to die! We must use our allotted time wisely so as to be without any regrets in the end."

"I think I came alive after landing on Gnaritus," Fergus said. "On Earth, a thick fog clouded my vision, and I never even saw where I was going. Surina, just forget Earth. There's so much to do on Gnaritus. You'll love it here!"

Even though Surina already felt at home on Gnaritus, she could not forget the Earth altogether, given the nettlesome issue of the Stinguard viral vector.

After Fergus and Tamarind had gone to their clinics, she remained in the lounge while waiting for her cancer clinic to begin just down the hall. Her favorite Scottish breakfast tea was a perfect complement to an incredible morning. Since the monastery-like silence in the lounge was conducive to contemplation and meditation, she tried at first to get into the lotus position, albeit without success. She opted to rest with her feet up and savor a warm raisin scone with her tea. For once, she made no particular plans and just enjoyed being in the moment. Before she knew it, it was one o'clock.

Despite having only two slots filled on her schedule that day, she was excited to see her first patients on Gnaritus. The nurse in charge, Joyce Herring, met her at the nursing station. She wore a nurse's hat with a Red Cross emblem and a hip-length white coat over her green jumpsuit. Patience exuded from every line of her face, which offered considerable comfort to patients and physicians alike. She had a reputation for being unflappable even in a crisis.

"Good afternoon, Dr. Mathew," Joyce said in a muffled voice stemming from the early stages of Parkinson's disease. "Welcome to Gnaritus! Your first patient is in room twelve. Vital signs are normal. I drew blood for labs, and the results should be back soon. I took a buccal swab as well in case you need a genetic analysis. The patient had low-grade lymphoma for several years that transformed into an aggressive lymphoma a year ago. He's here for an immune-cell booster infusion."

After thanking Joyce for her efficiency, Surina entered room twelve. To her surprise, it was Toben and Diola Okafor, Mercy's parents. Similar to Tamarind and Fergus, neither of them had aged a day after so many years. However, she did not remember them having such translucent eyes that blazed across the room and obscured the outlines of their faces.

From his supine position on the exam table, Toben raised his head as she entered. "We're so glad to see you, Surina. You look well. How is Mercy? We pray every day that she's safe. I wish we could see Mercy again, but what can we do? If only Mercy would also relocate here out of the strife on Earth. Although we sent her many messages about my lymphoma diagnosis, I doubt she knows since we last heard from her twelve years ago when she got married. Most children on Earth may not even be aware of their parents' illnesses on Gnaritus. Do we have any grandchildren?"

Surina told them about Mercy's wonderful family. The news of Janet and Darren left Diola struggling for words. She finally spoke after she had wiped away the moisture from her eyes. "It's such a blessing to have two grandchildren. We never even knew! With the passing years, there are fewer messages from Earth. Soon communication will cease between the two planets, and we will go our separate ways. In essence, we already have. Is Mercy aware of Toben's lymphoma diagnosis?"

"She never mentioned it to me, and I'm sure she would have," Surina replied. "It's too sad for words."

"Perhaps a reason for them to filter messages about births or illnesses in families is to curtail requests for interplanetary travel," Toben said in a mellow voice. "Or maybe, they just want to limit all communication to a bare minimum. You'll like it here, Surina. Rest assured, there's so much to do here that the only limitation is time. For example, I work at the Gnaritus Aerospace Engineering Firm, where our goal is to shorten interstellar travel times. We're happy here! Your parents were content on Gnaritus as well, and their only wish was for you to join them as soon as possible."

"Were you there when my parents died, Mr. and Mrs. Okafor?" Surina asked in a halting voice.

Diola combed her fingers through her buzz-cut hair as she relived the painful memories. "Yes, they both died of cancer within a month of each other. Almost to the end, they went every day to Algonquin Beach to meditate. They wanted us to tell you never to be sad about anything, least of all them because they are still here among the stars. When you connect with cosmic consciousness, you'll feel them there. Of course, it's cruel of the World Governing Body not to allow you to visit them in their final days on Gnaritus."

"It's such a relief knowing my parents were happy here," Surina said.

Then she measured Toben's lymph nodes with the pocket scanner and analyzed the laboratory tests. "I have some good news for you. All the lab results are normal, Mr. Okafor. The genetic analysis shows no new mutations other than those present at the diagnosis. You have only minimal residual disease in the lymph nodes, so we're on the right track with the immune-cell therapy every three months to jump-start your immune system to eradicate the lymphoma. Are you ready for the next dose today? Do you have any adverse effects? Fatigue is the most common."

"I have no side effects at all," Toben replied.

Surina infused the immune-cell therapy and discarded the empty syringe. "Well done. Please rest here, Mr. Okafor, for at least half an hour. Our nurse, Joyce, will monitor you in case of any reactions. Your next appointment is in three months."

"Surina, you must come for supper one day," Diola said. "We have so much to discuss! Next Wednesday evening is a good time for us."

"Sounds perfect," she replied, hoping to learn more about her parents' life on Gnaritus. "Is your address the same as on your chart?"

"Yes, we still live on Douglas Fir Lane in the Terra borough," Toben said. "See you then."

After leaving the room, Surina let Joyce know about monitoring Toben for at least half an hour before sending him home.

"The next patient in room five made a special request to see you as well," Joyce said, handing over his chart. "He has Hodgkin lymphoma without any relapse for the past eighteen years, which is such a blessing! He comes once a year for a physical checkup, although he's early this time. I hope he isn't relapsing."

Inside the room, Mr. Nachton Arthbutnott waited on the edge of his seat. He fiddled with his hat while his brooding owl eyes searched Surina's face as she entered. Although his medical record stated eighty years as his chronological age, Surina thought his laboratory tests and muscular appearance put his biological age closer to sixty years. Despite his long Santa Claus beard, button nose, and rosy red cheeks, he was anything but jolly, for he had a curious, penitent expression on his face. Moreover, his eyes did not share the characteristic luminosity of most other Gnaritonians. Although laconic by habit, he was loquacious about one topic only. Try as she might, she had difficulty remembering the dour Nachton Arthbutnott. Why did he request to see her in particular?

"Dr. Mathew, I'm so glad to meet you," Nachton said in a taut, anxious voice. "By the way, how is the Greysville Quadrant Hospital on Earth? I know someone who works there—Rod Stinguard!"

Like fingernails grating on a chalkboard, the sound of Stinguard's name reverberated in her ears. She cringed as her heart sank to the floor since Stinguard was the last person she wanted to discuss. Feeling a little queasy, she mustered enough strength to carry on the conversation. "How do you know Stinguard? Is he a relative of yours, Mr. Arthbutnott?"

Nachton bit his lower lip and stroked his untamed, bushy whiskers. Then he gave a cryptic reply. "You could say he was once, a long time ago. I read you worked at the Greysville Quadrant Hospital, so you must have run into Stinguard. I made an appointment with you hoping to learn whether his judgment day ever arrived."

The vehemence of his commination caught Surina by surprise, for he was the first infuriated Gnaritonian that she had encountered. He gave the distinct impression of being another one of Stinguard's victims.

"Please tell me a little bit more from the beginning," she said, trying to decipher his sphinxlike answers.

He flinched as if in pain. "My little sister, Robena, was Stinguard's first wife. She died of acute myelogenous leukemia at twenty-six years of age. Stinguard sent his solicitor with divorce papers to her deathbed since he couldn't wait even three more weeks to let her die in peace. His solicitor hounded her until she signed the wretched documents to finalize the divorce. In fact, Stinguard had no more time for Robena as soon as she got sick with leukemia earlier that year. Instead, he made other plans rather than following through on his marriage vows of being true to her in sickness or health. I learned much later of his designs on Nathara Miller, the sister of the vice chair of the World Governing Body, as his ticket to hobnob with the ruling elite. Even though Robena had delayed motherhood to juggle two jobs to support Stinguard through his medical school years, he forgot all about that. She scrimped and saved to fund his education, but it meant nothing since he never bothered to visit her during her final days. Only I was at her bedside on the day of her death."

He paused, gasping for air. Surina was about to rush toward him to check his oxygen level, but he was adamant that he was all right. He shooed her away and spoke in a wheezy voice. "I get a panic attack whenever I recall the pain and humiliation my sister suffered. I curse the day Robena met Stinguard since he finished her off by draining all the life out of her drop by drop. I believe the stress of her toxic marriage caused her to develop leukemia in the prime of her life. I blame myself because I never warned her not to marry him. I needed to shield her from harm, but I failed. I'm an utter and miserable failure. Stinguard duped me with his charade. By the time I saw through his clever disguise, it was too late. Nathara Miller became Stinguard's second wife only two months after my sister's death.

"That marriage sealed his meteoric rise through the ranks of the establishment since every door opened for him afterward. No matter what he does, the power of the ruling elite insulates him from any scrutiny. He was always full of bravado and now even more so after he snagged numerous scientific accolades and humanitarian prizes. Given the unreliability of the censored information from Earth, I try to talk with the new arrivals like you to see if the tide is turning against him. I am waiting for his day of reckoning. Did you work with him? What was your impression of him?"

While listening to Nachton, Surina had considerable difficulty picturing women throwing themselves at someone like Stinguard. Even so, Nachton's inner turmoil was palpable from across the room, for he brought to mind a frantic castaway in a stormy sea, searching in vain for a lifeboat to carry him ashore. He sat on tenterhooks, waiting for her to speak. Heeding the instructions of the council members, she decided not to mention the Stinguard viral vector.

"Stinguard's sobriquet in the hospital was *poison arrow*," she said. "He was a petty despot, who would brook no criticism or opposition. If ever anyone dared to disagree with him, he would hector that person into submission. If they didn't comply, he would retaliate by engineering their exile to Gnaritus. For example, I found a place in his black book because my experiments contradicted his data. I wish I had never met Stinguard either. Sometimes, it's best to avoid such people, but a sense of complacency and indolence lulled me into staying at my job, where I languished as a victim when I should have quit right away.

However, it's important to realize Stinguard flourished because he fits into the ruling elite on Earth so well. I'm glad to leave the cold, money-hungry, power-seeking society on Earth far behind. Gnaritus threw me a lifeline; otherwise, I would have no future. Tell me, Mr. Arthbutnott, did coming to Gnaritus provide you with any solace?"

"We are lucky to live on Gnaritus," he answered with a mirthless smile. "I wish my sister could have come here as well to heal her broken spirit. Who can argue with such laudable ideas as the knowledge of all things, cosmic consciousness, and the developmental singularity? On a practical level, though, despite being on Gnaritus for twenty years, I'm still waiting to attain cosmic consciousness. My meditation instructor, Eoin Dunbar, told me that letting go of all my sorrows is a prerequisite for soaring free into cosmic consciousness. However, I'm haunted by the terrible injustice that befell my sister."

"Eoin is right," Surina said. "Although I can't be sure, I may have connected with cosmic consciousness a few days ago, albeit for only an instant. It felt like coming home, for it neither judged me nor asked anything of me. Somehow, I sensed the presence of my parents there as if they stood right in front of me. Everyone lives on in the cosmic consciousness. Your sister is also there. If you want to attain cosmic consciousness, you'll have to let go of the past."

"How can I ever forgive such an ugsome, evil despot like Stinguard?" Nachton asked, looking aghast at her. "He has committed a mortal sin rather than just a trifling, venial offense. It's unpardonable."

"You have to forgive yourself first," Surina said. "Besides, blaming yourself is unreasonable because humans are such frail, fallible creatures in reality, with much less control over events than we believe."

Nachton squirmed in his chair while his frenetic eyes darted around the room as if searching for absolution. "Well, my goodness, you've given me a lot to chew on, Dr. Mathew," he said in a disconsolate tone. "I wonder if redemption is even possible for me after I failed my sister in every way. If cosmic consciousness exists, why are the scales of justice never in balance? Among all the lies and deceit swirling about everywhere, is there any room for the truth? Will Stinguard ever get his comeuppance?"

He paused as he stared at the floor with abject misery before he turned his pessimistic gaze toward her. "In any case, Dr. Mathew, is the Hodgkin lymphoma under control?"

Surina measured his lymph nodes with the pocket scanner and reviewed the laboratory results in detail. "Great news! You have no evidence of the lymphoma. The next checkup is in a year. Please come back anytime, Mr. Arthbutnott, in the event of new symptoms or more questions."

After thanking her, Nachton trundled out the door, still seeking reparation for the terrible injustices that his sister had endured. Today, Surina had encountered Fergus Wittenberg and Nachton Arthbutnott, another two of Stinguard's victims. She wondered how many other casualties Stinguard had left in his wake. Were they victims of Stinguard or of the ruling elite that nurtured and protected him? Worse still, how many other innocents would have to suffer on Earth after the launch of the Stinguard viral vector?

23
SOS

DR. BRUCE ARTAIR popped into Surina's lab the next morning. Instead of his usual green cape, he wore a white lab coat over his green jumpsuit. His galaxy-blue, twinkling eyes shed a prodigious light and blurred the rest of his facial features. He plopped down on a chair at a workbench beside Surina.

"I hope you're settling in well," he said in a soft, clear voice.

Surina nodded. "Oh yes. I've been making an inventory of the equipment. This lab is phenomenal. These gadgets are unlike any I've seen before."

"If you need any help, I'm in the next-door lab," he said. "Would you like to join my team? My research delves into the developmental singularity. The experiments will introduce you to the scientific methods for studying this complex topic firsthand. There are also evening classes in astrophysics twice a week at Gnaritus University. The autumn session begins tomorrow on September third, so you still have time to enroll."

"That's a good idea," she said. "I can't wait to begin. I'll register for the astrophysics classes at Gnaritus University right away. I also just learned you have no trade-secret laws on Gnaritus."

Bruce stroked his winter-white goatee as if he was pondering a perplexing question. "The absence of trade secret laws has fostered an exponential increase in the number of innovations on Gnaritus. Without the burden of proprietary ownership, patents, copyrights, or competition for research grants, we can share data openly instead of concealing it. Information flows for the benefit of everyone. How can anyone patent knowledge? How can the laws of physics operating in the universe be subject to proprietary ownership as they are on Earth? I remember my time on Earth. The trade secret laws led to many small-minded activities such as backstabbing, surreptitiousness, and trying to get ahead by withholding vital information. I'm glad I left all that mean-spiritedness behind, and you will too. Are you also working on cancer research?"

Surina handed him her research file. "That's my research proposal. What do you think? I'm hoping to apply a genetic analysis to measure the biologic age of patients. My hypothesis is that Gnaritonians reverse their biological ages over time. Perhaps, Gnaritus's atmosphere nurtures the human body to allow the toxic insults from Earth to heal, in a process of regeneration and renewal. The reason for the plunging cancer rates on Gnaritus has to lie in the genome of long-term inhabitants. Somehow, cancer-causing mutations are healing. It's uncertain if external environmental influences, internal mechanisms, or both factors trigger the repair of these genetic mutations."

"Maybe, cosmic energy provided the spark," he said, grinning. "Whoops! Look at the time. I have to go to the welcoming ceremony. If you come to my lab tomorrow afternoon, I'll introduce you to my team, and we could discuss some projects we're working on."

"I look forward to it," she said.

After he had left, Surina put on her lab coat to go to her clinic. She had a packed schedule today. The resilience of the patients astounded her, especially those over a hundred years of age. Since it was impossible to guess a person's age on Gnaritus, she would need to tailor therapy according to the biological age rather than the chronological age of her patients. Other than the specter of the Stinguard viral vector launch on Earth gnawing away at her, she felt content, without a care in the world.

· · ·

Surina relished those halcyon days in September. Although the days did not wane, the weather changed in September. Of course, in the absence of any foliage that could change color or pumpkin fields and apple orchards to harvest, only a fresh crispness in the air heralded autumn's arrival in the space colony. Along the coastline, sudden sandstorms also became more frequent, blocking the light of the three suns and turning the day into the only night seen on the planet. However, the mountain range protected the space colony from the ferocious winds that swept in from the ocean and stirred up the dunes lining the shore into whirling sandstorms. When the fury of the sandstorm ebbed about an hour later, the heavens opened. The torrential downpour cleared the air of any dust and left the beach spotless.

Surina thought the founding pioneers had built the meditation center on the shoreline on purpose, for a walk on the pristine beach after a sandstorm felt like starting over with a clean slate. She also enjoyed the soothing, healing thermal lake and the lessons from Eoin Dunbar in establishing a constant connection with cosmic consciousness. However, she wished her connection with cosmic consciousness would be more than just fleeting. Afterward, walks on the beach or philosophical conversations with Gowan under the shade of the outdoor umbrellas filled the languorous autumnal days.

To catch up on the events in their new lives on Gnaritus, Surina, Alfonso, and Stefan had decided to meet on occasion in the cozy Easter Rose Tea Shop. Soon Gabriel, Rafaela, the Cavaceccis, the

Ellisons, Norval, Gowan, Berenice, Toben, Diola, Nieves, and Fergus joined the group as well. In fact, everyone was welcome. In the beginning, the gathering occurred on a sporadic schedule of every few weeks. However, the subtle textures and exquisite flavors of the delicious food could entice any customer to become a habitué of the Easter Rose Tea Shop. In due time, the unbeatable combination of the tempting menu, together with their discussions about all manner of topics, made for such an enjoyable evening that the club became a regular weekly tradition every Wednesday.

Surina savored the club's debates about thought-provoking questions, which more often than not had no answers. For example, the conundrums included whether a grand design to the universe existed, what lay beyond the edge of the universe, and how many universes could fit into the multiverse. On other occasions, the topic of discussion was more mundane, such as how to improve the curriculum offered at Gnaritus University. The evening's uplifting camaraderie made Surina remember her friends on Earth, wishing they could join the club as well. Despite sending Mercy, Heidi, and the Lofgrens frequent messages via the communal computer, she had yet to receive a single reply.

After one of the club's meetings toward the end of September, Alfonso updated Surina and Stefan on a most puzzling development. "Although I had some success in removing many of the layers in the firewall, new layers spring up to replace any weak spots in the system right away. When I worked at the Rochester Manninghouse Corporation, I learned of the secret Muralis Team that maintains the firewall's integrity. The team used to respond to any threat by creating new software to plug any holes, so I could never reach the impervious core layer responsible for the major interruption in the free flow of information. However, of late, the Muralis Team is no longer as assiduous as before in reestablishing the integrity of the firewall. In the next few days, I'll take advantage of this unique opportunity to assail the firewall with a full-scale barrage to reach the fundamental core and disable it, if possible!"

"Why would the Muralis Team slack off?" Surina asked.

Alfonso and Stefan shrugged.

• • •

Then another inexplicable event happened. All of a sudden, the music from Mohawk Park stopped playing. The twice-weekly welcoming ceremonies offered the entire commercial center the good fortune to experience the exhilaration of a live orchestral performance. In fact, Gabriel and Rafaela's Celestial Violin Concertos had garnered a faithful following in the space colony.

One day at the end of September, during her rounds on the cancer ward, Surina went in search of a few patients missing from their rooms. Since it was a Tuesday, she knew they were most likely in the sunroom. She found Gillian Blyton, a tiny, birdlike woman with a pigeon breast, resting in a wheelchair by the window in the sunroom. Like many other patients, Gillian often came to enjoy the music drifting in from the General Assembly Hall every Monday and Tuesday. Despite her failing vision at the age of a hundred and twenty years, her green eyes glowed in their sunken sockets all the way across the room. Surina examined her with the pocket scanner and found everything in order.

Gillian grimaced. "I liked listening to the Celestial Violin Concertos. I miss the music so much. It reminded me of the haunting Pillars of Creation nebula I saw during the voyage to Gnaritus. It's three weeks since the music stopped playing, or am I losing my hearing also?"

"Your hearing is perfect," Surina replied. "I can play a recording of the Celestial Violin Concertos."

Gillian shook her head. "I like the live performance the best."

Soon, other patients grumbled, griped, and moaned about the lack of music from Mohawk Park.

"I haven't heard the vrooms of any starships landing on

Gnaritus in a long while," Gillian said. "The spacecraft have stopped coming here from Earth, so there aren't any new settlers either."

Surina decided to ask Gabriel and Rafaela about the absence of the music from Mohawk Park when the club met the next day on Wednesday evening at the Easter Rose Tea Shop. Had the World Governing Body ended the Relocation Policy to Gnaritus?

. . .

The monsoon forced the club members to abandon their usual Wednesday evening meeting place on the outdoor patio of the Easter Rose Tea Shop. Even though the patio had an awning, the blustery wind thrashed the rain at an almost horizontal angle against the bay windowpanes and soaked the tables as well. A heartening fire greeted the drenched club members as they poured into the bustling tea shop, full of shoppers taking shelter from the rain. Like a sullen immovable owl, Nachton Arthbutnott surveyed the raucous crowd from his perch alone at a corner table.

Despite the inclement weather, almost everyone arrived, including little George and Elizabeth Ellison with their parents. However, Gowan and Berenice sent word that the deluge would keep them at the meditation center at least until the storm subsided. The delectable appetizers of crab cakes soon made them forget the tempest raging outside. Halfway through the second course, consisting of a vegetarian pizza with a garlic herb crust and grilled eggplant, Surina became concerned about Alfonso's unexpected absence. She reckoned that the wailing wind and pummeling rain could have dissuaded him from venturing outside. Then she told Gabriel and Rafaela about all the patients who missed the sound of their music.

Gabriel's smile widened. "Our last performance was three weeks ago because no other starships have arrived since then. Now, there are no starships from Earth on Gnaritus. The *Odyssey* left long ago with the two space tourists onboard, so there are no

Earth citizens on Gnaritus either. Before the last spaceship lifted off a few days ago, the crew asked mission control on Earth whether there was a change in the Relocation Policy. They learned it was nothing more than a planned momentary pause in the resettlements. When I asked Somerled Knightly, it confounded him as well. He did say how unusual it was since the starships used to arrive as regular as clockwork, rain or shine. What do you think happened?"

"Maybe there was a revolt on Earth, and they refused to come to Gnaritus," Justin Hargreaves said.

A few snickers met his facetious pronouncement, followed by an ominous silence as their imaginations ran wild, searching for possible reasons.

Stefan leaned back in his chair and stopped eating the crunchy pizza. Gooey strings of mozzarella cheese dripped on his nose and chin, which he wiped away with a serviette. Despair hung over him as he spoke in a weary voice. "The all-pervasive World Governing Body on Earth would bulldoze any seedbed of rebellion. Besides, who is there left to instigate a putsch on Earth? It's hard to imagine there are any agents provocateurs or agitators on Earth. Most of the remaining ninety-nine and a half percent of the population are too downtrodden, demoralized, or docile to question anything or foment a revolt. They have capitulated their free will to the other half percent: the ruling elite and their cronies in the World Governing Body. In so doing, they have given their tacit support to the elite whose sole mercenary agenda is to maintain the status quo at any cost. For this, they built an invincible android army to do their bidding and ensure nothing will ever change by clamping down on any seditious behavior.

"The elite is waging a war of attrition against the poor and marginalized. Even though there is some good on Earth, what chance is there for goodness and truth to prevail under such circumstances? The batteries powering the heartless society on Earth will never run out of juice. It will carry on the same in perpetuity until the day things reach a breaking point. Rather than a revolution, I'm more worried about whether the starships made it through the treacherous comet fields of the Kuiper Belt and the Oort cloud in one piece."

Francesca shook her head. "Maybe, Earth just ceased their relocation programs to Gnaritus. Since we are nothing more than an inconvenience for them, perhaps this is a way to sever the last remaining connections with us forever. It feels funny to be alone in this corner of the universe, although Gnaritus was on its own from the start, so it doesn't matter one way or another. In any case, I much prefer being on Gnaritus!"

Without warning, Surina developed butterflies in her stomach along with a dry mouth while thoughts of the Stinguard viral vector surged through her mind. What if lethal mutations had developed as predicted? Then, she kicked herself for overreacting since many benign reasons could also account for the absence of the starships. Meanwhile, Stefan was so busy gobbling up the pizza that he failed to notice Surina staring at him with increasing concern.

In contrast to the heady boisterousness of the other denizens of the tea shop, a subdued silence now engulfed most of the club members. Linda and Giuseppe Cavacecci exchanged worried glances, wondering how their children fared on Earth. Toben and Diola Okafor's minds drifted to the Lake District, hoping that Mercy was safe. However, David and Mary Ellison watched over their playful children with as much merriment as before since they had little regard for the Earth that had scrunched them up like waste paper and thrown them away. Nieves and Fergus could not give a toss about any events on Earth either. They had neither kith nor kin on Earth, and their memory of their home planet was dimming after so many years away.

In the noisy clamor of the Easter Rose Tea Shop, no one noticed Alfonso running in from the rain in a drenched green jumpsuit. His disheveled clothing had streaks of mud after bolting from his home without a coat or umbrella, but he was oblivious to his attire or the inclement weather. Instead, he wore a Cheshire cat grin while his sparkling eyes danced with merriment.

"The wall is down!" Alfonso said from the entryway. "I got through to Earth!"

The good cheer in the tea shop drowned his booming voice. As nobody heard him, he moved closer to the large table by the bay window hosting the club members. The rain dripped from his green jumpsuit and fell on Surina, stirring her from her gloom.

"I got through to Earth!" Alfonso repeated, still trying to catch his breath from his sprint to Mohave Square.

Surina's jaw dropped. The rest of the group stopped eating as they looked up at Alfonso with mystified expressions.

"Is there a computer here we can use?" Surina asked, rushing her words.

"Remember, we have to use the communal computers in the squares to communicate with Earth," Alfonso said. "I went to the General Assembly Hall first where I unblocked the computer for the five council members and gained their approval to do the same with the remaining communal computers. We have to be quick. The latest images from Earth are shocking and blood curdling!"

It dawned on the remainder of the group that Alfonso had torn down the firewall blocking communication between Gnaritus and Earth. Except for the Ellisons, they stood up in unison. Without any hesitation, they ran out into the unrelenting deluge, pushing hard against the gale-force winds that whistled past their ears and hampered their progress. The suddenness of their departure startled the rest of tea shop, but only Nachton Arthbutnott rose from his corner perch to join the frantic exodus. Outside, the heavy raindrops pelted down on them in sheets, leaving a lingering taste of the fresh, cool rain and drenching their clothes right through.

After only a few hours of rain, a raging torrent cascaded down the gentle slope of the hill. As they waded across Mohave Square, water seeped into their black clogs. They climbed four steps to enter the gazebo that stood on an elevated foundation, safe above the river lapping all around it. The wind howled through the gazebo, but the overhanging eaves diverted the rain away from the interior, protecting the communal computer in the center. Even though the gazebo was small, somehow they crammed in like sardines.

Wasting no time, Alfonso worked on the computer at a frenzied pace. His fingers became a blur across the keyboard as he punched in the codes that only he knew. On occasion, a series of beeps and electronic twitters emanated from the computer. Then, he slowed down and applied the final fluid strokes on the console with a flourish. The computer whirred and purred to life. The light from the screen shone on their slack-jawed faces and even broke through the thick dusk enveloping Mohave Square now that the dark nimbostratus clouds obscured the three suns. Instead of the usual Earth Page, a search box appeared, in which Alfonso typed "Global News."

"In London, it's Wednesday the first of October at eight o'clock in the evening!" Alfonso said. "In other words, this satellite feed has only a two-minute lag! How that's even possible, don't ask me. Perhaps, it's due to the series of communication towers constructed on other planets relaying the signal from Earth."

An unrecognizable Stacy Smith appeared on the screen. A "breaking news" ticker tape banner in bold red letters crawled across the bottom of the screen. Instead of her trademark lustrous blond locks, she wore a greasy ponytail from which loose strands sprouted at odd angles. A wrinkled gray T-shirt replaced her customary expensive couture suit. Rather than her habitual fixed toothy smile, she pursed her dry, cracked lips together. Without her usual layers of pancake makeup, her scaly skin, with blotches and black circles beneath her eyes, leaped out from the screen. Even though her trendy purple cat-eye eyeglasses covered half her face, they failed to hide the panic in her eyes. She spoke with a brittle voice, for she was on the brink of tears.

"This is Stacy Smith bringing you *Global News* from London," she said, trying to maintain a semblance of normality. "We have live updates from across the globe on the crisis gripping the world. First, let's recap the latest developments. Since the launch of the Stinguard viral vector six weeks ago in Africa, the casualties are mounting. The first deaths occurred a week ago in sub-Saharan Africa and the towns in the Himalayan foothills. Now the scourge has spread to pockets of Europe, such as Tuscany, the Swiss Alpine villages, and Normandy.

"Even though the World Governing Body suspended the administration of the viral vector a week ago, three-quarters of the world's population had already received it by then. There is a fifty percent chance of developing lethal mutations up to five weeks after receiving the viral vector. These lethal mutations result in the inability of the body's cells to use oxygen for metabolism. Death occurs within twelve hours from the onset of air-hunger symptoms but can be instantaneous. The survival rate is fifty percent because lethal mutations don't develop in half of the recipients of the viral vector. Thus far, no deaths have occurred in those who have not received the viral vector. Although the viral vector is most likely noncommunicable according to extensive testing, a quarantine of the planet Earth is in place for two months out of an abundance of caution. The Ministry of Space Travel has grounded all starship flights to and from Gnaritus for the next two months. Any starships en route to Earth will remain in orbit until the quarantine ends. Let's go live to Aibne Waters, our reporter outside the National Gallery in Trafalgar Square, where demonstrators are demanding justice and accountability."

A rapid succession of astonishing images flashed on the screen unlike any Surina had witnessed before. Even in the night, the crowd poured in from all the streets feeding into the well-lit Trafalgar Square. When there was no more room, they climbed on the stone lions guarding Nelson's Column. Although accustomed to flocking unhindered in the square, the feral pigeons sought refuge on Nelson's Column and the other sculptures instead. The android security guards tried to elbow their way through the crowd and disperse it. However, the unstoppable surging force of the multitude either mauled or flicked aside the puny android security guards like annoying insects. A spasm of anguish convulsed through the beleaguered crowd that wailed, "Down with the World Governing Body."

The plangent cries for justice drowned out the intrepid young reporter standing by the Fourth Plinth, now hosting a Celtic spiral sculpture. Few in the crowd noticed the sacred spiral motif symbolizing infinity and the journey from the outer world to the center or inner soul. Indeed, the harmonious Celtic hierogram contrasted with the torment in the crowd that bemoaned, "Down with the World Governing Body."

The reporter screeched over the ululations. "This is Aibne Waters reporting from Trafalgar Square. With me is Rebecca Strudwick from Gloucester. Rebecca, what motivated you to come here?"

The current maelstrom had swept away Aibne's usual impeccable grooming. He appeared bedraggled in a rumpled khaki trench coat with buttons off kilter and an undone belt dangling from both sides. Since the makeup artist was ill in the hospital after receiving the viral vector, Aibne had foregone the makeup session as well. He had bags under his bleary eyes from a lack of sleep. The stubble on his woebegone face made him even more haggard. Pointing his microphone closer to Rebecca, he encouraged her to tell her story. She was in a swivet. A continuous stream of tears rolled down her flushed cheeks.

She turned her stricken face to the camera and squinted through her tears. "My whole world collapsed overnight. The fickle finger of fate has touched my family. My two little children died six weeks after receiving the viral vector. Their well-organized school follows the World Governing Body's health initiatives to the letter, so they were among the first to get the viral vector in England. Even I was about to have this cursed viral vector when they suspended it after the first deaths occurred a week ago in Africa. I escaped, but I wish I had taken my children's place rather than having them suffer such a terrible fate.

"My husband got the viral vector the day before they scrapped it worldwide, so we're preparing for the worst! I will be alone in the world soon, without a family. The shock of my children's deaths has numbed my senses and crushed my hopes. I came here to demand justice if that is even possible on Earth. I suspect the World Governing Body will ignore this and go on as if nothing is amiss. We're gullible in trusting this corrupt organization to do anything for our benefit since we mean nothing to them! Well, nevermore. We're no longer willing to bend the knee to the World Governing Body. These scam artists and swindlers will never hoodwink us again."

The frantic young mother's voice began to croak. Uncontrollable sobs racked her body. Her husband trembled with outrage as he tried to comfort her. Aibne Waters made an awkward attempt to console both of them but to no avail. Finding the tragic scene almost too much to bear, the camera operator swung the camcorder up to the sky. As they had done over the millennia, a blood moon and a galaxy of stars watched unperturbed by the turmoil and lament on Earth. Above Trafalgar Square, a rare white moonbow graced the sky. Somewhere in that sky were the three suns of Gnaritus as well. How did the camera man know, wondered Surina, that ten thousand light-years away tears also flowed down the cheeks of a group of Gnaritonians observing the heart-wrenching scenes from a gazebo on a distant planet?

The program shifted back to the studio, where Stacy Smith showed similar gritty scenes of protest from every capital city in the world. The crowded streets throbbed with pain. For example, the Royal National City Park in Stockholm overflowed with thirty thousand citizens, clamoring for justice. The lame android security guards viewed the proceedings from the fringes after giving up on their bootless efforts to subdue the demonstration. In an instant, Surina recognized the tall, wiry man who leaped onto the stage on which a mega screen projected images of the other demonstrations around the world. She hoped that somehow Liam and Bergitte Lofgren had escaped from receiving the viral vector.

Liam Lofgren's mellifluous voice rang out through the hushed silence in the park. "My fellow citizens, for the past two months I have fought against the distribution of the Stinguard viral vector. However, the World Governing Body drowned my voice with its underhanded campaign to tarnish and vilify both my wife and me. They crushed any dissenting voice against this viral vector, such as that of our good friend, Dr. Surina Mathew, who they sent away to Gnaritus after impugning her character. No publication or television news outlet would air our concerns either. Due to the wanton recklessness and moral turpitude of Stinguard and the World Governing Body, there is a potential for millions of deaths from this pandemic. Since every life matters, these lives also have value, and we will never forget them. The World Governing Body will never drown our voices or trample on our rights again! There must be justice and change! Therefore, we demand both Rod Stinguard and the World Governing Body stand trial at the World Body Criminal Court for their crimes against innocent victims!"

Thunderous applause erupted in the grieving crowd, which had mushroomed to seventy thousand demonstrators. People swarmed into the park in droves and soon covered every inch of the ground. When there was no more space, the younger members clambered up the trunks of the giant oak trees and perched on the sturdy branches like birds. The call for justice reverberated through the night with chants of "down with Stinguard" and "down with the World Governing Body." The mega screen on the stage, projecting a composite shot of the worldwide demonstrations, also burst into a simultaneous chorus of "down with Stinguard" in a paroxysm of inconsolable lament.

In Sweden, Liam took the microphone again to issue the clarion call that "every life matters" until a tide of "every life matters" rippled through the Royal National City Park.

The impassioned pleas from Stockholm sparked the demonstrators from all the capitals of the world to proclaim "every life matters" in unison. Linking hands with their neighbors to form a symbolic human chain of solidarity around the globe, they sang, "Every life matters." Surina felt sure that the heartfelt cantillations traveled throughout the entire universe as well.

Meanwhile, in the *Global News* studio, Stacy Smith's face became an ashen color as the devastation snowballed into an uncontrollable avalanche and overwhelmed her. When she froze, unable to utter a single word, the program shifted to Aibne Waters instead. The chaotic scenes from earlier in the day of the crowd's unbearable suffering now culminated in the rallying cry of "every life matters." After facing the grim horror of the inexplicable loss of countless innocent lives, they seemed to gain some measure of solace from chanting. Aibne Waters, deciding to embody the spirit of "every life matters," interviewed a homeless man. Wearing threadbare clothes, the itinerant soul carried his meager worldly possessions on his back in a ragged green canvas rucksack. He tied his long, wrinkled black plastic raincoat at the waist with a frayed string. Despite the sooty grime clinging to his rugged face, his eyes were like saucers and sparkled with energy. Even though he had lost his two front teeth, he continued to beam in wonder that anyone would want to interview him.

"Sir, what is your name?" Aibne asked. "Please tell us a little bit about yourself."

"I'm Lamond McNab," he replied in a lilting voice. "After graduating from Newcastle University in art history, I tried to eke out a living selling my paintings, albeit without success. I fell on hard times because nobody is interested in outer-space art depicting the stars, supernovas, nebulae, and other planets.

Somehow, I never managed to paint earthly objects well, even though I tried. Despite everything, I love art, and all my money goes to buying tickets for gallery exhibitions, although none of them even show celestial paintings. People have forgotten the Earth occupies only a tiny corner of the universe. We are a minuscule fraction of the vastness out there in the universe."

"Did you receive the Stinguard viral vector?" Aibne asked with concern.

"I never mattered even a brass farthing for anyone to chase after me just to give me the Stinguard viral vector," Lamond said, grinning. "I slipped under the radar because I'm indigent. In a way, there are advantages to every situation, even being homeless. At present, I have no symptoms of air hunger, so I doubt this virus is communicable. At least, I hope the virus is not transmissible from person to person. I never expected to hear that every life matters. I hope they mean it. If nothing changes after this crisis, then it never will."

"Why did you come here today to demonstrate?" Aibne asked.

Knowing that the program attracted a worldwide audience, Lamond decided to make a global appeal. "First and foremost, I came to express my solidarity with the call for justice for all the people who suffered in this terrible calamity. It's important to realize the Earth occupies only a tiny corner of the universe. There is much more to the universe. The responsibility for these countless deaths on Earth rests in the hands of humans. Humans alone created this evil because they lack harmony. Instead, an insatiable greed for power and dominance consumes this world due to a lack of respect for all life. We can't even recognize the humanity in each other, let alone have respect for all life. Since the universe is in perfect harmony, there can be no such thing as any evil perpetrated by the cosmos. The universe's actions are for the benefit of all. For the most part, the actions of humans on Earth are for self-aggrandizement rather than the greater good."

Lamond turned his face to the night sky and basked in the light of the blood moon for quite some time before he spoke. "I hope to see Gnaritus one day. The World Governing Body bandies around so many horror stories about Gnaritus that nobody should trust. How could anything be as hellish as the events happening on Earth now? If the viral vector turns out to be transmissible from person to person after all, and the curtain falls on the human race here on Earth, at least there is still Gnaritus. I wonder if anyone can hear us up there in the heavens. Earth needs to send out an SOS signal to the universe. Please save our souls!"

His words galvanized the vox populi and reignited the long-forgotten memories of their sister planet Gnaritus. Soon, rallying cries of "Gnaritus," "every life matters," and "SOS" echoed in all the capitals on Earth.

In the gazebo on Gnaritus, Surina shivered in the rain. "I think Earth fears a Permian-like extinction, this time of only humans. Two hundred and fifty million years ago in the Permian period, volcanic eruptions spewed carbon dioxide and sulfuric gases into the atmosphere to trigger the Great Dying of more than nine-tenths of all species. In contrast, this time humans on Earth face extinction at the merciless hands of other humans."

"The Age of Humans could end on Earth," Alfonso said.

Nachton recoiled in horror. "Stinguard has decimated the Earth. He finished my sister off too. In this instance, though, I can also hear the death rattle of the World Governing Body and Stinguard."

In Trafalgar Square, Aibne Waters tried to continue the interview with Lamond. However, Lamond disappeared into the crowd, to join in with the deafening roars of "Gnaritus," "SOS," and "every life matters!"

Instead, Aibne ad-libbed and updated the audience on the latest developments in the global crisis. "Breaking news from Keswick in the Lake District. Earlier today, the police arrested several prominent World Governing Body members, including John Jones-May, the chief executive officer; Cuthbert Miller, the vice chair; and Jane Woodford, the director of personnel. Additional arrests include Dr. Robert Hurpan and Dr. Ed Kadison of the Greysville Quadrant Hospital. Hurpan and Kadison also cochaired the International Scientific Committee on Human Evolution that approved the distribution of the viral vector. Dr. Robert Hurpan served as the chief executive officer of the Rochester Manninghouse Pharmaceutical Company, which manufactured the viral vector.

"Scotland Yard is conducting a sweeping investigation, with more arrests sure to follow. In fact, they detained the entire board of directors of the Rochester Manninghouse Pharmaceutical Company as well. At present, we are going live to Rod Stinguard's home in Keswick in the Lake District. There has been a worldwide manhunt for the absconding Stinguard for the past four days. It turns out he was holed up in a secret underground shelter in his home all along. Since he faces prosecution at the World Body Criminal Court for crimes against humanity, Scotland Yard police detectives are at his home to apprehend him."

On the mega screen at Trafalgar Square, an aerial view appeared of a sprawling Tudor mansion on the banks of the River Derwent. In the pitch-black darkness, a battalion of aerial spy drones guarded the perimeter of the estate and shone a glaring spotlight on the mansion. The ticker tape at the bottom of the screen revealed that the estate boasted fifty rooms, an ornate garden, a swimming pool, and two tennis courts. The elegant garden was resplendent with purple-blue rhododendrons, chrysanthemums, perennial sunflowers, and blooming red roses. An empty white party tent stood by the swimming pool as a vestige of one of Stinguard's high-society parties. Now, a swarm of forensic scientists combed through the estate in the grisly task of compiling evidence.

All of a sudden, a burly Scotland Yard police detective, followed by a group of five androids and a small man, emerged from the front door. When the aerial camera drone swooped in for a closer view, it showed the androids carrying Stinguard, who continued to kick and scream despite the unbreakable manacles around his wrists and ankles. Even so, his young, flaxen-haired wife, Nathara, rushed after him with feline lissomeness in a desperate attempt to stymie the group's progress down the cobbled garden path to the waiting police air van. She gave up and collapsed in a blubbering heap.

Stinguard's wizened face filled the mega screen as he sniveled and whimpered. His eyes had sunk even deeper into their sockets and almost vanished. As the androids approached the row of vans, Stinguard made a final feeble attempt to escape. In an offhand manner, the android security guards walloped him to thwart his anemic efforts and shoved him into a van. With its quarry in a secure cage, the police van ascended and jetted off. Meanwhile, a cast of thousands of spy drones, police detectives, forensic scientists, and android security guards remained to complete the investigation at the estate. In Trafalgar Square, the crowd vented its distemper in raucous cheers and pumped their fists in the air.

In the meantime, on Gnaritus, the nimbostratus clouds had drifted away to the south, carrying the rains with them and leaving behind a brilliant, sunny evening. The frenzied scenes from Earth so transfixed all those in the gazebo that they forgot it was well past the midnight hour. When Surina saw Stinguard's unceremonious detention, a part of her wished things could have turned out better for everyone. How had it come to this? However, no one on Gnaritus—or, for that matter, on Earth—believed with more fervor in the harshest retribution for Stinguard than Nachton Arthbutnott. In fact, Nachton had inched his way crabwise from the back of the gazebo so as to have a front-row seat to the unfolding events. A relaxed megawatt smile replaced his usual tortured scowl, frenetic angst, and continuous handwringing. Instead of his usual taciturn demeanor, he was chatty.

"My sister will be able to rest in peace in her grave," Nachton said with a sigh of relief. "They exposed Stinguard's true colors today, and it's not a pretty sight, to say the least. His blunders have gutted the Earth. He deserves everything coming his way and even worse! It's beyond comprehension how he can even live with himself after everything he has done."

"These are dark days for Earth," Stefan said. "It's teetering on the precipice without a safety net or parachute."

"Alfonso, can we send a message to Earth?" Surina asked.

"Yes!" he replied with glee. "If I connect to the television studio's mainframe computer, our message will go live worldwide."

"Maybe, we should get Somerled Knightly's approval first," Stefan said.

Alfonso stopped typing. "The council members have given the green light to communicate with Earth. I asked them earlier today. Somerled indicated he would prefer someone who had just arrived here on Gnaritus to make the first contact with Earth. He said he left Earth ninety years ago, so he has little memory of the customs there."

Francesca frowned. "Do you think Earth is ready to listen? What if we make matters worse?"

"How can anything be as bad as what's happening already?" Nachton said.

"Their SOS means they need our help," Surina said. "If we don't try to help them, then there is no one else who can."

Alfonso's eyes gleamed as he became absorbed in punching in another series of codes at a dizzying pace. "The video link connection is complete. Once I press this button, we'll appear on the mega screen in Trafalgar Square. Bingo! Here we go!"

On Earth, Aibne Waters remained at his post, anchoring the broadcast from Trafalgar Square. After updating his audience on the flurry of arrests, he began a fruitless search for someone else in the crowd to interview. The chants of "Gnaritus," "every life matters," and "SOS" continued unabated through the rest of the night and well into the morning. As the edifices of society collapsed, few in the crowd wanted to go home to face their plight alone. Many had received the viral vector and knew their time on Earth could be limited. Even though others had escaped from receiving the Stinguard viral vector, most of their family members had succumbed to it. While the foundations and fallacies that they had built their lives on crumbled, the populace felt stripped naked, with their faith in the justness of their society in tatters. They weltered in confusion and misery. In essence, standing together as one gave them some level of consolation from their existential anguish and assuaged their fears.

All of a sudden, the mega screen showing the worldwide demonstrations changed to an image of about a dozen eager faces with luminous eyes. They peered at Earth from a gazebo in an alien desert landscape with three suns and a planet with colorful rings in an endless blue sky. For the first time that day, shocked silence fell in Trafalgar Square.

With Alfonso prodding her to say something, Surina spoke in a quavering voice. "Hello, Earth! We are from Gnaritus responding to your SOS. Along with messages of condolence, we wish to tell you that all is not lost. In fact, we thought we had lost everything when the Earth cast us out, but we found so much more on our journey to Gnaritus instead. Always remember hope is the foundation of existence as well as the fundamental currency of the universe. Therefore, there is always hope. You are not alone in the universe. We on Gnaritus stand with you!"

24
The Bass Rock

AIBNE WATERS REALIZED that he could have the scoop of the century, but he vacillated. Were these *really* the humans from Gnaritus? Why were they all wearing rain-soaked green jumpsuits? Were these the little green humanoid creatures with radiant eyes that the golden oldie movies had popularized? Was someone playing a prank? While he debated whether to interview them, an elated voice spoke from the Royal National City Park in Stockholm.

"Surina, is that you?"

"Yes, Liam, I made it to Gnaritus," Surina replied. "Our computer whiz, Alfonso Diaz, cracked the firewall blocking our messages to Earth. There is nothing to fear about Gnaritus since it's flourishing. Money has no currency here, so there is no obsession with materialistic possessions. Instead, the goal on Gnaritus is to seek the knowledge of all things and to avoid repeating the mistakes of human history."

By then, the mega screen in Trafalgar Square had shifted to side-by-side images of the Gnaritonians and the demonstration in Stockholm. Surina explained all about the many advances in the

New World, such as the quest for cosmic consciousness. The protestors listened with rapt attention. After she had finished, cheers filled the Royal National City Park.

"We are in dire need of your help on Earth," Liam said. "One of our most pressing concerns is whether the Stinguard viral vector is transmissible from person to person."

Surina shook her head. "None of my experiments revealed even the remote possibility of human-to-human transmission. I doubt there's a threat of a mass extinction of humans on Earth."

A groundswell of relief rippled through the gathered multitude.

Liam addressed the worldwide audience in the hope of uniting the tattered remnants of Earth's society. "We need the help of our friends on Gnaritus. Gnaritus is a beacon of hope in this quagmire. First and foremost, we should mourn and bury our dead. Then, the onus is on us to conduct a far-reaching investigation to understand the confluence of factors leading to this catastrophe. Our quest for the truth will be without any bias or fear. In one week, the first trial at the World Body Criminal Court will bring swift justice to the principal parties causing this tragedy. After that, as we learn more from the investigation, all those responsible for this catastrophe will also face justice. Only if we restore probity, integrity, and decency in our society can we guarantee that these events will not happen again in human history.

"We have to overhaul the archaic governance on Earth to make it more equitable and inclusive, where every life matters. During the difficult days ahead, we will need guidance from Gnaritus. Most of all, we hope to learn how those cast off by an unjust society forged a more sophisticated and enlightened civilization on Gnaritus since we on Earth have to start over from scratch as well. We have been here all night, and now it is a new dawn. It's time to go home to gather the courage and determination for the journey on the long road to redemption. Nothing in this quest will be easy because all our former assumptions will also be on trial.

However, we are not alone in this enterprise, for our friends on Gnaritus have come to our aid. Like a shining light, they will guide us through our dark days ahead."

The demonstrators from around the world rallied behind Liam's clarion call to action and erupted in a prolonged round of cheers. They gained additional reassurance in knowing that they had the unexpected support of their long-forgotten sister planet, Gnaritus. Soon, the first rays of the sun peeped through the clouds on the horizon in Stockholm's Royal National City Park. Still unruffled by human folly, the birds broke into song as they always did in honor of the new day. While the sun ascended to its throne in the sky, the exhausted protesters resolved to change course and move humanity forward. They staggered home, and the crowd in Trafalgar Square followed suit. The feral pigeons cooed as they reclaimed their turf and refreshed themselves with morning baths in the fountain pools.

Standing in a now-deserted Trafalgar Square, Aibne Waters decided to end the program. "To our viewers on Earth and Gnaritus, thank you for joining us for our live coverage of these fast-moving events. Oh, we have more breaking news from the Lake District. Events are happening at a lightning pace. The new House of Humanity will take over the defunct World Governing Body's headquarters in Keswick. By popular consent, Liam Lofgren is the new president of the House of Humanity. Please join us tomorrow for our broadcast on this global crisis from the Aodh Logan's World Body Criminal Court in Scotland."

The mega screen in Trafalgar Square faded to black as Aibne Waters and his camera crew hurried home after their all-night stint covering the demonstration. Meanwhile, the image on the communal computer in the gazebo on Gnaritus switched to the *Global News* studio. First, there was a recap of the previous day's tumultuous events, including the sudden change in the fortunes of Stinguard and the World Governing Body. However, the dolorous scenes of the mourners singing dirges at one of many death marches through the mazy streets of Chislehurst, Kent, were too much to bear for Surina. She felt enervated by the tumultuous events on Earth.

"Can we send an e-mail to my daughter, Mercy, on Earth to make sure she's all right?" Toben asked.

"The firewall is down, so e-mails should go through," Alfonso replied. "Well, we'll soon find out."

While Alfonso opened the e-mail page, Surina heard the murmur of about forty people on Mohave Square. She guessed they were waiting to communicate with their relatives on Earth. However, the crowd was smaller than she expected. Then, she realized that most Gnaritonians had few ties left to Earth. For example, second-generation Gnaritonians would not have seen the mother planet other than in the history books. The long-term residents' memories of Earth could be fading as well. For the rest, maybe they thought no more of the planet that had cast them away.

Once Alfonso had established a link to the e-mail page, he stepped aside. Toben typed his message. "Greetings, Mercy. We are well. Did you get the Stinguard viral vector? How are Darren, Janet, and Jari? Please let us know you are safe. Hugs and kisses from Mom and Dad on Gnaritus."

Toben and Diola had a nervous wait. Both of them were almost on the verge of going home when their hearts skipped a beat as Mercy's reply flashed across the screen. With elation, they read: "Mom and Dad, we are doing well. Surina had warned me about the Stinguard viral vector before she left for Gnaritus, so we made sure to avoid it. Incredible to see you and Surina on television last night! You looked healthy and full of life. Is all of Gnaritus a desert? It seems beautiful with three splendid suns and a planet with colorful rings in the sky! I'll keep you updated on events here. Give my best to Surina as well. I hope we can visit each other one day when all this is over. Darren, Janet, and Jari are also well. Love, Mercy."

Toben and Diola fizzed with exuberance at the good news. Next, Surina sent an anxious e-mail to Heidi and the Lofgrens. Much to her relief, they had not received the viral vector either. Likewise, Francesca breathed easier after learning her son was safe.

Alfonso looked bleary-eyed. "I'm bushed. I forgot all about the time. It's already seven o'clock in the morning. Can you imagine we've been watching the news from Earth since yesterday evening? I can barely keep my eyes open. Do you want to have some breakfast at the Easter Rose Tea Shop before heading home?"

"Yes," Surina, Francesca, and Stefan replied in unison.

Surina, Alfonso, Francesca, and Stefan managed to push through the eager crowd milling around the gazebo. They lumbered across Mohave Square, splishing and sploshing in the water. The floodwater had receded a little during the night and now reached their ankles. Slimy mud splashed on their green jumpsuits with every step they took.

They trudged into the Easter Rose Tea Shop for breakfast. To Surina's surprise, all five council members occupied a table by the bay window. The rest of the tea shop was empty. Dishes, pots, and pans clattered in the kitchen.

Somerled Knightly waved to the beleaguered group. "Come and join us."

As Surina sat down next to Eoin Dunbar, she thought of how the five council members' impassibility comforted all those fortunate enough to be near them. In fact, their knowledge and experience of cosmic consciousness gave them a profound understanding of even the most abominable acts without the need to pass judgment or apportion blame. Even though the Earth shook at its core, they comported themselves with a serene and equable dignity, for their minds remained steadfast and at peace. Their inner peace seemed to be the same regardless of whether fortune was good or bad.

"Many thanks, Alfonso, for your hard work in disabling the firewall," Somerled said as he passed a plate of croissants around the table. "Only through your diligence and persistence did we learn about the dire circumstances on Earth. Otherwise, we would still be oblivious to the unfolding catastrophe there. Surina, how do you know Liam Lofgren, the new leader of the House of Humanity?"

"I met Liam and Bergitte Lofgren by chance on my holiday to Greece the week before I left Earth," Surina replied in between bites of a warm, buttery croissant. "He's a history professor at Stockholm University as well as a polymath with a wide-ranging knowledge of philosophy and the humanities. In fact, there can be no better leader on Earth to chart the right course out of these dark times."

"Liam's equanimity impressed us as well when we spoke to him this morning," Eoin Dunbar said. "He said the founding principle of the House of Humanity is that every life matters. His interest in learning about Gnaritus was apparent, including his hope of replicating our money-free society on Earth one day. Like all of us, Liam wished he could have done more to prevent this carnage. However, our letter would have been too late to avert the disaster since the viral vector's launch was a fait accompli more than a month ago. Although we tried to prevent this catastrophe, many things seem to be beyond our control. It's a relief that none of the new settlers on Gnaritus have received the viral vector. Dr. Ailbeart Ross verified your data, Surina, that this viral vector is not communicable, so there is no need to quarantine any of the new arrivals."

"Next week, there will be a trial at the Aodh Logan's World Body Criminal Court," Bruce Artair said. "Surina, the prosecution needs your testimony about how Stinguard and his cadre of friends ignored the results of your experiments and brought on this disaster. Stefan, they asked for your evidence as well, regarding the suppression of your article about the dangers of the viral vector. Alfonso, your knowledge of the firewall will also be vital. Since the Earth is under quarantine for two more months, the only way to testify will be by video link. On Monday, October sixth, please be at the General Assembly Hall by nine o'clock in the morning to give evidence by video link to the trial at the Aodh Logan in Scotland."

"No practicing solicitors remain on Gnaritus due to the long-extinct judicial and penal system," Eoin said. "Francesca, could you put aside your painter's brushes for a while in exchange for your former solicitor's robes and accompany Surina, Alfonso, and Stefan to the proceedings?"

Francesca hesitated. "I wish I didn't have to, but I guess I must. We can spend this week preparing the testimony to be ready for Monday. It will involve whittling away extraneous information not relevant to the case and learning how to give succinct answers."

All of a sudden, Justin Hargreaves burst forth through the front door and collapsed in an armchair by the hearth. A monastic silence descended on the tea shop as the others watched him lighting the electric fire to guard against the crisp October chill. Then he sat motionless in the same dejected pose as Rodin's statue of *The Thinker* at the Gates of Hell. He stared into the depths of the desolate flames and wallowed in the abyss of misery. Just as Surina was on the verge of asking him what had happened, Torree emerged from the kitchen with a platter of puffy chocolate-filled croissants. She stopped dead when she glimpsed the morose form of her husband slouching in a chair. Right away, she plopped down in an armchair next to him, holding his hand in both of hers.

"I sent a message to Tristan," Justin said in a funereal tone. "Our grandson Sean would have graduated this year from Oxford University Law School. His diligence at following the World Governing Body's initiatives got the better of him since he was among the first to receive the Stinguard viral vector in England. Sean died a week ago along with many other students who heeded the call to get the viral vector. Tristan and the rest of the family are not at risk because they never found the time to get the cursed viral vector. Only serendipity saved them. For some reason, Tristan blathered on about the end of the continuous line of succession at the Hargreaves and Thomas law firm. Of course, Sean was such a bright lad, with his whole life ahead of him, but Stinguard finished him off. Is there any point in putting Stinguard on trial? Is it even possible for him to atone for what he has done? No punishment could ever match the grievous harm he has inflicted by decimating entire families!"

For the first time, the Easter Rose Tea Shop closed early that day.

The turmoil on Earth had rippled across the Milky Way galaxy, for many families on Gnaritus shared the plight of the Hargreaves to greater or lesser degrees.

• • •

Over the weekend, Surina went to Bob and Betina Pagett's house on Seneca Square to pay her respects. Alfonso was already there. A recording of Gabriel and Rafaela's "Pillars of Creation" violin concerto played in the background. Sitting in an armchair by the blazing hearth, Betina dabbed her eyes with a tear-soaked handkerchief. She straightened her slumped shoulders when Surina entered the darkened room. All the window blinds were down, and only two candles on the mantelpiece lit up the room.

"Thanks for coming, Surina," she said.

Surina sat down on the sofa. "I can't express in words how sorry I feel about your son and daughter's sudden deaths from the viral vector."

Betina choked back her tears. "It's a tragedy. Our only blessing is our fifteen-year-old granddaughter is still alive. She escaped the viral vector by a miracle when she stayed home sick the entire week that her school was dispensing it."

Her voice cracked from the strain, and her head drooped.

Alfonso put down his cup of tea on the side table. "My paternal uncle and maternal aunt succumbed to the viral vector as well. Mom and Dad are taking it hard."

Bob came in from the kitchen and placed a plate of cucumber sandwiches on the coffee table. "I heard Francesca's son dodged the viral vector."

"The Cavacecci's three children escaped as well," Betina said.

"A plague of necrology is sweeping the Earth," Alfonso said. "The Gnaritus Orchestra has resumed its evening performances in Mohawk Park in the hope of comforting the bereaved. I transmitted a performance of Gabriel and Rafaela's music to Aibne Waters. Now the *Global News* ends with the 'Pillars of Creation' violin concerto as a tribute to the victims."

"I think it's an appropriate choice to conclude the harrowing news of all the funerals on Earth," Bettina said. "I keep playing the 'Pillars of Creation' soundtrack as well. That's the music you hear today. Somehow, the canorous music articulates my inexpressible grief. It's almost as if my soul grows wings. I soar across the solar system and into interstellar space to seek refuge among the stardust. After all, we will one day return to our origins in the stardust."

Bob nodded. "In a way, this soulful requiem provides hope. The poignant music makes me believe there is a grand design in creation so that our suffering will not be in vain."

The lyrical music was still playing as Surina left to see Francesca and prepare for the trial.

• • •

On Monday morning, Surina arrived at eight thirty on the outskirts of Mohawk Park and hurried toward the General Assembly Hall. Even though she was just a witness at the trial, she still had the collywobbles and a hard time controlling the butterflies in her stomach. The unpalatable thought of seeing Stinguard again, even if only by a video link, further exacerbated her apprehension.

While waiting for Surina in the shaded portico of the General Assembly Hall, Francesca, Alfonso, and Stefan went over their testimonies with a fine-tooth comb once more. They had little enthusiasm for the grim proceedings, but as soon as Surina joined them, they followed a steady stream of Gnaritonians inside. No one spoke as they inched down the corridor at a snail's pace toward a door that was emblazoned with an "Amphitheater" sign. The amphitheater hosted all the town hall meetings but served today as a makeshift courtroom, with enough seats for a thousand spectators. Only four seats in the front row remained vacant. The audience muttered and stared in eager anticipation at a giant screen dominating the wall in front of them. Francesca led the way down the precipitous stairs, past the semicircular terraced seating, to their first-row seats in the central orchestral area.

Surina sank into the comfort of the cushioned leather chairs with relief in having a few minutes to collect her thoughts. She recognized the five council members sitting together in the fifth row, but recent arrivals to Gnaritus comprised the majority of the audience. For example, Gabriel, Rafaela, the Cavaceccis, and the Ellisons were waiting on tenterhooks for the trial to start. In the second row, Bob Pagett tried to console his wife, Betina, who sobbed in despair over the loss of her children. However, a few long-term residents were in the audience as well, such as the Hargreaves, Gowan, Berenice, Norval, Nieves, Fergus, Nachton, and Ailbeart.

Surina wondered why there was standing room only in the amphitheater. Why had so many people come? Some would have come to seek justice for their dead relatives, although indemnification was impossible since nothing could compensate for their tragic loss. Earth seemed to have left an indelible mark on many others, even though none of their relatives had died from the viral vector. Perhaps they came in the hope of making sense of the society that had forsaken them so that they could break free from its tentacles, which ensnared them still.

Nachton Arthbutnott leaned over from the seat next to Surina's and whispered in her ear. "Get ready, Dr. Mathew, for the trial of the century! It should be a real barn burner. Stinguard belongs in the deepest, darkest dungeon! Do you think this catastrophe is a watershed moment for Earth, or will it just be business as usual after this trial?"

Before Surina could reply, Francesca handed each of them a file outlining key components of their testimony. She sat down next to Surina and gave last minute advice. "Just give the facts as they happened, and you'll never go wrong."

Sitting on the other side of Francesca, Alfonso thumbed through his file once more. "I hope this trial will be over as fast as possible," he said. "The evidence against Stinguard and the World Governing Body is overwhelming, but then again you can never predict the outcome on Earth."

All of a sudden, the gigantic screen in front of them flickered to life. The composite shot showed Aibne Waters in a leafy park awash with variegated flowers outside the Aodh Logan on one side and the amphitheater on Gnaritus on the other panel. Stillness permeated the amphitheater as the audience sat agog on the edges of their seats, listening with eager attention to every word from Earth. Aibne had made every effort to look smart by wearing a crisp, brand-new navy-blue suit with a complementary maroon tie. However, even the intensive makeup session could not erase the dark circles under his eyes from his many sleepless nights since the beginning of the swirling maelstrom on Earth.

"Welcome, Earth and Gnaritus," he said. "This is our live coverage of the trial of Rod Stinguard and the World Governing Body at the Aodh Logan in Scotland. We are here at the World Body Criminal Court in the dune landscape of the Aodh Logan, next to the North Sea coastal city of North Berwick. After a tour of the World Body Criminal Court complex and the Bass Rock, we will go inside."

The audience in the amphitheater saw images of the coast from the aerial camera drone as it swept over the World Body Criminal Court. It went past a dune field of spindly marram grass, prickly saltwort, and thistly sea holly in full bloom with metallic blue flowers. Then, it lingered over the beach, which was an amalgam of brown sand and gray pebbles. Occasional rumblings of thunder broke through the coal-tar clouds hiding the sun and threatening rain. In the distance, a bolt of lightning pierced the gloom.

The tempestuous North Sea vented its fury by spuming over the seawall. Soon, merciless waves clobbered the craggy shoreline, sending fountains of salt spray into the air. Offshore in the distance were the three extinct volcanic islands of Fidra, Craigleith, and Bass Rock, which served as sanctuaries for thousands of seabirds. In contrast to the other islands, the Bass Rock had a white color due to the large colony of nesting white Atlantic Gannets. Razorbills, kittiwakes, guillemots, and puffins added to the deafening squawks from the island. The white color of the Bass Rock also came from the mounds of seabird droppings that left a pungent stench in the air.

The aerial camera drone swept along the ocean, where puffins wheeled and dived into the turbulent waters to catch fish for their pufflings, which were nesting in the crevices of the rocky cliffs. Then the drone ascended the steep precipice to the dramatic white volcanic rock surface of the island, teeming with a horde of screeching white Gannets. However, the saxicoline nesting seabirds were oblivious to the desolate gray building at the center of the Bass Rock, a twelve-story maximum-security prison. Although each cell had a barred window, the windowpane could open without difficulty. In spite of that, few prisoners dared to let in the putrid odor of the bird droppings or the deafening caterwauls of the seabirds, which were reminiscent of quarreling cats. A thick lawn of fresh seabird droppings also besmirched the deserted open-air exercise yard for prisoners. Alongside the playful seabirds circling overhead, an ominous battalion of drones guarded the perimeter of the island like hawks.

Next came an aerial view of the truculent, shackled prisoners in beige jumpsuits shuffling in a single file on a carpet of seafowl dung to a waiting windowless gray air van. A caption accompanying this bleak image read: "Rod Stinguard, John Jones-May, Robert Hurpan, Ed Kadison, Cuthbert Miller, and Jane Woodford are to stand trial at the World Body Criminal Court." As they trekked across the courtyard, the thunder growled; the rain began to spit down, and thousands of seabirds battered them with pellets of fetid dung. Meanwhile, the security guard carried a black umbrella and wore a protective mask to keep out the noisome vapors on the island. The air van bearing the reviled prisoners hovered briefly before an angry flock of thousands of screaming seabirds chased it off the island, believing it to be a threat to their nests. Much to Surina's surprise, Nachton Arthbutnott began clapping, and soon the entire amphitheater broke out in raucous applause.

While the van flew across the fierce North Sea, it tossed back and forth, much like the mighty waves in the gale-force wind that wailed a mournful dirge. It landed in the courtyard at the back entrance of the World Body Criminal Court just as the thundering heavens opened up with a deluge. The relentless rain lashed the prisoners and drenched their beige uniforms as they hobbled along the cobblestoned path. Even so, the pellets of the seabird excrement still clung to their faces, hair, and clothes like glue and refused to rinse free in the rain.

After they had disappeared into the receiving area for prisoners, the broadcast returned to Aibne Waters as he raced to the front entrance of the World Body Criminal Court to escape from the rain. He ran on a bridge over the crystal-clear waters of the moat surrounding a twenty-one-story glass building. The glass symbolized transparency and openness. Over the ornate gold plated door, a silver placard declared the mission of the World Body Criminal Court to be *Veritas et Equitas*, or truth and justice. In his rain-soaked new suit, Aibne entered the three-story lobby of the judicial building that spanned two football pitches. The park outside continued inside the lobby with a verdurous oasis of innumerable plants and arboreal treasures from every country in the world to represent unity. The vegetation encircled the edges of the great hall and soaked the sun's rays through the glass.

Dominating the middle of the cavernous lobby was a row of abstract sculptures from all the corners of the globe in an endless array of shapes and colors. Aibne clawed his way through a crowd that stood shoulder to shoulder. Even though an undercurrent of disillusionment rippled through the crowd, they held signs demanding justice while keeping their eyes glued to a screen showing the interior of the main courtroom.

Soon, Aibne arrived at an impressive bronze sculpture of Earth outside the door of the main courtroom. After catching his breath, he wiped off the raindrops from his face before he addressed the worldwide audience. "Court will be in session in fifteen minutes. Today, the case is docket number twenty-two. The World Body Criminal Court's most senior judge is Marigold Harbottle. She will decide both the verdict and the punishment since there is no jury system. In addition, the chief prosecutor is Godafrid Kester, who has litigated many cases in the World Body Criminal Court. He has a reputation for incisiveness and insightful analysis that gets to the heart of the most complicated court cases.

"Contrary to the advice of the court, the prisoners elected to represent themselves in these proceedings and declined any defense counsel. Marigold Harbottle is a graduate of the prestigious Sorbonne University in Paris, where she also practiced as a solicitor. However, her friends claimed that the establishment blacklisted her from any promotion due to her infrangible ethical principles and outspoken defense of truth and justice. All that changed with the unexpected death two weeks ago of the long-term senior judge, Nestor Jones-May, from a heart attack. Soon after, Marigold Harbottle's peers elected her to fill this vacancy. In any case, another judge would have been necessary for this trial to avoid any conflict of interest since Nestor Jones-May was the brother of one of the accused, John Jones-May.

"The courtroom is almost full, but I have a reserved seat in the spectators' gallery next to the prosecution team. Only *Global News* has exclusive rights to televise the trial worldwide on Earth as well as to Gnaritus. Throughout the broadcast, you will see a split-screen image of the courtrooms on Earth and Gnaritus. First, I would like to welcome our friends on Gnaritus to this broadcast. Thank you for joining us."

A smattering of polite applause in the amphitheater on Gnaritus accompanied Aibne's announcement before reverting to a breathless silence. When Aibne opened the unwieldy oak-paneled door with both hands, the camera drone followed him in before it went to roost above the spectators' gallery. At the head of the courtroom, the judge's oak bench stood on a pedestal. In fact, all the furniture was made of oak. Next to the judge's bench, on level ground, was a witness box. On both sides of the courtroom, against the walls, were two simple rectangular tables for the prosecution on the right and the defense on the left. A square screen in the center of the courtroom would relay the testimony from the witnesses on Gnaritus. Even though only a small wooden fence separated the spectators' gallery from the prisoners' dock, a special encasing of bulletproof glass would protect the accused for this contentious trial. After squeezing past a row of seated spectators, Aibne sat down beside the prosecution table and began writing copious notes on his tablet computer.

The chattering in the packed spectators' gallery died down in an instant as a door in the corner of the courtroom behind the witness box opened. A tiny, frail woman in a black robe with an ermine collar entered and settled into a tufted, plush black-leather high-back chair at the judge's bench. Judge Marigold Harbottle's waist-length gray hair with a central parting framed a placid face that was rippling with wrinkles, which cascaded down her neck and hid her chin. Peering with steely determination through hefty, round black-rimmed Wayfarer glasses at the courtroom, she thought of how she had become a judge after a lifetime of being passed over for promotion. In fact, only three weeks ago, she had been in the midst of packing after receiving her relocation notice to Gnaritus. Now here she was, presiding over her first case as the senior judge in the world's highest court.

However, Judge Harbottle knew this case included many other precedents. For example, under the leadership of the former senior judge, Nestor Jones-May, the World Body Criminal Court prosecuted cases primarily from the African continent. The case before the court today heralded a paradigm shift since it was the first to involve the World Governing Body. As she opened the files on her desk, she was still in shock over her ascendancy to the bench a week ago at the age of fifty-five years. Perhaps, long overdue changes are coming to Earth's hidebound society, she thought.

Moments later Godafrid Kester, a towering, brawny man in his fifties, bounded into the courtroom through the same door, carrying a brown-leather briefcase. He took a seat at the prosecution table, whereas the defense table remained unoccupied. In one fell swoop, he emptied the contents of the briefcase onto the table, arranging six files in a row. His valuable online personal assistant materialized on his desktop computer to discuss the day's strategy.

The aerial camera drone showed Godafrid Kester examining the files, jotting down last-minute notes in the margins, and whispering to his online personal assistant. His task that day was to expose the morass of unbridled malfeasance, conceit, unscrupulous greed, subterfuge, hypocrisy, chicanery, duplicity, and lust for power and domination running rife in the World Governing Body. However, it did not daunt him since he had borne witness to treachery many times before in his career spanning three decades, except never on this scale. He often wondered what if anything would prevent the vicious circle of human history from repeating itself on Earth.

His mission was to conduct the trial with efficiency rather than to make a production of it and prolong the agony. Perhaps an expeditious verdict would provide closure for the grieving world population, he thought. Despite the enormity of his assignment, his impassive face had a set smile displaying the gap between his two front teeth, which highlighted the glow of his black-satin skin. Due to his wish for at least one distinctive feature after becoming bald in his twenties, he had shunned cosmetic surgery to correct his diastema. Similar to the folklore of France and his parents' ancestral tribe in Namibia, he believed they were his *lucky teeth*. He would need some luck to wrap up this historic trial with a swift verdict.

25

Our Place in the Universe

THE FLOOR OF the prisoners' dock creaked as it plummeted underground. After ten minutes, it crawled up. The spectators in the gallery gasped as the disheveled heads of the six defiant prisoners emerged. The scruffy prisoners looked as if they had been in a ferocious scrimmage. Despite the shackles on their wrists and ankles, they stood with overweening pride and nabob-like airs, albeit spattered with seabird droppings. Even though they wore identical beige uniforms, Stinguard was readily identifiable as the shortest prisoner. Otherwise, after being stripped of their lofty titles, they had little to distinguish themselves. The spectators crinkled their noses, for the prisoners reeked of the rancid smell of the musty prison and seafowl dung.

The sight of the prisoners inflamed the spectators further so that they unleashed their fury as the palpable tension in the courtroom boiled over. "Scum of the Earth. Scoundrels. Scam artists. Down with Stinguard! Down with the World Governing Body!"

The intensity of the public opprobrium caught the prisoners by surprise. They shifted in their shackles, and there was panic in their eyes. Even so, Surina doubted that it would make even a small dent in their immutable aura of invincibility. In contrast, the amphitheater on Gnaritus remained in a solemn silence, and only Nachton Arthbutnott joined in with the vociferous denunciation of Stinguard.

Judge Marigold Harbottle slammed her gavel on her desk and admonished the spectators. "Silence! We will have order in this court! There will be no more interruptions of this nature; otherwise, I will adjourn the court."

The spectators acquiesced with reluctance, and soon a respectful silence reigned in the courtroom such that they could even hear a pin drop. Meanwhile, the camera drone crept along the prisoners' dock, showing close-up views of the each of the accused as Judge Harbottle continued the business of the court.

"The prisoners are on trial for crimes against humanity," she said. "As is their prerogative, each of the accused has chosen to represent himself or herself at this trial instead of procuring defense counsel. The first accused is Dr. Rod Stinguard, the former chief scientific officer of the Cancer Unit at the Greysville Quadrant Hospital, who engineered the viral vector. Dr. Stinguard was also a member of the board of directors of the Rochester Manninghouse Pharmaceutical Company, which manufactured the viral vector. Please step forward. How do you plead, sir, to the charges of crimes against humanity?"

Ever since arriving in the courtroom, Stinguard had been searching the spectators' gallery in a frantic state. When the judge reminded him again to step forward to enter his plea, he twisted around to face her so that his dyspeptic countenance filled the screen in the amphitheater on Gnaritus. Instead of his perpetual scowl, he wore a shell-shocked, bewildered expression, for he realized none of his influential friends had come to support him, not even his wife. Moreover, he resembled a cadaver, with eyes that had disappeared into sunken sockets. His blanched skin looked as if it was either drained of blood or coated with powdery mildew from the dank prison cell.

The question seemed to flummox him, for he frowned and mumbled in a toneless voice. "Not guilty, my lady."

Judge Harbottle continued. "Next is John Jones-May, the former World Governing Body's chief executive officer. In essence, your signature finalized the approval for the distribution of the Stinguard viral vector. How do you plead, sir, to the charges of crimes against humanity?"

John Jones-May's dyed-blond locks had been the only striking feature of an otherwise nondescript face. However, his few days in the damp prison on the Bass Rock had stripped away the lustrous sheen of his hair and left only moldy, white hay on his scalp. A querulous sneer replaced his hail-fellow-well-met camaraderie. He considered the proceedings to be nothing more than a temporary nuisance, for only one possible outcome existed in his mind: his acquittal.

He lifted his chin up, puffed out his chest, and spoke in a bilious voice. "Not guilty, my lady."

Even though the declarations of innocence puzzled the judge, she maintained her composure. "The third accused is Cuthbert Miller, the former vice chair of the World Governing Body and the past chair of the Relocation Council. Your signature also authorized the launch of the Stinguard viral vector. How do you plead, sir, to the charges of crimes against humanity?"

Cuthbert Miller's rotund habitus attested to his many indulgences as a discerning gourmand, connoisseur of fine dining, and consummate bon vivant. He glowered at Stinguard with resentment. "My brother-in-law, Rod Stinguard, bamboozled me into approving this viral vector. He told me it was safe. None of this is my fault!"

Judge Harbottle silenced his coward cry. "Please only answer the question!"

"Not guilty, my lady!" he said with rancor.

After clearing her throat, the judge resumed. "The fourth accused is Dr. Robert Hurpan, the former medical director of the Greysville Quadrant Hospital. You were also the cochair of the International Scientific Committee on Human Evolution and the chief executive officer of the Rochester Manninghouse Pharmaceutical Company, which manufactured the Stinguard viral vector for worldwide distribution. How do you plead, sir, to the charges of crimes against humanity?"

All the way on Gnaritus, when Hurpan's scruffy, pugnacious countenance filled the screen in the amphitheater, he still reminded Surina of a stonyhearted vulture. He seemed unaware that his spectacles were askew on his beaklike nose. Of course, his current circumstances would have given anyone pause, but he continued to fume and bellow like a caged bull or a volcano about to erupt.

Peering at the judge with bloodshot eyes, he slavered at the mouth as he spat out his plea in a stentorian voice. "Not guilty, my lady."

After making a few notes, the judge resumed her questioning. "The fifth accused is Dr. Ed Kadison, former cochair of the International Scientific Committee on Human Evolution. The responsibility for reviewing the scientific validity of the Stinguard viral vector prior to its worldwide distribution lay in the hands of the committee you cochaired. Therefore, how do you plead, sir, to the charges of crimes against humanity?"

Ed Kadison's paunch had shrunk in half from his drastic weight loss on the Bass Rock. Without the benefit of his habitual natural-tears ophthalmic solution to soothe his dry eyes, he grimaced and squinted in pain under the intolerable bright light shining on the prisoner's dock. Throughout his career, he had always turned to his mentor, Stinguard, with meek subservience for guidance even before speaking; however, on this occasion, his stern gaze remained fixed on the drone camera.

With the realization that no amount of soft soap would get him out of the pickle he was in, he brandished a sly smile as he babbled his caustic reply. "Not guilty, my lady."

The judge paused to scour her notes on the next prisoner's multifarious past titles. "Jane Woodford, you are an ex-member of the board of directors of the Rochester Manninghouse Pharmaceutical Company, which manufactured the Stinguard viral vector. You also served as the head of Human Resources at the Greysville Quadrant Hospital and as the World Governing Body's director of personnel. How do you plead, madam, to the charges of crimes against humanity?"

Jane Woodford's patina of concern that she had perfected after many years in the Human Resources Department had cracked. Only a perpetual look of cantankerous disgust remained on her sallow face. She clenched her jaw and pursed her pale lips in indignation. "Not guilty, my lady," she shouted.

Judge Harbottle turned her attention to the prosecution table. "I will enter the pleas in the court record. Chief Prosecutor Kester, you may begin."

The spectators' gallery on Earth had respected the judge's call for silence to such a degree that even the rustling of the papers from the prosecution table was audible. At the same time, while each of the accused pleaded not guilty, the horror in the spectators' eyes spoke for them instead. Godafrid Kester stood up at his desk with a flourish, knowing that an audience on two planets was watching. Then, straightening his flowing, black robe with its ermine collar around him, he began building the case against the accused.

"My lady, the prosecution will furnish irrefutable proof that the prisoners are guilty of crimes against humanity," he said with polished eloquence. "In fact, each of the accused in the dock conspired to profit from the distribution of the Stinguard viral vector. Witnesses will also expose how those with the courage to question the nefarious practices of the World Governing Body received prompt relocation notices to Gnaritus from where, until recent times, all communication was impossible. In the same vein, Rod Stinguard sought to eliminate his scientific rivals by engineering their transfers to Gnaritus, ten thousand light-years away. The first witness is Dr. Surina Mathew of Gnaritus."

Being the first to testify caught Surina by surprise. As her image appeared on the screen in the well of the court, Stinguard snarled at her with bared teeth like an inimical gargoyle.

"Please state your name and occupation," Godafrid said. "Also tell us who your supervisor was on Gnaritus and Earth."

"I'm Surina Mathew, a physician at the Spatium Borough Hospital on Gnaritus," she replied. "While on Earth, I worked at the Greysville Quadrant Hospital. I have no supervisor on Gnaritus, whereas it was Stinguard on Earth."

"Tell us about your research findings," Godafrid asked.

"In brief, my experiments showed the instability of Stinguard viral vector integration site into the human genome," Surina answered. "The aim of the viral vector was to produce the DNA repair enzymes necessary for healing the cancer-causing mutations. However, I found the viral vector induced life-threatening mutations in about half of those who received it."

"For those like myself who are not in the medical profession, please clarify scientific terminology such as *DNA*," Godafrid said.

"Some other names for DNA are the genome or the building blocks of life," Surina said. "The DNA contains the genes that carry the code for each cell of the body, much like an instruction manual. The synthesis of a viral vector requires genetic engineering. First, we modify the virus so that it doesn't cause disease in humans. Next, we insert the engineered therapeutic gene, carrying the code for enzymes to repair mutated genes, into the viral genome. These enzymes are specialized proteins. Once injected into humans, the viral genome has to integrate at precise points in the human cell genome to produce a functional new gene. For example, the Stinguard viral vector contained the genetic code for DNA repair enzymes to mend the cancer-causing mutations.

"Instead, the viral vector induced life-threatening mutations because it failed to integrate at the proper sites in the human genome. In essence, my experiments predicted that the viral vector's integration site is not stable and can cause lethal mutations in half of the patients. My data also showed the viral vector would offer negligible long-term benefits for the fifty percent of recipients who survive. In fact, over time, the human cellular machinery will bypass the DNA repair enzymes that the viral vector produces. Due to the unknown side effects of the virus, the survivors of the Stinguard viral vector will also need lifelong follow-up."

"Did you succeed in publishing these percipient results?" Godafrid asked.

"No scientific journal accepted my research," Surina said.

"My lady, given these points, I am submitting notarized documentation of Dr. Mathew's thirty-four rejection letters to your computer," Godafrid said. "This evidence is available to the public on the World Body Criminal Court website as well. Stinguard was on the editorial board of all thirty-four of these journals and served as editor-in-chief for eight of these publications. My lady, the most compelling evidence is that the date of submission and rejection occurred within moments of each other on the same day. The prompt rejections attest to the lack of a proper peer review of the scientific merits of the research. I contend that the rejections were due to an irrational desire to suppress the research findings. Stinguard also deleted the research files that Dr. Mathew forwarded to him on her last day in the hospital instead of heeding their grave warning. Dr. Mathew, has anyone authenticated your research?"

"Yes, Dr. Ailbeart Ross, the medical director of the Spatium Borough Hospital, validated the data," Surina answered.

Godafrid sat down to search his computer and whispered to his online personal assistant. Then he stood up to address the court again. "My lady, for the court record, I am forwarding to you the detailed documentation from Dr. Ailbeart Ross. He conducted extensive testing to substantiate Dr. Mathew's research. It is fair to say, the millions who died also corroborated Dr. Mathew's research!"

Hissing and growling from Stinguard's direction prompted a swift reprimand from the judge. "Inasmuch as I have instructed the spectators to be silent, I am also warning the accused to refrain from making any comments unless asked a specific question!"

No sooner had the judge chided him than Stinguard slithered back into the corner of the prisoners' dock, still seething in anger. His beady, saurian eyes oozed poison as he hexed Surina's image on the screen.

"Dr. Mathew, you relocated to Gnaritus on July twenty-eighth of this year," Godafrid said. "Who informed you about your transfer to Gnaritus?"

"Robert Hurpan and Jane Woodford handed me my relocation notice," Surina said, thinking about that fateful day in the medical director's office.

"My lady, as the chair of the Relocation Council, Cuthbert Miller, handled all the transfers to Gnaritus," Godafrid said. "After a lengthy forensic analysis of Stinguard's computer hard drive, we unearthed evidence of his clandestine videoconferences with his brother-in-law, Cuthbert Miller. In fact, on July twentieth, Stinguard spearheaded the plan for Dr. Mathew's immediate relocation to Gnaritus. I am forwarding the documents to you with the dates, times, and contents of these conversations. The evidence also includes a list of many other physicians who Stinguard had a personal vendetta with and exiled to Gnaritus, such as the prominent researcher Dr. Fergus Wittenberg. By ousting these scientists, Stinguard sidelined many promising careers. In fact, the paper trail chronicles all of his communications with Cuthbert Miller that occurred before the expulsion of each of his scientific rivals. In every instance, Stinguard masterminded their exile to Gnaritus."

As the evidence mounted against him, Cuthbert Miller squirmed with uneasiness in his shackles. He longed to escape from the blinding light flooding the prisoners' dock. Why had his sister married a scoundrel like Stinguard? Then, he cast Stinguard a venomous, accusatory look for dragging him into a bottomless pit.

"Dr. Mathew, did you give a verbal warning to Stinguard or anyone else of your reservations about the viral vector?" Godafrid asked.

"Yes, I shared my grave concerns with Stinguard, Hurpan, and Woodford," Surina replied. "Since the clinical trial in Africa had only twenty healthy subjects with a short two-week follow-up period, it could have missed the possibility of life-threatening mutations occurring in half of the cases."

Godafrid turned to the judge. "My lady, in light of this new evidence, I am submitting documentation of these conversations. We found a recording of Dr. Mathew's comments on Rex's hard drive. Rex is the android security chief of the Greysville Quadrant Hospital, who was also present at these meetings. The crux of the matter is that Stinguard, Hurpan, and Woodford gave short shrift to Dr. Mathew's warnings. Furthermore, Kadison's computer contained the results of the trial in Africa that showed no ill effects at two weeks, but after five weeks ten of the twenty subjects died without warning from asphyxiation. The remaining ten patients in the clinical trial have had no benefits from the viral vector whatsoever.

"With willful, craven negligence, Kadison flouted the rules by withholding the data from the International Scientific Committee on Human Evolution, which was tasked with assessing the viral vector's scientific merit. When Stinguard received these results, he dismissed them rather than following the proper course of action by scrapping the distribution of the viral vector. Both Stinguard and Kadison shirked their responsibilities and abdicated their moral duty to society. Dr. Mathew, please stay with us, for I have more questions to ask you later, but at present I would like to call Stefan Stohl of Gnaritus."

Stefan's image soon appeared on the screen in the courtroom. For anyone on Earth who had once known him, he would have been unrecognizable, for a renewed sense of purpose and hope reignited his once-lugubrious eyes. Moreover, his rubicund, chubby cheeks were a far cry from his former lantern jaw.

"Please state your occupation on Gnaritus and Earth, Mr. Stohl," Godafrid said. "Also, describe your final assignment before you went to Gnaritus."

"I'm writing a book about my exciting journey to Gnaritus through ten thousand light-years of space," Stefan answered. "On Earth, I was a newspaper journalist, and my last assignment was to interview Stinguard about the launch of his viral vector. In my investigation, I discovered Stinguard and Jane Woodford were on the board of directors of the Rochester Manninghouse Pharmaceutical Company. Also, Robert Hurpan was the chief executive officer. I had to dig for this information since it's not available in the public record. In other words, they each had a financial stake in the worldwide distribution of the viral vector. Although my article exposed these associations, it never saw the light of day. Sloan Arrol, my editor, lambasted and rejected it on the spot. He most likely got scared of losing his job. Even though I attempted to circulate my article on the World Wide Web in the hope of halting the viral vector's global distribution, the authorities clamped down on it. The next day, I received my relocation notice to Gnaritus."

After the rumbling from the spectators' gallery had subsided, Godafrid resumed. "My lady, further evidence gleaned from Sloan Arrol's computer hard drive, proves he deleted Mr. Stohl's column as soon as he received it. Together with this, I am forwarding the specific contents of Mr. Stohl's article. Remember, these documents are on the World Body Criminal Court website as well for the benefit of the public. Here is a list of the clandestine Swiss bank accounts of Stinguard, Hurpan, and Woodford, showing large deposits of money after the launch of the viral vector. In particular, Stinguard, who holds the patent for the viral vector, pocketed the munificent sum of three hundred and forty million pounds. Hurpan has recent deposits totaling two hundred million pounds. Likewise, Woodford's coffers ballooned to thirty million pounds.

"Stinguard flaunted his newfound wealth with a shopping spree for items such as a Swiss chalet for skiing holidays and an indoor swimming pool. These ill-gotten gains also financed Hurpan and Woodford's profligate spending, with the illicit purchase of yachts, holiday villas in the Mediterranean, expensive jewelry, and clothing from Paris. Of note, this evidence also reveals three transfers of ten million pounds each from Stinguard's Swiss bank account to those of John Jones-May, Cuthbert Miller, and Ed Kadison. In fact, all six of this gang of spendthrifts colluded to profit from the launch of the viral vector! The ringleader of this gang was Stinguard. In light of these circumstances, we froze these funds pending the outcome of this trial. Thank you, Mr. Stohl. My next witness is Alfonso Diaz of Gnaritus."

Another plaintive murmur erupted in the spectators' gallery. They were dumbfounded. They always had a staunch faith in the edifices of their society, believing them to work only for their benefit. Now, the revelations in the trial had yanked the carpet out from under their feet. Was their society nothing more than a virtual reality created by the charlatans in the World Governing Body? Why had they lived with blinkers on for so long without ever seeing the blatant injustices and skullduggery until now? Were they only timid, disposable pawns in a game without any rules of ethical conduct? They ruminated on this during the lull in the proceedings until Chief Prosecutor Kester's eloquent Shakespearian voice drew them back to the courtroom.

Alfonso's image appeared on the screen in the courtroom. He

stared with raised eyebrows at the Byzantine complexity of the political imbroglio on Earth.

"Mr. Diaz, please state your occupation on Gnaritus and Earth," Godafrid said.

"I'm a computer engineer with the Gnaritus Computer Firm," he replied. "In the past, I worked at the Rochester Manninghouse Corporation, the largest computer company on Earth."

Godafrid paused to wipe off beads of sweat from his forehead. "Please explain, sir, how you came to leave the Rochester Manninghouse Corporation as well as how you used your technical acumen to restore communication between Earth and Gnaritus."

"The Rochester Manninghouse Corporation wiretapped all communication on Earth," Alfonso said. "The majority of employees knew about this, but they looked the other way. In fact, this surveillance also involved censoring news organizations. Later, by chance, I stumbled upon the existence of the Muralis Team, which maintained the firewall between Earth and Gnaritus. When I asked my supervisors why such programs even existed, they got the ball rolling to send me to Gnaritus. After arriving on Gnaritus, I used my knowledge of the structure of the firewall to bring it down bit by bit. I only succeeded when the firewall became more permeable over the past two weeks, perhaps due to the loss of some of the members of the Muralis Team to the Stinguard viral vector."

"My lady, I am forwarding to you the computer codes that Mr. Diaz used in restoring communication between Earth and Gnaritus," Godafrid said. "Our forensic scientists dredged up a treasure trove of information on the surreptitious censoring and surveillance techniques of the all-seeing Rochester Manninghouse Corporation. In fact, the Rochester Manninghouse Corporation relayed all the information from their surveillance programs to the World Governing Body. The evidence also proves that the Rochester Manninghouse Corporation erased Mr. Stefan Stohl's article from the World Wide Web. Thank you, Mr. Diaz. My next witness is Mr. Liam Lofgren."

From the back of the spectators' gallery, a lanky, athletic man bounded with a few giant strides past the prisoners' dock to the witness box beside Judge Harbottle's bench. He sat sideways since his spindly legs would not fit under the desk. John Jones-May glared at Liam with wild, choleric eyes.

"Mr. Lofgren is our new president of the House of Humanity," Godafrid said.

Unable to control his wrath any longer, John Jones-May brayed and blustered. "Remember, *I am* the chief executive officer of the World Governing Body! Lest you forget, the population of the entire world elected me not only once but also three times from a field of five candidates in lengthy contests. That makes this man nothing more than a usurper anointed by his cadre of friends. The House of Humanity is a junta that seized power by illegal means."

The spectators in the courtroom recoiled in horror and disgust at his outburst.

Judge Harbottle wielded her gavel five times to end the obstreperous prisoner's vitriolic tirade. "Mr. Jones-May, as a matter of fact, you are no longer the chief executive officer of the World Governing Body, for that organization is obsolete. Under your leadership, the World Governing Body promulgated disinformation to obfuscate and confuse, rather than to enlighten the population. Even though the world's population elected you, it was impossible for them to make an educated decision. It seems that the World Governing Body controlled every aspect of the dissemination of the news for the sole purpose of indoctrinating the public in its dangerous ideology. You cannot browbeat witnesses. In case of further interruptions, I will remove you from this court. Please continue, Chief Prosecutor Kester."

Like an irascible old man, John Jones-May cowered in the corner as the irrevocability of the loss of his stature in society dawned on him.

Maintaining his sangfroid, Godafrid resumed his line of

questioning. "Please tell us, Mr. Lofgren, why you campaigned against the launch of the Stinguard viral vector, albeit without success."

"I learned about the dangers of the Stinguard viral vector from Dr. Surina Mathew during our serendipitous meeting on holiday in Santorini," Liam said. "I will always remember her hesitancy in telling me about her research findings since she believed I would dismiss her as just another stranger, who was either disgruntled or tilting at windmills. However, as a history professor at Stockholm University, I am also a student of our shared history that binds us forever."

"Mr. Lofgren, please explain the meaning of *our shared history*," Godafrid asked, looking puzzled.

Liam answered in a poetic voice. "Every human alive today came from a single mother in Africa, who lived about two hundred thousand years ago. Later, when the sea levels receded about ninety thousand years ago, a small tribe of a few hundred traveled out of the plains of Africa. After crossing the Red Sea through the Gate of Grief passageway, they fanned out and populated the entire world. How can there be any strangers among us when we all share a single common ancestor? From the beginning of human society when we huddled together in caves in front of the fire, interpersonal connections ensured our survival. In recognition of our shared humanity, rather than dismiss Dr. Mathew as a stranger, I listened to her advice, which is the only reason I am alive today. I am indebted to her forever. That is to say, you can never know when and where your path will cross with the messenger who will save your life!

"I researched the viral vector and read everything I could lay my hands on after returning to Stockholm. In much the same way as Mr. Stefan Stohl, I learned of Stinguard's connections with the pharmaceutical company. In other words, Stinguard and the pharmaceutical company stood to make windfall profits from the viral vector. Though I sent my article to many newspapers, none would dare publish it. Perhaps, they looked the other way because they thought it would be more politic. Most people pay attention only when events directly affect them. Until then, they gild reality and cloud the truth. Just like Mr. Stohl, I then tried to disseminate the information on the World Wide Web, but the authorities axed the article as a way of silencing my voice. Since the cataclysm sweeping Earth has afflicted all of us now, we have awoken from our slumber of complacency to realize we can no longer afford to marginalize messengers of the truth if we are to survive. Nor can we ignore our shared humanity and our shared journey if we hope to recover and flourish as a species!"

"My lady, I am submitting in its entirety Mr. Lofgren's article that nine newspapers rejected," Godafrid said. "Once again, there is documentation of how the Rochester Manninghouse Corporation purged Mr. Lofgren's article from the World Wide Web. Compelling evidence indicates that the wanton disregard for the freedom of information came at the behest of the World Governing Body. In fact, the office of John Jones-May issued point-by-point instructions commanding the media to expunge news in any way injurious to the World Governing Body or its branches. The obeisant news organizations bowed down to these edicts, for noncompliance meant facing the threat of closure. As a result, they fed us untruths, which paraded as the news. Thank you, Mr. Lofgren. Before we proceed further, we must establish whether any of the accused received the Stinguard viral vector. First, Rod Stinguard, did you or your children have the viral vector that you synthesized?"

Stinguard shuffled his feet. After a considerable delay, he prevaricated. "In September, I was busy applying for a research grant, but I planned to get it last week after my wife and children returned from their vacation in Bali."

After hearing his weasel words, Godafrid fired back. "This is no time to be coy, Dr. Stinguard. Why did you delay having the viral vector that bore your name? Why did you force this treatment on others, like those in Africa, when you were unwilling to have it yourself? In other words, did you avoid it on purpose, knowing of its dangers?"

As Stinguard had become tight-lipped, Godafrid asked each of the accused in turn the same question. In a similar way, their bromidic replies were that neither they nor their families had received the viral vector because of their busy schedules. They did not elucidate further. After exhausting this line of questioning, Godafrid called Surina back to the stand.

Much like the spectators in the gallery, Surina reeled inside from the virulent treachery at the highest levels on Earth. In fact, these officious paragons of excellence had set the benchmark for all to follow. On a daily basis, these august organizations had judged her and always found her lacking. So, they had condemned her to the margins of society on Earth along with 99.5 percent of the population. She felt like such an ignoramus in squandering her time, trying to follow such bankrupt standards.

Although Godafrid tried his best to hide his dismay at the extent of the corruption running rife in Earth's society, he spoke in a strained tone. "Dr. Mathew, you worked with Stinguard for many years. How did the scientific community regard him?"

As a rule, Surina clouded her replies to questions such as these for the sake of politeness and propriety; however, this being a court case demanded complete frankness. "Stinguard's ideas never had the novelty or genuineness to propel him to the upper echelons of the great scientific pioneers. In reality, his stature came from his connections in the ruling elite due to his marriage to Cuthbert Miller's sister. He advanced in the scientific community only because he eliminated his rivals using his powerful connections. Even so, the quality of his scientific method was always questionable as shown by his viral vector. Nonetheless, he has won every accolade except the Nobel Prize in Medicine. Despite his money, power, and fame, only a Nobel Prize could have allowed him to join the pantheon of the greats in science. Perhaps, winning the Nobel Prize became his primary motivational force. Otherwise, on the whole, his scientific legacy is of marginal significance."

Godafrid turned toward the prisoners' dock. "In the final analysis, Dr. Stinguard, what motivated you to foist a faulty viral vector worldwide to the detriment of so many? Why did you bungle the launch of this viral vector? Why did you act with such temerity and jeopardize countless lives? Were their lives of less importance than yours? Did their lives matter at all?"

Seeing that the game was up, the cockalorum began to crow. "Ever since she arrived at the Greysville Quadrant Hospital, Surina Mathew always questioned everything, including my experiments. That troublemaker should have stayed in her country of India. Why should I answer your mumbo jumbo questions, Mr. Chief Prosecutor or whatever your name is? Who are you to interrogate me? Go back to your country in Africa where you belong! Why did I let the viral vector launch go ahead? With a survival rate of fifty percent, the gamble was worth taking. In other words, part of the population is expendable. After all, riffraff plebeians like all of you in the courtroom are disposable! Your inane drivel means nothing. We are the masters of the universe! Only masters of the universe shape history rather than rabble like you. Remember, the sun will never set on the masters of the universe!"

The spectators in the gallery booed Stinguard. With nothing left to lose, the prisoners in the dock lurched forward, trying to break free from their shackles. Without any compunction, the megalomaniacs yelled, "We are the masters of the universe." During this magniloquent performance, Chief Prosecutor Kester glanced at Surina's image with pity. Her tremendous longanimity impressed him. He wondered how anyone could survive the impossible situation of working with Stinguard for even a day, let alone ten years like she had done. Perhaps going to Gnaritus had saved her. Despite knowing he needed to conclude the case, he longed to go to Gnaritus right away, just to escape from the destructive madness engulfing Earth.

He decided against cross-examining the accused, for they had already declared their intentions. "My lady, may I begin my closing arguments?"

The vainglorious cacophony from the prisoners' dock did not abate until the judge read them the riot act; however, they maintained their sardonic, malevolent smiles.

"Do the accused have any exculpatory evidence to bring forward to refute these charges?" Judge Harbottle asked.

The intransigent prisoners lunged at the judge and pounded on the bulletproof glass with their fists. Then, they trumpeted their solipsistic reply in unison. "We are the masters of the universe! We are the masters of the universe! We are the masters of the universe!"

After noting the prisoners had mounted no defense, the judge advised the chief prosecutor to proceed.

Regaining his poise and mustering every ounce of his brio, Godafrid summed up the salient points in the case. "My lady, the incontrovertible evidence points to each of the accused being guilty of crimes against humanity. Overall, the supporting notarized documents expose the dark underbelly of our most hallowed institutions. Moreover, the shameful, derogatory remarks of the accused in court today mocked humanity and reason. Rather than atoning for their sins, they have shown neither remorse nor contrition. How do we make sense of the bloody aftermath of these events and arise like a phoenix from the ashes? These six accused are on trial, but humanity is in the dock with them too. Through our complacency, we allowed the accused to act as masters of the universe. We gave them unfettered powers and let their hopeless, divisive vision of the world flourish. As a consequence, arbitrary distinctions of race, color, creed, caste, socioeconomic status, and geography polarize our world. In fact, our xenophobic society assigns greater or lesser value to lives according to the predefined criteria that deviants such as the accused in the dock formulated to debase humanity. Worse still, certain lives do not matter at all!

"The grievous deaths in the past month occurred on an unprecedented scale. However, humanity has been dying by incremental degrees in our stereotypical society on Earth, with its insular and parochial worldviews. Today, humanity is in critical condition on life support in the intensive care unit. There is a distinct possibility we may not survive on Earth. If we understood *every life matters*, then would we have launched the Stinguard viral vector in Africa or anywhere else? If we believed *every life matters*, then would we have allowed the rapacious World Governing Body to act with impunity? Would we have supported the marginalization of large swathes of the population for so long while empowering the elite few?

"The miscreants in the prisoners' dock are only the tip of the iceberg threatening to destroy *Homo sapiens* on Earth. We are at a critical juncture. In essence, we cannot alter the past; however, we can ensure the survival of humanity on Earth only if we value each life. Our only way forward is to embrace Gnaritus's ethos. We must rebuild a more just, nonhierarchical society from scratch, where every life matters. In conclusion, any association with these hardened career criminals would be ruinous, injurious, and deleterious to humanity. All things considered, the prosecution recommends lifelong solitary confinement for each of the accused on the Bass Rock, with contact only with the androids. Thank you, my lady."

The spectators muttered under their breath and shifted in their seats.

"We will have a two-hour recess," the judge said. "I will then give the verdict."

Godafrid breathed a sigh of relief as he sat down, for never before had a case left him so shaken to the core. He tried to revive himself with green tea from the carafe on his table. In the meantime, the accused cast Godafrid spiteful glances for calling them hardened career criminals.

During the break, the spectators remained in the courtroom so as not to lose their seats. They had such little faith in any institution providing even a modicum of justice that they expected to hear an innocent verdict or a lax punishment rather than the hoped-for rhadamanthine judgment. Several spectators rushed to Liam and peppered him with questions about the future. He soon allayed their fears when he promised to redress their grievances and reform the business-as-usual mentality.

On Gnaritus, stunned silence shrouded the amphitheater. Francesca dreamt of returning to her true métier of painting. Although she hoped this would be her last stint as a lawyer, she knew by now that life had a way of throwing a few curve balls. Meanwhile, Nachton's former zeal gave way to a quiet reflection of his poor sister's cursed fate in marrying a monster like Stinguard. His understanding was in the incipient stages, but he acknowledged it was a well-nigh impossible task to extricate his sister from the tangled net ensnaring her. She was a victim, just like the millions who had succumbed to Stinguard's malodorous machinations. Providence and grace had freed others like Surina by sending them to Gnaritus. In fact, everyone in the amphitheater, including Surina, wanted to kiss the ground on Gnaritus for providing them with a refuge from the cesspool of corruption on Earth. Who would have imagined they were the lucky ones after all?

When Judge Marigold Harbottle returned from her chambers, an expectant silence permeated the courtroom. In fact, stillness filled every nook and cranny on Earth all the way to the amphitheater on Gnaritus.

The judge cleared her throat and began her perspicacious summation. "The case before the court today is of crimes against humanity. When I first agreed to serve as the judge in this case, I thought it set many precedents. However, I soon realized it is only another instance of history repeating itself. To illustrate this, I will discuss a few of the deplorable examples in history where human life meant nothing. In 1932, researchers in Tuskegee, Alabama withheld life-saving medications on purpose in patients with syphilis so as to study the natural history of this deadly disease. This reprehensible experiment showed an utter disregard for the value of African American lives.

"During World War Two, Dr. Josef Mengele conducted unconscionable research on innocent Jews and Romani Gypsies in concentration camps to advance the Nazi racial ideology. The Final Solution was the euphemistic term for the erasure of an ethnic group. He performed innumerable heinous experiments. For example, he injected chemicals into the eyes of children to turn them blue and caused blindness instead. After each of these atrocities, the entire world pledged never to repeat this tragic history.

"There have been acts of kindness and generosity in recognition of our human solidarity in history as well. For example, in 2085 Germany provided a sanctuary for countless refugees fleeing from the drought-stricken plains of Mongolia. By welcoming the homeless multitude to their shores, they embodied the principle that there are no strangers among us. Even so, the insatiable thirst for power and domination drowns goodness and truth. There is an inexorability to the way the same grim history keeps repeating on an even larger scale than before, as in the present case. Ever since the World Governing Body came to power a hundred years ago, the world has sunk into an even greater darkness."

The spectators waited on tenterhooks as the judge sipped some water. Meanwhile, the prisoners scowled and sneered in the dock. Turning her stern gaze to the accused, the judge continued. "Here we are once more discussing the case of Stinguard, who, without employing rigorous scientific methods, launched his viral vector on an unsuspecting population. He did this first in Africa, and then in India and, later, the rest of the world. An insatiable hunger for power, dominance, money, and the Nobel Prize spurred him on in his diabolical wickedness. He and his family used artful and ruthless means to dodge the viral vector that he concocted.

"Stinguard has caused the deaths of millions of innocent citizens on Earth. In essence, the World Governing Body aided and abetted Stinguard in his nefarious aims. Even more troubling is how the World Governing Body misled the public. For example, Kadison suppressed the results of the clinical trial in Africa that revealed ten of the twenty subjects died five weeks after receiving it. Mr. Stohl and Mr. Lofgren's newspaper articles, exposing Stinguard's links with the pharmaceutical company, never saw the light of day. The scientific journals lampooned Dr. Surina Mathew's research about the lethal mutations developing in half of those receiving the viral vector. All of these provided lost opportunities to halt the distribution of the Stinguard viral vector."

After another sip of water, the judge resumed. "The accused anointed themselves as the masters of the universe. Their spurious reasoning that they control the universe beggars belief. Copernicus and Galileo disproved the geocentric theory of the Earth as the center of the universe long ago; therefore, the accused are not the masters of the universe. In fact, the Earth occupies an infinitesimal part of the universe, and now even this little corner is at risk of annihilation by greed and hate. Besides, the planet has no more of its limited resources to offer to human arrogance. Alas, these pretentious people who have the gall and brazen effrontery to claim they are the masters of the universe presiding over a disposable population are destroying our most valuable resource: humanity.

"Overall, these are grave times for Earth, but humans have been on the brink of extinction before. For example, seventy-four thousand years ago, the population dwindled to about fifteen thousand during the ice age from the cataclysmic volcanic eruption of Mount Toba in Sumatra. Annihilation threatens us again today, albeit this time at the hands of unworthy, witless humans! In essence, the complete disregard for the profound value of each human life led to the deaths from the Tuskegee experiments, the Nazi concentration camps, and the Stinguard viral vector. Who can envisage what the future holds for the Earth? The cataclysm sweeping Earth is a tocsin for humanity, but will we heed the alarm?"

She paused for a considerable length of time as she searched each of the spectators' faces in the courtroom for an answer. "Is the Anthropocene epoch, or the Age of Humans, ending on Earth?" she asked in a melancholy tone. "Will we return to this courtroom in a few months to discuss yet another case of crimes against humanity? We need guidance to escape from the abyss we alone created. Where can we turn for help out of our moribund condition? Valiant, trailblazing Gnaritus, our forgotten sister planet to where Earth banished many of the marginalized, built a new world, vowing never to repeat the mistakes of human history. Even though there are two planets of *Homo sapiens* in the Milky Way galaxy, Earth is only a mere unsatisfactory simulacrum of Gnaritus. Gnaritus eclipsed Earth and soared light-years ahead by creating an egalitarian society where every life matters. Like Gnaritus, we must also value knowledge more than money. An unhindered flow of knowledge and information is a necessity if we want to move forward. In other words, we too can no longer afford to retrogress and repeat the errors of human history!

"Today, compelling evidence showed how the idea of every life having intrinsic and equal value posed such a danger to the survival of the draconian World Governing Body that it blocked all contact with Gnaritus. The sacrosanctity of every life is anathema to the elitism of the World Governing Body. I hope the restoration of communication with our enlightened sister planet will resuscitate our woebegone world, but we must have the courage to embrace change. In this way, we can rid our planet forever of its fusty worldview and ignoble practices so as to move forward instead of always going backward to repeat history!

"In conclusion, Chief Prosecutor Kester, you have made cogent and convincing arguments. I grant your request for a sentence of lifelong solitary confinement on the Bass Rock for each of the accused. The prisoners will live out their days in ignominy and disgrace. As the rules stipulate for the most dangerous criminals, only the android security guards will have contact with the accused. Once again, let me remind the defendants they are not the masters of the universe, for every life matters! Every life has a profound and equal value, with a right to live without fear and actualize its full potential! Remember, every life matters!"

All of a sudden, the prisoners started to heckle and jeer the verdict. They pumped their shackled fists in the air, stamped their feet, and taunted the judge. "We are the masters of the universe. We are the masters of the universe. Remember, we are the masters of the universe!"

No one clapped or cheered as the rabid-eyed, unrepentant prisoners plunged underground into the bowels of the court, where an air van awaited to consign them to oblivion in the Bass Rock maximum-security prison. As the contorted, malign form of the obdurate Stinguard disappeared, Surina hoped it would be the last time she saw him. Soon, the prisoners' cackles fizzled out, much to the relief of the spectators.

While Godafrid put his files back into his briefcase, he wondered whether he could even place this trial in the *cases won* column. Only if humans emerged from the fog clouding their judgment to acknowledge and embrace the core value that every life matters would there ever be a real victory. Judge Harbottle waited for Godafrid, and they exited the courtroom together. They knew their work had just begun. Next on the docket would be the Rochester Manninghouse Corporation's board of trustees. That case would include some prominent names, like Philip Jones-May, the son of John Jones-May, the erstwhile chief executive officer of the bygone leviathan World Governing Body.

Standing up from the spectators' gallery by the prosecution table, a weary Aibne Waters addressed the *Global News* audience. "Ladies and gentlemen, that concludes our program. Thank you for joining us. Our future broadcasts will be from the House of Humanity in the Lake District. The House of Humanity will occupy the premises of the former World Governing Body in Keswick. Mr. Liam Lofgren, our new president of the House of Humanity, will hold a series of debates on how best to resurrect the Earth for a new beginning."

The spectators bundled out of the courtroom in a mournful silence. Despite the relief of seeing at least some measure of justice, the worldwide audience on both Earth and Gnaritus quailed in horror from bearing witness to the depths of darkness in the human heart. Surina felt glad to leave the amphitheater and close that chapter in her life. An invigorating Indian summer breeze drifting through the colonnades greeted her as she stepped out into the portico. Alfonso paused to gulp lungfuls of fresh air. Up above, the three benevolent suns shone on the subdued crowd spilling out of the General Assembly Hall.

"Want to go to the Easter Rose Tea Shop before going home?" Stefan asked.

"That sounds like music to my ears," Francesca replied.

Surina and Alfonso joined in with a chorus of eager yeses. As they hailed an air cab at the edge of Mohawk Park, Nachton decided to join them as well.

26
Change at Last

AFTER THE RESTORATION of interplanetary communication, Surina often watched the *Global News* from London. She was curious to learn whether any change would come to Earth. On one occasion, toward the end of Earth's quarantine, Surina went to the communal computer in the gazebo on Huron Square to catch up on the latest news. Aibne Waters stood with Liam Lofgren outside the new House of Humanity in Keswick in a garden awash with winter jasmine and Christmas roses. In the background, sparrows and starlings chirruped and trilled in the sunshine.

Aibne wore a camel duffle coat. He no longer had bags or dark circles beneath his eyes. Instead, his eyes had a spark as if reignited with hope. "Welcome to our viewers on Earth and Gnaritus. The quarantine is over. No cases of human-to-human transmission of the Stinguard viral vector occurred as predicted by Dr. Surina Mathew of Gnaritus. However, for the first time since 1710, the Earth's population is seven hundred million due to about three hundred million deaths. Today I'm interviewing Liam Lofgren, our new president of the House of Humanity. Mr.

Lofgren, you gathered opinions from all over the Earth and Gnaritus on the way forward. What is the consensus opinion on the vision for the future of Earth's society?"

Liam's craggy face lit up with a reassuring smile. "The Earth's society will honor the memories of those who perished by embracing the innate value of every life. By recognizing that every life matters, we will shift our focus away from alterity, or otherness, to acknowledging the shared humanity among all people not only on Earth but also on Gnaritus."

"Mr. Lofgren, how are you implementing this vision?" Aibne asked.

"We are still in mourning, but as the miasma of despair dissipates, the pendulum is swinging in incremental steps away from the past and to the future," Liam replied. "There are many pressing concerns in our society. Who belongs? Who matters? Well, everyone belongs, and everyone matters. There is room for everyone. We will leave no one behind. For example, we are building free housing for the homeless in every country. Education is now a human right and is free. We recalibrated the core curriculum in schools to teach each child how to become a citizen of the universe with love for all life and matter in the cosmos. Rather than promoting citizenship of a village, city, or country, our hope is to foster the development of citizens of the universe. Education, knowledge, egalitarianism, and compassion are the keys to our survival as a species, for we can no longer afford to see through the distorted prism of fear and otherness.

"To achieve our vision of a more inclusive society, we dismantled several former World Governing Body organizations, including the behemoth Rochester Manninghouse Corporation. The population also voted to demolish the Greysville Quadrant Hospital a month ago. Due to its association with Stinguard's infamy, no one dared to go to the hospital. The demolition of the derelict hospital has restored the breathtaking panoramic view of the shores of Derwentwater Lake that it once obscured. The lush vegetation of the Lake District has reclaimed the razed site as it did with the ancient ruins of the Earl of Derwentwater's home on Lord's Island."

"Will you be restoring the Relocation Policy to Gnaritus, Mr. Lofgren?"

Liam shook his head. "The House of Humanity voted to eliminate the Relocation Policy. Now, citizens of Earth and Gnaritus can decide on which planet to live. We asked Gnaritonians for help in repopulating the Earth, but we haven't had any takers so far. It seems no one can bear to leave Gnaritus. On Earth, only Chief Steward Pars requested to relocate to Gnaritus."

Aibne furrowed his brow. "It's puzzling that no one else from Earth wants to relocate to Gnaritus."

"We're conducting surveys in the hope of understanding the reasons for this, Aibne. Perhaps, the fresh wounds from the catastrophe two months ago have to heal first before Earth's citizens can embark on the journey across ten thousand light-years of space. Most people cite the desert terrain of Gnaritus as the primary reason for their reluctance to relocate. Others say the fear of venturing into the unknown keeps them earthbound. The resumption of interplanetary communication and travel will enhance our understanding of Gnaritus so that the decision on which planet to live could become clearer over time."

"Mr. Lofgren, tell us more about the interplanetary cultural exchange programs you've organized."

"Your show, Aibne, has led the way in interplanetary cultural exchange by featuring the Gnaritus Orchestra's live performances. Interest in outer-space art is also skyrocketing on Earth. In fact, Lamond McNab has achieved great acclaim for his paintings of celestial bodies. I visited his art studio in Chelsea, and he suggested we have an *Art of the Cosmos* exhibition. In two months, London's National Gallery will hold its first *Art of the Cosmos* exhibition, celebrating the avant-garde works of Lamond McNab. It will also include the new genre of Gnaritus art by two

Gnaritonian artists: Linda Cavacecci and Francesca Lenzi."

"Thanks, Mr. Lofgren. That concludes our show for today. To our viewers on Earth and Gnaritus, we'll go live to the London Symphony Orchestra, which is performing the 'Pillars of Creation' violin concerto. Gabriel and Rafaela Higgins of Gnaritus composed this masterwork."

The melodious sounds filled Huron Square on Gnaritus. The children in the playground paused for a moment and smiled. Then, they returned to their games with more vigor. Surina also grinned as she dashed to the Spatium Borough Hospital to do the night shift on the cancer ward. Humanity on Earth is healing, she thought.

. . .

With the lifting of the iron curtain between Gnaritus and Earth, everyone had the opportunity to catch up with their relatives and friends. During a video chat with Liam and Bergitte Lofgren, Surina described the sensational voyage to Gnaritus, including the stars, planets, nebulae, and supernovas.

"What's more, the infinitesimal singular point of the big bang created all the matter existing in the universe today, including humans, and forged the intangible web of cosmic consciousness," Surina said.

Liam mulled over these revelations. "Although visible threads connect us, such as our shared genome with a single ancestor in Africa, invisible links also exist. Rather than only by happenstance, perhaps the imperceptible strings of cosmic consciousness drew us together so that our paths crossed on the holiday in Greece. Maybe, there are no such things as random events since cosmic consciousness provides messengers and signposts to guide us on our way. In fact, the beneficent universe wants only the best for everything it created. However, the arrogance of humans in considering themselves as the masters of the universe rather than an equal part of the whole tips the balance existing in the cosmos."

"I hope we can restore the equilibrium on Earth," Bergitte said. "Please come back to Earth, Surina. We could use your help."

Surina was in a quandary. How could she leave her studies at the Gnaritus University in astrophysics and her research in the developmental singularity at Dr. Bruce Artair's lab unfinished? She would miss her patients and all her new friends too! Thus, on a Saturday, she went to the Algonquin Beach Meditation Center, hoping to resolve her indecision.

Due to Norval Gilmer's interest in exploring the full gamut of vistas in the volcano fields, no passage through the chain of volcanoes was ever the same as before. This time, when they flew much further south along the edge of the region of active volcanoes, they lingered to watch the eerie dancing blue flames spilling down the steep slopes.

"Oh wow," Surina said. "How is that distinctive blue color formed?"

"After exposure to the oxygen in the atmosphere, the heated sulfuric gases in the lava ignite to produce the dazzling neon-blue fire," Norval said.

On the horizon, active volcanoes erupted in rivers of fire that fumed and sizzled as they snaked down the mountainside into a fiery lava lake in the foothills below. Up above, an eye-popping green aurora embellished the sky. All of a sudden, the air cab lurched upward to avoid a shower of cannonballs barreling toward them.

Norval tossed his head back and laughed as a cannonball whistled past the air cab. "Yikes! We're lucky to see these lava bombs shooting out from that volcano. The only problem is it could be the opening salvo of a full-scale eruption!"

Deciding not to press their luck, he veered the air cab northward past an orderly array of perpendicular basalt columns of cold lava. Later, they marveled at hydrothermal fields that were resplendent with a jigsaw of varicolored abstract sculptures of sulfur and potassium salt deposits resulting from the evaporation of the fiery groundwater. Nature had indiscriminately embraced all the hues of red, pink, white, black, yellow, and brown salt deposits as well as sculpted them in every shape and size.

In due time, the geysers, mud pots, and hot springs gave way to the glass building enclosing the thermal lake where Gnaritonians reveled in the healing waters. Surina knew the advanced meditation center on the chalk clifftop remained out of her reach for now. Well, the novices' classes in the thermal lake provided more than enough hurdles for her to surmount. She was uncertain where her quest for cosmic consciousness would lead; however, the journey itself was exhilarating. What an improbable odyssey it had turned out to be for humans, venturing out of Africa to the rest of the Earth and all the way to Gnaritus.

Once on the seashore, Surina searched for her friends under the multicolored beach brollies. To allow more time for their debates, they had moved their Wednesday evening club meeting from the Easter Rose Tea Shop to the beach on Saturday mornings. The unexpected sight of a carefree Nachton Arthbutnott, enjoying the briny ocean breeze, reaffirmed to Surina the ascendancy of time in bestowing forgiveness. Due to the trial tearing asunder, link by link, the fetters binding him to the past, he had managed to free himself and progress forward without turning back. As Surina strolled past him, he beamed at her as the foamy waves sprayed mist on his face.

"I never expected so much change to come to Earth!" he said. "Who would have ever thought it possible!"

"Just like the moon and stars, the truth can't be hidden for long," Surina replied. "Perhaps cosmic consciousness is balancing the scales of justice. Coming to the meeting?"

They trekked together along the beach and found the club members by the eolian rocks resembling a Gothic church archway. Right away, the conversation turned to whether they would accept the once-coveted invitation to return to Earth.

"Since I was born on Gnaritus, my decision to stay here is an easy one," Norval said without hesitation. "I'll just go to Earth on vacation."

Meanwhile, Gowan expressed the sentiments of many long-term residents. "My memories of Earth had almost faded until the trial made me even more grateful to be on Gnaritus."

"I have no family or friends on Earth anymore to draw me back," Stefan said.

Alfonso nodded. "Neither do I."

Nachton, Gabriel, and Rafaela concurred.

"We don't want to leave Gnaritus either," Toben said. "We pleaded with Mercy to relocate here, but she just wants to visit. Maybe when she comes, she'll grow to like Gnaritus and want to stay."

Francesca and the Cavaceccis revealed their children on Earth would also come only for a holiday on Gnaritus. In contrast, Surina remained silent, for she was still torn between the two planets. Indeed, the thought of returning to lay the foundations of a new society on Earth sounded exciting. As with the generations of explorers before, the Delphian ocean beckoned her, promising answers to life's uncertainties. Only a few footprints dotted the beach at that early hour in the morning, allowing her to leave the signature of her trail across the pristine porcelain sand to the shoreline. Soon the sharp, tangy salt air awakened her, making her remember all the unplanned journeys leading her to the seashore of another world at the edge of the Milky Way galaxy.

Here and there, the shimmering rays of the three suns in a cloudless, turquoise sky played in the ultramarine surf. While peering at her reflection in the crystal water, she was taken aback by her sparkling, large eyes, which seemed as deep as the fathomless ocean. Although she combed her hair in front of the mirror every morning, she had never before seen herself so clearly as in the sea. To be sure, the gaze of the sybilline ocean pierced right through her to say that Gnaritus had transformed her on the inside and outside forever!

Despite the detours, fate had never led her astray, for all the signs pointed to where she stood now. Gnaritus was her home and had always been the refuge her heart had longed for, even during her time on Earth. In an earthly dream, she had taken a ride on a blue comet, searching for the place where she belonged, and she had found it here on Gnaritus. She was home.